ALSO BY MAX SALT

Worlds Collide

Worlds Apart

HAROLD'S WORLD

Max Salt

This book is a work of fiction. It should be understood that, except for the occasional passing reference to a public figure, the names in this book are made up and the characters are fictional and not intended to represent anyone real, living or dead. There are factual inaccuracies in this novel, some of them deliberate, and undoubtedly some unintentional ones as well. The author is responsible for all of them.

ISBN 978-0-578-04805-5

Published by the Zelkova Press in 2010

I have always admired women who shrug off the roles and stereotypes society hands them, instead finding an inner strength to chart their own course and stand up for what they believe in. This book is for them: the warrior women.

God is day and night, winter and summer, war and peace, surfeit and hunger.
Heracleitus, *The Cosmic Fragments.*

. . . in truth we are responsible to all for all, it's only that men don't know this. If they knew it, the world would be a paradise at once.
Fyodor Dostoevsky, *The Brothers Karamazov.*

…though she be but little, she is fierce.
William Shakespeare, *A Midsummer Night's Dream.*

HAROLD'S WORLD

Prologue

"Take the shotgun," Stansfield told his partner, Jerry Kinch.

"Got it," he said, pulling the weapon from its rack and operating the mechanism to chamber a round.

Dispatch replied over Stansfield's radio: "287, negative knowledge on the front door. Be advised, suspect *is* inside, and he may be injured or deceased. Rescue ETA is about five minutes."

Stansfield drew his issued automatic and the two men approached the door. Kinch took up a position on one side of the door while Stansfield tried the old-fashioned thumb latch over the door handle. The latch clicked but the door was locked. "Let's look for another entry point."

The officers circled around to side of the house, where they found another door, slightly ajar. They again took up positions on either side of the door, and Stansfield pushed it a little more open. "Police! We are armed and prepared to shoot! If you can hear me, place your hands on your head and face away from this door!" He nodded at Kinch, who used the toe of his shoe to push the door open wide. Both peered in to the dark, empty garage, illuminated only by their large flashlights.

The two took turns covering each other as they crossed the garage and entered the house. They announced themselves again, worked their way through a short corridor and a dining room, then found and climbed the stairs. The staircase terminated in the middle of a corridor, where Stansfield observed light coming from rooms to his left and right, somewhat illuminating the hallway. "Shit."

"What?" asked Kinch, a couple steps below.

"There's a body in the corridor to our right. Looks like a lot of blood. What's her name again?"

Kinch's brow furrowed. "I forget..."

"Miss! Can you hear me?"

"Help!" The weak, panicky voice came from Stansfield's left.

Stansfield moved to the side of the stairway nearest her voice, allowing Kinch to move up on his right and cover the other end of the hallway and the body with the shotgun. "This is the police! We are armed and prepared to shoot. Anyone who can hear me should place his hands on his head and face the nearest wall. Miss, are you alone?"

"Yes," said the small voice.

"OK, stay right where you are—don't move—I'm coming to you, all right?"

"Yes."

"Don't move."   Stansfield stepped into the corridor, sweeping the doors in view with his eyes and weapon before taking three steps to the near side of the lighted doorway and pausing while Kinch closed on him, still covering the other end of the hallway with the scatter gun. Standing with his left shoulder blade to the wall, Stansfield quickly peeked his head around the door jamb, glanced, and pulled back to process the image. "Oh God."

"What?"

Without answering, Stansfield rotated his body and entered the room, leading with his weapon and checking both sides for danger. Seeing she was alone in the room, he lowered his gun and looked at the small girl wrapped in some kind of blanket, drenched in blood from her matted hair to the thin rivulets running down the insides of her lower legs. "Oh God..." he whispered.

One

July 1998
Kansas City, Kansas

Around two a.m. the beams from my car's headlights bore a tunnel through the warm, humid darkness. The sky is cloudy and moonless, and I'm doing about forty on the unlit industrial road. There's a dim glow from the tank farm way off on my right and I know from the map I looked at earlier there's a rail yard in the black on my left.

I kill the tunes when I see headlights coming at me, but it could be just some late-night worker—a security guard maybe. Or the police: they're patrolling these roads too, for the same reason I am. As our cars get closer, the doubt vanishes. The scar running a few inches down from the bottom of my sternum starts to itch; I tense and squint, bracing myself. A second later the deep, stabbing pain comes whamming through the center of my body, as if the killer in the other car—a low, long blur of a sedan—pierced me with a javelin on his way by. Then the pain goes with him and, except for me gasping a little, it's as if nothing happened.

Finally. The problem with this mission, with the two Kansas Cities, has been the size of it all. The cities are sprawling and there's no shortage of lonely roads along the rivers and past industrial sites. He—the guy in the other car—has dumped bodies all over the area in places like these. I've also been prowling his hunting grounds, but there's no shortage of places to hire prostitutes here either.

I come off the gas and watch his tail lights in the rearview mirror. After several seconds I hit Stacey's brakes and kill her lights before coming around in a tight U-turn. I felt a little crazy when I did it, but I'm glad I painted Stacey flat black last year because now I'm invisible. I hit the gas.

I'm still too far back to read his license plate when his brake lights come on. I automatically come off the accelerator, but I'm still gaining too fast so I hit the brakes.

His car's lights vanish.

Huh? I stop pretty fast—not so fast that it leaves rubber on the pavement, but fast enough that I'm still out of sense range—the scar below my heart isn't registering him. I wonder if he could have turned off somewhere, but there was no change in the orientation of the brake and tail lights before they went out. *OK, so stopping in the middle of nowhere— what's up with that?*

He could be dumping a body, meaning I can wait for his lights to come back on, then follow him like I've been doing. Eventually, the plan goes, I follow him home, get a license plate number, home address, maybe a name off a mailbox or door buzzer, and whatever else I can find out, then call it in to the police.

The other possibility makes my stomach crawl up my throat: If the person with him is still alive, then really bad things are about to happen to her.

I lean forward and reach under my seat. My hand closes over the compact angular shape of the Glock 26 and I pull it free, the Velcro making a tearing sound as I do. I'm careful to keep my finger outside the trigger guard—the only real safety on a Glock—as I tuck it into the top of my jeans. I shift into first and press the accelerator. Stacey is a Geo Metro sub-compact and the small one-liter, three-cylinder engine doesn't make much noise. As I shift into second my scar starts to itch. I accelerate for another second, then shift to neutral and kill the engine. Now I'm coasting and almost silent. When it feels like the scar is tearing open and the sharp hurt is moving deeper into me, I slam on the brakes and flip on the lights, nailing him from thirty feet away just as he's hauling a person out of his trunk.

He freezes, his face pale and alarmed in the glare.

I should have gotten closer. I haul up on the parking brake and jump out, pulling the Glock from my jeans as I do. He drops the body, leaving it hanging half out of the trunk, and bolts for the open driver's door on his big old boat of a car. I sprint after him, both arms outstretched holding the gun just above chest level, finger on the trigger now. I put the laser sight's red dot on his back and fire. He pitches forward against the door, falls sideways into the driver's seat, and pulls the door shut.

"No, no, *fucking no!*" I shout and dig harder into the road's loose, pebbly shoulder with my feet, pulling even with the driver's side window just as the car's tires start flinging dirt and squealing against the pavement. I point the weapon where I think his head is and fire repeatedly through the open window. The pain of the sense—that stabbing where my scar is—winks out. The car angles off the road and I have to stop short to avoid colliding with it. I hear it go crashing into the low, woody vegetation, then the horn starts blaring.

The absence of pain tells me my mission is over. There's nothing I want more than to get the fuck out of here and be done with this, to start trying to put my head together again. But I don't trust the sense that much.

I run down the path of flattened bushes, then slow to a fast walk as I reach the car and start pushing through the intact shrubs pressed up against its metal skin, my weapon aimed as much as possible at the open driver's side window. Staying even with the edge of the window opening, I peer in but it's even darker in the car and I left my Maglite back in Stacey's glove compartment. I shine the laser sight around and I'm able to discern the edges of his head. I put the red dot of the laser in the middle of it and squeeze off one more round.

Suppressing the urge to vomit, I push through the branches again then haul ass back up to the road. There probably are cops around here somewhere, and all the shooting and horn sounding will have them on me any second now.

When I reach the pavement I glance over my shoulder and see the body, illuminated by Stacey's headlights. The woman is nude, lying on her back, her brown hair fanned out on the asphalt around her head like some kind of sunburst or aura, her pale skin almost shining in the glare. I hesitate, then trot over. *WHORE* is carved into the skin of her upper chest, and I wonder if the man I just killed believed he was doing God's work, punishing sinners or some such bullshit. Her face is all slashed up too: deep gouges crisscrossing her features, part of her nose nearly cut loose, laying limply on her upper lip, the lips themselves ragged with teeth showing through in places, the right eye is gone—just a dark socket—

I look away, up at the sky.

Shit like this makes me wish I were still an atheist.

I can actually see a few stars, reminding me of the whole, huge fucking clockwork, right down to the unfailing sense that led me to this spot at this time so I could turn out the lights on another horror show. That big clockwork is why I stopped being an atheist, but there's no comfort in the idea this world is not an accident.

I look back down at the woman and hope all the carving happened after she was dead. I know it's pointless, but I squat and press two fingers into the groove next to her voice box. The skin is cool and there's no pulse. In my mind I see one more murder victim falling onto a mountain of bodies ruined by violence. "I'm sorry," I whisper.

Gotta get the fuck out. Still squatting, I pivot and launch into a sprint back to my car.

Skipping the even gears, I put the hammer down for the first half minute or so, then slow to forty-five, checking the rearview every other breath.

Two

July 1998
Kansas City, Kansas

Silas "Mac" MacIlwane can see the blue white glow reflecting off the early morning mist more than a mile from the crime scene, and wonders what Jeff Roberts, the agent in charge of the FBI's investigation, meant. When Jeff's call woke him twenty minutes ago, Mac asked if KC had hit again.

"Yeah, but…it's weird…" was Jeff's reply.

What was that supposed to mean? Mac found himself regretting again his choice to become a behavioral analyst—a "profiler." He'd always been out front—a "doer," not a support person—until he transferred to the Bureau's Behavioral Analysis Unit. It seemed like a good idea at the time—keep the same home base for more than a few years for the first time in his adult life, take a little pressure off himself, whatever. But now he's what his former, Army persona would've derisively called a "REMF": rear echelon mother fucker. It's not that he doesn't like this work, but he was always in charge—the guy who got stuff done. Supporting role isn't his style.

Well it is now, hotshot, he thinks.

They've got the whole road blocked off, and a uniformed local cop—from the *Kansas* Kansas City this morning—signals for Mac to stop. Mac holds his badge out the open window and the officer walks up and puts a light on it.

"Parking over there?" Mac asks, looking at a line of cars parked nose-in, half off the road.

"Yes sir," the kid says.

Mac's started doing this lately—thinking of people who look like they're in their early twenties as "kids," even though he can remember being in his twenties and how adult he felt. The attitude is probably an inevitable part of getting older, and he did turn forty-six a couple months ago.

He parks then walks over to the nearest concentration of lights. There's another grouping of lights and crime scene investigators several feet off the road, probably where KC left the body. He finds Jeff at the cluster on the road, looking every inch Hoover's ideal G-man in his conservative haircut, dark suit, and crisp white shirt. "What are we looking at up here?" Mac asks.

"The vic."

Mac steps closer and looks between the light stands, cases, and people in white Tyvek coveralls. At the center of it all, lying face up on the pavement, is a woman's naked body, the pale skin glowing under the intense glare of the lights. "Has she been moved?" Mac asks. It seems odd that KC would leave the body practically in the road; he's been less concerned about hiding the last couple bodies, but leaving his victim in the road would be a significant development, and Mac is already considering its implications.

"This is where the responding officers found her. They had a report of gunfire from a security guard at the fuel storage complex over there, and she was the first thing they saw. It's pretty clear KC was interrupted, and that's him in the car over there," Jeff replies, motioning with his thumb toward the other grouping of lights and technicians.

Mac automatically looks over as he processes the information. "Alive?"

"No—no, dead at the wheel. Shot up pretty bad, too."

"Why do we think that guy's KC?"

"The trunk was open and they already found blood and long hair from what looks like three different people in it. DNA analysis will tell us for sure."

"I wasn't expecting this."

"Who was? That's what I meant when I said it's weird."

"Yeah, I get it. But..."

"Who did him?" Jeff offers.

"Yeah, I'm trying to imagine a sequence of events that would end this way. I mean, was this some kind of random drive-by shooting? A robbery? What would get him shot and killed out here in the middle of the night?"

"Beats me," Jeff says. "I was just over there looking at what I could, but they're still processing the scene. The car body's not really shot up, and he still had his wallet on him, with some cash in it, so I don't think it was a drive by or a robbery, unless the robber freaked when he saw her body. I don't know—you ever see anything like this?"

"Not really," Mac says. He's seen multiple murders at a single scene before, of course, but usually it was pretty easy to discern the story leading up to what he was looking at. The one exception was over a year ago, in Trenton, New Jersey. That was another serial killer—a guy who'd been raping and murdering little boys—and he was found on the floor of his bedroom with a small kitchen knife sticking out of the base of his skull. Whoever did that knew something about killing quickly and efficiently, and he'd also obviously entered by smashing through the window leading to the fire escape, but why he broke in to that particular apartment and left without taking anything remains a mystery. It crossed Mac's mind then that it could have been the work of a vigilante. As it turned out, there'd actually been an anonymous phone tip about the dead guy a week or so before they found his body, but as far as Mac knows the case on who killed him is still open. "You say he was shot, huh?"

"Yeah, coroner said one in the back, one in the shoulder, one in the neck, and one in the head. Looks like soft-nosed ammo because it really made a mess out of him. There are parts of his head and neck all over the inside of the car."

"How 'bout the woman? She line up with the other bodies?"

"Yep, strangulation, face and genitals carved up, "whore" inscribed in her chest, just like the others."

"I don't suppose there was a phone tip relating to the guy in the car, was there?" Mac asks.

"I don't know—I'd have to go through the records."

"Yeah, just a thought."

"His name's James Wainwright, according to the license in his wallet, but that doesn't ring any bells with me."

"Me neither."

"Wait, are you thinking someone knew what this guy was doing and then went after him when we didn't?"

Mac shrugs. "It's one explanation."

Three

October 1998
I-84 South, Massachusetts

At 65 miles per hour the sensation on my upper abdomen goes from light itch to burning pain to itching again in a matter of seconds.

What?!

The sensation is gone all together and my mind is still registering it. The road surface continues rushing by a few feet below me, as if nothing happened, and every part of me is ready to pretend it didn't.

Well, not every part.

I look around and check the rear view mirror. It's early enough on a Saturday morning and I'm far enough from Boston that the road is mostly empty. There's an SUV too far back to cause the pain, and a big rig too far out in front of me. Plus it came and went so fast: I must have passed the source. I look left toward the other side of the highway, but the thick band of trees in the median blocks my view. Anyway, with me driving in the right lane, that side's too far away to trigger more than a scratch. Judging from the level of pain when it peaked, the source had to be within about a hundred feet of me. Someone is back there, in the trees on the side of the highway.

I look for a way out: By the time I get turned around he'll be gone; I'd never be able to find him in the trees anyway. *Seriously, what am I gonna do? Pull over in the breakdown lane and go hunting in the woods for him?* This goes on pointlessly in my head as I take the next exit, cross over the highway, and get back on it going northeast, my gut cramping with dread, my mouth dry, my brain buzzing.

I hit the accelerator and feel Stacey surge forward, running hard. I sense the bad guy again, but this time the peak is only a scratch and the whole thing is over quicker. He's still there, but I'm further away this time. He's on the southbound side—not over here, and not in the median. I take the next exit and reverse direction so I'm heading south again, more slowly this time, scanning the woods on the right side intently.

This time I see the sign for the rest area, and before I even reach it the itching starts on the scar in the upside-down V formed by the two halves of my rib cage. I move my foot from gas to brake and spot the opening in the pine and spruce trees, then the pavement for the off ramp. I press harder on the brake and turn the wheel slightly as the itch becomes a scratch. As I move down into the thick grove of trees, a hot line seems to burn on my skin, and I spot a beat-up, dirty white van.

"Fuck," I breathe, and try unsuccessfully to swallow. It feels like the skin below my breast bone is starting to tear open, but I ignore it. My skin is fine; it's all in my head. *It's in that van.*

It's not much of a rest area—no phones, no bathrooms, not even picnic benches. Just some parking spaces, maybe a dozen, in a paved area surrounded by a wall of trees on the highway side and more open but still shadowy forest on the other. Except for the van and me, the place is deserted. I take the time to back in to a space, so it'll be faster to get out when I need to. I botch the parking job. *Fuck it.* Automatically I reach up to kill the engine, but leave it running and instead put the gear shift in neutral and pull up on the parking brake. In front of me the trees completely block sight of the highway. I slide my eyes right and see the van is also parked nose out and its hood is up. The side of the vehicle has a logo painted on it—Mathews Cabinetry—and a New Hampshire address.

I'm about thirty feet away, and the pain has deepened to severe twisting cramps inside me, but they're not. That's important: reminding myself there's not really any physical damage makes it easier to take the pain.

I lean forward, reach under my seat, and pull the weapon free from the Velcro. I place it in the large right side pocket of my rain shell. I chose this jacket in part because it has pockets big enough to accommodate the gun, Glock's smallest nine-millimeter model. I lean back again and, looking through the passenger window, I see a man behind the wheel of the van, looking out at me. Unless there's someone else I don't see, maybe in the back of the van, then the guy I'm looking at now is the source of the pain. I check the rear view mirrors and look out the window to my left, but it seems to be just him and me. *Shit motherfucker here we go.* My stomach is twisting and I feel light-headed as I get out of the car. He rolls down his window and waves, hesitantly, more to get my attention than to greet me. He puts his left hand to the side of his head, miming using a phone.

"Do you have a cell phone I can use? I pahked heah to rest and now it won't staht. I can't figyah out what's wrong." His accent tells me he's from around here—somewhere in eastern New England.

"Sorry, I don't have a phone," I lie, working hard to keep my voice relaxed and steady. I stand by Stacey, hands in my coat pockets, like I'm just stretching my legs.

He drops his head in disappointment. "Damn, I just can't catch a break." He looks up at me again. "I don't suppose you know anything about fixing cahs, do you?"

I shake my head and watch him, tensing the muscles in my arms and back to keep from trembling. "No, sorry." *I should just take him out—no fuckin' around, just take him down.*

He opens his door, steps out of the van, and gestures with his left hand at the side of the van. "I'm a cahpentah, not a mechanic." He smiles self-effacingly; he seems harmless, friendly. He looks like a regular guy, clean-cut, maybe in his early thirties. His hands are empty. In fact, the right sleeve of his flannel shirt is unbuttoned and stretched over a cast.

The pain rages inside me; I don't let it show. It gets worse, becoming a sharp stabbing as I walk slowly, casually toward him, my hands thrust into the deep pockets of my open coat, my right hand cupped around the handgun to hide its shape. "Sorry, I don't know much about engines either. Has it done this before?"

"This piece of crap is always breaking down on me," he says, making another frustrated wave at the vehicle with the cast he's wearing and taking a few steps toward the front bumper. "It's probably my own fault, though—I don't take very good cayah of it. Always mean to, but somehow time gets away and 'Hey! Haven't changed the oil in a yeeah and half or so!'"

"Even I'm not that bad," I say, keeping my voice natural-sounding despite the pain just below my diaphragm and the fear moving through me like an electric current. I glance quickly back at my car, and at the trees surrounding the small parking lot. *It's definitely him—just shoot him.*

He moves to the front of the van and stands looking down at the engine.

I know what he is. The safe, smart thing to do is just kill him now, but that'd be crossing a line. Killing just on the pain's say-so would make me too much like them: killing just because something inside me said to. I always make sure; I have to be sure.

The normal thing is to join him at the front of the van, so I do. As I approach, I look through the van's windshield. I don't see anyone inside, but there's a tangled pile of sunglasses on top of the dashboard on the driver's side. I don't allow my eyes to linger on them, but my mind does and my heart's hammering. Standing next to him, looking down at the engine, the pain is at its peak; I glance around again, but see no one else.   I focus completely on him, on every movement he makes, every word he speaks. *Have to be sure...*

"Yeah, I've been driving all night, headed down to Hahtfuhd for a trade show to exhibit some of the furniture I make, but I stahted nodding off, so I pulled in heah for a nap. I was hoping if I looked unda the hood theah would be something obviously out of place that I could fix, like a loose wiyah aw something.   But everything looks fine to me, I mean, dirty, but—aw hell, I have no clue."

I lean toward the engine, pretending to look, but my eyes are actually shifted all the way to the left, watching his arms.   I reach my left hand out as if to tug on one of the cords coming out of the distributor, and as I do I see his right arm, the one with the cast, go up and out of my field of view.   I shift away from him, simultaneously turning my head and body to look at him and see the cast-clad arm swinging down.   I duck away; the blow lands on the outside of my left shoulder, square on the deltoid muscle, rather than the back of my head and neck. It hurts, but I'm kinda preoccupied to do more than register the sensation.   The force of it makes me stumble backward and bump into a corner of the van, but I manage to point the Glock, still in the big coat pocket.   At this range it'd be hard to miss, and I don't.   Surprise registers on his face as the Hydra-Shok bullet knocks him back a few steps.   I back up too, frantically fighting to get the handgun out of my coat.   He sees this and lurches toward me, but then the weapon is free. Before I can fire again, though, he drops to his knees, a bewildered look on his face.   I aim, fire into that confused expression, knocking him backward.   The pain in the center of me vanishes.   I quickly step up to the body and fire one more round into the head, then sprint to my car.

I jump in, turn the key, hear the grinding racing noise because the engine is already running, put the car in gear and start to pull out when I think of the pile of sunglasses under the van's windshield. *What if he has someone in there?* There's no more pain in the center of me, so I know there are no more bad guys around, but what if he has another victim confined in the back? That seems unlikely, and I want to get the fuck out of Dodge before someone else comes along and finds me with the dead guy, but I need to make sure. I take Stacey out of gear, pull on the parking brake and realize it's still engaged. "OK, OK, let's get this done," I mutter as I get out and sprint over to the back of the van.

I reach for the handle on the back door and notice my bare hand. I stop short of the handle, then tug the sleeve of the rain shell down over my hand before opening the door.

As the door swings open my mind flashes to the interior of another van, three and a half years ago in a field in northern Florida. That vehicle was a mobile torture and killing room; the woman inside had already bled out by the time I got to her. So I'm expecting the worst now.

The interior is dim—there are no windows except a small bubble skylight in the ceiling, but after a couple seconds I can see there's nothing inside—no carpentry tools, no furniture, no prisoner, no dead body. There are dark stains on the floor, and metal rings, a couple inches in diameter, set into the floor. I remember having the same things in the helicopters I flew in the Army, for securing cargo. There's no cargo on the floor of the van, but there are long plastic ratchet ties threaded through four of the floor rings. The ties haven't been closed yet; I imagine they would've been if his plan had worked and he'd loaded me in the van.

OK, let's get the fuck out.

I run back to my car, toss the Glock under my seat, and pull out, carefully driving around the body and then speeding up to the highway. I pause a second, realizing it would be bad to be seen pulling out of the rest area. A car whizzes by, but there is no one else in sight behind him, so I accelerate into the right-hand lane. Stacey is responding sluggishly and I realize

I still have the parking brake on. "Sorry Stace," I whisper as I release the brake. The speed limit here is 65, so I take it up to 70 and hold there, covering ground as fast as possible without attracting attention.

After a couple minutes I notice my forearms are burning: both hands are balled like fists on the wheel, the knuckles pale. I relax my hands then wipe the palms one at a time on my jeans. The skin on my head and in my armpits feels prickly, and a drop of sweat runs down the left side of my face. I wipe at my eyebrow and my hand comes away wet and trembling. Luckily, as I cross into Connecticut I see a sign for a welcome center up ahead. I take deep breaths and suppress the growing sick feeling, hanging on. *Just a little further.* Another sign for the welcome center, and there's the arrow pointing to the off ramp. I take the exit, follow the sign for cars, and pull all the way to the back edge of the parking lot. I kill the engine and get out, my legs almost giving way as I do. Bracing myself on the car, I bend over and retch. Breakfast was a couple hours ago, so there's nothing in my stomach to throw up, but I pull a muscle deep down in my crotch before I get myself under control.

I straighten up and tilt my head back, breathing deeply through my nose while the cool October air dries my face. Gradually my heart rate slows to normal and the nausea and tremors subside.

There's a sharp, throbbing ache in my left shoulder and I think of that cast-clad arm coming down. I carefully poke at the area, assessing the damage and finding the edges of the injury. It hurts like a bastard. I can move it, so I guess it's not broken, but any use of the delt hurts badly: a really bad, deep bruise that'll be with me for a long time.

I see a picnic table a little ways off in the grass beyond the lot's pavement. I get my keys from the car and lock the door since my weapon is inside, then walk slowly over to the bench, feeling much older than twenty-eight, tired, and filthy.

I'm contaminated not only by what I've done, but by who I did it to. The sense—that pain in my center—and contact with the fuckers it's linked to takes me back to the Bad, my first run-in with human monsters. Every interaction with them is exposure to their disease. Killing them is participation in their cult of violence.

I sit on one of the attached benches and lean back against the picnic table, gazing at my car and the half empty parking lot beyond. The flat black paint I put on Stacey last year makes her look like a little storm cloud.

Along with the taint of what happened, there's also an emptiness—a deadness—inside me. I kill, then go on like nothing's happened. The killing has become part of my life, like it's a job I do. The normal person who wouldn't even think of murder is disappearing. Each homicide is a little suicide.

How much of me is left? How many more times can I do this?

I don't have to do this. I could turn Stacey around, head back home. This slow death doesn't have to be my life anymore.

But going home means aborting my mission, which was not that bastard with the van and the sunglasses collection. *He* wasn't even on my radar.

What are the odds I'd find a psychopath on the way to find another psychopath? Harold must really have it in for me. A more superstitious—or religious: same thing really—person might say Harold is guiding me, using me as "his" instrument of justice or whatever. But I know better. Harold doesn't give a shit about any of us, or if it—*it* not *he*—does, then it's a fuckin' sadist, not a righter of wrongs, and certainly not a protector of innocents. I really don't know *what* the deal is with Harold; it's taken me years to even accept its reality. But the existence of murdering freaks in the world it created says something about what it's like.

Anyway, my mission is in Philadelphia, where another monster the press is calling the "Pink Slasher" is torture-killing gay men. Going home now would most likely mean horrible deaths for more young men in Philadelphia, and I can't allow that. I identify with the victims. They're different with each mission, but they all make me think of that teenage girl years ago.

Four

November 1985
Byfield, Massachusetts

"What's the difference between mitosis and meiosis? I mean, I get mitosis, but..." Shailene asked, looking up from the textbook in her lap. She was sitting on the narrow battered bed in Derek's dorm room, studying for a test coming up in their tenth-grade biology class. She was pretty sure she already knew the answer, but was having trouble finding the section on it in the book and wanted to be sure. Plus, they hadn't said anything to each other for the last several minutes.

Derek, a poster for *Star Trek: The Undiscovered Country* looming over him where he sat at his desk, looked up from his book and over at her.

She realized they were looking at each other's eyes, which was good, but in a weird way made her nervous. She looked down at her book again. "I've been searching, but I can't find the section on it."

"Meiosis is cell division that produces egg cells in women and sperm cells in men—cells with..."

Why did you have to ask that *question?* she silently demanded, annoyed with herself. *AWK-ward!* She isn't sure why exactly—maybe the sperm and egg thing. *It shouldn't be, but why is it?* She realized he'd stopped talking. "Isn't this stuff cool?" she said. "The best was when we did that lab where we looked at our own cheek cells. I looked at that little blob in the microscope and was totally blown away by the idea I was looking at all the plans and instructions to make me—all of me—but even under the 'scope it was too small to be more than a dark blob all scrunched up in the nucleus. It totally blows me away. The world is so amazing." She felt herself smiling big. It really was the coolest.

Derek smiled back, and that made her feel even better—accidental awkward patch successfully gotten through. She liked his smile, liked that he was wicked smart. He was smarter than her in some ways, but she was also better at some stuff, like math. It was like they balanced each other out—wherever he had a hard time, she was pretty confident, and the other way around.

"You're right, it is pretty amazing; almost enough to make you get religion," he said, smiling some more, but different now because he was teasing her.

She liked it though—liked when they debated. He made her think harder and back up what she thought. Leaning forward, she rested her elbows on the textbook in her lap. "It *is* hard to believe this could happen randomly, isn't it? I mean, what seems more likely—that this all happened by accident, or that it was organized by something that wanted it this way?"

"I don't know—give randomness plus natural selection billions of years and it's not so hard to believe it could happen on its own, I think. I guess I need more convincing."

Shailene smiled. "Always the scientist—tangible proof, reproducible results!" she said with exaggerated deepness in her voice and an expression on her face to match, but only for as long as it took to say that. He never mocked her opinions, and she didn't want him to think she didn't take his ideas seriously. She leaned forward and rested her fingertips on Derek's arm—well, really the sleeve of his Byfield Academy sweatshirt, but she could feel his arm and its warmth through the fabric. "I'm just teasing—you know that, right? You're probably right. I think I'm just more willing to listen to my heart as well as my head, and it's all so extraordinary, from the cells that make us to the atoms that make them, to the supernovas that make *them*. You've got to feel some of that too, otherwise you wouldn't like this stuff so much." She noticed her fingertips were still resting on his arm. She pulled her hand back, and leaned against the wall behind her, but her fingertips felt tingly, like they were sort of still touching him.

Derek smiled at her, but in a nervous way, and shifted in his chair. "I love talking to you," he said.

She felt something quiver in her stomach—not a bad feeling, but not something she really understood either, and it made her nervous.

"I mean, you're really interesting. So, they're running a van to the mall on Saturday—you want to go?"

She did want to go; at least, part of her did. Part of her, though, felt like things were changing in a way she didn't get, and she wasn't sure it was for the better. Still, it'd be kind of fun to go someplace with Derek... "What time is it leaving? I have a game on Saturday."

"I think it leaves around four—I'll check and let you know."

Suddenly she remembered: "Oh wait—I told my parents I'd go home this weekend. They're coming up for the game, and then taking me home with them—you know, long weekend and all—sorry. It really would be fun to do something like that sometime, though." For a second she thought she should invite him home with her, but that would definitely be weird, and her parents would be all like "so, what's up with this Derek?" and Shailene didn't need that. Becky, Shailene's best girlfriend, would find out too, and not long after that Derek and Shailene would officially be dating, whether they actually were or not. Why did this have to be so complicated?

"That's OK," Derek said.

They both looked down at their books: major awkwardness.

"Just so you know," Derek said after a few long seconds.

Shailene looked up at him, but his eyes were still pointed down at his book.

He continued, "I wasn't asking you on a date; I know how you feel about that—'too much other stuff you want to do,' 'crazy dramas,' all that—but I really was just saying we could just go and whatever, have fun—*not* date—you know?"

Erg! He said it! But he sounded sad, and that's the last thing she wants him to be. Plus, she really did want to go with him—he should know that. She leaned close and touched his arm again. "I really would've gone with you if I hadn't already made plans with my parents."

He looked up at her. He wasn't smiling exactly, but he didn't look sad either. "OK, I totally get it. They'll probably run another trip eventually—maybe we can go then."

"I'd like that," she said softly.

"Cool," he said, smiling.

Five

October 1998
Connecticut Welcome Center, I-84 South

For several seconds, maybe a minute, I imagine myself safe in the little world of my apartment, maybe reading or whatever, done with going after bad guys. No more fear, free of the sick anticipation of what lies ahead, cured of the infection of violence.

I stand up.

No one knows who the so-called Pink Slasher's next victim is—maybe not even the Slasher himself who will, according to the articles I read online, first be the young man's lover and then his murderer. The Slasher relies on his appearance as a normal person to gain access to people's trust, then his targets' homes, where he kills them. My one advantage is not only does his disguise not work with me, but I can even sense him from a ways off—about a city block, give or take. This makes me uniquely qualified to stop the Slasher. But if I go home now then the odds of the targeted young man's survival get slimmer.

Which is why I'm getting back in my car and continuing south to Philadelphia. Not because Harold wants me to—it doesn't care. I'll find this Slasher fucker and stop him because no one should have to endure what that teenage girl went through.

Six

November 1985
Lincoln, Massachusetts

The red glow through her eyelids woke Shailene. Confused, she opened her eyes to slits against the glare of the lights in her bedroom. "Mom? Dad?" she asked groggily, trying unsuccessfully to see.

"Mom's here, but Dad's dead."

The male voice sounded amused like he's about to reveal some big joke. It was unfamiliar and brought Shailene instantly to full, confused alertness. She saw her mother: tears running from bulging, panicked eyes, head held tightly against a pale, dark-haired man's shoulder, his hand clamped over her mouth. A knife was pressed against her mother's neck, the shiny blade beaded with bright red. *Nightmare.* She tried desperately to wake up while staring dumbly at her mother's eyes, the knife, and the hungry grin on the stranger's face.

"Having a hard time grasping the reality here?" the stranger asked. "I get that sometimes, Shailene."

She thought this must be a bad dream after all—how else could he know her name?

"Let me tell you," he continued, more angry-sounding now, "you *are* awake, and we're just getting started. On second thought, why don't *you* tell her, Mom?" He dropped his right hand from Mom's mouth to her upper chest.

"Shailene, *run!*" she screamed, "*Ru—*"

Her voice was abruptly cut off as the man, his face contorted with the effort of working against Mom's attempt to pry his knife hand away, pressed and pulled the blade across her neck, releasing a spray of blood and a gurgling sound from her neck. Shailene, still stunned silent, saw the helpless anguish and suffering on her dying mother's face, then leaped off the bed and threw herself at the man, instinctively reaching for his neck.

Still holding his adult victim, the stranger raised his leg and kicked Shailene in the chest, knocking her backward and sitting her down hard on the floor.

Both the man and her mother toppled over, with her mother on top. Her mother's eyes were big and staring at Shailene, and her mouth was moving as if she were trying to speak, but the only sounds were the wet grunts coming from the gaping wound in her throat.

"Mom!" Shailene scrambled across the floor, but her mother's eyes were already unfocused and her mouth had stopped moving. The man, his hands drenched in blood, was getting to his feet, the wet blade clutched in his left hand. Shailene launched herself at the door, but he caught her around her body and dragged her back across the room. She struggled, arms flailing at him while striving for purchase on the carpet with her feet, then sharp pain exploded in her back as the corner of the dresser impacted near her spine. She cried out and tears ran down her cheeks.

"OK, *Shailene*," he hissed loudly, his face inches from hers, "all you need to understand is that *I* am in charge now— it's *my* turn. That means you do what I tell you, got it?"

"Why?" she got out between breaths. "Why?" She meant to say more, but that was all that came out.

"Because you're hot," he said, as if it were obvious. His voice was softer, especially compared to what it had been moments before. "*You* want *me* too—I can tell."

Her eyes flicked down to see where his crotch was, thinking she might be able to kick him in the balls, but at that moment he pressed her harder into the corner of the bureau, bending her backwards and making it impossible for her to do anything except gasp. The knife was at her throat, the tip of the blade actually slicing through the thin skin under her jaw as she stared into a coldly impassive gray eye.

"Look, this is going to happen." The edge was creeping back into his tone. "You can't stop me, and deep down, you don't want to stop me. But you want it 'hard' or 'easy'? I can do either; I like 'em both. I'm going to let go of you, and when I do, you're going to tell me how you want it: If you want easy, take off your clothes and lay down on the bed. Do anything else if you want hard."

His words crystallized an understanding for her, but not the one he intended. Not only was this going to happen, but it was also going to kill her. There was no way he was going to let her live.

The gray eye didn't blink, but she felt the pressure on her throat ease, then the blade left her, then the empty right hand released her. He took a step back, nodding and smiling a little, and she was able to come off the corner of the dresser. The pain in her back eased slightly. Still watching him, she kept her eyes locked on his face, but was aware of the knife now dangling loosely at his side. She lifted the hem of her oversized T-shirt and tucked her thumbs into the elastic of her panties. She bent at the waist, preparing to slip the underwear over her butt and down *please God help me* and instead launched herself head first at the center of his body.

There was no pain, just the registering of the impact, the sense of uncontrolled movement, and the sudden stop on the floor. Slightly stunned, but determined, she pulled her limbs under her body, but before she could rise, her head was jerked back, and she was being lifted by her long hair. Her scalp stretched and felt like it would pull loose from her skull. She gasped, cried out, and tried desperately to stand and ease the stress on her skin, but before she could get her balance he pushed her forward to the bed and drove her down onto the mattress. She moved her arms and legs frantically, trying to use the momentum to get away, but he still had her hair, reigning her in. She kicked, and grabbed and pulled at the far edge of the mattress, but he was on her now, turning her onto her back and pinning her with his weight. She began thrashing violently in place, moving whatever she could, and then there was a fist clenching a knife sailing toward her face.

* * *

She felt herself tearing as she was pierced. Nausea rolled over her, tears ran down her cheeks, but when she heard herself screaming she clamped her teeth together. She wouldn't scream: he wouldn't get that satisfaction.

"Knew you'd wake up soon," he said, a little breathless.

She felt his body between her legs pushing her rhythmically, felt his hands on her hips. Her own hands and arms were free. She opened her eyes to slits and saw the gray eyes staring back. He smiled. She punched his face.

After a moment of surprise, he smiled more broadly. "You want it rougher? I can play rough." He was almost laughing as he said this.

She felt the hands on her hips tighten their grip, the fingers digging into her flesh. There was a momentary pause in movement, and then—incredibly—the pain low in her body increased as he began slamming into her harder. She closed her eyes, but that did nothing to ease the sickening hurt.

Without slackening his pace, he shouted, "How do like that? You really want it hard, don't you, you little slut!" His spittle sprayed her face.

Despite the pain, she tried to figure out how much she could move and what she could do to him. Her legs were free, but he was between them, so all she could do was kick him lightly on the backs of his legs. She quickly stopped doing that because any movement below her waist added to the hurt. Her arms were free too, laying at her sides, but punching him had only made things worse. Wriggling away was impossible with both his hands clamped onto her hips.

Both hands—where's the knife?

Without opening her eyes, she rolled her arms slightly, feeling for the weapon, but sensed only piled sheets and blankets on her left and open mattress on her right. He paused for a second while he leaned back and lifted her hips off the bed. He began thrusting again, his pace faster now. She opened her eyes slightly: he was leaning back and his eyes were closed. His breathing was heavier, faster, and he was making grunting noises. *Please,* please *God, stop him, stop this, help me. Please God please.* She rolled her head to the right, and looked down the length of her body, still searching for the knife. The sight of her nakedness and him between her legs—*the knife, find the knife.* She saw her arm and, further down, just beyond her hand, the weapon, the tip of the blade pointing up at her. She moved her arm, stretched her fingers, and just touched the blade when his tempo sped up dramatically, sending new bolts of agony up through her body, blurring her vision and shoving her and her hand away from the knife. She glanced at him to see if he had noticed what she was doing, but his eyes were still closed. Just then he yelled and his fingers dug hard into her hips and buttocks.

He looked at her, a crazed smile splashed across his face. Keeping her eyes on his, she reached blindly for the knife one last time, even though it was now well out of range.

"Shailene, I came so hard I'm surprised you're not choking on my spunk," he said. He ground his hips into her one last time and pulled out. "You are so *good.*"

Instinctively, she closed her eyes. The disappointment, after being so close, after *touching* the blade, was crushing.

"What? Don't want to see it? I think you do—I think you want to lick it clean." The mattress moved as he repositioned himself. She felt his legs, still wearing his jeans, on either side of her torso, and opened her eyes when he placed the cold blade against her neck. He was straddling her, his thing, almost unrecognizable to her, red with her blood, was a foot or so from her face, smelling like wet metal and his stink. She looked up and locked eyes with him, daring him to put it in her mouth, because if he did he'd never put it anywhere ever again. He must have seen this because he stopped and the expression on his face changed from sadistic excitement to uncertainty, then anger. He backhanded her, the force knocking her head sideways. "Fuckin' cunt. I'm not done with you yet. I'll show you who's in charge." He swung his right leg behind him and climbed off her and the bed, pulling his jeans up as he did. He was still fully dressed, the blood-soaked gray sweatshirt hanging on his wiry frame. The knife was in his hand.

Shailene barely noticed the new pain in her face, given all the kinds of hurt below her waist: burning in some places, deep ache in others, and a sharp, eye-watering torture deep inside her. She rolled on her side and pulled her knees to her chest to try to ease the suffering while she watched him. Warm liquid ran out of her and sideways across the back of her thigh, down to the mattress. He was standing a few feet from her, near the doorway, looking at her posters: the mist-shrouded redwoods, the Horsehead Nebula, the sea otter floating on his back and holding a mussel shell. She watched the monster, forcing her mind off the pain, off the wetness running out of her, and on to what she could do to him.

"Your room is just like I imagined it—a good girl's room." His voice was soft, friendly. "You know, just because you want me doesn't make you bad. I believe you *are* a good girl." He stepped past—

Don't think—

Mom

Do NOT think about it!

He moved around the foot of the bed and stood in front of the orders of magnitude poster. "You like science, don't you? That's great—beautiful *and* smart."

His back was to her. If she could just get off the bed without him hearing, she'd have a head start... *No, he's still too close to the door.* She watched, lifting her head slightly as he moved further from the door. He was by the desk now, and hadn't looked back once. *God, I need you now—please help me get out of here...* Slowly, silently, she extended her legs, tensing her jaw against the pain.

"Hey!"

She froze.

"I recognize *this*."

She looked back at him, saw he was standing over her desk, looking at her field hockey team photo.

"So you're a fan of my work," he said.

The photographer. It clicked in her head—how he knew her name. She'd thought there was something vaguely familiar about him.

"Although this shot of you isn't my favorite. I like the ones where you and your friends are flirting with me. Especially you—when I developed those and saw the way you looked at me, wanting me, I knew we had to be together."

She was frozen, watching him over her shoulder. His words were confusing her. *Go—think about it later! Got to go now!* She resumed the movement she'd started, fully extending her legs.

"I have those pictures hanging in my bedroom. I have one where I cropped out your friends, so it's just you, posing for me, the way you wanted it to be. I blew that one up really big—it's my favorite."

Don't listen to him. Her lower legs were over the edge of the mattress now, and she was half sitting up. She saw how it would happen: sit up and feet on the floor in one movement, then out the door, down the hall, and away. *Please God, please...* She glanced back at him; he was still studying the field hockey photo.   She looked back at the rug, where in another moment, her feet would impact as she began running. The mattress creaked softly as she swiveled upright.

"You know, this—*fuuuuuck!*"

His shout was the starter's gun going off in her head; she shoved herself off the bed, her feet touched the floor, and she was bolting for the door, leaping over—*Mom*—and out the door and away, away—*please God please*

As she got through the doorway, she opened her stride, her feet thudding on the hardwood floor in the hallway, but he was already right behind her.

Oh please, oh please God help me oh please God—

The impact from behind sent her sailing forward and further down the hall, past the top of the stairs.   She landed hard on her chest, but her arms took the impact for her head. His arms were around her waist; his body pressing down on hers.

"You *cunt!*" he hissed in her ear.   "We're *together* now! Can't you get that through your fucking head?   *I'm in charge now!*"

Shailene was still kicking her legs, her knees thudding against the floor, still trying to run, even though she could hardly breathe.

"Stop it!   Stop it!" he shouted.   He was straddling her waist now, pressing down on the place between her shoulder blades, pinning her to the floor.   There was a quick, hard hit to the back of her head—

* * *

An intense burning at the top of her belly awakened her. The pain was sharp as the knife cut a few inches from the bottom of her breast bone down, but it seemed a long way off; she felt it, but it was like it was happening to someone else.

Her eyes were closed, but she could tell when the blade left her skin. *He's stabbed me now; I'm dying.* With that thought she relaxed, let go. She thought of her parents. *They're already dead.* She felt sad, then thought she might be with them soon.

Her eyes popped open and tears ran down her cheeks as a jolt passed through her body. *Now* she was being stabbed; she could feel the blade slide into her, again just below her breast bone. Suddenly it hurt to breathe. She took shallower, quicker breaths, shrinking from the pain normal breathing brought. The blade slid out again. Through tear-clouded vision, in the dim light spilling out of the open door to her bedroom, she saw him looming over her.

"You think you're tough? We'll see how tough you are when I fuck your cunt heart."

She heard the sound of something metal being dropped from a low height on to the wooden floor, then the zipper on his jeans. There was a pause, and Shailene, still apart from what was happening, waited for the next assault, beyond being afraid, now just wanting it to end. She closed her eyes as his body lowered toward her. He stabbed her again, this time not with the blade. She closed her eyes and tried to go somewhere else in her mind, but couldn't ignore the pain of him pushing into the wound below her heart. She tried not to think of it, focusing instead on if she would throw up and breathing as shallowly as possible. His weight pressed her body into the floor rhythmically. He was thrusting like before, but now while straddling her body. She hoped it would end soon, hoped for darkness, wondered what it would be like.

Seven

October 1998
King of Prussia, Pennsylvania

The motel room on the outskirts of Philadelphia is low-end and generic, but clean and in decent shape. In other words, the usual: as inexpensive as possible while still being reasonably safe and sanitary. I drop my luggage—a garment bag, soft-sided suitcase, and black canvas gym bag—on the floor and close the door, securing it with both the deadbolt and a hinged metal lever that closes over a metal spike. The orange and gold drapes are already drawn, but I check there are no gaps between or around them. Exhaling loudly, I sit on the bed and rest my forehead in my hands. The adrenalin tremors subsided hours ago when I was still in Connecticut. Now I just feel tired—wicked tired. And hungry, but weapon and personal maintenance come before food and sleep.

I take my sneakers off, then get up and take the Glock from the black canvas bag. I only fired three rounds, so I'm not going to clean it, but I'll replace the used rounds with three more from the box of ammo I brought. I pull on my thin, tight Nomex gloves, then eject the magazine, clear the chamber, lock back the slide and inspect the barrel. I press two rounds into the magazine, which I then replace in the weapon's handgrip. I release the slide to chamber a round, eject the magazine again, and push the third round into it. Re-insert the magazine and put the Glock and gloves back in the gym bag with my soap and toothpaste and stuff.

Next I strip. The T-shirt and tank top smell like the fear from the rest stop hours ago. I'm sure the same goes for my underwear. I put everything I wore except my jeans in the big green Army duffel I use for laundry; get a clean tank top and underwear from my suitcase; and carry those, the gym bag, and my jeans to the bathroom.

I flip on the light and notice my reflection in the mirror over the sink. The pain below my sternum has been gone since taking out the guy at the rest stop; the old wound is only a shiny, faded pink line. As if it were healed.

Eight

November 1985
Lincoln, Massachusetts

She thought again of her parents, if she would see them again after—

That sound—what was that sound? She remembered hearing something hard hit the floor right before she heard the zipper.

Where's the knife?

She opened her eyes. The hallway was dimly lit by the light coming from her bedroom, but all she could see was his body, covered by the bloody sweatshirt. Looking straight up, she saw his shoulders and, tilting her head back slightly, she saw that face she wanted to claw to shreds. His eyes looked closed, his mouth was open. He was grunting softly in synch with the thrusting of his hips, and his arms were on either side of her head, propping him up. She turned her head to the right, in the direction of the sound she heard, but saw only her arm lying on the floor. She closed her eyes, felt her body being rhythmically pushed into the floor, squeezing the air out of her each time so she had to synch her breathing with his movement. She swept her right arm quietly toward her body, and felt the blade of the knife press lightly against the skin of her forearm. She curled her hand in and her fingers touched the handle of the switchblade. She bent her fingers around the handle, still warm from him, then slowly pulled it into the palm of her hand. She tightened her grip, squeezing the handle hard, and lifted the weapon a fraction of an inch, feeling its weight.

He was thrusting faster now, breathing harder, grunting, and forcing the air out of her in quick gasps. She opened her eyes slightly and saw his head thrown back, eyes still shut, mouth open wider. She focused on his neck, stretched taught above her head.

One chance.

She looked back down and raised the knife, its blade held back against her forearm. Carefully, carefully, she avoided touching his body and brought the knife up to her shoulder, in the space below his chest. She turned her fist, pointing the blade up and moving it over her face. She tilted her head back again and pointed the weapon at the stretched neck.

One chance.

His grunting was getting louder, like it did before. He was completely unaware of anything beyond what he was doing. His thrusting made it hard for her to hold the knife steady.

Do it!

She held her breath, tensed her body, then threw all the strength she had left into her right arm. The blade leapt up. She felt but didn't hear the blade's impact. He froze, and she pulled the blade back and hit again, and again, stabbing furiously at him as he raised himself away from her. A hot spray hit her face, stinging her eyes even after she closed them. He made a strange noise—a strangled, choked shout, and his hand hit her shoulder and pressed down, but she was still inside his arms and kept stabbing blindly. She could feel the blade connecting with something on him. The blood kept raining down on her, more on her neck and chest now as he pulled back and away from her. His hands found her arm and grabbed on to it, stopping it. For a full second there was almost no movement, and then his weight was bearing down on her, pinning her arm and then her whole body under him. She turned her face from the torrent of blood running out of him, soaking her hair. Her left arm was still free and, unable to fight any other way, she pounded his back and side with her fist.

She gasped for air and immediately felt sharp pain at the bottom of her chest, but the need for oxygen trumped the hurt. It was getting harder to breathe though; the monster had stopped moving, and he seemed to be getting heavier, pressing down on her, suffocating her. Frantically, she pushed against the body with her left arm, but couldn't budge him. Her right leg was free too and she kicked with that, trying in a frenzy to get out from under him. By kicking her free heel against the floor, pushing with her free arm, and doing a sort of wave movement with her body, she was able to finally pull her upper body out. She gulped air while trying to ignore the pain under her lungs and the sickening salty taste of his blood in her mouth. Pushing with both arms, she pulled the rest of herself out from under him.

Free, she backed away as quickly as possible, moving crab style as best she could, her dragging butt leaving a red smear across the floor. Everything hurt bad but, even if he was dead, she wanted to get as far away from him as possible. She bumped into a wall and used it to steady herself as she struggled to her feet. The intensity of the pain made her dizzy and she almost passed out, but by staying bent over at the waist she was able to hang on to consciousness.

Gotta get help. But running to the neighbors and trying to wake them seemed impossible since she couldn't even stand upright. She thought of the phone in her room, but choked when she remembered her mother. She felt her face crumple and tears flow. The crying made her breathing ragged, increasing the agony in her lower chest. *No, I gotta get help.* She calmed herself and thought. The door to her mother's study was a few feet away, and there was a phone on the desk in there. Still hunched over and leaning heavily against the wall, she staggered to the doorway and, holding on to the jamb, flipped the light switch. She knew the room wasn't very big, but just the idea of crossing it was exhausting. *Get to the phone, make the call, then you can rest.* She staggered across, sat down heavily in the desk's chair, and rested her upper body on the writing surface. She extended her right arm and pulled the phone closer.

"9-1-1 operator, what is the nature of your emergency?"

"Please—" Her voice was cut off by a sudden fit of sobbing.

Nine

October 1998
Philadelphia, Pennsylvania

"So do you have any more questions?" Detective Bradley Fogarty, the lead investigator from the Philadelphia Police Department, asks, his voice as rough as his face is lined and craggy.

The old detective smells like stale cigarette smoke. Mac leans back, making the movement casual, like he's just getting comfortable in the swivel chair, and looks sideways at the legal pad with his notes on it. "Just confirm or correct my understanding here: Five male victims, all found dead in their homes—apartments in every case."

"Correct."

"And all five victims had semen in their rectums."

"Yes."

"The first one was strangled, without ligatures, just the hands, and then had his skull caved in with a table lamp."

"Right—that's the actual murder weapon. The strangling apparently wasn't the cause of death, but probably caused the victim to lose consciousness."

"Makes sense. Second victim was hit on the back of the head with a cast-iron frying pan, then stabbed repeatedly with a kitchen knife."

"Yes."

Fogarty nods and still looks interested, Mac is glad to notice. It's rare, but sometimes he encounters skepticism in the cops he works with—cops who had a feeb profiler forced on them by their superiors, and perceive this as a vote of no confidence in their own abilities. Mac is good at dealing with this, at putting the cops at ease and eventually showing them he really does have something to contribute, but it's a distraction from his real job. Fortunately, that's not necessary with Fogarty, who attended a National Academy session at Quantico years ago and is pretty comfortable with the Bureau and its resources.

Mac continues, "The last three all had their throats cut, and the knife was not found. He refined his technique, found a method that worked for him, and started bringing a knife of his own and carrying it away when he's done. It's probably a switchblade since that'd be easy to conceal in his pocket, but also quick to deploy.

"His signature has also evolved. The first victim was left in a heap, with no postmortem damage aside from the excessive bashing of his head. With the second victim, our killer stabs and mutilates the anus after the killing. Then, with the last three we get the progressively more careful and elaborate excision of eyes and genitals and, with the last one, writing his message on the wall with the guy's blood—the gay epithet."

"'Fag'."

"Yeah: we hate most in others what we hate most in ourselves. Obviously our killer is homosexual, but he'd never admit to that. He didn't plan the first victim. After years— several years because he's at least in his late twenties—after years of amazing repression and self-discipline, he finally lapsed briefly and had his first gay encounter. He couldn't handle the truth, so in a fit of remorse and self-loathing redirected toward his sex partner, he reacted violently. He was disciplined violently as a kid, and that's how he reacted in this situation. Of course, it's pretty hard to strangle someone with just your hands, particularly if you haven't been taught how, so out of desperate frustration he grabbed that lamp and hammered away until the victim was very dead, then bolted.

"He spent a lot of time thinking about that afterward. On the one hand, deep down he really wants more sex with men.

He's had relationships with women, but he's just not into them—both figuratively and, probably, literally. He's single, never married, and probably has sexual performance problems with women, but not with these men, as we know. So deep down he wants to be with a man, but he also can't accept that about himself, probably because he was raised by parents with very traditional ideas about gender roles and sexual orientation, and about how to raise and discipline kids. Psychologically he's in a bind, but if there's one thing our big fat brains are good for, it's figuring out ways to justify doing whatever the id wants to do. In this case, he's telling himself these men he has sex with are bad—he may even use religious language like 'abomination,' or he may just dismiss them as 'fags'—sub-humans. What he thinks he's doing is verifying these men are gay, conveniently by having sex with them, and then taking them out. He sees it as a service to society, but really he's just trying to kill the homosexuality in himself."

This is an example of the far-reaching damage done by prejudice and teaching hate to children, but Mac doesn't say this to Fogarty. Given the color of Mac's skin, he thinks it would come across as militant, or at least political, neither of which is true of Mac. Instead, he summarizes "So what we have here is a man so afraid of his own sexuality he's compelled to lash out murderously at those who reflect back the truth about him.

"It's even more tragic when you consider he's intelligent—probably above-average. He can also be charming and socially adept; it's not hard for him to get men to invite him home. As I mentioned, he's disciplined and well-organized. His home is meticulously neat, as is his car, which is only a few years old at the most and is probably a sports car. Could be an SUV, but my money's on the muscle car, which he drives from somewhere else to Philadelphia. He doesn't live here—given his inhibitions, he wouldn't go looking for male companionship near where he lives and works.   I'm guessing he lives in Wilmington. He's an urban dweller, and Wilmington is pretty convenient to Phillie. Could be somewhere in New York City too, though. This is just a hunch, but I get the feeling his occupation has something to do with money—could be a broker, or maybe a banker: some line of work where he controls other people's finances. He's a college grad, most likely a four-year degree, and possibly an advanced degree—MBA maybe."

Fogarty smiles, showing gray teeth beneath his bushy gray and yellow mustache.

Mac smiles slightly in response, but asks "What? Which part?"

"The whole thing," Fogarty says, chuckling. "Don't get me wrong—I'm sure you're dead on about this guy. Years ago I worked with one of your predecessors—Paul Morneault?"

"He was one of my instructors."

"He did the same thing—it was like he'd met the guy. And you know, he was right about almost all of it."

"Well, he kind of did meet the guy, like I've met this one: through the killer's work. What he does with his victims is intensely personal and expressive. Sounds kind of weird—touchy-feely—but this is the most personal thing this guy has ever done, so it's a window on who he is.

"But what really matters," Mac goes on, "is how we use what we know to catch this guy. He doesn't care about the victims—this is all about himself, about what's going on inside him, so trying to elicit sympathy by humanizing his victims won't work, and he doesn't have any interest in visiting the graves or attending memorial services. That works with some, but not with this one.

"It's obvious from the removal of the victims' eyes, and the last time actually grinding them into the carpet, he's obsessed with how others see him. His victims saw his homosexuality, so he destroys their eyes. He writes 'fag' on the wall to prove he hates gay men—to prove he's not gay himself. If we let him know we're on to him, it might confuse him enough to slow him down and, ideally it'll provoke him into contacting us to set us straight."

Fogarty nods as he writes in his notebook. "The men he has sex with are mirrors he smashes; you want us to hold up a mirror, let him try to smash that one."

Mac smiles. "Exactly. Get him to over-extend himself and hopefully screw up in a way we can exploit. Either one— or both—of us can do it, but we need to give a press conference in which we lay out the profile, emphasizing the UNSUB's sexual orientation. I can write a script that will maximize provocation. We also need to promote the tip line you set up. He probably already knows about it—he's following news about the case—but I doubt he bothered to write down the number. We also need to coach the staff answering the tip line so they know which calls to re-direct to us. He'll ask for whichever of us makes the statement, but there'll also be the usual nutcases asking to speak to us too. We only want to talk to someone who claims to be the Slasher and who wants to set us straight about his orientation."

"OK, we'll probably still end up talking to some nutjobs—"

"Undoubtedly, but hopefully it'll be a short enough list that we can follow up on them. Even the phone numbers that call us might be helpful; if we get a payphone in, say, Wilmington, if the call is credible it'll at least give us someplace to look for him."

"OK, worth a shot. Anything else we can try?"

"The ostensible purpose of the press conference will be to ask people to contact us if they know someone who matches the profile, particularly someone who has become either more withdrawn or more vehemently anti-homosexual over the past couple months. That's our ruse to draw out the UNSUB, but it's not just a trick. The profile information we give will be accurate, and there might be people out there who know this guy well enough to recognize him. That'll generate a bunch of calls, but briefing the call center staff will help to sift out the helpful tips from the crap. They should all have summaries of the profile and should question callers who claim to know the Slasher about specific points in the profile, looking for correspondence."

"OK, sounds good. When do you want to do the press conference?"

"I can have our scripts written today, so sometime tomorrow if your guys can get the call center and its staffing set up and the conference scheduled with the media."

"I'll find out and let you know."

"OK, one more thing: I don't think waiting for calls to come in should be our only plan. The UNSUB may never call us, and we may get nothing helpful from the public. We want to put some of our people in the same place as him, but like I was saying before, this guy has no interest in visiting gravesites, memorial services, and probably not even murder scenes. Once he's killed his victims, he's done with them. And since he's not taking the bodies anywhere, we can't try to anticipate his next dump site."

"OK, so what do you suggest?"

"Normally we'd find officers who appear similar to the victims and deploy them in the places the UNSUB is hunting. The last four victims were all at gay bars the nights they were killed, so I recommend we place gay cops undercover in these places to see if they can spot this guy based on his behavior and the profile."

"Why do the cops have to be gay? Isn't it enough for them to be men in their late twenties or early thirties?"

"The cops working undercover have to be convincing: if they're not, and word gets out about cops working undercover, then the UNSUB spooks and goes somewhere else, and we have to start over again looking for him. We can't afford to mess this up with someone who's awkward and obviously doesn't belong."

Fogarty looks down and leans back away from the table, exhaling loudly. "Yeah, I don't know about that one. I'm sure it's a good idea in theory, but I don't know of any gay cops except this one lesbian who's been trying to organize some kind of a gay police union or something, which isn't going anywhere, probably because there aren't any—or hardly any—gay cops. The mayor and the commissioner have been pushing this gay-friendly thing, putting ads in the gay newspapers and coffee shops, but so far they've only gotten one gay guy to enroll in the police academy. You ask me, he won't last. I don't think gays have the personality for police work, and most of us aren't really interested in working with them. I mean, can you imagine being partnered with some fruit and all he wants to talk about is redecorating his apartment?" he smiles and looks up, but Mac doesn't return the smile.

Mac's familiar with the attitude, but he suppresses his irritation. It was the same in the Army: this perception that gay men all conform to the stereotype of being absurdly effeminate, or that gay men are obsessed with sex and will try to come on to every man they meet and so create chaos and incite violence in the ranks. Personally, Mac has almost no direct experience with homosexuals, but ridiculous stereotypes and animosity based on ignorance seems not so different from racism. He didn't always feel this way; in fact, years ago his attitude wasn't much different from Fogarty's. Mac can't recall a specific conversation, but Tracie was probably responsible for changing his outlook. She was such a good influence on him.

But Mac isn't here to preach or take a political stand. The mission is to help catch a killer, so he says simply, "OK, well look, this guy's going to be tough to catch. He's smart, motivated, and operating in a world that's hard for us to penetrate, so at least think about my idea. We need every resource we can come up with. That's all I have for now. I'll get going on the press conference script and the profile summary for the tip line people."

Ten

November 1998
Philadelphia, Pennsylvania

I watch the cops exit the apartment building, the badges on their dark uniforms glinting in the light from a fixture over the stoop. It's just the two of them: no prisoner, and I feel the weight of what has to come next press down on my head, compressing my neck and making my shoulders bunch up. Did I really have any right to expect different? They get an anonymous call sending them to an apartment where two consenting adults are continuing their date. Throw in a history of police harassment of homosexuals plus the present-day potential for bad press and lawsuits, and you've got two cops who can't get away from the apartment fast enough.

They don't notice me across the street and several addresses down, wearing dark clothes and standing in the shadows. The police car pulls away; I stare at the narrow three-story brownstone they came out of, the persistent itch of my scar confirming what's inside. It's all come down to me.

"OK, now what?" I sigh, a little tremor in my breath as it passes through my tightened throat. In the past I've looked for some corroboration of what the sense is telling me. I don't understand how the sense can even be possible, so I'm inclined not to trust it. The problem with verification is sometimes it means innocent people get killed—that was true on my first two missions. More often lately it means my ass is on the line, like in that rest stop—my shoulder still aches from that run-in, and that was three weeks ago. But not being a man, I couldn't put myself forward as a potential victim this time. Now it's too late for that anyway. Waiting, on the other hand, means standing by while the guy who lives here gets butchered. *I don't think I can live with that.*

Which leaves trusting the sense enough to kill someone on its say-so. "Fuck," I whisper. *Murdering on the basis of a gut feeling—tell me again what makes me different from them?* But it's either take out the target now or wait until another innocent person is dead first.   The sense has always— *always*—been right: never wrong, never mistaken. And if I'd trusted it when I ran into that kid in Trenton, the one who was dissecting a live cat, then the even younger child he killed months later would still be alive.

I look down at the sidewalk, polka-dotted with dark rounded shadows left by discarded chewing gum, and think about what I need to do. I walk through it in my head, try to anticipate how it could go wrong, then look back up at the lighted doorway diagonally across the street. I unsnap the front of my coat, reach in and touch the grip of the Glock with my gloved hand as if to confirm it's still with me, and step out of the shadows.

I almost forget to check for traffic before stepping off the curb, but there's no one. I stride quickly across the pavement, forcing myself into the present moment, thinking only about what I need to do, and accepting the increasing pain in my scar. On the other side, still walking, I take the black ski mask from my coat pocket. I pull it over my head and face as I reach the steps out front, and then I'm pulling the door open and squinting as I step inside. The lights in the building's other units have been out, and I don't want to wake them, so I move swiftly but quietly up the stairs, my sneakers tapping lightly on the wooden treads.

Even if I hadn't seen where the lights appeared after the target and his date entered, the sense would tell me which floor they're on, and there's only one unit per floor. There's a small oriental carpet and a little wooden end table with a vase and some dried flowers on the third floor landing. I pause in front of the door, rehearsing once more in my head. There's a moment of hesitation, but I draw the Glock and pound on the door, my head swimming a little as I realize there's no stopping now. "Police! We have a couple more questions, sir!" I call out in the deepest voice I can—the same voice I used when I called 911 a little while ago. My voice is on the low side for a woman anyway, so I can sound passably male.

"Oh for god's sake!" I hear one of them exclaim. "This is outrageous—did I *mention* that I work for a *law firm*?! Did you *miss* that part?!"

There's no peephole, so I stand in front of the doorknob, take a two-handed shooting stance, and put the red laser dot on the door where the opening will be. My finger is on the front of the trigger guard since the door will probably be opened by the guy I'm protecting—this'll be his place if the Slasher is staying consistent with his pattern and if the profile that FBI agent gave is accurate. I feel a slight vibration in the floorboards right before the deadbolt snaps back, the knob turns, and the door gets jerked open.

His face, a mask of anger and indignation, freezes, his mouth open to say something that doesn't come out. His eyes go wide and his skin gets noticeably paler. You hear about this, but I've never actually seen it happen before.

I was right about who would open the door; at least, I can see he's not the target, who is taller, has a bigger frame, and heavier facial features. "Back up motherfucker!" I say in the deep voice, loud enough to sound like I mean it and get through to him, but hopefully not loud enough to wake his neighbors on the floors below. He doesn't respond immediately, so I say it again, gesturing with the weapon as I do: "Back the fuck up!" I've got to make this happen fast.

He backs up, hands half-raised on either side of his body, palms open. I follow, keeping the red dot on his chest. The door is on my left, so I quickly check right and see the target across the apartment's open floor plan, back in the kitchen area. I look back at the would-be victim. "Get in the bedroom and close the door! Now!" I order, swinging the apartment's door shut behind me with my left hand. "Do it and you won't get hurt," I promise, trying to get the truth through to him.

"Take what you want, just take it and leave—I don't care," he says, backing toward an open doorway.

I glance over at the target—the Slasher. "You—don't move! Don't do anything!"

The resident is still backing up, and he says to his date "Do what he says—just let him take whatever and go. It's all insured anyway."

I like what he's saying, but I have to get this done. "Just get the fuck in the room and close the door!"

"OK, OK," he says, still backing up.

I take a couple steps toward the other and point the Glock at him, and when I do the resident turns and quickly disappears into what I guess is the bedroom, closing the door behind him.

He could have a weapon of his own in there—another reason to get this done fast. I cross the room quickly, gun outstretched in both hands, my finger inside the trigger guard now. The target starts to raise his hands, showing they're empty, but as soon as I see the red dot on his chest I pull the trigger. The impact knocks him backward, bending him back over the counter and bouncing his head off a cabinet door.

The sound of the shot is deafening in the closed space. I walk faster, putting the dot on his face and squeezing the trigger again, firing over an island with three stools lined up in front of it. His whole body drops suddenly, as if the wires holding it up had suddenly been cut, and the stabbing pain below my heart vanishes. Even so, and maybe it's stupid, but I side-step into the kitchen, pick out what's left of the face at the top of the crumpled heap, put the dot on it and fire once more. The head jumps and a section on the side of it shatters with a spray of blood.

I turn and run for the apartment's door, glancing toward the bedroom as I go, but the door there is shut and stays that way. I hit the stairs running, gloved right hand on the banister, Glock in my left hand now. Fortunately, the doors to the other units stay shut.

I tear off the ski mask and switch from running to walking when I get a few doors down from the building. I holster the Glock and button my coat even though I'm soaked in sweat and feel like I'm burning up. I turn down the next side street, put my hands in my coat pockets, and start thinking about how to get back to where I parked Stacey.

Eleven

November 1998
Philadelphia, Pennsylvania

"Be careful," she tells him, her dark eyes shiny. Her face has always looked regal to him, with its perfect ebony skin and prominent cheekbones made even more dramatic by her short hair being curled tightly against her head.

He reaches out and strokes the skin of her cheek with his thumb, feeling its soft smoothness. "You know I will," he replies, the weight of his son light on his arm, the child's wet face pressed into his neck. He drops his hand to her shoulder and pulls her close. "Come here, my queen." But there's a sound—he turns to locate the source, realizes it's the phone and he has to answer it. But Tracie—he looks back: she's gone and his eyes are opening to the semi-darkness of the hotel room, and the phone is still ringing. There's a stab of painful, sad realization. He reaches for the handset.

"Special Agent MacIlwane" he says, sounding wide awake.

"Mac, it's Brad Fogarty."

"Did he hit again?" Mac sits up and swings his legs over the side of the bed.

"I don't know. I just got a call from the late-watch detective and I'm on my way there now. The short of it is someone was killed in the gayborhood and there's some connection to the Slasher, but this one is different from the others. It'll be easier to have him explain it to both of us once we get there."

Mac is perplexed but asks only "OK, where am I going?"

Fogarty gives the address.

"I'll meet you there."

Mac hangs up and rubs his face again, trying at once to remember and push aside the dream, or rather the memory it was replaying. He wills himself out of bed and turns on the overhead light. He spreads his Philadelphia street map on the room's small table and locates the block containing the address Fogarty gave him, circles and dates it. The crime scene is about ten minutes away. A glance at the clock shows it's almost one-thirty in the morning.

* * *

Mac sees the flashing blue and red lights blocks before he reaches the address, the strobes bouncing off the close-packed buildings along the street. He finds a parking spot close to the brownstone and walks up to the police line. Because it's still early, there are few onlookers besides the press contingent—a couple TV news vans and a knot of reporters clustered against the police line. A uniform turns to him as he walks up, but he already has his FBI identification clipped to his suit jacket. They nod at each other and Mac ducks under the yellow tape.

There are more uniforms standing around securing the crime scene, but he doesn't see Fogarty. He climbs the stairs to the front door, greets another cop, and goes inside.

As he enters the building he is already scanning, looking for anything relevant, totally in the moment, completely attentive to his surroundings, the sights, the smells. He knows the crime scene technicians are going over everything carefully, but another observer might yet spot something unnoticed by others. He knows the killer almost certainly entered this way, and he tries to see what the killer saw, feel what he felt: anticipation, lust, power, guilt...

The building is so narrow there is only one apartment per floor. The door to each level's unit is open, and Mac sees uniformed cops conducting interviews inside, but no crime scene technicians, so he keeps going upstairs.

The third floor landing is small, occupied by an oriental carpet and a little table with a vase of flowers, and Brad Fogarty in his wrinkled tan trench coat, the lines on his face even deeper and the bags under his eyes bigger than usual. "Good morning Mac."

"Hey Brad. So what's going on? Are we still waiting on the crime scene people?"

Fogarty nods. "Yeah, it'll be a few more minutes. I just spoke with the ME: looks like cause of death was a couple bullets in the brain."

"Bullets?"

He nods again. "Yeah, this one is different—it may have nothing to do with the Slasher, so I apologize in advance for dragging you out here if it doesn't. I talked to the late-watch detective, and he tells me the responding officers had actually been to this same apartment about fifteen minutes before the call came in for the gunshots. Apparently there was an anonymous phone tip to 911 saying the Slasher was in this apartment with his next victim. So our guys show up, and it's just two fa—two gay guys hangin' out together. Our guys leave, figuring it was some kind of practical joke or something, but then about fifteen minutes later dispatch sends them back here to check out shots fired. They find the guy they talked to the first time, the resident here, screaming about some masked guy what burst in and shot the other guy here— his date or whatever. So now we're wondering if the first call, saying the Slasher was here, was just a few minutes early for some reason."

"Except it's the *'Slasher'*—he's never shot any of his victims as far as we know, and he always has sex with them first. What you just described is an assassination—get in, kill the target, get out."

Fogarty shrugs and nods, an "I know, what can I tell ya?" look on his face, his hands open and palms up at his waist.

"My guess would be someone with a personal connection to the guy who lives here or the dead guy was unhappy about them being together," Mac speculates. "Maybe it's a jealous former lover. So he tries to piss on their parade with the prank call to the police, and when that doesn't work he goes in and shoots one—either his former lover or the new guy in his ex's life. Maybe the survivor can tell us—he actually saw the killer, so maybe he recognized him from his shape and size and the way he moved."

"Jerry—he's the detective I mentioned—is interviewing him now downstairs in the second floor unit. I was just headed down there."

Detective Jerry Kuhns, a tall, pale, angular man in his thirties with straight brown hair and a matching bargain rack suit, takes a break from interviewing to tell them the witness has no idea who the killer was.

"That means the vic was probably the killer's former lover, right?" Fogarty asks Mac.

Mac nods noncommittally, rethinking the situation, which is starting to remind him of a couple other cases he's seen in the past two years. "Maybe, but you say the witness claims to have just met the victim tonight, right?" he asks Kuhns.

Kuhns nods. "That's what he said—they met earlier this evening at," he glances at his notepad "a club called 'Manhole'." He smiles and looks up. "Jesus, who comes up with these names?"

"So the—what's his name?" Mac asks, nodding at the visibly shaken man sitting at his neighbor's kitchen table and staring into a cup of coffee.

"Brent Stevens."

"So Stevens," Mac continues, "meets this guy at a gay bar and they decide to come back to his—Stevens'— place to hook up. *That* sounds like the start of a Slasher scenario. How long were they here before the police got the call?"

"Not long—they were here only a few minutes when our guys showed up the first time."

"In response to a call saying the Slasher was here with his next victim."

"Right."

"Have we identified the vic yet? Any ID on him?" Mac asks.

Kuhns shakes his head. "I don't know—I've been down here while they're working."

Mac turns to Fogarty, who says "Let's go find out."

Back upstairs Fogarty introduces Mac to a balding middle-aged man with pink skin and a cheerful expression, wearing Tyvek coveralls. The criminalist's name is Cashin, and it's immediately clear he loves his work more than most. "You can come in now, look around, but don't touch anything yet," Cashin tells them as he turns and leads the way back into the apartment.

As they cross the room, Mac notices a lot of blood and bits of tissue stuck to a couple of the kitchen cabinet doors and the tile beneath them. *Soft-nosed rounds*, he muses. Now that they're close, he can smell the cordite and blood, and urine too, undoubtedly from the dead body.   Once they're practically in the kitchen, Mac sees a technician bent over the body taking samples of fluids and scrapings from the skin. The sight of this always strikes Mac as surreal. In his Army experience he saw corpses, but they usually fit in with the general destruction and mayhem of their surroundings. The bright lights and clinical detachment of the crime scene technicians with their bottles, bags, and tools—everything neat, well-lit, and methodical—seems at odds with the grotesque aftermath of violence they study.

"Henry, we'd like to see the ID the vic had on him—did you bag that yet?" Fogarty asks.

"Yep, right here." Cashin takes a small white paper bag from a row of them on the counter-topped island separating the kitchen area from the rest of the room, and dumps a wallet and keys on a clear part of the counter. Cashin glances at his gloved hands, then picks up the wallet and opens it.

"Delaware driver's license?" Mac asks.

"New York, actually," the criminalist says, extracting the plastic rectangle and holding it up for them to see.

"That was my second guess. What's that on the keys?"

Cashin glances down at the counter, pokes at the key ring. "Corvette key chain."

"Makes sense."

Fogarty looks at him. "Wait, are you saying…are you saying the vic is the Slasher?"

"I think we need to check it out—fingerprints for starters. We have those consistent prints from the other crime scenes that we haven't been able to ID, so let's compare this guy's and see if they match. Do a DNA comparison to the semen in the Slasher's victims to find out for sure. But yeah, I'm guessing this is the guy we've been looking for."

"No shit," he says, looking over at the crumpled body in its puddle of blood.

"Sometimes you get lucky," Cashin says brightly.

"What do you think, Brad?" Kuhns asks. "Did we get lucky, or did the doer know who this guy was?"

Fogarty shrugs and looks at Kuhns. "Mac was saying it seems like some kind of love triangle turned violent. I guess it could still be that and we got lucky. But if the witness is telling the truth and doesn't know anyone who matches the killer, then that'd mean the Slasher was the killer's ex, right?" He looks at Mac for confirmation. "Does that fit what you know about the Slasher?"

Mac is actually thinking of the other two cases this one reminds him of—the other two cases where the bad guy he was trying to help catch turned up dead. The killer's signature matches the one here—quick, efficient execution of a serial murderer. There was an anonymous phone tip before the rapist-killer of children in Trenton turned up dead too. He wonders if the murder weapon in this case will turn out to be a nine-millimeter like the one in Kansas City. "I really couldn't say based on what we know—it's just an idea. I think it's unlikely the Slasher would have a homosexual lover who is still alive. If it were up to me, I'd question Stevens some more: see if he's absolutely sure there's no one he knows, even just a little, who matches the height and build of the killer. And did the killer say anything? Maybe the voice is a match. This person may not have actually been close to Stevens, but could have been stalking him. It's entirely possible he had no idea he was killing the Slasher, any more than Stevens knew he was dating him."

"Well what's the alternative? That this is the work of a vigilante who found the Slasher before us? How would he do that?"

"Maybe he was more hooked into the gay scene than us," Mac says quietly. He can sense the detectives looking at him. Point made, he continues, "But you're right: it's unlikely someone would find this guy before us, and if he's a vigilante, why'd he call the cops first?"

Mac notices he's pushing the personal connection theory, as if to deflect attention from the idea this is the work of a vigilante. But if the same guy killed all three of these serial killers, in three different states, then it's federal jurisdiction anyway. *I can compile the evidence on these cases back at Quantico and see if they match up.* "Mind if I interview the witness?" Mac asks.

Fogarty and Kuhns glance at each other, shrug, and look back at Mac. "Be our guest," Fogarty says.

Back downstairs, Mac accepts a cup of coffee from Mrs. Barsamian, a tiny woman about the same age as his mom, and sits down across her kitchen table from Stevens. After introductions, Mac asks "So how long have you lived here, Mr. Stevens?"

Stevens looks at him, blinks once, then says, a little dazedly, "Uh, about three years now."

"Good neighborhood?"

"Um, sure," he says, pressing his open hands together and setting them edge down on the table in front of him, as if trying to focus his thoughts. He looks at the hands, then back up at Mac, meeting his eyes.

"And what kind of work do you do?" Mac goes on, keeping his voice light and conversational.

"I'm a paralegal—a paralegal with Clermont, Jones, and Feinberg. Not to sound rude, Agent MacIlwane, but what does this have to do with someone barging into my apartment and gunning down my date?" Mac notices the hands have gone flat on the table now, and Stevens is leaning back a little, but otherwise his non-verbal cues haven't changed much.

"I like to take a holistic approach to my interviews," Mac says, trying to deflect the witness' irritability. Impatience at the baseline questions isn't unusual, and is usually a good indicator for innocence. "I just want to get to know you a little before we get into the heavy stuff, but in the interest of moving things along, why don't you tell me about the victim: his name, how long you've known him, where you met, like that."

"His name was Scott—I never got his last name. I just met him tonight at a club called 'Manhole,' and yes, I know it's a funny name, but that's what it's called. We hit it off and decided to come back to my place." He's still making occasional eye contact, and his hands are still on top of the table, pressed together and pointed at Mac again. Voice is a little high-pitched and stressed, but not much more than during the baseline questions.

"So you get back here and you're in the apartment for how long before the cops arrive?"

"I don't know—ten minutes maybe? Just long enough for it to be really annoying when they started pounding on my door."

"And what did the police say when you spoke with them?"

He sighs loudly, looks down at his hands. "I've already been over all this with Detective Kuhns—don't you guys talk to each other? Probably not." He looks up at Mac again. "I don't remember exactly, but the officer said something about a phone call saying someone dangerous—the Pink Slasher, I suppose—was in my apartment."

"Any idea who would have made that call? Or why?"

"That's assuming there *was* a call. You're probably from out of town, but the police in Philadelphia don't have a reputation for treating the gay community with respect, you know? Honestly, we just figured it was harassment; they probably saw us go in together, watched to see which lights went on, and decided to have some fun by trying to scare us. And it's only because of the police having just been by that I was so quick to open the door the second time. The killer actually said he was the police coming back, and I was furious, so I just threw the door open because I was going to get their badge numbers and file a complaint and maybe talk to one of the lawyers I work for in the morning."

"So the killer knew the police had just been there—is that what you're saying?"

The angry light in his eyes dims a little as he pauses to think. "God, it's so hard to go over this—it's like going through it again."

"I know, and I'm sorry, but we want to catch the guy who killed Scott, and what you tell us will help."

He nods, looking down at his hands, which are clenched together in a two-handed fist, but still on the table. "He said he was police, and said something about having a few more questions."

"So he actually said *more* questions, right?"

"Um," he tilts his head, thinking, then starts nodding again. "I'm pretty sure, yeah; I mean, whatever he said, I understood it was the same cops coming back again, which is what really ticked me off, that these guys had the nerve, the freakin' *audacity* to just keep coming back and openly harassing us." He makes eye contact. "Are you saying there *was* a call, and maybe the killer made it? But why would he do that?"

"I don't know; I was hoping you'd have an idea. Maybe there's someone who would be unhappy about you dating Scott? An ex? Someone who's been interested in you, but you didn't feel the same way about him? A stalker? Any of this ring a bell?"

He sits back and a look of concentration comes across his face. "I hadn't thought of that." He crosses one arm across his chest, grasps an elbow, and puts his fingers to his lips. "But no," he shakes his head, "no one I've dated would do something like this—I don't date violent people."

"You'd be surprised at how good people are at hiding what they're really like." Mac wants to add that he probably brought the Pink Slasher home with him earlier tonight, but doesn't. "I'd like you to make a list of everyone you've dated in the past couple years, or who's been interested in you in the past six months or so, and give it to the detectives."

"You've got to be kidding me," he says indignantly, crossing his arms.

"Look, Mr. Stevens, someone just came into your apartment and gunned down your date. If you want to help bring this guy to justice, then please, work with us. At this point we just want to broaden the investigation. Even if you're right and none of your acquaintances would do something like this, maybe one of them knows someone who would. Right now, you're the best lead we have—our only witness. So please, make the lists.

"Now, can you tell me anything more about the shooter? Is there any chance he could be someone you know? Think about him—how he moved, his size, his voice…was there anything about him even a little familiar to you?"

He closes his eyes for a few seconds before shaking his head. "I'm sorry, I'm just so…exhausted. God, this is hard. Can't we do this later?"

"We can, but I'd like you to give it a shot now because your memory of the details is unlikely to ever be better than it is now. Why don't you just describe him to me, and if that reminds you of someone, just let me know, OK?"

He sighs loudly, leans forward again and puts his hands on the table. He stares across the room for a few seconds, then closes his eyes and nods. "Mostly what I saw was the ski mask and the gun. But you know, now that I think about it, and don't have the gun in my face, I'd have to say he was probably shorter than me—yeah, I'm pretty sure of that."

"How tall are you?"

"Five-seven, so I'm not very tall either, but he was shorter."

"Does that match up with anyone you know?"

"Oh, probably—look, I'll make your list, but not now. Anyway, he was shorter than me, I'd guess around five-five? I'm not sure about the build—he had a coat on, a green, pretty shapeless, ugly coat. I don't know anyone with a coat like that; I mean, this was a really drab, dirty-looking dark green."

"What else was he wearing?"

"Well, the aforementioned ski mask—I guess that was black or navy, with holes for the eyes, but that's it."

"His eyes—what can you tell me about those?"

Stevens gives Mac a look that says "you've got to be kidding me."

"No, think about it—maybe you can't give me the color of his eyes, but what about the skin around them?"

Stevens closes his eyes again and thinks. "Well, he was a white guy—pretty pale, actually.   But that's all I can remember."

"Pants?"

"I don't know—jeans maybe?"

"Blue? Black? Did you see what color they were?"

He shakes his head. "Like I said, I was mostly looking at the gun, which was up high and pointed at me, so I wasn't looking down at his legs."

Mac realizes he should have thought of this sooner: "How did he hold the gun?"

"Um, well, in both hands, sort of," he sits up straight and holds his hands up, the right index finger extended like the barrel of a handgun.

"Were his arms out straight?" Mac wants to demonstrate, but doesn't to avoid replacing whatever memories are there with new ones. "Or held in close?"

Stevens' eyes roll back, then he flexes his elbows and pulls his arms in a little. "I think they were like this. Oh, and there was a light on the gun—a red light."

"A red light? You mean a laser?"

"Yes!" he says, pointing at Mac. "It looked like a laser pointer! But why would he have a laser pointer on a gun?"

"It's a sight—the laser points to where the bullet will go."

"Oh," he says, his face a mixture of interest and distaste.

"That's really helpful," Mac says.   "Can you tell me anything else about the weapon?"

"It was black."

"OK, anything else? How big was it?"

Stevens shrugs. "I don't know—it looked big from where I was standing."

Mac pulls out his own side arm, a Beretta 92FS Vertec and displays it.

Stevens automatically looks away and puts his hands up. "I really don't want to look at another gun."

"Mr. Stevens, please: I'm not pointing it at anyone and I'm not touching the trigger. Did it look like this one? Was it bigger, smaller, same size?"

Stevens looks askance at it. "His kind of looked like that, but—well, I don't know. I really can't tell if it was bigger or smaller."

Mac holsters the weapon and lets his suit jacket close over it again. "How about his voice—he said some things to you—what did his voice sound like?"

Again he closes his eyes. "You know, he was mostly yelling at me, but now that I think about it, his voice seemed a little off, like he was trying to make it sound different— deeper, maybe?" He shakes his head and looks at Mac. "I don't know—it could have been that his voice sounded a little unnatural and forced, but I'm starting to feel like I might be imagining things to fill in details. I really couldn't say for sure, other than it was a mid-range voice—not high, not low."

Mac questions him for a few more minutes, but it's clear Stevens has given up all the useful information he's going to for now. Mac thanks him and reminds him to get the lists of acquaintances together for Fogarty and Kuhns. Then he heads back upstairs to look for them.

"Hey Mac, the criminalists found something they missed the first time they went through the vic's pockets." Fogarty holds up a switchblade in his gloved hand.

Mac nods, not really surprised. "I think that's our guy."

"Anything useful from Stevens?" Kuhns asks.

Mac shrugs. "He's telling the truth. I asked him to come up with a couple lists for you, of everyone he's been intimate with for the past couple years, and anyone else who's exhibited interest in him in the past six months. You'll have to remind him about it, though. He's not too keen on doing it, but I think he will if you keep reminding him he's the only real lead here."

"So you think it was someone jealous of him?"

"I really don't know. It could also be someone connected to the Slasher, but I doubt the Slasher had any intimate male partners who lived. Could be someone stalking him but we can't get his list, so Stevens is the best you can do for now. At least it'll expand the investigation; throw the net wide enough and maybe you'll catch something."

Again Mac doesn't mention the bodies in KC and Trenton—those wouldn't be their problem anyway. It makes sense to let the Phillie cops focus on the local possibilities while he explores the other connections. This serial vigilante, if he exists, can be Mac's own investigation, his own operation to run.

Twelve

November 1998
Somerville, Massachusetts

"Thanks for taking the time to answer our questions," I say, finishing up the last interview of the day. I give the doctor the number to call if she doesn't receive her honorarium check by the end of next week. At least I'm ending on a good note; this doctor was polite, and forthcoming with her answers without droning on. I hang up the phone, take off the headset, then log out of the computer terminal that's been feeding me the survey script and taking the answers I typed. Time to go home and get some dinner.

Doing phone surveys is pretty boring, and feels like a waste of most of the years I spent in school. I have a masters in information technology; I could have built the network these terminals are on. I had a job like that, when I first got out of the Army. Then my other life intruded.

Trenton.

Now I have three jobs, more or less, and they all allow me to take extensive time off when I need to, which has been a lot lately—a month last December, three weeks over the summer, and then six weeks just recently in the fall. My other life is incompatible with a full-time job, or even a part time job that expects you to keep a regular schedule. The phone bank would rather I was around more, but I guess they have a big enough pool of people that they're able to deal with my absences. The courier gig and the landscaping work are the same way. I don't need much, so between the three I'm even saving a little, though I don't really know what for.

Stop it.

I pull on my coat and the dark blue knit cap I wear in the cold weather. I use electric clippers to cut my hair down to about an eighth of an inch every weekend, so my head gets cold if I don't wear a stocking cap from November through March.

The room is getting noisy now. The night shifts here are usually bigger and louder than the day shift. Most of my day shift co-workers are older people—moms and semi-retired people looking for easy work with flexible hours. The night shift is completely different—fully staffed, and mostly kids still in high school and college students. I go over to the table by the door and sign out.

"See ya tomorrow, Shailene."

I look up at Dale, the guy who manages the computer network here. He's about my age, I guess, and looks his part: skinny with thick-framed glasses, hair that's perpetually damp-looking, and side burns extending down below his ear lobes. He's a nice guy, I guess, but makes me nervous. Not because he's dangerous—obviously I'd know if he were. I think he wants to be friends *(or something)*, and that weirds me out. It's messed up, but the more time I spend alone, the harder it is for me to be friendly and talk to people, and the less I want to be around them.

Although it would be nice to have someone besides myself to talk to once in a while.

"See ya," I say.

I take the back stairs down. The treads are wood, and old enough there are dents worn in them from all the feet that have stepped on them, back to when this building was still used as a factory instead of an office building. I push through the door at the bottom and walk out into a little dead-end alley with a row of triple-decker houses across from me.   It's dark, drizzling, damp, and December chilly. I start walking home.

It's cold, but also beautiful. Everything is shiny because of the rain. The beams of the headlights of passing cars and buses bounce off the wet pavement and glistening light poles, and the tail lights and traffic signals shine like jewels.

I cross College Avenue, one of the six streets leading into Davis Square, then the brick-paved area between the two subway entrances, passing through the scattering of three-quarter size statues of people: a flower vendor, an elderly couple, a family of five watching a mime frozen mid-performance, depicting something I've never been able to figure out. I have to wait for traffic before I cross Holland Street. Then I pass the other subway entrance and start down the bike path that'll take me out to Massachusetts Avenue.

The path is lined with tall lights, made to look like old gas street lamps, and this time of night there are always commuters on foot, headed home from the T station, but even if it were darker and less well-traveled, it wouldn't bother me. The attack on my family and me when I was fifteen happened in our home—a big, well-built, secure house in a safe, high-end neighborhood. No place is completely safe. If I were going to be scared, I'd be scared all the time. I don't believe in being afraid; I believe in being ready. I have a canister of pepper spray in my pocket, I know something about fighting, and I can run like hell if I need to. My legs are a little sore now from the weight training I did this morning and yesterday's wind sprints, but adrenaline will take care of that if I need to run.

The drizzle has turned to a full rain now, the droplets zipping down. My knit hat is already pretty wet, and my semi-water-resistant coat and canvas high top sneakers will be soaked through by the time I get home. When I get there I'll change into dry, comfy-warm clothes and heat up some cider in the microwave. I think I have a can of lentil soup in my cupboard—mixed with some instant rice, that'll be dinner. Until I get there, though, I'll walk fast to generate heat.

Before taking a right on Mass Ave, I glance left, as usual, toward Porter Square and the cozy restaurant Mike and I had dinner at. In a few months it'll be two years since I told him to leave me alone, but I still think about him. I figure he's probably doing well; he was pretty squared away. I imagine he's found a girlfriend by now.

I'm a pretty rotten person sometimes, and to such good guys, too. It's embarrassing. I cringe at the memory of the last time I saw Derek, the guy who was my best friend in high school, who probably would have been my first boyfriend, if not for the Bad. He was a sweetheart; he even came to visit me in the hospital after the Bad. I told him to leave me alone too.

So here I am, left alone.

With Mike there was a minute or two when I almost forgot about the Bad, about the answer the monster gave when I asked him why he was attacking my parents and me:

Because you're hot.

I *almost* forgot, but then Trenton happened and my other life stomped all over what I'd been trying to build—both the job and the friendship with Mike.

Well, I don't really want to be anyone's girlfriend. The implications of being a guy's girlfriend move through my brain and I actually shudder.

Now it's just me and Harold. I feel one corner of my mouth tugging into a half smile. Harold isn't much of a boyfriend, or any kind of friend, but trying to figure him out gives my brain something to do and distracts me from the cold, now that my coat and hat are soaked with rain.

His name isn't really Harold; I guess he doesn't have a name. I don't think he has a gender either—"it" is probably the more accurate pronoun. But thinking of it as Harold is sort of a private joke for me. When I was very young, before I even started going to school, I thought it was called Harold because of the prayer: "Our father, who art in heaven, Harold be thy name..." I believed the father part long after I found out I had his name wrong, but the Bad set me straight on that:

What kind of a father would let something like the Bad happen to his children? Even if I deserved what happened, my parents didn't. I really shouldn't have needed the Bad to figure this out: if Harold is any parent at all, he's a sick and abusive one. History is full of examples—holocausts, wars, and plagues on the grand scale; murders, rapes, and torture on the individual level. If Harold made this world, I hold him ultimately responsible.

Actually, after the Bad I decided Harold didn't exist at all—I had enough trouble sleeping without believing in a psychopath god. Conspiracy theorists like to think there's some organization, some design—even if it's malevolent— behind what happens, but not me. I'd rather take my chances with randomness.

But that was the problem: the *lack* of randomness. Ironically, it was the weird sense that enables me to find psychopaths, that legacy of the Bad, which undermined my atheism, the other legacy of the Bad. The sense is so consistent in its function—dependably accurate and predictable in the way it varies with distance—it's the opposite of random. That got me thinking about all the other regularity and order in a world that at first seems crazy and unpredictable. Once I started looking for it, the order was everywhere: mathematics, the laws of nature, even me—my body, the brain it sustains, and that brain's ability to string thoughts together. Science is part of it too. There don't have to be any explanations or patterns of cause and effect at all, but there are. We don't need a bioengineer god to create my body and its brain when we have billions of years for natural selection to work its magic, but even the mechanism of evolution is a kind of pattern, a way of carving order out of chaos. *Something* is going on here, and I want to know what. If there is some Harold at the heart of it all, I'd like to know what his freakin' problem is.

Maybe our traditional ideas about Harold are all wrong. If they are, I'd like to know *that* too.

Either way, even if it sounds weak to someone who was a devout atheist three years ago, and who's still skeptical of the whole God and religion thing, I know deep down I'm hoping to find something that makes sense out of the mess that is my life. It'd be easier to deal with if there were some reason for it, something beyond the boredom and the senseless violence.

But I'm a long way from that. I didn't even get serious about this hunt for Harold until after Trenton. I'd killed three...for lack of a better word...*people* before Trenton, but those were "them or me" situations. Trenton was the first time I knew what I was going to do, more or less, before I did it. The final, irreversible step in that apartment was quiet, relatively slow, even intimate. Hundreds of showers later, and I still have its trace on me, plus the accumulated stains of the killings since—not on my skin, of course, though sometimes it feels that way. If I believed in a soul, I'd say that's where the damage is accumulating, but I don't believe in a soul. Not yet, anyway.

I meant to take my mind off the cold and wet, not creep myself out. *Fucked that up.* I've crossed over into my town—Arlington—now. Up ahead is the Capitol Theatre's lighted marquee; I focus on that. As I pass the movie theater's entrance, I check out the posters and think about maybe taking in a movie sometime this week, but I don't stop. I just want to get home.

At the next corner I pass a pizza place. A delivery guy comes out and gets in a car right before I go by, and I walk through the smells of the fresh-baked dough, cheese, and tomatoes. I haven't had pizza in years, but my stomach growls and I look longingly as the guy pulls into traffic and drives off. *OK, almost there.*

A couple more blocks and I turn down Marion Street, and then right on to my street—Belknap. I'm only a block off

Mass Ave, but the densely-packed houses, a small storefront, and a big church effectively screen out most of the traffic noise. I really like where I live—it isn't, but it feels almost secluded.

I climb the three steps to the front porch of the triple-decker I live in and enter the left-hand door. The mail for the second floor unit and the two third floor units gets dumped on the stairs inside this door, so I spend about a minute sorting through the envelopes, catalogs, magazines, and flyers to see if any of it is for me, and come away with an electric bill and—very happy—a new *National Geographic*. Outside again, I go around to the back of the house. Five doors, two porches, and two sets of stairs later, I arrive at my door. I like the complicated route to my apartment, even though it makes carrying groceries up a pain. All the doors and stairs make it harder to find me. Plus, I can hear every door and stair from inside my apartment, so it would be hard to sneak up on me when I'm at home. I unlock the deadbolt I had installed, then the knob lock, and pull the door open. Inside I key the deadbolt locked again, twist the button on the knob lock, and use a snap link to attach the chain from the wall across the stairwell to the eyebolt I installed low on the door. Even if someone picked the locks and busted the glass on the door's window, it'd be pretty much impossible to reach the chain down near the floor, much less open the snap link and unhook it, and with that chain in place the door isn't coming open easily.

I hang my coat on one of the hooks just inside the door, then climb the last set of stairs up to the main level of my space. At the top I glance around, seeing everything just as I left it in the morning. I flip off the stairwell light and flip on the ceiling light in the middle of the room, then sit on the brown-orange carpet that came with the apartment and take off my sodden sneakers, leaving them in their usual place on the top stair.

There's another door up here, leading out to my deck. I flip on the light out there and look around, seeing only the buckets and flower boxes full of dirt and compost left over from last summer's container garden. This side of the house faces south, and in the warm weather I grow sweet and hot peppers, tomatoes, eggplants, and okra. My harvest wasn't so great last year because when I went to Kansas City I had to move everything down to the second floor's back porch. The light isn't as good there, and my neighbors, who very kindly kept things watered, didn't notice the aphid infestation. By the time I got home at the beginning of July I'd lost half the pepper plants. Still, if it hadn't been for Pete and Liz watering the plants, everything would have been dead, and I really didn't expect or ask them to do anything else.

I close the inside door to the deck. I left it open in the morning so during the day the room and the two small cacti I keep in pots would get as much sun as possible through the glass of the storm door. There's really no way other than a really big ladder, or a grappling hook I guess, to get to my deck from outside, so I don't worry about leaving that door open during the day. Still, I close and lock it now, both the knob lock and the deadbolt I had installed, and then I put my keys on top of the half wall separating the stairwell from the rest of my space.

I go to the bathroom to pee, glancing inside the sliding doors to the shower-bath combo as I go by. Then I change out of my wet clothes, draping them over a folding wooden rack, and put on sweatpants, a hoodie, and thick fleece socks, which feel like a warm miracle on my cold, damp feet.

In the little kitchen area I nuke a cup of cider while I dump a can of soup, instant rice, a chopped up dried cayenne from my deck garden, and olive oil into my Pyrex bowl. Cider comes out, dinner goes in and gets nuked for five minutes. While I wait, I put on my Walkman and Public Radio's *All Things Considered* comes out of a pair of big, propped-open headphones.   The voices are familiar and homey. I sit down at the drafting table I got at a used furniture store and write a check to pay the electric bill.

After dinner, I check on my pet cacti. I thought about getting a real pet, like a rat or a hamster, but it'd be alone a lot, and I don't know what I'd do with it when I have to go on missions, so instead I got these two cacti. One of them has a dry, kind of hard textured surface that makes me think of a lizard, and the other has really long spikes all over it. These guys are good for me because they can go for weeks with no water and I like how they're kind of bad-ass with their needles and armor. Supposedly they can both flower, but I haven't seen that yet. Maybe they know they don't need to do that to impress me.

I turn off the radio and settle into my basket chair with the book I've been reading. I bought this chair from a guy on a Cambridge sidewalk. It was cheap and all I had to do was clean it up and run the cushion's covers through the laundry. It's wicked comfortable—sometimes too comfortable because it's hard to stay awake in it.

Lately I mainly read books to help me figure out Harold. I'm still not totally sold on Harold—God—whatever— existing, but I heard if you want to understand an artist, look at his art. Science looks at Harold's art, so I mostly read science. Occasionally I mix in philosophy or, rarely, theology. I had enough myths fed to me as a child: I don't need to read more lies. It *is* helpful to read how other people have approached the questions I'm thinking about now, but I'm not looking to glom onto someone else's answers. I'm not going to trust anything I can't figure out for myself.

It's usually hard to make any connection to my hunt for Harold. Some nights the basket chair wins and I start nodding at the book, half-formed dreams mixing with the words I'm reading. Tonight, though, something clicks, and about forty-five minutes in I find something important.

Maybe. Often what I think is a big idea ends up being disappointing after a day or two, because once you realize something, it becomes sort of obvious. Still, I always write stuff down. I lever myself out of the deep round cushion and shuffle over to my desk, flip open my Harold notebook, and scratch out a few lines. *Another piece of the puzzle.* It doesn't necessarily mean I've dropped the piece in place; just finding the pieces to begin with feels like an achievement. When you're not sure the puzzle exists at all, finding pieces to it is pretty exciting. Eventually, when I have enough collected in the notebook, I'll try to fit them together.

At least that's the plan.

Thirteen

November 1998
Baltimore, Maryland

Flash stands back, feeling the moment fully, making it count. Ironically, he spends the least amount of his life doing what makes him feel most alive. The hours wasted just on sleep! And the rest of it: eating, shitting, showering... Most days are dominated by the grind of work with its office politics and bullshit small talk. Even the best parts of his usual life—training at the gym and watching those movies he special orders—are poor substitutes. All that shit just to get to these few perfect, worthwhile moments. So now he pauses, catching and holding each second as it slips by.

Even now the outside world is intruding on *his* time. Unfortunately, all the nasty, weak-willed humans who individually wouldn't have the guts to stand up to him—*couldn't* stand up to him even if they did—collectively have him outnumbered. Society and all the fucking governments appointed over him tell him how to live his life. They try to kill his spirit with their laws, stipulations, and constraints. He evolved his own set of rules to protect himself from the hordes, but the fact that he has to have rules at all intrudes on this precious, all too rare time and space he's carved out for himself. The bullshit day to day world shouldn't be allowed to detract from the few, best hours of his life. It's an inversion of the correct order of things. The strong should dictate to the weak, not the other way around. *They* should fear *him*.

Fuckin' bullshit, he thinks, riding the thrilling wave of rage that suddenly comes barreling through his head, blurring his vision slightly and making the honed muscles all over his naked body jump. Channeling the hot, red frustration, he reaches out and, grasping her big toe in both hands, he snaps it over sideways. There's a loud crack, but he's not sure it was a bone snapping so much as the joint. Her bones are small and thin, but it felt like the joint gave way.

Of course, her whole body jumps and strains against the belts and cords he's tied her with, and she screams, but the sound is almost completely muted by all the panties he shoved in her mouth—one of his rules. He'd like nothing more than to hear the full-throated, ear-splitting screams, but that would attract attention from the other tenants in the building, and not long after that the police. More tears are running down her face, and she makes some jerky heaving movements, but there can't be anything left in her stomach to throw up and choke on, not after earlier. There was so much of it—surprising for such a small woman. The smell of it hangs in the air, part of the full experience. It's all good.

He turns and goes across the short hallway to the bathroom, his sticky, tumescent cock flopping against his thighs. Despite the fullness of his bladder, it takes several seconds for the plumbing to switch over to piss and the stream to start. He doesn't wait for the dripping to stop; he simply turns and, on his way out, stops in front of the mirror.

He examines the hard cords and bulging muscles, the delts like cannon balls at the tops of his massive arms, his pecs swelling like rounded mountains when he flexes them. This body is the proof: he's taken charge of his life and who he is. He's become the antithesis of the cringing, scrawny, joke of a man that was his father. He has put things right.

But he could use more mass in his upper chest—one of his perpetual weak points. Maybe more negative work will help with that: he'll blast the area when he gets back to the gym this weekend.

He wonders if the woman could have ever imagined, all those mornings and evenings she spent looking into this mirror while she brushed her teeth, fixed her hair, applied and removed makeup, if she ever could have had any idea her fate would one day be reflected in this same mirror, or that it would look anything like Flash.

Back in the bedroom, he glances at the clock: it's almost four a.m. Unfortunately, this means it's time to wrap things up here—another rule. Despite being up all night, he feels like he could go another twelve hours, riding nothing but the excitement—a pure, clean high, without any shit like ecstasy or coke or anything else. Just the experience: the real, unaltered, unmodified intensity of what he's doing to her, with nothing separating him from that. This is his drug of choice, and except for the dianabol and growth hormone he uses to maximize his body's musculature, it's the only drug he uses.

But no matter how up he is now, the rules dictate he finish and get the hell out before her neighbors might start coming out of their holes. No one can see him leaving her apartment.

He goes to the kitchen in search of a blade and finds a nice sharp paring knife. This is the only time he uses anything besides his own body, or the gags and bindings, to do what he does. That's important—his body, his personal strength is his weapon. From when he first subdues them, to when he finally kills them, he doesn't need tools, except for this one part, because he needs to cut to take a trophy. There's more muffled screaming and bucking, even though she's only making it worse for herself every time she makes the tip of the blade slip. He presses down hard on her pelvis to hold her steady and takes his souvenir. It's dark like her nipples—darker than he'd imagined when he first met her hours ago at the bar. He finishes cutting and sets it on one of the bedside tables. Then he turns her head for her and makes her look at it.

Her tears feed his anger and hatred, and he fucks her once more, hard and fast. Now time is really getting away from him, so he finishes up with a series of hammering punches to her face before twisting her head for that last, satisfying *crunch*.

Fourteen

November 1998
Quantico, Virginia

All the offices in the FBI's Behavioral Analysis Unit, the criminal profiling department of the National Center for the Analysis of Violent Crime, are located in the basement of a building at the FBI Academy in Quantico, Virginia. Mac isn't sure why they're stuffed in the cellar, but the unit is relatively new—about twenty years old—so maybe all the choice offices were taken when it was formed. Being underground, there are of course no windows, but it works out since they use the unbroken wall space to spread out crime scene photos and diagrams. Depending on the case, and the photos, that can be pretty intense and disturbing.

Mac's boss, the BAU's chief, is Martin Helmbrecht, and his office is just down the hall from Mac's. Helmbrecht has been writing profiles of criminals longer than anyone else in the unit, and still pitches in, so his office is plastered with photos and diagrams too. There are also a couple white boards showing ongoing cases and the BAU personnel assigned to them, and a small part of one wall is devoted to Helmbrecht's diplomas and photos of him with Janet Reno and some other people Mac hasn't been able to see that well from the visitor chairs.

Today Helmbrecht is wearing a crisp, dazzlingly white shirt with a gold pin joining the corners of his collar to the tight, symmetrical knot on an intricately-patterned deep blue tie. He is not wearing his suit's jacket now, no doubt to avoid creasing it, so Mac sees gold cuff links and navy blue suspenders. Peering through the rimless round lenses of his glasses, Helmbrecht could be a corporate raider on Wall Street, examining his next target's report to stockholders.

"Nice work in Philadelphia," Helmbrecht says, looking up from an open file folder on his desk and motioning Mac to an empty chair.

Mac feels his brow furrow. "Sir?" *Is he being sarcastic?*

Helmbrecht's face is pleasant and he meets Mac's eyes when he says, "Good job. Your profile was right on the money."

"A lot of good it did: they didn't catch him."

"They would've. The main thing is, you did your part flawlessly. Well done."

"Thanks."

Helmbrecht looks down at the papers in the open folder again, but then a quizzical expression takes over. "By the way," he says slowly, and then looks up at Mac again. "Didn't something like this happen to you before? Was it over the summer?"

Mac nods. "Jerome McNeely—the Kansas Cities Killer."

"That's right," he says, nodding and leaning back. "Hmmm...weird."   Helmbrecht studies him for several seconds. "You're not offing these guys, are you?"

"What?" Mac says, almost laughing.

Helmbrecht smiles too. "Well, I know you're probably accustomed to doing things more efficiently, given your last assignment in the Army."

Mac forces a small smile, nods, then shakes his head. "Yeah...no." Mac's last unit assignment is actually classified, and glossed over in his personnel record, but Helmbrecht managed to find out shortly after Mac joined the BAU, and for some reason enjoys making references to it when they're alone together. Mac isn't sure if he does this to make a point about how well-connected he is, or if he really likes joking about it, but Mac finds these references annoying. "You know sir, that stuff was so long ago now, it seems like I'm carrying around someone else's memories." He means it; after eleven years, his time in the Army seems like another life, parts of which he misses. A lot.

"Anyway," Mac continues, "I think Philadelphia PD's theory is an associate of the Slasher's last victim, probably a former lover who didn't want to be former, took out the Slasher. That's the angle they were pursuing when I left them. As far as KC goes, the case was turned over to the local police there. The best they could come up with is some citizen who happened to be carrying accidentally came across Jerry McNeely when he was dumping his last vic's body, and the citizen decided to take matters into his own hands, then got scared and left."

"That's a hell of a coincidence."

Mac isn't sure if he's referring to Mac's involvement in two cases where the original object of the investigation was violently assassinated, or to the improbability that someone with a gun would just happen to come along an industrial back road around two a.m. when a body was being dumped. Maybe both, and Helmbrecht apparently isn't even thinking of Trenton, which was more than a year and a half ago. Mac could mention that now, but instead he hesitates for a heartbeat and the old Mac, the guy who used to get shit done himself, shoves the guy in the supporting role aside. "The thought crossed my mind too, but with all the body dumps McNeely did, odds were someone would run into him eventually. Besides, how would someone else find him before we did? We had more information and resources than anyone."

"Unless the someone else knew McNeely personally— maybe even was close to him," Helmbrecht offers.

"You want me to look into this? Follow up with the locals out there?"

"Nah," he waves dismissively. "Just thinking out loud. It's a local problem," he says, apparently discounting the possible connection he'd been making between Kansas City and what happened in Philadelphia. "If they want help they can call us—the fact they haven't probably means we'd be unwanted if we tried to force ourselves on them. No, I've got an abduction and demand for ransom for you to deal with," he says, tapping the open file in front of him. "There's some stuff in the kidnapper's communications I think you'll be able to work with. Mainly, they need you to help them narrow down the list of suspects."

* * *

It's about six-thirty at night. Mac often works late—no reason to hurry home anyway. He pushes aside the Chinese takeout containers and leans back in his chair, looking again at the large blank areas on one wall's corkboards. Besides the kidnapping case, Mac spent part of the day filing away the materials from a case he worked on a couple months ago. The local DA just indicted a suspect in the case, so Mac took all the related crap off the boards and organized it for use during the trial, making room for the inevitable.

He shifts his eyes back to his computer screen. The computer's operating system allows for a background picture on the screen, and this is the one mental oasis in Mac's office. Mac changes the picture, but it always includes his wife and very young son. His favorite pictures include him too, on one of the rare occasions when they were all together. Tonight, though, it's just Tracie and Malcolm, laughing while she tickles him. Actually, Mac was there too, but on the other side of the camera. He stares at their images, trying to transport himself back to that day about thirteen years ago.

But he wants to do at least some work on his project before he leaves. The vigilante has been on his mind since he got back from Philadelphia several days ago, and he wants to develop this profile while the ideas are still fresh in his mind.

Unfortunately, he's been unable to get to it, mainly because this profile is technically not work. Officially, the killings in Trenton, Kansas City, and Philadelphia are unrelated and, like Helmbrecht said, fall under local jurisdiction. Mac might have been able to change that, if he'd made a point of articulating his gut feeling about the homicides being the work of one person, and if he'd mentioned Trenton too. But the BAU is overworked and understaffed, and there are so many other urgent cases where innocent lives are at stake. It seems pointless to make a big deal about three bad guys getting killed, especially when their deaths may end up not being related after all.

But—also like Helmbrecht said—it's a hell of a coincidence, especially when Trenton gets added to the mix. The cases *feel* similar, and there's something about them, and the man behind these killings, Mac can't leave alone. So tonight he's not going home until he's completed at least an outline of a profile.

A couple clicks on the computer's mouse and a word processing screen obscures Tracie and Malcolm. They have interactive software for developing profiles, but Mac prefers a blank screen and the free flow of his thoughts for the first swipe at it. He begins to type.

White male

All three victims were white, and were sufficiently removed from one another to make it effectively impossible they had a mutual acquaintance between them, so it's unlikely the vigilante knew more than one of his targets personally. Serial killings of white strangers are almost invariably committed by white males.

This guy is different from the typical serial killer, though: he's not looking for a *type* of person, but rather specific individuals who have done something. The odds still favor the killer being caucasian, but Mac adds a question mark before hitting the Enter key.

In Trenton there was evidence of a struggle in which the target, a heavy-set guy in his late twenties, was subdued, probably rendered unconscious by a choke hold, before having his brain stem neatly severed by a paring knife. The vigilante would therefore be able to hold his own in a physical confrontation. This, along with the neat, professional style of killing, implies some kind of training and discipline in the application of violence:

Probably former, possibly current, military or law enforcement.

This guy clearly came prepared to take out his targets— he was armed, at least in the last two incidents, mentally ready to fight, and quick in his work and escape. He even took the precaution of wearing gloves when handling his ammunition to ensure his fingerprints did not appear on the shell casings.

Extraordinarily organized, focused.

This level of care and preparation indicates he is at least in his late twenties and intelligent. Probably has a college degree too. It also indicates his fingerprints are on record, possibly because of employment in the military or law enforcement, or because of a past run-in with the law.

Late twenties to

Mac thinks about it. It's hard to narrow the age down; after all, Mac's forty-six, and he could do what this guy has done. But he's probably under fifty.

late forties.

Some more characteristics follow along with great attention to detail:

Fastidious. He is clean and tidy, as are his clothes and his living quarters.

His vehicle is well-maintained, though not necessarily new.

Mac wonders about make and model. It would be something that seems practical, but it's hard to say what that would be to him? A muscle car to give him fast acceleration if he needs it? SUV for its off-road capability? Or something small, ordinary, and inexpensive that blends in and is easy to forget? Mac leaves the question unanswered and moves on to pieces he can be more certain of.

If not still in law enforcement or the military, he is retrained as some kind of professional—not a doctor or lawyer, but possibly a financial advisor or some other kind of consultant.

The consultant idea looks about right—if he has time to go and do these missions, he's not tied to a strict schedule. Maybe he's self-employed. Mac starts to type, then realizes he's making an assumption: maybe the vigilante doesn't need all that much time to do these missions. That goes back to one of Mac's original questions: How does the vigilante find the bad guys before the police and the FBI? But Mac isn't going to be able to answer that tonight either; God knows he's thought about it enough in the months since McNeely turned up dead back in Kansas City. Mac just doesn't see how it's possible.

Unless he's currently working in law enforcement…what if he's a rogue cop with access to data from ongoing investigations? *And what? He's some kind of criminological genius who is somehow able to sort out the identity of the unknown subjects faster than the rest of us?* That seems unlikely, but Mac mentally ticks off a list of people involved in the cases and can think of no one who worked all three—Trenton, KC, and Phillie—unless you count Helmbrecht, and he didn't really work them. No one except Mac himself. A small smile crosses his face. *Just you and me...*

But how are you doing it? How do you know who the bad guys are? Then it occurs to him: He didn't know. In Kansas City he killed McNeely when he caught him dumping a body. In Trenton the vigilante entered Wayne Lambert's apartment by busting through a window off the fire escape. There were no victims other than Lambert himself in the apartment when his body was found, but there was evidence of children—

fingerprints matching two of the victims they found buried in the woods, and fingerprints from one other child who was never found, on a remote control toy.   It's possible the vigilante waited until Lambert had his next victim in the apartment before he burst in on them.   He waited until the bad guy did something incriminating, to be sure of what he was before taking him out.   But in Phillie there was no victim: just two consenting adults in the apartment together when he forced entry and killed the Slasher.   Granted, he waited until the Slasher was making his move, but didn't wait until there was incontrovertible evidence.   Mac types some more.

OK, so he wasn't sure, and when possible he looked for corroborating evidence, but that doesn't change the fact that he knew *whom* to look at.   And in Philadelphia, even without evidence, he was right: he got the Slasher.

He also called the cops first, as if he would've preferred the police take care of things.   The vigilante only made his move when the police passed and he had to act to save someone's life.

It's not about the killing for him; he doesn't enjoy taking out killers.   He'd rather the police do it for him.   And he's careful, making sure he has the right guy before he attacks, unless someone else's life is at risk.

Mac wonders if he contacted the police about McNeely in Kansas City, but maybe he didn't have a chance to.   He does remember an anonymous phone tip regarding Wayne Lambert; Trenton P.D. followed up on it—actually sent a pair of detectives around to Lambert's apartment and questioned him a week before he was killed.   Mac doesn't know the details of the tip, so he looks up the phone number for Jonas Vidian, the lieutenant there who was in charge of the case.   He calls and leaves Vidian a message asking for any information about who gave them that tip.

"OK, so he's probably not a sociopath, and he's probably not a cop either since he wouldn't need to *call* the cops if he already were one. And he can't be completely without faith in the criminal justice system if he's trying to refer his cases to it." Mac types some more.

Mac considers what else he knows: There's the 911 call the vigilante placed in Philadelphia. Mac has listened to the tape several times, but finds the voice doesn't reveal anything except the caller was trying to disguise his voice. Obviously distorted, it's mostly devoid of inflection and accent neutral— just a generic, TV anchorman American dialect.

And there's the witness description he got from Stevens in Philadelphia. That's not a lot to go on either. The vigilante is short, knows how to handle a gun, and…well, that's about it.

The KC Killer and the Pink Slasher were both killed with nine-millimeter Hydra-Shok ammo—hollow-point bullets designed to deform on impact. This ammunition is typically used in law-enforcement because it's safer for bystanders: the distorting bullets don't ricochet or pass through walls as much. But this ammunition is available to the public, and many gun owners choose it for both the safety aspect and stopping power: instead of passing cleanly through, deforming ammunition flattens and clears a bigger path through the body it hits. Mac could request comparison of the ejected shell casings and recovered slugs from both scenes, but that might attract unwanted attention to this project. Besides, even if it wasn't the same weapon at both scenes, that wouldn't rule out the same perp doing both killings. And it wouldn't tell him who the vigilante is.

He needs more information from somewhere. The profile only describes what the vigilante is like, and now Mac really wants to know who he is, to locate this guy and find out how he works. Mac opens up a search interface for the ViCAP database. The Violent Criminal Apprehension Program's database is an exhaustive electronic compilation of violent crime case histories. He defines a query to include all the homicides of known criminals in the United States since 1993. As he expected, this yields way too many hits, so he filters the results to include only killings of violent criminals.   This narrows it somewhat, but it's still too broad, so he screens out all the cases ending in arrests. Although the initial search took a while, the additional filters do their work in seconds, and he finds he now has a list of a few dozen cases. As a sanity check, he verifies the three cases he knows of—Trenton in '97, and Kansas City and Philadelphia this year—are still included in the list. He's not really sure what he's looking for, but he's hoping a pattern will be evident, or he'll at least get an idea from looking through the cases. After about a half hour, though, he realizes he still has too much data to sift through.

He chucks the empty Chinese food containers from dinner in the trash can by his desk and leans back in his chair, interlacing his fingers behind his head, the lightly-stubbled scalp warm against his palms. He's not sure how to crack this, but it's good to be on the hunt and calling the shots again. He really misses being in charge.

OK, let's think about motive. He looks at photos of the three victims—three dead murderers—spread out on his desk. There's the motive right there: killing killers before they can kill again, but what drives him to do it? These guys couldn't have all been connected to him personally, so why run the risks to do these hits? *Something in his past, maybe.*

Like me, Mac thinks. Maybe this guy lost someone to violence too, and now he's fighting a war, same as me. *Well, not exactly the same. I send the bad guys to court, not to hell. Shit, now I don't even do that; I help someone else send the bad guys to court, and hopefully to jail, and* maybe, eventually *to hell via lethal injection.* "I like his way better," Mac mutters, surprising himself, but it's true.   This guy is dangerous and has no right to do what he's doing, but Mac can't help feeling…what? He doesn't exactly *like* him, but maybe there's a little grudging admiration.

Or envy.

Mac types the note about motivation; it might help him find this guy eventually. Whatever happened to him or his is likely in the ViCAP database.

He closes his eyes. *What else? What do I know about his signature?* He realizes he hasn't added the dead murderer factor to his ViCAP search. He leans forward again and types, modifying his query to screen out all the victims who were not themselves suspected of homicide. This list is considerably smaller, but still contains his three known incidents. He reads through the other cases, which turn out to be drug or organized crime-related, or incidents where a cop was the one to kill the murderer.

There's one exception: a bizarre mystery. In May 1995 a pair of hikers in northwestern Florida discovered a van parked in a field beside a dirt road, its side door open. Noticing a strong smell of rot, they approached the vehicle and found the bodies of two women—one just outside the van's open door, and the other inside on the van's floor. The subsequent police investigation discovered a third body, a man, in the tall grass near the front of the van, his head smashed in. The blunt trauma to his head killed him, but there was also a post-mortem bullet in his skull. Mac lingers on that detail, wondering: both McNeely in KC and Skufka in Phillie also had bullets in their brains; in fact, Skufka had two. As for the female bodies, the one inside the van had her throat ripped out, apparently by the woman on the ground outside the van who was still gripping the knife she used to do it. This second female was killed—two bullets to the head—by the same .38 Smith and Wesson that put the bullet in the male's head. Neither the handgun nor the blunt object murder weapon were found.

The dead man, Alan Hayes, was the registered owner of the van and, incidentally, a .38 Smith and Wesson that was never recovered, and the knife-wielding female was his live-in girlfriend Denice Horn. Neither had a prior criminal record. The knife victim, Kristen Reese, was a twenty-year-old college student attending Florida State in nearby Tallahassee. She had been reported missing a couple days earlier by her roommate. Besides the fatal knife wound in her throat, Ms. Reese had also suffered several other injuries, inflicted by someone wielding a vice grip, a box cutter, and a soldering iron, all of which were also found in the van. Apparently Hayes and Horn had been torturing Ms. Reese, and trace evidence in the van indicated other women had been attacked there in the past. Through DNA analysis of this trace, the investigation was able to tie the couple to one other missing person case, in Mobile.

Clearly a fourth person interrupted Hayes' and Horn's activities, killed them, and left with the murder weapons. The police questioned Ms. Reese's acquaintances who were or might have been in the area at the time of the murders, but they all had solid alibis. There were some tire tracks in the clay surface of the adjacent road, but rain and the passage of several vehicles, including the hikers', had made obtaining useable imprints impossible. Except for some bloody prints left by sneakers—small Converse All-Stars sneakers—on the floor of the van, no evidence of this person's identity could be found, though the police pretty much disassembled the van searching for clues.

"Was that you?" Mac whispers.

Fifteen

December 1998
Arlington, Massachusetts

I adjust my backpack as I stand at the top of the broad granite steps in front of the library's main entrance. Arlington is not a huge town, but it has a big library in a massive stone building, and I think that's really cool. It's one of the reasons I've always liked Arlington.

This evening I've checked out several books because, with Christmas merging into the weekend this year, it looks like I'll have three days off from my jobs and will be doing a lot of reading. I'm really looking forward to it. I'm jazzed about the other night's insight, which still feels important—a good sign. Most of the time I'll come up with a thought which seems huge, but after a couple days I either find something wrong with it or end up thinking "so what?" This one, though, really does seem like a major piece of the puzzle.

I was reading about chaos theory: a kind of science that looks for patterns in unpredictable systems like weather. We tend to think unpredictable events are random, but often that's just us not wanting to admit our ignorance. Chaotic systems are dependent on so many subtle, small causes that we can't have anything like enough information to predict what will happen next, but the systems' behavior is still caused and patterned, not random.

One startling thing about chaotic systems is the complex, beautiful, and repeating patterns called fractals that are formed when some of these effects are quantified, described by surprisingly simple mathematical expressions, and graphed. Out of what looks like a random and boring series of events, like drips falling from a leaky faucet, appear these amazing, intricate patterns. Maybe this kind of observation isn't something a real philosopher or scientist would consider significant, but stuff like this got me doubting my atheism in the first place.

It's hard to accept all the natural rules and order we see around us are an accident. I'm not arguing for something hokey like "intelligent design" or, worse, "God's plan"—a phrase I hate. But when I see stuff like this, it makes me want to know more. I mean, why should mathematics, with its consistent results and logical inevitability, not only exist, but actually describe the universe—everything in it and the way it works? And the more we look around, the more order we find, even in places we weren't expecting it.

That last bit is what I'm excited about now—the first major piece of the puzzle I've found in a while: *Paradox is typical.* Chaos theory is an obvious case of apparent opposites occurring together, in connection with each other, but once you start looking for it you find examples everywhere. In a universe that's blasting apart, and spreading its energy out, living organisms are pulling stuff together and concentrating energy. Or take something like steel—so hard and heavy, but now we know it's mostly empty space, with each neutron in an atom of steel smaller than a fly compared to the stadium-sized atom all around it. Even in ourselves: each person can be so compassionate and giving, and also so full of hate and destruction.

I wrote all this down in the notebook I keep. There are lots of pages full of writing, but it all boils down to only a few ideas I feel any certainty about: First, I know something exists, because otherwise I couldn't be here, reading, thinking thoughts, and writing them down. Even if things aren't as they seem, and they're probably not, it's hard to argue against the idea that *something* exists, and I might as well believe I do.

Given the existence of anything, it's hard to avoid asking where the edges are, and if there are edges, what's beyond them? Maybe there aren't any edges to Harold; maybe he's—it's—infinite. Put another way, if you believe in cause and effect, and you start following the pattern back, you quickly find out there's either no end to the chain, or there's some ultimate causeless cause that's the source of everything else. Either way, it smells like infinity to me.

And now this idea of paradox: I'm not sure how it fits in, but it's definitely another piece, another glimpse of Harold.

It's only about five p.m., but it's fully night. As I walk down the sidewalk I notice Arlington Center is decked out for the holidays with strings of white lights adorning the lampposts and trees by the town's biggest intersection. Snow has started falling, and I'm relieved and a little surprised to actually feel cheerful. Since graduating from West Point I've spent most Christmases alone, and I've learned to keep busy with things I'm interested in instead of moping around feeling sorry for myself. But it's been a long time since I actually felt happy about the holidays.

The last time was when I spent Christmas with Miranda, but that was three—no four—damn, *four*—years ago. We put up a little artificial tree in her apartment. We couldn't get her string of lights to work, so the tree was unlit, but the ornaments caught the light from the room and we were happy with it. We exchanged gifts Christmas Eve. She gave me a book—*Maia* by Richard Adams. I think she thought I'd be able to identify with the protagonist, a girl who loses her family, survives dangers, and overcomes obstacles. Maia is stronger and better-adjusted than I am, but I did like the book. I gave Miranda a pair of stud earrings with small stones which matched the deep violet of her eyes. She always wore plain gold ones before that, but I hope she liked them; she did wear them until we broke up. Maybe it was a little of my suppressed girly-ness from before the Bad coming out, but I thought they looked great on her.

We were doomed from the start, but it was mostly good while it lasted. We met at night school while we were both working on master's degrees in computers, and started talking in the parking lot after the class we had together. The time we spent standing there next to my car or her jeep got longer each time, and when my birthday came up in October she really wanted us to go somewhere together. She'd invited me out before, but I'd always resisted. After the Bad I just wanted to stay by myself, and the more time I spent alone, the harder it was to be with other people. By the time she came along I was a hermit girl, but Miranda was persistent.

"Oh no you don't," she said after class. "I know that smile, and you're not backing out of this."

I looked up at her, wondering *Am I that obvious?* "What smile?" I asked.

"That's your 'maybe some other time' smile—the one you always use when I ask you if you want to go to Boomer's with me and meet my friends."

"What? I don't—" I hesitated, unsure what to say because obviously she was right, but not about tonight.

"Only because I stopped asking you," Miranda jumped in, her smile and Alabama drawl softening the words. She touched my arm lightly and spoke more softly. "Hey, I'm just teasin' you—you know that, right? I know you don't like a big crowd, and that's fine by me. It's just us tonight, I promise."

"Sorry I'm...I don't know...so anti-social. I just feel awkward, never know what to say..."

"You fooled me—you always seem to have plenty to say here in the parking lot. Look, seriously, it's just us tonight, and I want you to have a good time—it's your birthday, woman! But if you'd rather not, just say so—we don't have to do anything. I know I come on kinda strong sometimes. I just get...enthusiastic, you know?"

"I really like hanging out with you—you're my best friend." I paused, decided not to add the rest of the truth: *You're my only friend.* Instead I explained, "I'm just not used to celebrating my birthday. It's no big deal to me, and I haven't really paid attention to it in years." Nine years, to be exact; the last time had been with my parents. The first couple years it had seemed wrong to celebrate anything, and my father's parents reinforced that feeling. As if it needed reinforcing. Since then, not celebrating anything had become habit, a sort of penance.

"Why not? Are you feeling your mortality? Now that you're an old woman of...what? Twenty-three?"

The feeling was more like guilt, but I didn't want to explain it: "Oh no—try *twenty-four*!"

"Ancient! In that case, we must eat, drink, and be merry, for tomorrow you may be gone. Not me though—I won't be *that* old for another year! But if it makes you feel any better, you don't look a day over...twenty-three, same as me."

I smiled and felt myself relaxing a little. It wouldn't hurt anything to be with Miranda for my birthday.

"See! I can always get you to lighten up," she said, looking at me. "And when you smile you look like you're about sixteen."

She was smiling too, but also appeared hesitant, as if she wanted to say something but wasn't sure if she should. "What?" I asked, searching her eyes, which in the dim light of the parking lot looked as dark as her nearly black hair.

"I'm just memorizing your face, before it dissolves in wrinkles now that you're getting so old." She smiled and started walking away. "My jeep's over there—follow me, OK?"

"Where are we going?"

"Surprise—just follow me."

When we arrived at an apartment building across town, I figured out where we were even before Miranda announced "home sweet home."   We took a well-lit flight of stairs down to her one-room basement apartment.   "It's not much, but it's affordable.   Anyway, I'm comfortable here, and like being in the basement.   In the summer it stays cool down here, and who cares about having a view in this town anyway.   No one underneath me to complain about noise either."

"I live in a studio too—I like it.   The small space feels safe; I can see everything except the bathroom as soon as I walk in the door," I said as I stood just inside the doorway beside her, looking around.   The walls were covered with pictures of female athletes; the only one I recognized was Jackie Joyner-Kersee.   Part of one wall was almost a shrine to a blonde bodybuilder.   "Who's she?" I asked, nodding at the collection of images.

"Kathy Unger—best abs in the business," Miranda declared, stating the obvious.   "Wish mine looked like that."

"I didn't know you were trying to really bulk up—I mean, wouldn't you need steroids to look like that?"

Miranda shrugged.   "Yeah, I mean, I wouldn't *really* want to look like that, not *that* big.   But I would like to rip up more, y'know?   Really cut up.   I'm too smooth.   You're closer to what I'd like to look like—when we were working our arms last weekend I could see every fiber in yours."

I shrugged, a little embarrassed.   "Product of a vegetarian diet and lots of running.   So who are these guys?" I said turning and looking at the only picture of males in the room— four youngish men, one with a saxophone, another with a large upright bass, and all wearing sort of retro-looking suits and hats, as if they'd just stepped out of the 1930s or '40s.   "I mean, I can see from the poster they're called the Birmingham Bruisers, but..."

"Swing band.   Now you're learning my guilty secrets.   Actually, swing dancing isn't really guilty or secret.   I was hoping I might get you interested."

"I don't know anything about it—I'm not even sure what swing music is. Isn't it really old?"

"Ever heard of Count Basie?   Glen Miller?   Duke Ellington?"

"Oh—Duke Ellington—I've heard of him. I thought he was jazz."

"He was—swing *is* jazz, like an old form of jazz. I can't really explain it better than that—I'm no musicologist. But I know swing when I hear it. Here, I'll put some on and you can listen while I'm gettin' dinner ready." She walked over to the one bookcase in the room and selected a CD from a small collection. "The Bruisers play some Ellington tunes on this album," she said as she put the disc in the portable stereo.

I immediately recognized the line *It don't mean a thing if it ain't got that swing!* "Oh yeah, I've heard this song! This is really cool!" I didn't listen to music much—didn't own any of my own. I'd lost interest in my collection of eighties pop about the time I moved in with my grandparents, and had never really gotten in to music again. But this—the way they used drums and their voices, the honking saxophone, and the upright bass plunking along underneath it all, made me want to forget everything else and move my body. I'd taken ballet as a girl and liked it, but hadn't danced since I'd stopped listening to music. I wandered around the small apartment, gazing at the posters and swaying a little to the beat.

"That's what I was hoping to see!" Miranda said, turning around from the kitchenette part of the room.

I turned and smiled. "I really like this."

"If you're a good girl and eat all your veggies then after dinner I'll show you some dance steps."

By about midnight we were both flushed red in the face from dancing and I felt like I at least understood what the Lindy Hop was, even if I couldn't quite pull it off. I'd had fun trying; it had been the best time I'd had in years. A big part of me didn't want it to end when I suddenly noticed the time.

"Whoa! I should get going—it's late and I have to work tomorrow."

"Stay."

"Oh, I can't—I left my flight suit at home. I had no idea I'd be here so late," I said, looking around for the sneakers I'd taken off earlier. I spotted them in a corner and walked across the room to retrieve them. "Miranda, this has been the best! I had a great birthday—thank you so much! You're the best—" I turned and discovered Miranda had followed me across the small apartment. Our eyes met and I saw something serious, hopeful, and vulnerable. "...friend I've ever had..." I finished, my voice trailing off.

"Stay with me tonight," Miranda said quietly, evenly.

"Oh." Suddenly I got it: the awkward moments when she stood face to face with me but didn't say anything, the little touches, which made me nervous at first because I don't like being touched but I'd gotten used to, the excited look she got in her eyes sometimes. It all made sense now. "Oh," I said again, feeling stupid and panicked and clueless.

She turned and walked away. "I'm sorry—I didn't mean to put you on the spot, but I had to know. You have no idea how hard this has been for me, how many times I almost just—well, anyway, let's forget I said anything, OK?" She turned and forced a smile. "Happy birthday! Don't forget your present!" she said.

"Miranda, I—"

"Nope, let's just forget it, OK?" She opened the door and I stepped through, carrying my sneakers in one hand and the present she gave me in the other.

The door closed and I found myself standing in the stairwell, suddenly overwhelmed by the thought that I was losing Miranda's friendship. There was something more, too. I was twenty-four and I'd never been close to anyone, and that wasn't likely to ever change for me with any guy. The idea of dropping my guard in the presence of a man was...it just wasn't going to happen. I knew that, and how lonely it was. *Could it work?* I looked back at Miranda's closed door, then at the stairs leading up, then back at the door and knocked. "Miranda?" Silence. I knocked again. "Miranda, please? Can we talk? Will you give me a chance?"

Several more seconds passed before the deadbolt slid back and the door opened. Miranda stood slouching, as if annoyed at the interruption. Her eyes were a little red and puffy. "What?"

"Can I come in, please? I have some things I want to tell you, but not all your neighbors."

She looked at me for a couple heartbeats, then looked down and slowly walked the door open. I entered, and she closed the door again and stood a few feet away, looking alternately at the floor and the refrigerator.

"This might be hard to believe, but I had no idea you were, you're a, that you—"

"That I'm a lesbian? Are you kidding? Do you honestly expect me to believe that?"

"Look, this isn't easy for me," I said, my voice rising to match hers. "I'm not exactly worldly, all right? I've never met a lesbian before, and I'm not experienced with guys either. I've never had a boyfriend, never been on a date, never even held hands."

"What—are you looking for some kind of sympathy?"

"No, dammit, I'm trying to make you understand how it is I could be caught so completely off guard by you. I've never even considered being with a woman, but—"

"Oh, well don't let *me* sully you with my worldly ways!"

"Will you shut up and let me speak?"

"Well hurry up!"

"What I'm trying to say is I'd like—" I almost said "try," but sensed that would sound bad. "Look, I don't know if it would work or not, but I...I want it to. Work. With us." I felt like I needed to say more, but decided to stop.

Miranda slowly looked up at me. "What are you telling me?"

"I've never felt this way about anyone else, and I don't want to lose you, if it's not too late already."

"I don't know if I like the idea of being a lesbian experiment."

"Well, that's the best I can do, Miranda. I'm not going to lie to you. It's scary for me too."

She looked down. Several long seconds crept by before she slowly looked up again, a small smile on her face. She took the few steps between us so she was standing close, and I felt something deep inside my stomach contract thrillingly. Miranda's eyes shifted down and her smile broadened a little. She took the sneakers and present from me and set them on the floor before resuming her position facing me. She was just a little taller, and I stared into the deep, dark blueness of her eyes. She placed her hands lightly on the back of my neck and moved closer.

I closed my eyes and forced my mind to go silent. Our lips touched, and I was all physical sensation—the soft pressure of Miranda's lips, the heat of the hands on my neck, the presence of another all down the length of my body, the feel of the small of her back under my hands. A tiny spark of panic ignited, but I stamped it out: *It's OK, it's Miranda; I'm with Miranda.* I inhaled her scent; Miranda didn't wear perfume either, but she still had a flowery feminine fragrance—her soap or something. The smell reassured me, made this closeness possible. She pulled back and I opened my eyes, met her gaze.

"You're going to crush me," she said softly.

Embarrassed, I let some of the squeeze go out of my embrace. "Sorry," I whispered.

We closed our eyes and kissed again. This time I felt her lips part and her tongue flick against my lips. Instinctively I opened my mouth and let the tongue in. The slippery, wet sensation was new and exciting, and I kissed back hard. *Miranda, I'm with Miranda.*

I wonder how she's doing now.   I still miss her. Sometimes I listen to the swing CDs I bought later and remember getting dressed up in retro clothes and going dancing together. You'd think that'd be depressing, but it's pretty much impossible to be depressed while listening to swing. Instead, it cheers me up because it makes me think she's probably doing great, with someone who's a better match for her. I wish it could've been me; I'd change if I could. When we had sex the first time it was fun, but not so much the second time, and then I began avoiding it. I wanted to stay friends, but Miranda wanted a real relationship. Selfishly, I asked her to give me more time. "Women aren't oysters—we're not an acquired taste," she'd said. "If you're not wired that way, then you're not."

I guess I'm not wired at all anymore.

Sixteen

December 1998
Memphis, Tennessee

"So? How is it? Turkey too dry?"

"No, Mama, it's great," Mac replies honestly. "I'm just trying to figure out why you continue to make so much when it's just the two of us."

"It freezes. I'll get I don't know how many more meals out of this dinner. You would too, if you'd move back here."

"It'd be kind of a long commute to Quantico from Memphis, don't you think?" This always comes up, and Mac's response is automatic. The next question is too, but he means it, and catches his mother's eyes before he asks, "Why don't you move to Virginia, Mom? You could stay with me until we find you a nice apartment nearby."

"What, and leave all my friends?"

"You make friends faster than anyone else I know— you'll have a whole new gang inside of a month. And it's not like you can't keep in touch and come back to visit here sometimes—I'll give you the tickets I would have used to visit you."

"Silas, forget it. You're not going to get me to move to Virginia any more than I'm going to get you to quit the FBI and move back home."

They look at each other grimly for a few seconds then begin to smile, and soon they're laughing. "Mama, you are one tough old broad."

"Well, you're a stubborn young man."

"Not really young—not anymore," Mac says, still laughing a little.

"Hmm! You got that right. So tell me, my not so young son, have you met any nice ladies lately? Are you seeing anyone?"

Mac's smile fades and he looks down at his plate. This line of questioning is also familiar. "No, Mama, I'm not."

"You'd probably meet more women if you weren't still wearing a wedding ring."

"Mama—"

"No, I don't want to hear it again. I know what you're gonna say, but son, she's gone. You're not married anymore, and I don't think Tracie would want you to be lonely for the rest of your life."

"I still feel married. I still feel like she's with me. You know I still dream about her?"

Mrs. MacIlwane reaches both her bony hands across the corner of the table and grasps Mac's right hand, removing the fork from his fingers and setting it gently down on the plate as she does. "Silas, that's wonderful and noble—for the first year. Even the first two years. But son, she's not coming back, no matter how much you want her too. Malcolm neither."

Surprised, Mac looks up at her face. She almost never mentions Malcolm, so painful was it for her to lose her grandson. Her eyes are compassionate, but there's also a firmness there.

"That's right, I said it. They're gone, Silas, and it's been *twelve* years now. More than twelve. And you may be not so young anymore, but you're not so *old* neither. You're too young to give up on life, to stop living."

"Well what about you? You didn't re-marry after Dad died, and that was five years ago."

"But I *am* old—"

"Not so old—sixty-six."

"I *know* how old I am! And it's a damn sight older than you. You're too young to be livin' they way you do, spendin' all your time at work or alone in your condo and not sharin' your life with anyone!"

"All right!" Mac says, throwing up his hands.   "I surrender—you win."

"So you'll try to meet someone new when you go back to Virginia?"

"I'll think about it, Mama, all right? I'll think about it— that's the best I can do." Mac knew, even as he said this, it wasn't really true, but it seemed pointless to go on arguing, especially on Christmas Eve. He knew from a lifetime of experience she wouldn't give up until he admitted she was right.

"Well, think hard, 'cause I'm right about this one."

"I will, Mama, I will. Now," he said, changing his tone and picking up his fork again, "why don't you tell me what your church group is up to—aren't y'all planning a trip to Branson?"

* * *

The next morning, as he has almost every Christmas morning since he lost his family, Mac rises early and drives to the cemetery to visit them. The air is surprisingly chilly and the frosted grass crunches underfoot as he walks through two rows of markers to the stone that will eventually mark the graves of all three of them. For now, though, there's a blank space where his year of death will go. Mama had been unhappy with this arrangement, said she didn't like seeing her son's name on a tombstone, but Mac knows, has known since not long after he first met Tracie, that she is it for him. He never even considered removing his wedding ring.

And then there's Malcolm—

Mac can't even think about Malcolm while looking at the grave marker without losing his composure. Like a child himself, Mac feels his face contort and his eyes burn. He shifts his eyes from Malcolm's name to the phrase he had added to the stone a year or so after it was put in place here: "A Love Supreme."   After a while he regains control, and contents himself with looking at their names and the phrase above the potted poinsettia he has brought and centered at the base of the stone. He says nothing; he knows he doesn't need to, that wherever they are, they know his thoughts without his speaking them. They know that every day he wishes, more than anything else, he could have been there when they needed him, and misses them so badly he sometimes imagines ripping his heart out to ease the pain.

By the time he leaves, the sun has melted the frost off the grass.

Seventeen

December 1998
Matthews, North Carolina

Flash watches them munching contentedly on the food he brought. They eat well, dining on fresh carrots, greens, and apples, safe in the shelter he provides. He smiles and snorts a little at a thought he has: Do they see him as a god? The Bringer of Food, the Protector of Life? That's giving them too much credit; they are, after all, just rabbits. Still, there's something appealing about being the linchpin in their existence.

His nose tells him, god or not, he'd better clean the hutches this weekend.

The day's light is fading fast, and it's getting chilly, so Flash pulls the old blankets over the hutches' screen doors and then walks the short distance across his back yard to his small house. As he closes the door and locks it, he wonders what to do next. It's only five p.m.—too early for dinner. He's not hungry anyway. A day of watching movies and reading has left him feeling numb, flat, and agitated.

Still, he's glad he declined Dan and his wife's invitation to their dinner party. He prefers his own company over hours of superficial, inane interaction and chatter, but today has been way too sedentary. He wishes again the gym were open. He needs physical intensity, to feel something.

He goes to his bedroom. He installed a chinning bar in the doorway for occasions like this. He thought about buying one of those home gym sets, but the gym he goes to is only closed one day a year, and there's no way he could afford enough equipment and iron. Even if he could, it wouldn't fit in the house. The chinning bar is a good, simple solution.

The diamond-pattern grip presses into the calluses on his hands, making his grip secure, and he executes the movement slowly. It takes several repetitions before the muscles in his upper back and arms catch fire, but when they do the pain is a relief. He moves almost continuously, pausing only briefly at the top and bottom each time until he finally is unable, no matter how hard he tries, to raise himself again. He lowers his feet to the floor and takes the weight off his arms. There's some resistance as he peels his hands from the bar. He looks at the red, patterned imprints in his palms, and enjoys the minor hurt in the mounds of hardened skin at the bases of his fingers. He spreads his hands wide to flatten the mounds out again.

He's feeling better now, but needs more. He strips off his T-shirt and jeans and begins doing pushups on the bare wooden floor of his bedroom. He has to do many more pushups than pull-ups before his chest and triceps even feel it. He doesn't keep count, but at maybe repetition eighty or so the movement becomes difficult. He slows down, increasing the strain on his body. Perhaps two dozen more repetitions and his body is feeling tapped out. His arms tremble and his face contorts as he squeezes out another pushup, savoring the burning pain in his triceps and chest. It takes a lot of repetitions to get to this point when the only weight he has to move is his own body, but it's worth it to feel this scorch. He focuses on the pain, trying to magnify every neuron's output. He straightens his arms and pauses. He waits until he's confident of completing another rep before lowering himself again—slowly, *slowly*, relishing the pain. He is inside the muscles now, his whole world the burning caused by the concentration of lactic acid in the straining tissue. At the bottom, his chest just grazing the floor, he stops his body and holds it. The trembling in his arms becomes more violent, his elbows shaking back and forth rapidly until he forces them by the power of his will to steady. Still mentally inside his tri's and pec's, he forces them to contract. His body raises an inch or two, then stalls.   This is his favorite part: He continues squeezing, imposing his will on his body, which is vibrating with the effort. He realizes he's wasting energy contorting his face; he relaxes it and opens his eyes, which focus on a knot in a floorboard. He sees a drop of sweat fall and splat on the same floorboard, creating a tiny puddle, and then the puddle is receding, slowly, as his body submits to his authority and rises again. His muscles seem to be on the verge of tearing or spasming. That's happened before, and it's bad because, unlike the good pain of exercise, the bad pain of injury heralds weakness, not strength. He recognizes the signs and, hyper-aware of his body, is able to keep his muscles just this side of failure. He completes the pushup and locks his elbows, putting the load of his weight on the aligned bones and giving his triceps a partial rest. He knows he has extracted all he can from them now. He has been here enough times to know when it's used up. He begins to lower himself to the ground, but his arms are incapable even of controlling his descent and suddenly they collapse under his weight. His face hits the hardwood floor and he gets the unexpected treat of intense, wet pain radiating from his nose out to his sinuses and eye sockets.

His whole world is this pain, this overwhelming sensation that allows him to *feel* his existence, the fact of his being *alive*. He rides the wave of hurt until, after a few minutes, it subsides to an ache, and he opens his eyes on a bright red puddle spread out in front of and under his face. When he was younger traumas like this were his primary source of real sensation, beyond the bland, muted stimuli of everyday life. That was before he learned better ways. Self-destructive acts are for the weak, and, strictly speaking, he shouldn't have allowed himself to be hurt this way. But this pain is more intense than the good kind, and anyway, there won't be any real, lasting damage from this. His arms have recovered enough now to help raise him to a semi-sitting position. There is a lot of blood—*his* blood, which is unusual, but maybe *more* fascinating. Sitting on the floor, he stares at it, admiring the rich, bright red color. His injured nose registers only the heady, dark, liquid smell as blood runs out his nostrils. He licks his upper lip and tastes the salty flavor of life. He remembers and his sex responds. He puts his right hand, palm down, into the puddle, then grasps his erect penis and slides his hand up and down it. Closing his eyes, he replaces the room around him with the memory of her, his favorite. *Alexis.* There have been others, of course, before and since, but she was the best. He recalls penetrating her bloody cunt while she thrashed and struggled and tried to scream around the gag. He shared her intensity of experience; they were one in her terror- and pain-filled eyes, her spasmodic and writhing body.

After, in the shower, his thoughts turn to dinner. *Rabbit tonight*, he thinks. *It is Christmas after all.* There's one fat one in particular he's been noticing lately: shiny, brown and black, in the left hutch out back. He's hungry, so he won't take as long as he normally would to kill it, but then he thinks: *The back legs are the only part I really like—I wonder how long it could live if I just took those and cauterized the wounds to stop the bleeding?* He knows about cauterization, and it really works. Watching the animal's struggles while he eats its legs will be like dinner and entertainment in one package. He decides to use the indoor grill rather than roasting, and mentally debates about whether to go with the dry rub or the barbecue sauce.

Eighteen

December 1998
Arlington, Massachusetts

My right leg below the knee has gone numb. I'm not sure if that feels better or worse than the sharp ache in my left leg, especially in the knee. I push the thought from my mind, trying not to think, just to breathe, as I sit on the round black cushion in the middle of my floor. It feels like I've been in the lotus position for hours, but it's probably only been about thirty minutes. I stop myself from thinking about how much time has elapsed, but now I'm thinking about not thinking. *Just shut up*, I tell myself. *I wonder if I'm getting worse at it.* I started practicing Zen meditation five years ago, but I still suck at it, so it's a relief when I hear the answering machine click on.

I keep my phone's ringer turned off; I always wait to hear who it is before picking up anyway. The volume on the answering machine is up just loud enough to hear. First there's the monotone, gender-neutral voice I use sometimes, saying the ten digits of my phone number, then the beep, then a familiar Boston-sounding voice.

"Hey Shailene, you theah? It's Chahlie from Cambridge Cuhriah."

He knows my deal with the phone, so he waits a few seconds on the line. I manage to untangle my legs and stagger over to the phone. When I pick up the machine clicks off automatically and rewinds. "Hi Chahlie, you gut a job fa me?" I say, noticing the same Boston accent creeps into my speech when I talk to him, as if I were some kind of linguistic chameleon.

"Yeah, you know the deal. It's yah's if ya can do it now."

"Sure," I say, making an effort to pronounce the R and flexing my legs to get the circulation back into them.

"A'right, I'll have the package ready when you get heah."

"I'm leavin' now." I hang up, change out of the soft baggy gym pants and into jeans, pull on my high top sneakers, and grab my coat as I head out the door.

I've been expecting Charlie to call at some point. I put myself on his call list the previous Christmas too, and it worked out well. Inevitably there are holiday parties running out of booze, and Charlie discovered the niche and exploited it, creating a miniature black market in alcohol for a day each year when the state closes the liquor stores. It's not legal, but by comparison...I just smiled when he asked me if I had a problem with breaking the law.

The courier job is a regular thing with me—one of the part time gigs that doesn't mind me taking a few weeks off on short notice from time to time, and isn't interested in what I do with those weeks. When I first came back to Massachusetts after leaving the Army, I got a job taking care of the computers for an architecture firm in Cambridge. The Trenton mission wrecked that when I had to spend two weeks down there. I'd only been with the firm for a few months, so this was way beyond the vacation time I'd accumulated, and I couldn't even tell them why. I quit over the phone from Jersey before they could fire me.

Most of the year the courier runs are just regular stuff, mainly carrying large envelopes or small boxes of paper between offices around town. One time I even delivered something to the architecture firm I worked for, but the receptionist was new since I'd left, and I didn't see anyone else in the thirty seconds I was there dropping off the package.

Stacey, being so small, is perfect for delivery work because her small size allows her to squeeze through road construction sites and park in spaces too small for most vehicles. The occasional parking ticket is inevitable, but

Charlie splits those with me and most deliveries end up paying well if calculated as an hourly rate, unless I get caught in rush hour traffic or ensnared by the ever-changing mess around one of the Big Dig sites. And it's a good change from doing phone interviews, which is my least favorite but most dependable job.

These Christmas runs are the best deal of all. There's hardly any traffic, so the time investment is less, and the pay is triple the usual rate. Charlie knows rich people hosting holiday parties are too stressed, too drunk, or too both to care how much they pay to avoid running out of social lubricant and looking stupid in front of their guests. He gouges them on the booze as well as the service charge, but he's been working this for years, so apparently he knows what he can get away with.

Charlie's office and home is a former gas station on Massachusetts Avenue in North Cambridge. Charlie runs a Ryder franchise as well, so there are a few rentable yellow trucks and vans parked in the lot and around the boarded up gas pumps. I back Stacey up to the old service bay Charlie uses as a warehouse since that's where he'll have the boxes prepared. I get out and walk around to the front door. The air is cold, the sky completely black, the stars mostly invisible because of the city's glare.

The front of the office part of the small building is mostly glass. Light leaks out between the slats and around the edges of the blinds, which Charlie always keeps down and shut. As usual, the door buzzes as soon as I walk up to it, so I grab the metal handle and pull it open.

The first thing I see is Dog—Charlie's watchdog—standing a few feet in from the door, watching me intently. There is a moment of silent appraisal, then the tail starts wagging. Dog is a mutt, but his rottweiler ancestry is obvious in his massive, jowly head. He steps close to me and looks up happily.

"Hi Dog." I pat the big skull, then look up at Charlie in his usual position behind the desk. "Hi Charlie. Merry Christmas."

"Too soon to tell yet," he replies in his somewhat high-pitched voice. "But this run is a good staht. These jokahs need a lot of stuff—I got it all ready in the garage." As he speaks, he gets up from behind the desk. His usual flannel shirt and dark pants hang on his rail-thin frame, the trousers held up only by dark green suspenders. For some reason he always makes me think of the stereotypical crusty old Yankee farmer, though for all I know he might never have set foot on a farm in his life. He walks briskly over to the door leading to the service bay.

Dog follows us into the big, chilly garage. Charlie pushes a button and one of the doors raises, revealing the back end of Stacey.

"Shoot, I fuhgut you had that little cah. Think it can handle all that?" he asks worriedly, gesturing at the stack of boxes and a keg of beer.

I look at the pile, then at Stacey, then back at the pile. "Yeah, she holds more than you think."

The keg ends up riding shotgun, but we manage to get everything in. "OK, where'm I takin' it?" I feel the warm weight of Dog's head against my hip and reach down to scratch behind his ears.

"It's a ways out, so you'd bettah get goin'—needs to go to Lincoln. Evah bin theah?"

"Uh, yeah..." I say, absorbing the surprise, keeping it in. "Yeah I know it."

"Rich town, pretty high end. Prob'ly take ya about half an hour to get theah if you don't get lost, so don't get lost. Heah's the duhrections they gave me ovah the phone," he says, handing me a yellow sheet from a legal pad.

I look at the directions. Charlie's penmanship isn't so great, but it's readable, and anyway, I remember the street from when I lived in Lincoln. The address is actually not far from—

"Can ya read my writin' OK? Any questions? 'Cause if not, you should get goin'—they might already have run out by now."

I nod and look up, meeting Charlie's watery, pale gray eyes. "No problem—I know where this is," I turn and walk toward the driver's side door of my car.

"All right, see ya soon with the check."

"See ya," I slide behind the wheel.

During the drive out I'm not sure how to feel, or more accurately, I'm afraid to feel anything. Instead, I focus on driving, keeping my speed no more than five miles per hour over the speed limit, just in case there are any cops around. Getting pulled over would not only put me hopelessly behind schedule, but could also lead to some difficult questions about the cargo. I have the directions handy, but end up not using them until the last mile; I remember the roads and landmarks as soon as I see them. The directions describe the mailbox, which is embedded in a stone pillar. A metal plate on top of the pillar gives only the house number, but there's no house, just a narrow road leading into the woods. I turn down the road—actually a very long driveway, maybe a quarter mile from street to house. The house is, of course, huge. It's made of stone and dark wood, and looks like an oversized hunting lodge. Charlie's directions say to drive around to the far side, and there I see a lighted covered parking area already occupied by a caterer's van. I pull in behind the van and kill the engine. A few wood steps lead up to a plain door painted dark forest green. I knock and after a few seconds a man about my age, dressed in a white shirt, black pants, and a large white apron, answers the door.

"Are you the booze?" he asks.

"I brought it, yeah. Where's it going?"

"We'll bring it in here," he says, leaving the door open and stepping out. "Where is it?"

I lead the way down the stairs and to the back of Stacey. I open the hatch, show him the cargo. "Who's got the money?" I ask. "I need to get paid before we start unloading."

"Oh yeah," he says, digging in his pocket and pulling out an envelope.

I open it and turn it to the light: everything is correct; I fold the envelope and stuff it into a front pocket of my jeans. "OK, grab a box and lead on," I say, picking up a box of wine. Another member of the catering staff joins us, and the work is done in a couple minutes.

The question stands poised in my mind as I drive down the long driveway toward the street. Without really knowing why or evaluating the move, I make a left instead of the right that would take me back to Cambridge. About a quarter mile down the road I have a moment where I think the question may be moot because I'm not sure I know my way as well as I thought, but then I see a low stone wall and a sprawling house behind it; I take a right. A little further and I see the street sign for Albion Road. There's a tightness in my chest; my throat is constricted and my mouth is dry. *This is a bad idea.* I pass a few more houses and then see it for the first time since the ambulance took me away from it.

It's just a house. There's nothing remarkable about it, nothing setting it apart significantly from any of the other houses on the winding, wooded street. Nothing about it reveals what happened inside thirteen years and six weeks earlier. I pull over and stop in front, peering through the winter-bare trees at the place. Light passes through the sheer drapes in the front window, but other than these drapes, and some alterations in the landscaping, it hasn't changed much. I realize, with some relief, that seeing the house like this, from the outside, evokes happy memories of coming home from school, raking leaves in the fall with Dad, and playing in the street out front with the other neighborhood kids on warm summer evenings when I was little. The tension evaporates, but as the memories flood through, a different emotion gums up my mouth, and I feel my chin spasm. I know what I need to do...

First things first: I pull my cell phone out of a coat pocket and press the speed dial for Charlie.

"Cambridge Cuhriah."

"Charlie—" I tip the mouth end of the phone away from my face and clear my throat. "Charlie, it's Shailene. It went fine, and I got the check."

"Didja check it?"

"Yeah, it's fine. But listen, I have something else I need to do, so I'm gonna be a little late getting back to you. Don't worry, all right?"

"What's up?"

"Just something I need to do while I'm out here—it won't take long. I'll be back a little later with the money." He doesn't like this, but he's just going to have to deal with it.

"All right," he says slowly.

"OK, see ya later." I press the button to end the call, then turn the phone off and lay it on the passenger seat.

I think for several seconds, not about *if* anymore, but *how* to get there. It's been over thirteen years since I was last there too. I put the car in gear and pull away from the curb.

I get off track once, but soon find my way. Since it's after dark the gates are locked, so instead of pulling in, I park across the street in front of a house, then cross and climb over the low stone wall. I stand for a few minutes, again careful not to consider if, but only where. I want to do this but I'm afraid I won't. I start walking, my feet crunching softly on the thin layer of snow, hands shoved deep in coat pockets, wool stocking cap pulled low over my ears against the cold.

There is of course no artificial illumination, but the night is clear and the moon is full, which is better since the light is more widely and evenly distributed.   Visibility is, in fact, practically as good as in sunlight; only the colors are missing. I cross several rows of markers until I hit one of the paved roads.   It's clear of snow, and I walk quickly down it, occasionally glancing back at the main gate and comparing the view to the one etched in memory.

Because of the inexactness of the remembered images, I don't realize I've found it until I see the name across the top: CAMPBELL. I freeze in place, and my eyes drift down to the names below: WILLIAM and MICHELLE.   The polished granite stone—one stone for both marking side by side burials—gleams in the moonlight.   A pot of poinsettias is centered against the base of the marker. *From Grandma, no doubt.*

"I'm sorry." The pathetic weakness of the words smacks me hard in the face, and in my pockets fingernails dig deep into my palms. My knees weaken and then I'm on them, my head bowed forward, eyes clenched shut. "I'm so sorry," I whisper, but the words have a hard time escaping. *Who are you talking to? There's no one here; they're gone.* I wish I believed in some kind of afterlife, but I gave up trying to convince myself of that years ago. "I miss you." My cheeks feel hot despite the cold air and wetness on them. A sob escapes from deep in my chest and tries to choke me on its way out.

Nineteen

Mac is puzzled by the Fed Ex envelope for a second until he remembers leaving Lieutenant Vidian of the Trenton, New Jersey, police department a voice mail message back before the holidays. Suddenly excited, he tears the envelope open and dumps a cassette tape and a few sheets of paper onto his desk.

The cover letter confirms what Mac remembered: There was a call to the tip line regarding Wayne Lambert; in fact, there were *two* calls, both anonymous, both made from the same payphone at the Trenton Marriott. The attached sheets are transcripts of both calls, but the tape is of the second one only—the first was accidentally recorded over. According to the letter, two detectives from Trenton P.D. followed up on the tips and interviewed Lambert in his apartment but found nothing incriminating. Lambert claimed the tip was probably made by a disgruntled former employee at the restaurant where he was assistant manager.

Mac puts the cover letter aside and scans the transcripts. Both calls are brief, each giving Lambert's name, address, place of work, vehicle, and license plate. Mac knows anonymous calls are usually researched after the other tips, if ever. Trenton P.D. might never have gotten around to following up on these if the second call hadn't added that Lambert actually followed a kid who was walking home from school.

Without the first recording Mac technically can't tell if both calls were made by the same person, but given the similarities in content, order of presentation, and point of origin, it's extremely likely they were. Mac opens a drawer in his desk and pulls out a small tape recorder. He looks at the spools on the cassette Vidian sent, pops it in the recorder with side A up, and presses play. After a few seconds of quiet a woman's voice states that it's the child abduction tip line.

The voice of the caller is next, and it sounds identical to the one from the 911 recording in Philadelphia. "It's you!" he whispers excitedly. Without technical analysis and comparison of the recordings he can't be a hundred percent certain, but Mac is convinced the voices are the same, linking Trenton to Phillie. The nine-mil Hydra-Shok ammo and bullets in the brain link Phillie to KC, and the bullet in the brain probably links KC and Phillie to Florida too. The signature—efficient killing of recreational killers—unites all four incidents. *OK, so I have my trail.* Mac looks at the clock in the lower right corner of his computer's screen. It's only about eight in the morning—he'd wanted to get an early start catching up on the two work days he'd missed, but...

I need more data. What else has this guy done? Mac tears pages off a legal pad to get down to a clean sheet, and begins listing what he knows, starting with a timeline. He notices a nearly two-year gap between the Florida killings in spring of '95 and Trenton at the end of winter in '97. A little over a year after that there's KC this past summer, then Philadelphia last month. Four points of reference. The geography's not much help: except for two being in the northeast, they're all over the place. *Well, all I really know is the two in the northeast were both his. Maybe the other two are someone else.* It doesn't seem likely though. This kind of vigilante activity is really rare; in fact, he's never heard of anything like it before. He taps the tip of his pen on the pad, jots *phone* by the two northeastern incidents, then wonders if maybe there was a phone tip in KC but they never followed up on it. Mac could check—the Bureau was in charge of that one, so all the call transcripts would be close at hand in the FBI's own records.

Then something else occurs to him.   The two cases without the "phone" notation both had the bodies of other victims on the scene. In Florida there was the coed with her throat cut open by Denice Horn—one of the vigilante's targets. In KC, McNeely was apparently dumping the body of his last victim when the vigilante caught up with him. So maybe there was no phone in those cases because the vigilante didn't have time—he'd been trying to save, or simply reacting to the presence of, his target's victim. Or...maybe when he calls in tips, he isn't sure he's right and he wants law enforcement to look into it for him. When he catches his suspect in the act of attacking someone or with the body of a victim, then he's sure and acts.

Makes sense.   So... Mac wonders, *has it ever worked? Has he ever gotten the cops to do his work for him? Even if he has, I would have missed it when I searched ViCAP because I was looking for homicides, not arrests.*

Mac opens the ViCAP interface and initiates a new search, this time looking for multiple murderers who were arrested in the past five years. There's the usual assortment of hit men and guys who set out to do something like rob a bank or sell drugs and something goes wrong and they kill a few people, but only six are psychopathic serial killers—one thing all four vigilante incidents have in common. Four out of these six arrests resulted from phone tips, but all these are from identified sources: a brother, a landlord, a victim who escaped, and a co-worker. No anonymous tips. *Maybe he just didn't do anything for a couple years after Florida. If Florida was his first, maybe he was freaked out for a while.* Mac leans back and tries to think of other approaches. He could extend the search back further, in case Florida wasn't the vigilante's first.

Instead he closes his eyes and mentally goes over again what he knows: *Finds serial killers—psychopaths—but I don't know how.   Then he tries to get the police to arrest them if possible, either because he's not sure he has the right guy, or because he'd rather not get his hands dirty.   But when he is sure or if he has to act to save someone, he kills them himself.   Lately uses a nine-mil handgun, Hydra-Shok ammo.*   Mac could do a search based on that detail, but files that away for the moment.   *What else?   Calls to the police are anonymous—why?   In case he has to kill the target himself, like in Trenton and Phillie—he doesn't want to get in trouble.   But maybe the calls weren't always anonymous; after all, doing the killing himself seems to be a last resort.   Maybe...*

Mac sits up again and looks at the screen.   Of the four phone tips that led to serial killer arrests, three were from people who knew the criminal outside the context of his criminality—co-worker, relative, landlord.   But one was an escaped victim—what was the story there?   Mac brings up the details of the case again and reads more thoroughly.

Apparently the escaped victim, a young woman, first made *an anonymous phone call to the tip line.* "Ho...ly...shit," Mac whispers.   "Wait, no...a young woman—the vigilante's a man, right?"   Mac closes his eyes and tries to remember how he arrived at that conclusion. *Because the vast majority of serial killers are men.* But that's not conclusive, and anyway, the vigilante isn't *really* a serial killer—not a psychopath.   The vigilante kills only when necessary, and takes no pleasure in it.   *But in Trenton— Lambert was a pretty hefty guy, and he wasn't shot: there were bruises on his throat, and then the knife in the base of his skull.* Still, with the right skill set...

Mac looks again at the case description on his screen. This twenty-five-year-old woman not only made an anonymous call from a hotel payphone, but then she went back out looking for the killer.   She found him when he was

about to shoot a couple in a parked car—his usual signature—
and shouted at him. *Freakin' shouted at him.* Predictably,
this resulted in her getting shot. *Gutsy. Not smart, but gutsy.*
The woman then managed to get away and, despite her own
wound, flagged down a police cruiser and took them to where
she was shot, only to find the dead couple in the parked car,
and no killer.   Eventually, a month and a half later, she
returned to New Orleans and found the killer *again*, and this
time called the police without anonymity.   Police responded
and were able to apprehend the killer, James Lee Williams.
Mac reads through the rest of the case notes, learning this
woman was, at the time, an Army officer stationed at Fort
Rucker, Alabama, not all that far from the northwestern
Florida site where Denice Horn and Alan Hayes were found
killed.

And the incident in New Orleans occurred only about six
months after the one in Florida too.

Mac thinks, then opens a second search which brings up
the north Florida case from earlier that year. Alan Hayes, the
owner of the van, was a resident of Dothan, Alabama, and so
was his partner Denice Horn. Mac does a quick map check of
the proximity of Fort Rucker to Dothan: only about twenty
miles. *Damn.*

He smiles and shakes his head. *A woman?* He puts her
name into the ViCAP search engine. He has to check the
spelling because the first name is unfamiliar to him:

Shailene Campbell

Twenty

January 1999
Arlington, Massachusetts

Mac cruises slowly down the quiet residential street in his dark blue-gray Oldsmobile rental, the most official-looking ride he could get. Officially he's taking a couple days off, so he's not entitled to a government vehicle, but he doesn't want her to know this. He needs her to believe the full weight of the Bureau is dangling just over her head. Personally, he's looking every inch the G-man in his dark suit, dark trench coat, and fresh shave.

The street is densely-packed with houses, most three floors tall and at least half with two front doors side by side or metal panels with buttons, indicating the homes have been converted into mini apartment buildings. He spots "12" on a white triple-decker, pulls to the curb in front of it, and cuts the engine.

His watch shows about eight in the morning, a time he decided on after careful consideration of her history and the employers listed with her last tax return. He closes his eyes and takes a deep breath, holds it, then lets it out steadily, striving for the right balance between confidence in himself and regard for the suspect. He mentally reviews his priorities: confirm she is the vigilante, find out how she finds these guys before everyone else, gain control and shut down her vigilante activities.

Mac's a little fuzzy on that last point. He definitely wants to know how she's finding these guys so quickly, but what he does after that depends on the information she gives. The duty-bound federal agent in him knows vigilante justice is anathema to law and order; clearly he can't allow her to persist in what she's doing. If he has to, he'll arrest her, but he'd rather keep this unofficial. Mainly he wants to learn her methods so he can use them himself to find bad guys...in his capacity as a law enforcer, of course. *Right?* But the big mystery is how, with no background in police work, does she do it? What does she know that Mac, with his almost eleven years of training and experience in the field, doesn't? And it's not just him—there's all the other detectives, agents, and the rest at the police departments and FBI that have worked these cases. Could she be some kind of naturally-gifted genius? *Maybe she's not working alone.* He starts to consider that, then shakes his head to clear it. The answers will come if he stays focused on the task at hand.

He gets out of the car, walks up the short paved path, and climbs the three front steps. There are two doors off the front porch, one labeled 12, the other 12A. The IRS has 12 as her address, so he presses the button by that door. He doesn't hear any ringing, so he opens the storm door and knocks on the window set into the inner door. No one comes and he hears nothing inside. There's a curtain hanging on the other side of the window, so he can't see in. He glances over his shoulder, then tries the knob. It turns and the latch disengages. Gentle pressure eases the door open a couple inches.

"Hello?" Silence. He pushes the door in some more; it opens on to a stairwell. He steps inside, surveying the scattering of junk mail on the worn, dingy brown carpeting covering the floor and steps. Bending slightly and squinting, he is able to make out the addresses on a couple flyers without pulling out his reading glasses, but they're both addressed to "resident." He climbs the stairs to the second floor and finds two doors leading in and one out to another porch. He knocks on each of the inner doors, but gets no response; both are locked. Mac descends and steps out on the front porch again.

He's about to try 12A when a movement in his peripheral vision catches his attention. The person walking down the driveway alongside the house is wearing a dark-green coat and black stocking cap pulled low over her ears and forehead. He compares what he can see of her face with his memory of the three-year-old military file photo he saw the previous week. "Ms. Campbell?"

Startled, her head turns quickly toward him. He registers the feminine—some might say pretty—features, and the eyebrows that angle downward as they approach the center line of her face.

He turns and calmly, deliberately descends the steps to the walk in front of the house, then crosses the frozen lawn to the driveway where she is still standing, motionless, watching him. He doesn't show it, but he's pleased to see the concern on her face and the tenseness in her posture; he got the G-man look right. As he nears her, he uses his left hand to produce his badge, opening and displaying it clearly, wanting her to take a good, long look at it. "Good morning. I'm Special Agent MacIlwane, Federal Bureau of Investigation."

Her eyes shift from his face to the badge, then back up to his face, then back to scrutinizing the badge, her features a study in concern and suspicion. Suddenly she seems to relax, and she meets his eyes with hers. He already knew from her military records the eyes would be green, but the intensity of the color surprises him. The concern still lingers in those eyes, but she's making a good effort to hide it, and her voice is steady and just below normal conversational volume. "How can I help you?" she asks flatly. Her voice is on the deep side for a woman; she'd certainly be able to pitch it as low as the voice that called the tip line in Trenton and 911 in Philadelphia last month.

He also already knew she would be five-four, but in person it's hard to imagine this slender, small person as the vigilante whose work he's been seeing for almost two years. "Are you Shailene Campbell?" he asks, guessing at the pronunciation of her first name and making it sound like "Aileen."

"Yes."

"I'm investigating a series of murders, and I hope you can help me. I'd like to ask you a few questions."

"Now?"

"Yes, I'd appreciate it if you would accompany me to a coffee shop near here. You probably know it—it's just a couple blocks down Massachusetts Avenue."

The green eyes, which Mac finds a little distracting, look past him at the street, and she shakes her head. "I'm just on my way to work—maybe we can do this some other time."

"Actually, I need to speak with you now. As I said, I am investigating a series of murders and time is critical."

She looks back at his face. "What murders?"

"If you'd prefer, we can always go to the field office in Boston, but I think you would find the coffee shop more pleasant and less time-consuming than one of our interrogation rooms." Mac keeps his voice pleasant and polite as he says this, letting the words on their own do the work.

The downward angle of her eyebrows increases as they draw together. "I need to go back up to my apartment so I can call work and tell them I'm going to be late."

Mac expected this and pulls out his cell phone. "What's the number?"

The eyebrows get a little steeper. "How long will this take?"

"That depends on you. Let's say a couple hours."

She says the phone number. He dials it, listens. "Opinion Research."

"Just a moment," he says, and hands her the phone.

"Hi, it's Shailene—I'm going to be in late."

He notices she pronounces the first part of her name to rhyme with "May."

She pauses, then says, "Yeah, I'm fine, but something's come up. I should be there in a couple hours or so. OK, bye." She hands the phone back to Mac, who presses the button to close the connection. He gestures toward his car and they walk to the front passenger-side door. He opens it for her, then walks around the car and gets in.

Mac says nothing during the short drive, and neither does she. He finds a parking space on a side street and they walk silently back to the coffee shop, which is busy at this time of day, but the table in back is unoccupied thanks to his visit a earlier this morning and the compensation he paid to the shop's manager. As they enter, the manager heads for the table and removes the paper with RESERVED written on it. There are two chairs; Mac drapes his coat over the back of the chair in the corner and sits, leaving Campbell with her back to the rest of the small shop. Mac orders a plain black coffee and turns to Campbell, who shakes her head.

"No thanks."

Mac turns to the manager. "Bring her the same, please."

The manager leaves and Mac sits looking at her but saying nothing. It feels awkward and he does nothing to change that. Instead he visually assesses her, beginning with the amber-colored hair, which, now that she has removed her hat, he sees is cut to a uniform eighth of an inch or so. The effect of this is jarring. In the file photo, her hair was short, but not an unusual style for a woman. Although the face is the same, the juxtaposition of the crew cut makes her large eyes seem larger, and her features seem harder, less feminine. *Lesbian?* he wonders. Although she removed her hat, she's kept her coat on, but it's unbuttoned. Underneath she's wearing a dark gray, shapeless sweater at least a size too large for her. He shifts his eyes up to her face again, and meets the green eyes looking back at him.

"So how can I help?" she says, irritation apparent in her voice.

"Just a minute, please," he says. He looks over at the counter and watches as a young man with a tribal pattern tattoo on his neck and an earring in his left ear carries their coffees over and sets them on the small, round table. "Thanks," Mac says, handing him a twenty and telling him to keep the change. Mac removes the spoon from his mug, taps it lightly on the rim to remove most of the coffee from it, and lays it down on the table. He looks up at her again. "Why don't you tell me about your trips to New Orleans three years ago."

The irritated but composed expression on her face doesn't waver for a moment. "What do you want to know?"

"Why did you go there the first time?"

She waits a couple seconds before speaking. "I'd never been before. I went and saw the sights, listened to the music."

"You went alone?"

"Yes."

"Were you aware of the ongoing series of murders there when you went?"

"I'd heard about them, yes."

"That didn't make you hesitate to visit there? Alone?"

"The killer was targeting couples; if anything, I felt more safe by going alone."

"And yet you ended up getting shot by this killer."

She just looks at him. Mac registers this and decides to look back and tick off the seconds in his head, see how long it takes. At almost a full minute she says "I didn't hear a question. If you want me to confirm what you said then yes, I did get shot, but obviously you already know this. Mind if I ask what series of murders you're investigating? Last I knew James Lee Williams was in prison—has that changed?"

"You were shot when you tried to dissuade Williams from shooting another pair of victims—"

"That's right."

"You also told the investigating officer you had been following Williams for some time before getting shot, and you actually called 911 before you saw him threaten anyone. Why?"

"Why did I call?"

"All of it—why follow him?   Why make a call about him?"

"I had a bad feeling about him."

"What do you mean?"

"I mean I saw him walking around and something wasn't right about him."

"So you followed him?"

"Yeah—it's not like I was pal-ing around with him; I followed at a distance."

"But why? What made him stand out to you?"

"I told you, I had a bad feeling about him at first—"

"From the first moment you saw him?"

"Right away, and then the more I followed him—he seemed to be acting strangely. He kept walking up and down the streets, back and forth in the same area, as if he were looking for something, but never stopping in anywhere, and never really going anywhere."

"And you didn't get tired of following him around? You didn't mind taking time out from your vacation?"

"Like I said, I'd heard about the killings. I saw this guy, and the more I followed him, the more I thought he might be dangerous. So I called the cops on him, and then I went and found him again."

"Then what happened?"

She raises her eyebrows and looks at him with a confused and exasperated expression. "Then I saw him looking into a parked car and pulling out a gun. I shouted at him because I didn't know what else to do, and he spun around and shot me. But what I don't get is why you and the detective down in New Orleans both question me like *I'm* the criminal. I did my civic and moral duty by reporting this guy and trying to stop him from killing—how is any of that wrong?"

"It's not. But what *I* don't get, Ms. Campbell, is why you went *back* to New Orleans a month later."

"I'd seen his face—I could identify him and no one else could."

"You gave his description to a police sketch artist."

"Yeah," she says, drawing out the word a little, "and he did a good job, but it still wasn't exactly right. And in the month and a half I was away no one turned him in, so I went back to see if I could spot him again. I *still* don't see how that's a problem for the police. I mean, I'm not looking for a medal, but why harass me about it?"

Up until now Mac has kept his voice fairly soft, conversational. Now, to add to the punch, he allows an edge to creep in. "When you went back to New Orleans, did you bring the Glock 26 you'd just purchased?"

Her eyes narrow and he can see through them to the mental scrambling going on inside. She looks down at her untouched cup of coffee. "That would have been illegal," she says quietly, noncommittally, effectively answering his question. Suddenly she looks up, her eyes more confident. "I bought a cell phone too—why don't you ask me about that? I took it with me when I went back to New Orleans, and as you no doubt already know, I used that to help the police catch James Lee Williams. Last I heard he was in jail, hopefully for the rest of his life."

He watches her, letting the silence stretch out. She returns his gaze, but only for a few seconds, then looks down at her coffee, then at the wall behind him and to his left. "How did you find Williams the second time?" he finally asks.

The eyes shift to meet his. "Same way as the first. I walked around until I spotted him, then called the cops. The difference the second time was I didn't have to go looking for a payphone. Oh, and I think they took me a little more seriously since they knew I'd seen him before."

"So you identified yourself when you called them that time?"

"Yes."

"And you found him by just wandering around a large city until you spotted him on the street."

"I'd plotted his past killings on a street map, so I had an idea of his stalking ground. That narrowed it down some."

"You returned to New Orleans, illegally carrying a newly-purchased concealable weapon to get back at him for shooting you, right?"

"Who cares that he shot me?!" she says loudly. "He was—" she interrupts herself, apparently realizing how loud she is, and how quiet the people around her have become. She leans back and, again looking at her untouched coffee, she takes a deep breath. The red in her face abates and she smiles a tight, angry smile with only the right side of her mouth. When she speaks again it's much more quietly, and she keeps her eyes on the mug in front of her. "He was a serial killer. I was in a position to help the police catch him, so I did. That's it."

She leans forward, resting her forearms on the table, and meets his eyes. "Sir, what is this about? I don't understand why you're interrogating me about this. It's three years old, it's done, and I did nothing wrong; in fact, I put myself at risk to do a good deed. Where's the bad in that?"

Time to ease up again. Mac takes a sip of his coffee, then says gently, "I'm a behavioral analyst for the FBI. It's my job to study and understand human behavior, and apply that knowledge to support investigations. Your actions in New Orleans were noteworthy, and I want to understand them better."

She cocks an eyebrow at him, and he finds the expression appealing. He likes her face, even with the crew cut. He allows the silence to stretch out, hoping she'll match his change in tone and his personal revelation.

Instead, after perhaps another minute, she says, "OK, so is that it?"

"Actually, there's another thing I'm hoping you can help me with." Mac takes the small stack of photos from the breast pocket in the lining of his suit jacket, glances at it to check orientation, then peels off the top photo and sets it on the table in front of Campbell so it is face up and right-side up for her. He watches her face.

She leans forward slightly, but keeps her hands where they've been most of the time, out of sight below the surface of the table. At first her expression is blankly neutral. He can see her eyes shifting slightly as they scan back and forth over the photo, then they stop shifting. It's subtle, but he can detect a slight tensing of her facial muscles. She glances up at him, then quickly back down at the photo, and, after a second or two, her face relaxes and she says, without taking her eyes off the photo, "So what am I looking at here?"

"You tell me," he answers.

She looks up again, this time the picture of blank, unknowing innocence: "A van and a car parked in a field?"

"The habitual honesty they taught you at West Point makes you a terrible liar, Ms. Campbell."

The carefully-composed façade wavers for just a moment; her eyes flick away, then back to his again. "I haven't told a lie yet," she says.

"Strictly speaking, no, you haven't, but you are definitely exhibiting an 'intent to deceive'." Her eyes narrow and she stares at him. He returns her gaze and after a couple heartbeats says "Class of '74." Mac suppresses a smile at the rapid sequence of surprise and doubt on her face which predictably ends with her looking at his hands. He moves his right hand slightly to make his West Point class ring easier to see.

She goes back to staring at her cup of coffee, but Mac hopes he has subconsciously reduced her resistance to him and made her even less comfortable with trying to deceive him. He tries the honor angle again, probing for the limits of her conscience: "An honorable person would take responsibility for her actions instead of hiding behind a deception," he says gently.

She looks up sharply, a small line between deeply-angled eyebrows, the green eyes bright. "My integrity is intact."

Now hard again: Mac takes the next photo from the stack and places it in front of her, next to the first one. "Recognize the van in these pictures?"

"I've seen lots of vans like that."

"Look closely; this one was parked in a field in northern Florida, not far from Panama City Beach."

She stares at the photo, which is a closer view of the van. Through the open side door it's possible to make out part of Kristen Reese's body, and Denice Horn's body is visible in the partially trampled grass beside the van, but Campbell doesn't react beyond staring silently.

"How about this one—do you recognize this man?" he asks, laying down the picture of Alan Hayes' body sprawled in the grass, the bullet hole visible in Hayes' battered face.

She looks at it briefly, then flips it over and raises her eyes to his. "Maybe we should talk about duty instead of honor."

"I'm listening."

"If a person sees a crime in progress, isn't she obligated to try to stop the crime?"

"Yes, if there isn't time to contact the police. Do you have first-hand experience with this? Besides what happened in New Orleans, I mean."

"So you agree a citizen has a duty to protect others from violence if she can."

"Maybe you can provide me another example. Why don't you tell me about that van in Florida? What happened there?"

Twenty-One

"**M**aybe you can provide me another example. Why don't you tell me about that van in Florida? What happened there?"

I want to, I really do. *Shit, no, don't say anything. If he knew, he wouldn't be playing these games. He's trying to trap me.* I stare at the wall while my mind freezes up. *Need time to think...* "What company were you in? Back in school, I mean."

"E-2."

"Go Dogs," I reply automatically, the arcane information somehow emerging from the confusion in my head. I look at his face for some sign of what I should do, but it's unreadable, and watching me. "You know what I never understood? How you get 'Dogs' from the letter 'E'."

He shrugs. "Dogs are a better mascot than...I don't know, elephants, I guess, which would've been hard to say all the time. Anyway, 'Dogs' is better than 'Hamsters'."

"Hamsters?"

"H-3, right?"

How much does he know about me? I nod in response to his question. "Yeah: Hurricanes."

"H-3 was Hamsters when I was there—must've changed mascots. Good thing—hamster's a pretty lame mascot."

I nod again. "Yeah, I guess so." At some level I'm amazed and amused we're talking about this, but I know I'm running out of time, and following this conversation isn't helping me get my response straight. I look down at the back of the photo I flipped over, trying to focus, wishing desperately for more time to think, to go through the options. I really should have prepared for this by now, probably should have prepared for it right after I killed the one in the picture. Of *course* they would catch up with me eventually—wasn't it inevitable? But how? How did they connect me with, of all the missions, this one in Florida? But maybe he hasn't— maybe he's just guessing. If he had evidence, wouldn't he have just arrested me? How do these things work, anyway?

"Why don't you tell me what happened in that field," he suggests quietly.

Shit, got to think of something. Maybe this could be a good thing; maybe there's a way out of the endless pursuit of murderous freaks. If I can trust him, and if I can convince him about the sense... I open my mouth, then stop myself. *What am I thinking? There's no way anyone would believe this— even I have a hard time with it. And if I admit to anything—* I look up quickly at the eyes boring into my head, making me feel transparent. "So what are you investigating—just this van in Florida?"

"Unless it's connected to something else."

So he doesn't know about the rest. I feel a tiny bit of relief seep in. *If I can just get out of this one—* "And what makes you think I had anything to do with it? Just because it happened the same year as the investigation I helped out with in New Orleans?"

Those fucking eyes, like my face is a window or something. "I never said when we found the van."

Something heavy drops inside my belly and lands on my bladder, making me feel dizzy again. *Didn't he?* "Yes—yes you did."

He shakes his head slowly, the dark eyes pinning me down, the dark face impassive. "No, I deliberately did not. Come on, Ms. Campbell, tell me what really happened there. It will be bet—"

"I don't think I should talk to you anymore." I push away from the table and pick up my hat and lunch bag. *I should've never agreed to this—got to think this through before I really fuck up.*

"You can talk to me now, here, or I can get a warrant and arrest you, and we'll continue this conversation in an FBI interrogation room—the choice is yours, Ms. Campbell."

"I'm going to find a lawyer," I say, standing up. *I've got to get the fuck out of here.* I turn and head for the door.

"I'll be asking you about Trenton next time." *What? Keep walking.* "And Kansas City." *Oh shit.* Another heavy thing drops inside me, landing on top of the other, and my feet slow down. "And what happened in Philadelphia last month." My face feels hot and I want so badly to be outside, to feel the cold air on my face, to run away, but my feet have stopped moving. *This is bad, very bad.*

"Your choice," he says.

I wonder if I *can* run away, and what if they find me and then I'm *really* in deep shit for fleeing. On the other hand, if I stay, maybe this is my chance, maybe I can cut a deal, help them, and I won't have to go after these bastards on my own anymore: no more fear, no more violence—I could just point the bad guys out and let someone else do the hard part. I look back at the agent—I don't remember his name, but I think I've seen him somewhere before today—still sitting, watching me. If not him, then who? And he's a grad: maybe he would understand—*duty. Still, have to be careful...* I walk back to the table without looking at him, focusing instead on the cooling cup of coffee intended for me. I place my lunch and hat on the table and sit down, thinking, planning my words, my one chance to do this. Fortunately, the agent is quiet, allowing me to think. Finally, I look up at him. "I'd like to ask you a question."

The dark brown eyes meet mine, but the face remains expressionless. He nods slightly. "Go ahead."

"Hypothetically, let's say you know someone is a killer—you see this person, and you can tell he's the one killing people, but you don't have any evidence."

"Then how do I know?" he asks.

"You just do—you can *feel* it."

"What, like some kind of intuition?" he says, sounding irritated.

"No, not intuition. I mean you *feel* it—physically. Like you feel pain when you see the person, when you're near him." I watch him closely, looking for a sign that my words are connecting, but instead I see growing impatience. *Shit, I'm blowing it. I'm blowing it, and I'm going to jail.* "Look, it sounds crazy—even *you* have a hard time believing it. In fact, the first few times it happens, you don't know *what's* going on. Your doctors tell you it's a symptom of post-traumatic stress disorder caused by something really bad that happened to you when you were a teenager."

I pause and look at him, wondering how much of my history he knows, feeling naked and ashamed but also, for the first time, actually *wanting* someone to know about the Bad.

His eyes lock with mine and he nods. I think I see understanding in them. At least I hope I do.

"They told m—" I quickly correct myself: "They told you it's some kind of flashback, like combat veterans get, and you figure that must be what it is.

"But eventually you notice a certain person consistently triggers the pain, even if at first you didn't realize he was nearby. Not only that, but the pain varies predictably depending on how close you are to him, and you wonder what's going on.

"So the next time it happens—the next time you feel this physical pain—you try to understand it. You follow it, find the people triggering it, and then you follow *them*. Eventually you catch them hurting someone, out in the middle of nowhere—no police, no phone, so it's all on you." I see the van again, its windows glowing yellow in the darkness as I approach it through the tall grass, a tire iron in my hand. I'm already scared, then I hear her screams. I see her lifeless eyes and the deep, bloody gash in her throat—

"And you stop them."

Startled, I look at the agent, registering what he said. I open my mouth to reply, then remember I was asking *him* the question. "Is that what *you'd* do?"

His eyes shift down to the table and, after a heartbeat or two, he nods. "I get it."

The three words I've wanted so desperately.

Then he starts shaking his head "no," and looks up, his eyes angry, his dark face even darker. "You expect me to believe this bullshit? Don't insult my intelligence!" His voice is low, but the tone is yelling at me.

"I *know* it's hard to believe," I say urgently, then consciously lower my volume, aware of the people sitting nearby. "But if you think I did the things you mentioned then tell me how, all by myself, I found those guys faster than the police and the FBI?"

"That's what I want to know!"

"I *told* you!" I shout whisper.

He looks like he's going to start screaming at me, but nothing comes out.

"I just *told* you," I repeat quietly, leaning forward and holding his eyes.

Gradually the rage on his face dissipates until he seems only really ticked off. He looks away, past me. "This is absurd."

I study his face, which is lean but with a roundness to his features and a smoothness that makes him seem closer to my age than he must actually be. There's something familiar about it, and I briefly wonder again if I really have seen him somewhere before, maybe on one of the missions. I shrug the question off and try to think of a way to convince him of my honesty, but I'm coming up empty. I stare down at the coffee cup in front of me. "You're right," I sigh, suddenly feeling sad and tired at the truth. Several seconds pass and I'm almost surprised to hear the sounds of the coffee shop behind me, of people having normal days just a few feet away. "It *is* absurd. I'm not saying I understand it." I notice I've dropped the pretense of this being hypothetical, but it doesn't matter. We both know I'm talking about me, and I've as good as admitted Florida at least, so I keep going. "That's why I don't trust the sense alone: I look for confirmation, and I call in tips to try to get *you* guys to deal with the bastards. It's not my fault the cops usually don't pay attention, or even when they did, they didn't arrest him. I wish they would; the last thing I want is contact with these freaks. It scares the shit out of me, and getting near them means re-living the worst fucking unspeakable moments of my life." I feel tears starting; I close my eyes and swallow hard. *I feel so tired.* "But," I have to whisper to keep my voice from totally breaking up, "I can't let someone get killed...or worse..." I take a deep breath and it comes back out shakily, but I swallow, breathe again, and get my voice somewhat under control. "I can't allow that when I can do something to stop it."

My face feels hot and a drip runs down my right cheek. *Crap in a hat,* I think and wipe angrily at my face, then look up hoping he's still staring off into space and not looking at me. But my eyes meet his and my face feels even hotter and I look down and to the left at where the edge of our table meets a wooden strip stuck to the wall. Another tear escapes, and my nose feels like it's starting to run. I grab the little paper napkin that came with the coffee and wipe at my face.

"Here," he says.

Keeping my eyes down I look toward his side of the table and see his hand out toward me, a neatly-folded white handkerchief in it. I feel like he's mocking or patronizing me or something and look away again, but the napkin's wet and my nose is still running, so I just take the handkerchief. I blow my nose, wipe at my eyes, and clear my throat. The waterworks have stopped and I'm feeling in control again, so I hand the handkerchief back.

"That's OK—just keep it," he says.

I realize I'm handing him a bundle of snot. "Sorry—I'll, uh, wash it and get it back to you. Look, disregard the emotional outburst, OK? It's just hard to talk about, but everything I've told you is true. I don't know how else to tell it, how to make you believe me. I tried to explain the sense to the detective down in New Orleans, but he didn't believe me either and told me to keep quiet about it. He thought it'd hurt my credibility and their case. I don't doubt it; fortunately, they didn't need my testimony to put the bastard away."

I look up and he returns my gaze for a few seconds, then looks away and blows out some air, sounding frustrated. I don't know what more to say, so I wait in silence for whatever's next.

"Your explanation sounds literally incredible to me," he says quietly and matter-of-factly.

He lets the statement hang, long enough I start to feel sick, but I still don't say anything.

"Who are you working with?"

Huh? I look at him blankly; he looks back expectantly. "What?"

"Playing dumb isn't helping your credibility. Start leveling with me and maybe we can work something out. There's some wiggle room here, but you need to stop trying to bullshit me. One more time: who are you working with?"

What is he talking about? "I'm alone; I—there's no one else. Just me."

"Goddamn it, I'm trying to help you and you're lying to me, Ms. Campbell!"

"I'm sorry; I *am* trying to be helpful. I'm telling you the truth; I really am." The more I claim to be truthful, the more dishonest I sound, even to me, and I *know* I'm telling the truth.

"Not all of it. Who is helping you? Who took out that guy in Trenton?"

It's a trap—another trap. He's trying to trick me into admitting guilt over what happened in Trenton. I look at him, trying to figure out how to respond.

"Well?"

"I...work...alone," I say carefully and deliberately, holding his eyes to try to get the truth through to him. "That's my problem—I have to deal with this by myself. I'd *rather* work with the police. That's why I called them in New Orleans."

"You expect me to believe that *you*, by yourself, *unarmed*," his tone is mocking now, "killed an armed, violent man, *and* his armed accomplice in that field in Florida? By *yourself?*"

"Look, I don't know what you're getting at, if you're trying to trick me into confessing to something or what. I'm telling you the truth: *I work alone.* Why is that so hard to believe? Because I'm a *woman*? Because I'm five-four? What? Don't underestimate me, and don't make assumptions about me based on my size or gender; just because I'm a woman doesn't mean I'm helpless or weak or—or—or *timid* or whatever. I don't need a *man*, if that's what you're getting at, to do anything. I mean, are you saying I find them and someone else does the heavy lifting? I *wish*, because then I wouldn't have gotten shot in New Orleans! I *wish* that were the case. Why do you think I called the cops and tried to get *them* to do the dirty work? Or are you saying someone else is finding these fuckers? If that were true, I wouldn't be involved *at all!* Why would someone need *me?* I mean, I can take care of myself, but no one would seek me out as hired muscle. No, it's *all* on me. I hate it, but that's the truth."

He looks hard at me, his eyes narrowed, then shakes his head and looks down. "I don't know how else to explain it," he says almost too quietly for me to hear. He raises his eyes again. "A few months ago, Massachusetts State Police found a van and a body at a rest stop near the Connecticut line with a couple nine-millimeter Hydra-Shok rounds in its head. I don't suppose you know anything about that, do you?"

I drop my gaze and shrug, tired of this. "Target of opportunity," I say quietly.

"What do you mean?"

I look up, cautious again. He seems really interested in what I just said, or what I'm about to say, and I realize why. "I didn't know that guy even existed; I wasn't looking for him. I was just driving by and the sense picked up on him. And no one else could have told me he was there."

He studies me intently for several seconds, I guess trying to figure out if I'm lying or not.

I look back at him.

"Yeah, well," he says, dropping his eyes and seeming uncomfortable for the first time, "they found dried blood from four different women in the back of that van. Judging from the collection of sunglasses on the dashboard, there were at least twice as many victims over an indeterminate length of time. So…you were right about that one too."

"I know: he hit me with that cast on his arm, and I think there was a metal bar or something in it."

He looks surprised. "There was—you let him hit you?"

"Like I said, I don't trust the sense, so I make sure. I didn't know what he was going to do, only that he was bad. He was aiming for my head, but I ducked and he only got my shoulder. Hurt like hell, but luckily nothing broken. And by the way, I was alone: you think he'd have tried to club me if I'd had someone with me?"

But I can see by his face he's still fighting the idea. "Frankly Ms. Campbell, I'm not sure what to think." He pauses. "But I can't come up with another explanation for how you find these guys and how you're consistently accurate." He opens his mouth to say something more, then changes his mind and frowns instead, gazing past me again. After a few more seconds, "Let me get this straight: You're saying when you're near a murderer, you feel pain like you felt when you were attacked as an adolescent."

"Yes." I feel queasy as I realize he probably knows—from the police report and for all I know some doctor's report or something—he probably knows all about what happened to me. He's probably guessing at and imagining which pain I feel—"It's, uh, pretty specific actually. He—the—the guy—" I look at the agent, and he nods. "He stabbed me here." I point to the place just below where my breastbone ends and abdomen begins, in that angle formed by the two halves of my ribcage. "This is where I feel the pain. And it's not always pain; it starts out as just an itch or a scratch, and only gets bad when I'm really close, like within fifty feet. It doesn't tell me where he—or she—is, only how close they are."

"How close do you need to be to sense them at all?"

"About a city block...or a football field. Maybe a little longer than a football field, so between a hundred and a hundred fifty meters."

"And how often does it kick in?"

"When I'm in range of someone, it's constant, except it gets worse the closer I am."

"No, I mean how often do you sense someone who triggers it?"

"Oh," I shake my head, "not often. It's not set off by just anyone, not even by most criminals, I'd guess. I think it's just people like the one who came after my family and me, people who are—who have a compulsion to kill. That's my guess, anyway, because most of the time I have to go looking for them. Before I realized what the sense means, I only felt it two or three times over…whatever it was—something like ten years."

He nods, studying my face, then looks down at the table and touches his lips with an index finger. He seems unaware of the gesture, but it's as if he's telling someone to be quiet. He puts the hand down on the table again and looks up at me, leaning forward. "Ms. Campbell, I believe you're telling the truth as you see it, and I appreciate that. I'm not convinced you're right about this sense, but I don't know how else to explain all of this. So I'm not sure what's going on, but it's got to stop." He pauses, looking at me.

I start to say what I really want is to work with the police or the FBI, to have them trust me so all I have to do is point out the bad guys to them, but he puts up a finger and continues.

"I'm giving you a choice. I can arrest you now, take you into custody, and begin building a case against you. You don't want that, but to avoid it you need to agree to a few things: First, you have to check in with me every week, and I have to be able to get in touch with you at all times. Second, I need to know where you are, so you let me know if you're leaving the metro Boston area, even just for the day. If you try to run, I will find you again, and there will be no deals, just prosecution." He counts off another finger: "Third, the next time you sense someone, you don't do anything except call me immediately. There will be no more cowboy justice, got it? No more Lone Ranger shit. Are we clear?"

I nod, mostly relieved to not be going to jail, but also concerned. "What if someone is in danger?"

"Ms. Campbell, I'm not kidding around. You are authorized to contact me and only to contact me. Anything else invalidates our understanding." He reaches his left hand into the inside right breast pocket of his suit jacket and produces a business card, which he hands across the table.

I take the card and look at it. The FBI's seal is centered at the top. Below that, printed in sharp capital letters:

SPECIAL AGENT SILAS MACILWANE

"You'll find all my contact information on that card. I always have the cell phone with me—call that number whenever you need to be in touch. Call that number every Sunday evening at six p.m. Is what I'm saying clear to you?"

I nod.

"You have a cell phone, right?"

I nod again.

He takes out a small pad and a pen and pushes them across the table. "Write the number for me. Make sure you always have this phone on you. Our deal is I can get in touch with you anytime."

"OK." I push the pad and pen back across to him when I'm done.

"If I'm going to be unreachable," he continues, "I'll provide you an alternate contact who will understand you're an occasional source of information, and who'll know how to get in touch with me. Is *that* clear to you?"

"Yes." I glance down at the business card again.

"Any questions? Comments? Concerns?"

I do have questions, mainly about how I'm going to continue to stop bad guys since, given the sense, I have that responsibility. But at this point I just want to get the hell out of here and process what's happened, so I shake my head.

"When will I hear from you again?"

"Sunday evening at six."

"I think we have an understanding, Ms. Campbell. Thank you for your time today."

"I'll be in touch," I say, standing, eager to get away.

"You'd better be."

Twenty-Two

January 1999
Charlotte, North Carolina

Flash walks down the narrow corridor to his office, trying to hang on to the sense of calm happiness from the gym. Sometimes, when it occurs to him that he'll be doing this work or something like it for the next thirty-some years, he feels sick. It seems impossible. But at least he has another life—his real life is outside the office; he just does this to bankroll it. He wonders how other people do it, and figures they must also live for something outside of work, though he seriously doubts any of their lives compare to his. *Although Dan does that rock climbing thing—that might be fun. But really not in the same class...* Of course, maybe someone else he knows *does* have a secret life like his. *Yeah, right.* He smiles at the idea one of his co-workers might share his passion. He hangs his long coat on the hook on the back of his door.

His office is small, but at least he has an office—and a window—unlike those administrative drones and computer geeks in their partitioned cubicles. He picks up his mug from his desk and carries it back down the corridor to the kitchen.

Flash really likes this mug, which he bought at a mall kiosk where they imprinted the cup with a photograph he gave them. Most of the guys and—even better—some of the women in the office have commented at one time or another on how pretty his girlfriend is. He loves when that happens. Alexis was exceptionally attractive, which is maybe why she's still his favorite and why he had her picture, taken in the couple hours before she found out what he really likes to do, put on the mug. Seeing her picture at work helps keep him sane; it reminds him of his real life.

"Hey Erik," Dan—not rock climbing Dan, but the one from accounting—says.

"Hey Dan, how you doing today?" This guy is OK—quiet and courteous, so Flash doesn't mind talking to him. Not that it would matter; he is his own master and doesn't reveal how he feels about anyone.

"Erik" is the name the world associates with him, but he doesn't use it in his real life. His real name is short for Flashphaler—a good, strong name, and the only strong thing about his father. Flash's mother subordinated herself to her husband only once, when she took his name as hers. Unlike his father, Flash is worthy of the name. Mainly, though, he likes the sound and connotations of Flash, as in *flash of pain* or *flash of brilliance*: a burst of power and energy. This is his real name.

"I just started the coffee, so it'll be a few minutes," Dan says.

"That's OK—I'm just going for the water," he says, walking up to the cooler and operating the spigot.

"Oh yeah, I should have known that. You're really healthy and into fitness, aren't you?"

Flash smiles. "I drink coffee before the gym—it sort of primes the pump. After the gym, I'm just thirsty."

"Yeah, I'm trying to get going on an exercise program. My wife and I have a little competition to see which one can stick with the New Year's resolution longer. I wish I had your discipline—do you work out every day?"

"Three days on, one day off. It's really not a matter of discipline, though: It's easy to do the things you want to do. That's the best kind of discipline."

Dan shakes his head. "I wish I could get that. Right now the main thing motivating me is my wife's scorn."

It's like a switch flips in Erik's head, and he feels... *What? Sympathy?* "Hey, don't let her do that to you," he says. He represses the urge to reach out and touch Dan's shoulder.

Dan looks at him uncertainly, then smiles and laughs a little. "Oh, it's cool—it's good for me."

What am I doing? Flash wonders, and produces the socially conventional reaction: he laughs. "Yeah, I was just kidding. Well, whatever works," he says as he turns and leaves.

Back in his office he takes a few minutes to go through email and reviews his list of sales contacts to see who is due for phone calls. At 9:25 he goes to the conference room for the weekly sales meeting, run by Deb Waters, a shrewish little woman he despises. Fortunately, Flash excels at deception— that's why he went into marketing—so he's able to appear cheerful and motivated even as he's fantasizing about impaling her head on a sharp stick. He knows this fantasy can never go any further; doing so would break one of the rules that keeps him safe: Never kill close to home. His first kill was close to home, but that was unanticipated. After that he started making the rules he's followed since, and they've protected him for years.

He is first in the room and as usual takes a seat at the opposite end of the long table from where Deb will sit. Soon the other five sales reps, all men, trickle in. They're weak and boring but otherwise OK, which is good since he has to go on trips to various trade shows and conferences from time to time with each of them.

Deb arrives at exactly 9:30 as usual, carrying her whiteboard calendar. Flash is willing to give credit where it's due, and she does run a punctual, efficient, usually short meeting. She places the board on the room's easel, and soon she's talking about quarterly goals and business plans. Flash listens, but to make the situation tolerable he avoids looking at her. He pretends to take notes while actually writing down ideas for the phone calls he'll make after the meeting. He finishes that but she's still talking, so he rests his eyes on his hands, which he has folded on top of his notepad. He notices some dried blood under his right thumbnail, probably from the rabbit he killed last night. He casually scrapes it away, wishing it were Deb's dried blood he was removing.

As she begins to hand out assignments, Flash picks up his pen again, and makes eye contact with her.

"OK, we've got the Network Computing Expo coming up in Boston in a month. Jeremy and Erik, you two can have that one. It's a big show, so bring plenty of materials."

"Yeah, I worked it last year too," Jeremy says.

Flash copies the dates off the whiteboard calendar. He'll stop by the travel assistant's cubicle after this meeting and ask her to arrange his tickets and hotel. Then he'll call AAA after getting back to his office and order a travel book and map for Boston. He feels a stir of anticipatory excitement in his gut.

Twenty-Three

Mac gazes at the picture of Tracie and Malcolm on the desk in the one-bedroom apartment he owns. Malcolm is blowing out the candles on his fifth birthday cake. *His last.* It was a long time before Mac could even look at this picture, but now it's OK. He can't articulate the thought without losing his composure, but there's some comfort in the knowledge they were happy, and this picture commemorates one of those times.

He's been in California for the past few days, speaking at a law enforcement conference. He arrived home a couple hours earlier, had a sandwich from the shop down the street for dinner and went through the mail that had accumulated in the oversized mailbox he rents at the post office. After paying the electric bill, he found himself with nothing left to do but turn in for the night, but when he turned off the Miles Davis CD he'd been playing the apartment seemed too quiet and he was still too awake. Instead of going to bed, he ended up gazing at the photo, trying to put himself in it, in the moment when it was taken.

Which is an act of imagination instead of memory, since Mac was deployed overseas, "protecting America," when Malcolm turned five. Tracie's sister Sandra took the picture.

Mac was also deployed overseas when a couple crackheads broke into their home and murdered Tracie and Malcolm. He hadn't protected them; he'd been protecting a dictator the U.S. government needed but who was too distasteful to publicly endorse, which is why it had to be Mac's unit that did the protecting. Mac didn't even find out what had happened to his family until two days after they were killed.

He'd been fighting the wrong wars, protecting the wrong people. He was too late for Tracie and Malcolm. But in the time since maybe he's protected some people like them.

Except when Shailene Campbell is doing the protecting, he thinks, smiling a little. *Then I'm just cleaning up afterwards.*

And now he's shut her down, more or less.

Because vigilante justice is an oxymoron.

Right?

In the Army he didn't concern himself with justice; he just did what was needed to solve the problem and accomplish the mission. He got things done. But now...*Am I in this to protect the law and justice? Or did I choose this path to protect people?*

Am I fighting the wrong war again?

He thinks of Campbell, and of the man who was almost a victim in Philadelphia. He thinks of the fingerprints on the radio-controlled toy in the apartment in Trenton—the child's fingerprints that didn't match any of the bodies they dug up, maybe because the kid is still alive somewhere, thanks to Campbell. He thinks of the dead woman at that last scene in Kansas City—the *last* victim who implies all the women that didn't become victims because someone—Campbell again—killed the KC Killer.

And now I've shut her down.

It's been almost two weeks since their meeting, and almost a week since she called to check in, right on schedule, last Sunday evening at six. His gut told him she wouldn't bolt, but he'd changed cars and kept an eye on her for a couple days after they met to be safe. His instincts were right: she went on with a routine, solitary life, going to a gym, going to work, going home. The next test had been the first Sunday check-in a few days later, and she'd passed that too.

He's still puzzled by what she told him. Implausible as it seems, the very unbelievability of it is an argument for its credibility.   Clearly *she* believes her story, because if she didn't she would've picked a better lie. *So she's crazy?* Mac has more than a little familiarity with abnormal psychology, enough to know crazy people can behave and communicate completely normally and still be out of touch with reality. But like she said, how'd she find the killers she took out? Find them before law enforcement—before Mac and the task forces he was on—found them?

He thinks of her response to his mention of the body in the Massachusetts rest stop: "Target of opportunity," she'd said in what sounded like an automatic, tired, and honest response, only becoming alert again when he asked her to elaborate. It could have been an act, but she was at least telling the truth about being there—she knew the detail about the fake cast with the piece of rebar inside.

What happened in New Orleans backs up her version of things too. The fact that she was shot confirms she herself was encountering the bad guy directly, which argues against someone else working with her as the muscle. Plus, the witness' description of the Phillie shooter's height and build matches Campbell. But if someone else is *finding* the bad guys, why would *she* be picked as muscle? It's not ironclad, but as improbable as it seems, everything he knows backs up her story that she's working alone and doing what she claims—finding killers, trying to get the cops to take them out for her, and when that doesn't work or isn't an option, doing the job herself. And in every case he's aware of, she was right. He doesn't understand how it's possible, but she's doing it.

It's like when he was a child and for a few years his family lived in an old, supposedly haunted house in Memphis. It wasn't often, but every once in a while a piece of furniture would move from its usual location while no one was around, or a light they distinctly remembered turning out before going to bed would be on the next morning. There was no rational explanation, and after the first couple times they simply accepted it as "the ghost again" and left it at that. Sometimes things don't make sense but are true anyway.

Mac is also familiar with the phenomenon that some abused children are able to almost precognitively sense danger from a violent parent. It's a survival adaptation: apparently some kids are able to subliminally pick up on precursors to rage—possibly they can smell a change in the parent's body chemistry, or see a difference in the way the abuser moves, or hear a subtle modulation in the adult's voice. Something like this might be going on with her—a survival adaptation in response to the attack on her and her parents. Maybe she learned to subconsciously detect some characteristic unique to psychopaths on the hunt.

He thinks of what he read about the incident that killed her parents and almost killed her. The descriptions in the police and medical reports were typically dry and antiseptic, but even in those terms it sounded really bad. *The brutality...* In his position as handler he cannot allow himself to feel sympathy for her, and as any cop will tell you, everyone has a sad story. *Still...*

So what's next? I found her, supposedly found out how she finds the bad guys, and supposedly have her, at least for now, under control. Right? He doesn't think she'll run. She probably *wants* the deal he dictated. The phone calls to the police made it clear she really doesn't want to go after killers alone, and it's unlikely she wants to add being a fugitive from justice to her list of problems. And if she were going to flee, she probably would have done so already.

Unless she was waiting until after the first Sunday night check-in so she'd have a full week for her head start.

He dials her number—the home phone, not the cell. He hasn't called it before; there was no need to confirm it because he got it from the listing, not from her. It rings a couple times, then he hears a click and the static-y sound of a cheap answering machine. He recognizes immediately what comes next: the vigilante's voice stating her home phone number. Mac is surprised and pleased at this additional confirmation of her identity and the fact she has apparently overlooked a key bit of evidence he could use, if necessary, to tie her to the killings. The short message is followed by more white noise, then a beep.

"Ms. Campbell, this is Special Agent MacIlwane. Call me."

There's a click on the other end. "Hello Special Agent MacIlwane," she says, with what he thinks is a trace of irony in her tone.

A wave of relief washes over him. "You can call me 'Agent MacIlwane' for short."

"Thanks. So are you checking to see if I ran?"

Her directness surprises him a little, but he doesn't allow it to come through. "Yes."

"I didn't. I won't as long as our arrangement stands. Believe it or not, I like it."

"I suspected as much. Are you pursuing any targets now?"

"Like I said, I like our arrangement. I'd call you if I were." There's a brief pause, then she asks, "Are you working on anything now? Anything I can help out with? Because I haven't seen anything on the news websites I check at the library."

News websites? "I thought you had some sixth sense about these things."

"I do, but it only kicks in at about a hundred meters or so."

"I guess I don't really understand how you do this."

There's silence on the other end of the line, and Mac realizes he should have discussed this more with her in person.

Without the benefit of body language and facial expression, he doesn't know if she's clamming up, or thinking, or just confused by his question. He's about to speak again when she preempts him.

"Each week I check online for news about ongoing serial murder cases. I always hope to find nothing, but... inevitably..."

"I get it." He thinks for a couple beats then, "You don't need to do that anymore. I'll feed you your missions from now on."

There's a long pause before she replies, "Will you? Really? Because—don't patronize me, all right? It might sound crazy, but the sense is real, and I can save lives with it. You have to give me a chance to prove it to you."

"I don't *have* to do anything, Ms. Campbell," Mac says quietly but firmly. "And yes, I really will bring you in on the next serial murder case I handle. In the meantime, you stay out of trouble and in touch."

"I will."

"Have a good evening Ms. Campbell."

"OK, bye."

He hangs up, leans back in his chair and closes his eyes. He pictures the small woman with her pleasant, even pretty face dominated by green eyes, then imagines her caving in the skull of that man Hayes in a Florida field. Or gunning down the Pink Slasher, or the sunglasses collector at the rest stop in Massachusetts. It's not so hard to wrap his brain around. He's seen enough to know anyone is capable of violence under the right circumstances, and appearance is not a reliable indicator of what's deep inside a person.

Despite that, he finds himself looking at his memory of the face. It's not a face that would, even if it were possible, under different circumstances, appeal to him romantically or sexually, but there's something about it he likes.

Twenty-Four

February 1999
Arlington, Massachusetts

Using the business end of a pencil, I push aside a little of the damp soil, creating a shallow cavity. I press my fingertip against the seed lying on the table. The flat, roughly circular chip sticks to my skin and I lift it up, trapping it with my thumb. This tiny package of life is not much bigger than the tip of the pencil's dull point—too small, you'd think, for it to contain the stuff to make a new plant. What I'm doing feels like magic: an ancient rite which will conjure existence out of almost nothing.

Besides all the order in the universe, which first inspired me to doubt my atheism, I've started looking for examples of paradox as signs of Harold. Like pattern, coexisting contradictions are all over the place. Even in this: There's something counterintuitive about burying a diminutive speck in the mud and expecting a plant to appear in its place. There's also irony in the dirt, which is composed not only of sand, but also of organic material: the remnants of things once living. This mix of the inert and the dead provides necessary support for the living.

The real paradox, though, is in the natural selection that led to the evolution of the genetic code in the seed. Here's a process which uses destruction and death to make creation and life stronger and the power in the seed reliable. Even life itself is a paradox. The Second Law of Thermodynamics says energy everywhere in the universe wants to spread out, but living organisms gather up and concentrate energy. How do you get life out of a universe where entropy is the rule?

There's paradox in me too, carefully tending these seeds now, then eating them or throwing them away in the summer when I eat the hot peppers the plant will produce. Create, destroy, nurture, kill...I contain all these.

I wonder about the people I hunt, if there's more to who they are than the impulse to hurt and kill. The first two, Alan Hayes and Denice Hook, seemed to love each other. I found them at a shopping mall and followed them around for hours after that. I still remember her feeding him fries in the food court and thinking the sense had to be wrong about them. But that night I was cradling their naked victim's head in my lap as the last of her blood drained from the gaping neck wound Hook had opened. The one in Trenton, Wayne Lambert, buried most of his victims with toys, as if he wanted them to have something to play with in the afterlife.

Maybe I shouldn't think too gently about the enemy.

Still, knowing and ignorant, knowable and mysterious, we are each a nexus of opposing forces and drives: helping and harming, loving and hating, worshipping and defiling, living and dying.

The chip falls and balances on a small ridge of soil. Using the pencil point, I move the seed into the depression and push damp soil over it, being careful not to let the tiny beige disk stick to the graphite tip and get pulled to the surface again. I move on to the next cone-shaped cardboard section in the tray. The seed company recommends planting three seeds per compartment, but I only put one in each. I'm not good at untangling the fragile roots without wrecking them when it comes time to move the seedlings, and anyway I only have room on my porch for a few of each type of plant, so if a few cones in the starter tray are wasted, it's fewer seedlings I have to throw out. I don't like throwing out seedlings. I poke at the damp earth and make another small depression. I reach for the spill of seeds.

The answering machine clicks on and my hand stops in mid-air, waiting for my brief greeting to play out.

"Hey Shailene, you theah? It's Chahlie."

I cross the room and pick up the handset, causing the machine to stop recording and rewind the tape. "Hey Charlie, what's up?"

"Got a job fa you—y'intrested?"

"Sure," I say, kneeling in front of the phone table and picking up the pen by the pad of paper there.

"Good. I need you to go to Lexington, pick up a package, and take it to a booth at the Hynes—there's some kind of conf'rence or somethin' theah today. Ya ready to write?"

"Go 'head."

It's almost an hour before I take the Fenway exit off Storrow Drive with the box of pamphlets and promotional materials I picked up at the office in Lexington. Apparently the trade show is going well for this small software company, since there's so much interest in its product. I glanced at one of the pamphlets while loading the box in the back of the car and saw they're selling some kind of help desk product. Once upon a time I would've been one of their target customers. At least, that was the plan when I got out of the Army. But in the Army we used to say the first casualty of any engagement is the plan.

The itching starts as Stacey descends the ramp to the parking garage below the Hynes Convention Center.

Oh crap.

My stomach twists and I start to feel sick, but I breathe slowly and deeply through my nose as I stop at the guard booth and show the laminated card that identifies me as working for a legitimate courier service. As I head deeper into the underground garage, the scar over my solar plexus continues to itch. The persistence of this feeling kills my hope that the source was just passing by on Boylston Street, which would have made the issue moot for now, since there's no way

I'd be able to get out of here fast enough to catch up and find him. No, clearly whoever is triggering the sense is here in the convention center with me. My stomach gives another twist. "Crap in a hat," I sigh. *At least now I'm not alone—I can call in the cavalry.* I find an open 30-minute drop-off space and pull in.

I lock Stacey's door, walk to the back, and open the hatch. The box is pretty weighty, but fortunately there's only one. There's supposed to be a hand truck near the elevator— the wall is stenciled with words about returning it, but I've never seen it in the three or four times I've delivered stuff here, so if there's too much for me to lug in my arms I end up making multiple trips. I manage to balance the box on my hip with one arm and pull the hatch closed and lock it with the other, then head for the elevator.

On the way up the itching intensifies. I try to focus on what I'm doing by studying the floor plan they gave me when I picked up the package.

The elevator stops; I squat and pick up the box; the doors open. The noise of hundreds of voices washes over me. Fabric-covered partitions separate the concrete and steel of the giant room's outer walls from the exhibit floor. I walk the length of the partitions, turn the corner, and pause, getting my bearings. The floor plan changes every time I come here, but the map helps. As I make my way to the booth, the itching intensifies to a painful scratch that starts to dig deeper into me the further I penetrate into the exhibit area. My guess is it's a security guard. I read many sociopaths gravitate toward law enforcement-like occupations for the power and authority those jobs hold. Sociopaths usually don't pass the psych screenings to get work on police forces, so sometimes they gravitate to work as security guards and night watchmen. Plus, it seems really unlikely one of these computer geeks could be a killer.

Well, I was one of these geeks...

The people at my destination booth are glad to see me; or rather, they're glad to see what I'm bringing. They cheerfully sign my delivery receipt and I'm done with them in less than half a minute. Free of the box, I begin walking around the exhibit floor, not really wanting to, but...

I follow the pain to, generally, the center of the cavernous room. There are a lot of exhibitors and customers here, but I see no security guards. I walk the aisles, looking at the reps with their displays and pamphlets, laptop computers running demos, and TV-VCR combos playing infomercials, homing in as my scar seems to tear open. The deeper cramps begin, then sharpen. I stop for a moment and close my eyes, adjusting to the hurt, then open again and resume walking slowly. *Close now.*

Before the pain can peak, it eases slightly. I stop and turn around. The aisle is about ten feet wide; the target is on one side or the other, meaning my options are Axent firewalls and magusWare, which appears to specialize in human resources software. At least, there are pictures of people and clocks and paychecks on their backdrop. Axent has a woman and man working its booth, and magusWare has two men, so playing the odds, I move toward magusWare first.

I know immediately I guessed right: walking up to the booth is like walking onto a knife blade. I clench my teeth and pull in a deep breath through my nose. Fortunately, there are already a couple nerdy guys in T-shirts and jeans, and a professional-looking young woman in a business suit talking to the magusWare men. I stand slightly behind and between the visitors, absorbing the pain and reminding myself I'm not really being harmed, which doesn't reduce the hurt, but does make it easier to deal with and control my reactions.

At this point I can't tell who is the source. Since the magnitude of the pain varies only with distance, not number of bad guys, there could be multiple psychopaths, but that's extremely unlikely. One of the magusWare reps—the one wearing a maroon sweater and talking to the geeks—is a little older, in his forties or so I'd guess. Still playing the odds, I focus on the bigger guy with the blonde flattop haircut who's about thirty and talking to Ms. Business Suit while she taps some keys on a laptop he's turned around for her to look at. Flattop's looking very sharp himself, in a dark three-piece suit he wears well. His shoulders are really broad and the front of his jacket hangs straight down below his bulging chest— judging from the breadth of his upper torso and thickness of his neck, he's obviously into weight lifting. I move up next to the woman, taking the stabbing up another tick, to about as bad as it gets. I swallow hard and consciously relax my face.

Flattop looks at me and little wrinkles appear around his eyes when he smiles. He has a genuine-looking, very white smile which contrasts with his tanned, sharp-featured face. I guess he's good-looking, though I don't really think in those terms. "Hey, welcome," Flattop says. "We were just talking about magusWare's new suite of management utilities. Emily is looking at timeWare, our time tracking module," he says, referring to Ms. Biz Suit. There's a hint of the South in Flattop's voice, though different from the way people spoke in Alabama. "By the way, you lost your name tag," he says to me while pointing at his own to show me what I'm missing.

I look down, pretending to be surprised. "Oh! Must've gotten pulled off in that free T-shirt melee I was in over at the Symantec exhibit," I say, surprising myself with the improv, especially considering how much I'm hurting. My voice is steady too. Being female has its advantages, like a high tolerance for pain. As I glance back up, Flattop holds out his hand.

"I'm Erik," he says.

Keeping my face neutral, I take the offered hand. "Sharon," I say, automatically giving the alias I use when I'm doing phone interviews for Opinion Research.

"So what is your company using now to handle personnel functions?"

I'm stumped; all I can think of is the stabbing below my heart and the name "Symantec," and I don't know if that company offers anything like this. I can't remember the name of the software we used at the architect firm I was at before Trenton. Charlie uses an adding machine, and I have no idea what Opinion Research uses. "I don't know. I'm actually here for someone else—he told me to stop by and check you guys out, get any literature you're giving away."

Erik seems a little thrown by this, but just then Ms. Biz says, "Thanks, that was really helpful."

Erik looks at her. "Any questions I can answer for you?"

"No, it looks good, but I want to take a look at the demo disc back at my office."

"OK, well if you do have any questions, you have my card. Thanks for stopping by."

She leaves but the pain stays of course. I didn't think it was her setting it off.

Erik turns back to me. "So, I'm sorry—you said you're here for someone else?"

I nod. "Yeah, he couldn't make it but asked me to stop by, get a brochure or something."

"I don't suppose you have a business card for him?"

"No, sorry. That would've been a good idea, wouldn't it? It was kind of last minute. Sorry."

"Why don't you give me one of your cards and write his information on it?"

This guy is all about business cards, isn't he? But all these booths have boxes or bowls for collecting the things, and some even have prize drawings to give people an incentive to hand them over, so apparently that's big with the marketing set. "Sorry—I've run out," I say, and then I get a great idea. "But if you give me your card, I promise I'll pass it on."

"Sure," he says with faked enthusiasm.

I take the card, which is cream-colored with electric blue lettering:

Erik Flashphaler
Senior Account Representative
magusWare, Inc.

The address below this is in Charlotte. "So you guys are out of North Carolina?"

"That's right," Erik says as he hands me a glossy brochure and a square cardboard envelope. "This covers our full line of products, and there are demo versions of timeWare and payWare on the CD."

"That's great—he'll really be interested in trying them out," I say, thinking *OK, now I get the hell away from these guys and the pain.*

But if I'm going to follow them after they leave here, it'd really help to know where they're staying. Instead of bolting, I spout the first think I can think of: "So it must be a lot colder up here than down in Charlotte..."

"Actually, it gets chilly there this time of year."

"Yeah, but nothing like this," Sweater Man, the other rep, chimes in. "What was it—twenty-five this morning?"

I notice the pair of geeks have left and now I'm the only customer they have, leaving me two possibilities for who is setting off the sense. "Something like that," I say. "So how long are you up here?"

"Just for the expo," Flashphaler says.

I nod, "Well, stay warm. Where are you guys staying?"

"What's it called?" Sweater Guy asks Flashphaler. "The 'Twin Trees'?"

"The Doubletree," he says.

"Oh yeah," I nod, "how is it?" I ask, trying to sound conversational.

Flashphaler shrugs. "It's fine—pretty standard stuff."

"Erik doesn't really care about his room—he's always taking in the local color when we go on these trips. Me, I'm married, so after this it's a call home, then a room service dinner and a movie on HBO," Sweater says, smiling.

"Well, you should come back up and visit us sometime in the spring—Boston is beautiful then.   You can bring your family and do the tourist thing."

"Thanks, I might do that," Sweater replies.

"OK, well, good luck—have a good…expo or whatever," I say cheerfully, spinning on my heel to finally get out of here.

"Hey, do you think I might call that guy who's interested in our software sometime?   Maybe you could give me a number to reach him at?"

I've already turned away, and I'm intent on escaping, so I only slow a little and look over my shoulder at Flashphaler. "Um, I think it's probably better if he calls you—I'll give him your card.   He's out of the office a lot.   Thanks!"   I look forward again and walk quickly down the aisle, the pain below my breastbone mercifully dropping off as I go.

I get to the end of the aisle, turn the corner, and stop as soon as I'm out of sight of the magusWare booth.   There's one piece left before I can go, and that's verifying which of them is a bad guy.   Everything I've seen and heard points to Flashphaler as the likely candidate, but I've got to be sure.   I find the restrooms and position myself inconspicuously between them and magusWare.

While I'm waiting I take out my cell phone and call Charlie.   "Hey, it's Shailene.   I did the delivery, but I've got some other stuff I have to do before I can come back out there. I'll bring the receipt by later, probably sometime tomorrow."

Charlie's unhappy—he likes getting his paperwork back as soon as a job is done.

"Yeah, I know—just trust me, OK?"

"It's just that this has been happening a lot lately with you," he says.

"A lot?   One other time—the Christmas—"

"Don't say it!"

What does he think, his phone is tapped?   "One other time, Charlie. I've got the receipt right here in my hand, and it'll be in your hand tonight—I'll drop it off on my way home," I add hopefully.

I have to wait about half an hour or so, wandering back and forth in the swirling crowds and every few minutes peering between displays at the booth, but eventually Sweater walks by and there's no increase in pain. On my way out I pass behind Flashphaler, the sudden deep cramps double-confirming he's the one.

I find my way back to the garage elevators, snagging on my way out a flyer giving the dates and hours of the expo. I get Stacey out of the garage, luckily before someone ticketed her for overstaying her 30 minute welcome, and drive to a big municipal parking lot sandwiched between Soldier's Field Road and the Charles River. I point Stacey's nose into the sun before shutting down.

I pull out my wallet and find Agent MacIlwane's card. This is the first time I'm calling him, but I remember he said to use his cell number, so that's what I punch in on my phone.

"Special Agent MacIlwane."

"Hi, it's, uh, Shailene Campbell," I say, stumbling a little as I almost call myself "Ms. Campbell."

"Afternoon Ms. Campbell. What's happening?"

"I—I have a name for you."

There's a pause, then "You were supposed to contact me when you *started*, not wait until you identified him."

"This just came up—kind of a target of opportunity. I found him an hour ago at a trade show up here, and I got his business card—he's a sales rep with a North Carolina software company. I don't know what, if anything, this guy has done; all I know is he's bad. I'm going to keep an eye on him tonight; I think he's only here in Boston until tomorrow, when the trade show ends."

The silence on his side goes on for several seconds. "Agent MacIlwane?"

"I'm thinking." A few more seconds of silence, then "So what makes you think this guy is of interest? Just that sense thing?"

I feel the red light come on in my brain, but I swallow and reign in my emotions before speaking quietly. "Not 'just that sense thing.' I know it's hard for you to believe, but the sense is real, and this guy is bad. Maybe you can check around, see if there are some unsolved serial murders somewhere."

"There are always unsolved murders, and many of them are probably parts of series we aren't even aware of."

"Well, yeah, but maybe there could be some unsolved murders in Charlotte, North Carolina, where this guy is from."

"Tell me what you have."

"He works for a company called magusWare—"

"*Maggot*ware?"

"No, *magus*Ware—magus, as in—"

"The singular of magi?"

"I was thinking of the John Fowles novel, but yeah."

"I didn't read that one."

I give him the rest of the information off Flashphaler's business card.

"You know, when I was talking to him and his co-worker, the other guy mentioned something about Flashphaler going out at night when he's on these trips."

"That's not exactly incriminating."

"Yeah, but if we knew where and when he's been on these trips—"

"There might be a correlation between his trips and people dying in nasty ways. Good idea. OK, I'll look into it, see what I can find out. In the meantime, don't do anything."

"I've got to watch him tonight. Maybe he'll stay in his hotel room, but if he goes out, I've got to make sure he doesn't hurt anyone."

"Campbell, don't go vigilante on me; that's not our deal."

"I'm keeping my side of it, but that doesn't include letting this guy attack someone when I can maybe stop him. I've got to watch him tonight."

There's another pause on his side before he says, "All right, *watch* him, *call* me if it looks like there's going to be trouble and we'll figure something out. Make sure you have your cell phone with you."

"I'm using it right now."

"OK, use the phone if he does anything that looks dangerous."

"Fine with me. You should know by now I don't do this because I like it."

"Yeah, I got that."

"Let me know if you find anything out about him."

"That's not part of our deal."

I think the least he could do is let me know if I'm right or not, but I guess I already know I'm not wrong. And if I can actually hand this off to him, it really doesn't matter, so I decide not to argue. "Fine—whatever."

I call information next, get the number for the Doubletree Guest Suites, then call and ask to be connected to Erik Flashphaler's room. They put me through and I hang up.

Twenty-Five

I'm going to blame myself if this goes bad.

Mac goes over the alternatives in his head again, and reaches the same conclusion. There really is no provision for this in the normal FBI way of doing business. If they had evidence, a witness, *something* to go on, then he could call in all kinds of resources. As it is, though, he doesn't even know how to tell anyone what might be going on. Common sense says her story is impossible, but he doesn't know how else to explain what brought him to her in the first place: the killers she identified and stopped. His instincts also tell him she's on the level, and if he's right about her, then she's the most potent weapon there is against psychopathic killers. But the Bureau is too much itself: a big bureaucracy, closed-minded, mired in inertia, and unable to assimilate something like this. On the other hand, leaving Campbell to wield this power alone would be irresponsible. It's up to Mac as a professional, and as the only person besides Campbell to know of her sense, to take control and make the best use of her ability.

He glances at the clock display on the computer screen: 7:43 p.m. Activity on his desk phone is not only billed to the government, but also automatically logged, so he picks up his cell phone and calls her.

"Hello." Her voice lacks the questioning inflection people usually give the word when they answer the phone; she says it like a flat statement of fact.

"Where are you, Ms. Campbell?"

"I'm in my car, in a hotel parking lot."

"Is he there?"

"He's in the hotel."

"Alone?"

"I think so. He arrived alone, but I'm not sure if he has a guest or not. I was actually getting ready to go in and find his room, but I think it's safe as long as he stays here. I don't think he'd kill someone in a room registered to his name."

"You were going to call me before you went in, right?"

There's a pause. "Did you find anything out about him?"

"Are you armed, Ms. Campbell?"

"No."

There's no hesitation in her answer; he's inclined to believe her and feels slightly better. "I looked at the magusWare website. They still had listings for three trade shows that already happened, so I checked for murders in those cities on those dates. Only one of them happened to have a murder during the dates of the show, and that could easily be a coincidence. You might be wrong about this guy," Mac says with more conviction than he feels.

"What kind of murder was it?"

"The kind where someone turns up dead."

"Very funny," she says, her voice maintaining its flat affect. "I mean, was it someone killed in a robbery, or was it something sadistic?"

"It's one murder out of three possible place-time intersections."

"So it *was* something sadistic or sexual, maybe both; otherwise you'd be telling me it was a drug deal gone bad or a wife killing her husband."

"There's no way we can draw a conclusion or make a pattern out of this one event."

"What about Boston? Has anything happened up here in the past couple days?"

"If it has, I don't know about it."

"How about the Charlotte area?"

"Nothing like what you're talking about in the past year. Like I said, maybe you're wrong about this one."

"He's definitely triggering the thing in me—I hurt when I'm near him; I'm sensing him now. But I don't know—maybe he's not active. Maybe he just *wants* to hurt people, but he's not doing it. I'm not really sure how this works; all I know is every time I've followed up on it before, the source was someone dangerous." She's quiet for several seconds, and Mac isn't sure what to say next. "I'm going in to find his room, see if I can hear anything through his door."

"Campbell, they're not going to tell you what room he's in. Just go home."

"I don't need to ask the staff. I can find his room."

"What, with your sense?"

"It's like warmer/colder hints, only they hurt."

If she *is* right, then she's also right about the need to keep an eye on the guy. "All right, listen, you're just observing. If you suspect any trouble—"

"I'll call you—I know. But what good will that do if he's attacking someone?"

"You call me and I'll get someone there fast."

"How?"

"Trust me. Don't try to intervene yourself. You're really unarmed, right?"

"Yes, I'm unarmed."

"What hotel is this?"

"The Doubletree Guest Suites."

"Boston, right?"

"Yes."

"You have a number for them?"

"Hold on." He hears rustling around, a thud like she dropped the phone, then some more rustling.

"Sorry, I dropped you." She reads him a phone number.

"Call me if there's trouble. I'll get someone over there, and I'll call his room to stall him. Don't do anything besides call me, all right?"

"Believe me, I don't want to—I'd *rather* hand it off to you."

"You keep saying that, but you need to show me before I can trust it."

"You mean trust *me*.   That's fine—I understand your position.   But understand mine, too: If someone is being hurt, I'm not going to wait for long before intervening—'long' being about five seconds if it sounds bad.   I'll give you as long as I can, but if there isn't time and I have to do something myself, I will."

"Just be careful, all right?"   His own words surprise Mac.

"Always."

"Always" like when you got yourself shot in New Orleans? he wonders.

Twenty-Six

Flash sets the tray of dirty dishes and the remnants of his dinner—a porterhouse steak with fries and a salad—on the floor just outside and to the right of his hotel room, hangs out the do not disturb tag, and closes the door. As usual, although he's only slept for two or three of the past 36 hours and feels exhausted, he's too wired and restless to fall asleep. Sometimes mindless TV like the sitcom re-runs he watched with dinner tonight help him wind down, but not this time. As soon as his head hits the pillow he knows it's going to be difficult. He opens his eyes to the semi-dark room and listens to the sound of a waterfall coming from the travel-size sound conditioner by his bed. This dampens out most hotel noises like quiet voices in the corridor or a barely audible television in the next room. The glowing numerals on the clock by the bed tell him it's only about 8 p.m. He could, of course, watch more TV, but he really is tired and needs to make up for the sleep he missed the previous night.

His mind wanders to the stored images, sounds, and smells. Her perfume; the sound of her voice, her laugh; the look of confusion on her face, quickly replaced by fear—he loves that turning point; the smell of her blood, then of her soiling herself; the weird grunting noises she made against the improvised gag he put in her mouth. Masturbating usually helps him sleep when he's restless, so he retrieves a couple tissues from the bathroom and returns to the bed and his memories of the night before. He considers getting the plastic bag he put his souvenir in, but he would have to turn on the light to really appreciate it, and that would work against his goal of getting off and getting to sleep.

Soon he's almost home, remembering that final, culminating violation of her, his hand moving quickly up and down as the memory rolls, the pleasure building in him.

"Sir, can I help you?"   A man's voice in the corridor, sounding very close.

After a pause, a woman's voice, even closer, responds. "Uh...I'm looking for a contact."   She sounds like she's right outside his room.

"Sorry ma'am.   Did you say you lost a contact?"   The man's voice sounds a little closer.   *What the hell is going on out there?*

"Yeah..."   She's moved a little further away.   "But I don't think I'm going to find it.   Oh well—no big deal."

"I can get a flashlight if you like."

Now Flash's attention is completely refocused and he's lost all his momentum.   *This is ridiculous.*   Flash sits up and swings his legs over the edge of the bed.

"No, that's all right—it really doesn't matter.   Thanks anyway."   The female's voice is getting further away as she speaks, and this time the male voice doesn't respond.

Flash listens for several more seconds, but the corridor is silent again.   His erection and libido are gone and he's even more awake than before.   The corners of his mouth tug into a tight smile: *No rest for the wicked.*   Resignedly, he picks up the remote from the bedside table, turns the TV on again, and settles in for a *Seinfeld* re-run.

Twenty-Seven

Icarry the bowl of oatmeal from the microwave to my table and set it down to the side, leaving the middle of the table open for the newspapers. I picked up both a *Globe* and a *Herald* on the way home from the gym, but I start with the *Herald* since its focus is more local and murder-oriented than the *Globe's*. I don't have to look far. The front page is taken up with an oversized headline about cost overruns on the Big Dig project and teasers about sports stories. Page three, though, has four columns dedicated to

Young Woman Found Brutally Murdered

The sense was right, I think as the sadness floods me, *but too late*. I read the article, then walk over to the phone and dial MacIlwane's cell number.

"MacIlwane," he says, sounding a little out of breath.

"It's me—"

"Hey," he says, still a little winded, "you ever find that contact lens?"

I ignore the joke. "We were too late. He killed a woman night before last."

"What?" he says, his tone becoming urgent and serious.

"I just read it in the paper—the cops found a woman murdered in her apartment. The article says she was beaten to death."

"Shit." I hear clanking sounds in the ensuing silence.

"Where are you?"

"The gym. Listen, just because this happened doesn't mean your guy did it. I'll be at my office in about thirty minutes. I'll see what I can find out, see if there's any similarity to the one in Baltimore."

Baltimore—so that's where the murder he mentioned yesterday was. And like I thought, it was sadistic, since he's comparing to this one. "OK." I pause, thinking. "I gotta work at the phone bank today—I'll be there by nine, and I can't really take calls while I'm on my shift. All right if I call you on my break at about eleven?"

"Yeah, that's fine. Call the cell."

"OK." It seems like there ought to be something else to say, but there isn't. "OK," I say again, and hang up.

* * *

It's an overcast, cold day. The paved bike trail that passes behind the house I live in and leads into Davis Square, where the phone bank is, picks up again just beyond the phone bank's building, continuing east through Somerville. I walk down this section of the path now. It's quiet here; the path isn't nearly as popular in the winter as it is the rest of the year. I go a few steps then take out my phone and call MacIlwane's number. He picks up after the first ring. "It's me. Find out anything?" I ask.

"There are some significant commonalities between the two incidents—some signature elements not released to the press."

I wait through a few seconds of silence, then ask "So? What do you think?"

"It's likely the same guy did both murders. I haven't decided how to proceed yet; I'm weighing alternatives."

"Well, what's the big deal? Can't you have him arrested? Search his house? Or at least bring him in for questioning?"

"I guess you don't remember your law classes from West Point. To arrest or search in this situation I need a warrant, and to get a warrant I need probable cause. Your weird feeling plus a coincidence, minus any tangible evidence or witness testimony, do not equal probable cause. I could probably convince my boss and anyone else who might be interested that these two murders were committed by the same UNSUB—uh, unknown subject—but the only thing connecting the murders to *this particular guy* is your...instinct, and nobody is going to buy that, and his lawyer would have a field day with it. I could question him, and some people break down under questioning, but what I've learned so far tells me whoever did this enjoys it and is without remorse. He is also very organized and in control of his actions. Taken all together, I judge whoever did this is unlikely to break easily."

"OK, so what's the plan?"

"Let me think about it; I'll call you at home tonight."

Twenty-Eight

Mac swings open the door to his condo and clicks on the light in the entryway. The black trench coat goes on a hanger in the coat closet. There's a chair by the door; he sits and removes his shoes, placing them to the side.

He turns on the overhead light in the living room. The apartment is neat and clean the way he likes it, but as usual seems too quiet. He walks past the matching couch and recliner covered with off-white cloth that makes him think of sun-bleached canvas, like porch furniture at a beach house, and goes up to the media center. Like the desk, bookcases, and coffee table, this piece of furniture is made of blonde, varnished wood. On the shelves, along with the television, VCR, stereo, and the CD portion of his jazz collection, are some framed photographs: his mom and dad, a bunch of his Special Forces pals and him at Fort Campbell, and, of course, several pictures of Tracie and Malcolm.

On impulse his hand goes to John Coltrane's *A Love Supreme*. He begins to pull the CD from its place on the shelf, then hesitates. Trane's signature work was one of the handholds he used to steady himself after he lost Tracie and Malcolm, and it will always bear an added emotional charge for him. But for whatever reason this is what he craves tonight, and anything else, especially silence, is unappealing. He loads the CD and turns up the volume a little.

He washes his hands and changes into a worn pair of jeans and an old, fraying sweatshirt from his days as a New Agent Trainee at the FBI Academy, then goes in search of dinner.

The small but functional kitchen is separated from the living room only by a counter-topped island. Tonight he doesn't feel like cooking, so he takes a plastic container of lean sliced roast beef, a jar of horseradish, and a bag of bulky rolls from the refrigerator. As he's making his sandwich, Coltrane begins chanting the phrase "a love supreme." Mac, bulky roll in one hand and bread knife in the other, pauses and closes his eyes, listening. Coltrane was referring to God's love, but twelve years ago, when Mac found himself repeating the mantra in the depths of his grief, the love was his own, for his lost family. After a while the two loves seemed indistinguishable, and repeating the words became a source of hope and power: "A Love Supreme. A Love Supreme."

The first track, "Acknowledgment", ends and "Resolution" begins. Mac whispers the mantra once, like a prayer, then opens his eyes and goes back to making the sandwich. He returns the unused ingredients to the fridge, takes out a carton of orange juice, and pours himself a tall glass.

There are two black wrought iron chairs at the island. Mac sits and, as he eats, directs his thoughts back to the situation with Campbell and this guy Flashphaler.

None of this has turned out the way he expected, starting with Campbell herself. Even knowing the truth, it still seems strange to associate the small, slender woman he met with the murder scenes in Florida, Trenton, Kansas City, Philadelphia, and that rest stop in Massachusetts.

And then there's her strange ability: it's crazy, but it's crazier to argue against the evidence at all those murder scenes pointing unequivocally to the guilt of the people she killed. How else to explain her getting it right five times out of five— six out of six counting New Orleans?

Has she ever gotten it wrong?

If she has, he hasn't been able to find the incidents in ViCAP. Anyway, going forward it's his responsibility to make sure she never does.

Well, it's more than that. Mac thinks again of the killers she's stopped and, by extension, the people—*innocent* people, like Tracie and Malcolm—she's saved. Shutting her down is *not* his goal here.

Be honest with yourself, he thinks. *What are you* really *trying to accomplish?*

He rinses his empty, crumb-laden plate in the sink and places it in the drainer, does the same with the empty glass. Back in the living room the Coltrane disk has ended, and Mac replaces it with a Chick Corea solo piano CD and lowers the volume.

He lingers there in front of the entertainment center, staring at an old picture, centered above all the electronic hardware on the shelf below, of Tracie smiling tiredly down at the wrinkled and pudgy face of Malcolm. One of Malcolm's tiny fists is visible, poking out of the blue blanket, the little plastic ID bracelet encircling the impossibly small wrist.

Honestly, what are you trying to do?

The picture is all the answer he needs. He turns, walks over to the desk, and picks up the phone.

Earlier, in the afternoon, Mac called Flashphaler at the magusWare office, and actually got the guy and not his voicemail. Posing as an employee at one of the Bureau's front companies, Mac said he would be in the Charlotte area and would like to meet with Flashphaler in person, requesting a date that coincided with the dates for the Atlanta trade show mentioned on the magusWare website. Mac's guess proved correct: Flashphaler said he would be at the trade show then, and transferred Mac's call to another sales representative. Mac followed through with setting up the meet, then put a note in his calendar for next week to cancel the appointment.

Ascertaining the time and place of an opportunity was easy; coming up with a plan to exploit the opportunity is hard. What he's devised isn't foolproof, but it's as good as he can make it and minimizes Campbell's involvement. He'd rather leave her out of it all together, but the plan strays outside legal boundaries at a couple points, is based on her unbelievable assertion about Flashphaler, and he'll probably need her sense to pull this scheme off, so there really isn't anyone else he can use.

Mac punches in Campbell's home number.   After the answering machine routine, she comes on the line.

"Hey."

"How are you doing, Ms. Campbell?"

"Fine. I was starting to think you weren't going to call."

Mac glances at his watch. "It's only 8:30."

"I usually go to bed about nine."

"Nine? Why—? Never mind; so, I confirmed it—he's going to be at a trade show in Atlanta next month."

"OK. I called his hotel up here earlier and he checked out, so I guess he's on his way home now."

"Good.   He won't hunt on his home turf since he's organized and smart enough not to do that, plus there aren't any recent unsolved murders matching his signature there."

"So, Atlanta..."

"Yeah." Mac hesitates, then says. "I'm going to need your help with this."

"I figured; that's our arrangement, right? So, who do I meet up with, and where and when does it happen?"

"His trade show in Atlanta runs from nine through eleven March—that's a Tuesday through Thursday—so we should put feet on the ground the preceding Sunday, the seventh. Why don't you meet me for an early breakfast that day here in Virginia—you could drive down on Saturday, and we would drive the rest of the way after breakfast, should get there by that evening."

"Why doesn't the FBI just fly me down to Atlanta and I'll meet you there?"

"Because besides me the FBI doesn't know about you yet."

There's a pause on the other end of the line. "What?"

"The Bureau doesn't know about you."

"But—you said—when I met you—"

"I said I could take you in for questioning, and I meant it. But you chose the coffee shop, so the FBI didn't have to get involved."

"OK, but our deal—"

"Is just that: *our* deal. It's going to stay that way until I verify for myself how you're identifying murderers."

"I told you how. And if it's just you and me, what's to stop me from walking away from this?"

"Because then the FBI *would* know about you. From me."

There's another pause; Mac waits patiently. This had to come out, and so far it seems to be going well, though handling people over the phone is harder than in person where there are more cues to go on.

"All right, all right, but I think I'm missing something here: How is this going to work? I tell you where he is, and then you tell your guys?"

"It's just you and me on this one, Ms. Campbell. I need to see what you do for myself before I talk to anyone in the Bureau about your sense. At this point all I have is an outrageous claim from an unverified source against a citizen who has no criminal record and no evidence against him."

"But you *know* I've been right every time."

"Yeah, I count at least six victims you're responsible for: at best, you're a vigilante; some might see you as a serial killer yourself. Either way, I don't recommend taking your chances with the legal system until you have me on your side." Mac softens his tone, switching to good cop mode. "Look, Ms. Campbell, I believe you're doing *something* to find these guys, and I understand how you describe it, but even you admit it sounds crazy. There's no way anyone is going to buy your claim without something irrefutable to back it up."

"So bring me in—I'll give a demonstration. You guys have serial killers, right? Locked up, I mean."

Mac had actually thought of this. Initially, he couldn't imagine a way of doing it that wouldn't make him look ridiculous—at best—if it didn't go well. Now, as he's grown more certain she *would* prove her claim, he still doubts the Bureau would be able to accept her, even when confronted with irrefutable corroboration. Her background would come out, she'd go to jail, and he'd be back to supporting investigations instead of running his own show. Either way, the experiment would end badly, but rather than argue all that to her, he says simply "I'm not risking my reputation until I've verified what you do for myself."

"So it's just us on this."

"Yes."

"Great: you're not willing to risk your reputation, but you *are* willing to risk my ass and the life of the next victim."

"I'm not risking anyone's ass," he snaps, then takes a breath and says more reasonably, "Neither you nor anyone else, except maybe me and him, will be in danger."

"Fine, what's the plan?"

"You find him, put me onto him—that's the extent of your involvement. After that, I'll have him under observation the whole time, and there's no way I'll let him hurt anyone."

She's quiet, apparently thinking it through. "So how will you know I'm right before it's too late?" she asks, her tone quieter and more thoughtful now. "I mean, you know more details about how this guy operates than I do, but the one in Philadelphia...he looked and acted like an ordinary guy until his victims were alone with him behind their own locked doors."

"So how did you verify you were right about him before you acted?"

There's a long pause, then she says quietly "I didn't—but that was the only time, I swear. Every other time I had confirmation beyond the sense, but I couldn't just let an innocent man get killed to confirm something I was already sure of."

Mac thinks about this, realizing he should have understood as much before. "*Were* you sure?"

"No, not a hundred percent," she says, barely audibly. There's a tremor in her sigh, then some rustling around. "And if you think that was an easy decision—it wasn't. It still isn't. I tried to avoid it—I called 911 and sent the cops there. The sense has been right *every time*. Someone in that apartment was going to get killed, and it was up to me to make sure the bad guy got it. But you can bet I was all over the news feed on that one afterwards, until you guys confirmed I'd gotten it right."

Mac keeps quiet, thinking about where this piece fits, and waiting to hear what she'll say next.

She breaks the silence: "Look, I did the best I could. What I'm saying now is we might be headed for the same situation again; I mean, according to the paper the woman up here was murdered in her own home."

"I have access to a range of excellent surveillance equipment; I'll know what's happening, and I'll intervene if and when the situation turns dangerous, if and when it's clear you're right about this guy." Mac allows the ensuing silence to stretch out before asking, "Are you still there?"

She sighs, then says, "With all due respect, Agent MacIlwane, that plan is weak. I know this is what you do, but what if the equipment doesn't work for some reason, or worse, we think it's working but it isn't, so we're sitting there like a couple of momos while another woman gets beaten to death. There's a lot of opportunity for failure, and we've got no business risking an innocent, unsuspecting person. So if you're not going to bring in more resources—if it's just down to you and me—then let me run the risk. If you weren't involved, I'd...use myself as bait anyway. At least now I'll have you backing me up."

This is not how he wants to do this. This is his gig; she's just there to point out the target. There are always risks, but the odds are in the potential victim's favor. Which isn't to say Mac didn't consider the idea of using Campbell as bait, but it probably wouldn't work anyway. "With all due respect, Ms. Campbell, I don't think you're his type."

"I'm more his type than you are. I at least want to try. I think I could clean up pretty well; at least I used to be able to. Let me worry about that—you worry about protecting me. And if you're right and he's not interested in me, we'll do it your way—that'll be our contingency plan."

A mental image of Campbell flits through Mac's mind, juxtaposed with crime scene photos of the Baltimore victim, her face battered, bruised, and broken beyond recognition. "I don't think using you as bait is a good idea, and I'm in charge of this operation, so we'll do it my way."

"Since you're in charge, it's up to you to choose the best plan. So far you haven't described anything better than my idea. Furthermore, if this isn't an official FBI investigation, then we're just two people, and you've got nothing without my input. Now I'm fine with following your lead, but do your job right and either come up with something better or use me to catch this guy and don't risk some innocent woman's life."

"At this point, in this situation, *you're* innocent."

"It's too late for me." She says this matter-of-factly: no trace of drama, simply making the statement. "At least I know what I'm getting into."

Arguing with her would be stupid—not because she's surprisingly, aggressively stubborn, but because she's right. Still... "I'll work on this some more, but for now go ahead and make whatever preparations you need for your idea. Let's meet down here on Sunday, seven March at five for breakfast." Mac gives her the easy directions to a local diner near the interstate.

"I'll see you there," she says, and hangs up.

Twenty-Nine

I can't believe how much this stuff cost, I think as I drape the small pile of dresses over my basket chair and set the other bags down on the floor. I normally do my shopping in the boys department at K-Mart or Target, and I forgot how much women's clothing costs. *How do normal women afford all this stuff?* If I were a conspiracy kind of person, I'd think this was a plot to keep women poor and powerless. Wacko theories aside, though, the mark-up on women's clothes still feels like institutionalized sexism. At least it doesn't usually affect me, and even now I'll only keep two of the dresses and return the others. I could have made my choices at the store; I tried them all on there to make sure they would fit, but I want to see them juxtaposed with the wig and makeup. Besides, the woman at the store was making me feel weird—obviously I don't look like their usual clientele. I got out of there as quick as I could.

I decide to start with the wig, which is from a store on Newbury Street in Boston and was wicked expensive. It's made with real human hair—creepy—but it has to look real so I bought quality. I take the bags with the hair and cosmetics into the bathroom.

The wig fits snugly over my stubble-covered head, and I use adhesive to attach it securely, the way the woman at the store instructed me. She was nice to me; I think she thought I was a cancer patient. The purchased hair is honey-colored like my own hair so I don't have to worry about changing the color of my eyebrows, and it's a little wavy, also like mine would be if I let it grow out. I realize I'll need to get a hair brush; for now I use my fingers to tidy up the locks, which are parted on the left side and frame my face, covering my ears and reaching the base of my neck in the back. At its longest, when I was fifteen, *my* hair reached halfway down my spine, but it's been almost two years since I had more than a quarter inch on my head, so I feel positively shaggy. It tickles the sides of my neck and makes the insides of my ears itchy. I try not to think about this hair brushing the skin of the person who grew it.

Wig in place, I open the bag of cosmetics. Even before the Bad I wasn't big into makeup, but it's probably essential for this mission. I try to remember how to do this stuff, wanting to look "made up" without overdoing it. I start with several dabs of base and spread it around. I apply just a little blush on my cheeks, and decide not to use eye shadow after all since I'd probably screw it up. Instead I opt for a little eyeliner and some mascara, which should have been easy, but involved a lot of facial contorting and anxiety about ocular safety. Finally, I line my lips with dark pink and apply the slightly lighter-colored lipstick. I haven't worn makeup in over thirteen years, but I find myself automatically pressing and rolling my lips together to smooth out the color, which looks, I think, pretty natural, only more. Leaning close to the mirror, I inspect my work section by section. I guess I have it about right, though I should practice some more over the next three weeks to refine my technique and get faster. *I hope this doesn't make me break out.* I stand up straight again and smile a little at how weird the old West Point sweatshirt with its frayed collar and small holes looks next to the made up face. *Time to get dressed up.*

Back in the main room, I spread three of the dresses out on the basket chair and arrange the other two on my futon mattress so I can see all five at once. I choose the small red cocktail dress with the spaghetti straps and the plunging neckline first. Personal history aside, I still don't think I'd ever wear something like this, which is probably best characterized as a fuck me dress. Still, I strip down to my panties and pull it over my head, then into the bathroom for a look. I need a full-length mirror, but all I have is the one over the sink, so I only see the outfit from my waist up. That's enough though. While I appreciate the needs of my mission, this dress is just too much—or rather, too little—for me to stand. Turning and looking back over my right shoulder seals it because the small, shiny purple scar from the bullet I took in New Orleans is plainly visible over my shoulder blade. "OK, not attractive."

Back in the main room I take off the red dress and, arms crossed against the chill of my apartment in winter, I look around at the others. There's a silky green one I thought would work with my eyes, but it would show off the scar on my shoulder too. I can't believe I didn't think of that when I was picking these out in the store. What's more, I can't wear the padded bra I bought with the really little dresses, and my flat chest needs all the help I can give it for this mission. I put on the bra, and then try on the remaining three outfits, settling on a classy black dress with a fairly low V-neckline but intact shoulders and cap sleeves, and another of about the same design, but the color of celery with small, printed yellow flowers scattered over it. I don't think the green one is really typical nightlife wear, but there's something about it I like and it seems right.

I dump out one of my recycling bins and take it into the bathroom so I can stand on it and see all of each outfit, although without my head, in the mirror. The black one's hem is a little higher than mid-thigh, and the green one comes to just above my knees. There's no way I'll be able to conceal the Glock or my backup knife under either of these outfits, which makes me wonder about the specifics of the plan. Depending on how and when MacIlwane will intervene, I hopefully won't need weapons. I decide I'll bring them anyway, even if they only sit in the car under the seat. Better to have and not need them.

Wearing the light green dress, I step down off the inverted bin and push it out of the way. I move back as far as I can and look at my reflection, not studying the details anymore, but just taking in the whole picture for the first time.

A young woman with blonde hair, green eyes, and a pretty dress looks back at me and smiles, surprised and a little amused at what she sees. I close my eyes. When I open them again, the young woman is crying. I turn and leave, killing the lights as I go.

Thirty

Flash's eyes pop open in the darkness of his bedroom. Lying absolutely still, barely breathing, his mind races. *How could I have not thought of this before?* The idea is brilliant, stone cold brilliant. And obvious: *To think it's been staring me in the face for what? A year now?*

Of course, there would be a lot to get done, but one good weekend would probably be enough, and he has two more besides just in case.

He goes over the details of the dream that woke him, recording it into memory before it can evaporate. Just the idea of it makes his erect cock throb. He pictures the woman in the rabbit hutch again, her soft, wet eyes looking up, silently pleading. As he replays the dream, he embellishes it, teasing her with the carrots instead of just feeding her; holding the food inches from her face and then pulling it away just as she leans forward to eat. He watches tears well up in her eyes, hears her beg—no, *pray to* him, on her knees, hands pressed together, the whole deal. Eventually he lets her eat and she thanks him for his mercy. Unlike the rabbits, she's fully aware of her position and her dependence on him. She worships him because to do otherwise means death.

This, this, *is what I've wanted, what I've been building up to all this time.* A woman in a hutch—a *kept* woman. He smiles, then laughs quietly. *It's brilliant, absolutely fucking brilliant.*

He tries hard to remember what he saw the last time he was there, and begins visualizing what needs to be done, composing a shopping list in his head as he does.

Thirty-One

Mac savors the aroma of the coffee the waitress just brought and gazes out the window at the parking lot in front of the diner. As he watches, a flat black little hatchback with Massachusetts plates pulls into the pool of artificial light. He recognizes the car from when he was watching her apartment following their initial meeting. He glances at his watch, which shows 5:55 am, then looks back up. The black car pauses a moment before backing in to a space near an enormous forest green SUV at the far end of the lot, ignoring several spaces closer to the door. Wearing the same dark green coat and black stocking cap she had on when he first met her, Campbell crosses the lot, eyes and head sweeping her surroundings as she goes. The door opens and she enters, removing her cap as she does and looking around the diner. Mac raises his cup to her as she turns his way, and her mouth tightens in response. He's not sure if it counts as a smile of recognition or a grimace, but she walks over and sits down across from him in the booth.

"Good morning."

"Good morning Ms. Campbell, how you doing?"

"Fine—you?" she responds, making momentary eye contact before taking a menu from the caddy under the window and opening it.

He watches her eyes as they flit back and forth, reading. Something about them holds his attention, which is odd because she's done nothing to accentuate them: no makeup, no looking up at him. Maybe it's because the paleness of her face and drabness of her clothing make the bright green of her eyes the only real color on her, or the extreme shortness of her hair makes her eyes seem unusually large.

That was true with Tracie. She never straightened her hair; in her college pictures she had a big afro, but by the late seventies when he met her she'd begun wearing her hair short, which suited her. Besides making her dark almond eyes seem larger, it also emphasized her high, regal cheekbones, making him think of a Nubian queen. *My queen*, he used to call her sometimes.

"What?" The green eyes across from him shift up, locking with his.

Mac closes his eyes and shakes his head slightly. "Sorry, I was spacing out. The Belgian waffles here are pretty good. You can have them dressed up with whipped cream and sliced strawberries if you're into that."

"Not really," she says, her eyes returning to the laminated menu.

Mac looks at the fingers curled around the edges: they're slender and pale, and the nails are clean and neatly trimmed short. He has a hard time imagining these almost delicate-looking hands caving-in Hayes' skull at the northern Florida murder scene, or pushing the kitchen knife into the back of the Trenton pedophile's neck. It's almost funny that this petite, quiet woman left the trail of bodies he followed to find her.

The waitress appears. "You ready to order?" Mac asks Campbell.

"You go 'head," she says without looking up.

Mac turns to the waitress and orders three eggs over easy, bacon, toast, and grits.

Campbell closes the menu and looks up at the woman. "I'd like a glass of orange juice, a bowl of grits, and toast, please. And no butter, please."

The waitress nods and leaves.

"I like the paint job on your car," Mac says.

One corner of her mouth pulls a little tighter into what might be a smile. "Thanks—I did it myself. Now it's a 'black ops' Geo Metro, like those Task Force 160 aircraft."

Mac smiles at the reference to the Army's special ops aviation unit, which he worked with a couple times when he was in the Army. They usually operate at night, and for that reason paint their helicopters, inside and out, flat black. "It's about the same size as one of those little birds," he says, putting slightly more stress on the word 'little' than 'birds,' referring to the two-seat Hughes 500 model used by the Task Force.

Campbell nods, the tight, closed-mouth smile still on her face, and looks down at the table.

The waitress drops off Campbell's juice, and they sip their beverages silently for a minute.

"So why'd you park way over there?" Mac asks, nodding toward the parking lot.

Campbell looks out at the car, then back at him. The smile, such as it was, is gone from her lips, but now it's in her eyes. "Maybe you should tell me—you're the shrink."

"That's just it—I didn't think you'd want to cross that much parking lot if you didn't have to." Mac stops himself before saying more, not wanting to get too personal, or too candid about his assessment of her.

"I guess I was trying to analyze you back, and figured that SUV was yours. Was I right?"

Mac gives her a "get real" look. "What makes you think that's my vehicle?"

She shrugs. "I figured former military, current law enforcement, kind of got that macho, man in charge thing going on."

Mac raises his eyebrows. "And? You think I need to accessorize with a really big vehicle to prove it?"

"So it *is* yours." She's smiling with both eyes and mouth now.

"No. Try again."

She looks out at the lot, twists in her seat to see behind her, then looks back at him. "The beat-up beige Caddy."

"I think we'd better stick with me doing the profiling. I drive the black Civic right outside our window."

"Yeah? I figured you'd buy American."

"Most Hondas sold in this country are built in Ohio."

She nods. "It's hard to tell anymore. I thought I was buying American—the Geo line belonged to Chevy—but when I opened the hood there was a Suzuki Motor Corporation sticker on the engine. A Metro is just a relabeled Suzuki Swift."

"Welcome to the global economy."

They're quiet again but it doesn't feel awkward. Since this isn't a social meeting, there's no need to fill the spaces with chatter. Instead they gaze out the window as the morning's first light appears in the sky. The food arrives and they eat without comment for a few more minutes. The waitress checks in and they both nod at her. After she leaves, and aware that the adjoining booths are still unoccupied, Mac pauses from eating and leans forward slightly. "Any second thoughts about your plan for this?"

The green eyes flick up at him. She finishes chewing and swallows. "Not unless you've come up with something better."

Mac looks at her, silently wondering what she sees when she looks in the mirror.

"I have a wig—a good one," she says, apparently intuiting his thoughts. "It was expensive, but I think it's convincing. It's really close to my own hair color too. And I have makeup. And a couple dresses. I look different with all that stuff."

Mac looks down, feeling a little embarrassed, but unwilling to fault himself. "And if, despite all that, he doesn't go for you, then we fall back to my plan and follow him, keep him under observation, and intervene when he makes his intentions clear."

"That's one of the good things about my idea—it doesn't preclude yours."

Mac nods. "I've reserved us adjacent rooms at a Ramada. Based on the two crimes we think he was involved with, he'll want to go back to your place. It makes sense from his perspective because then he doesn't have to worry about the logistics of body disposal. I brought equipment to wire your room and monitor it so I can hear what's going on, and we'll work out a signal for you to call me in. When we check in, we'll get an extra key to your room for me so I can get in fast when the time comes. You with me so far?"

Campbell nods. "Sounds good."

"I also brought surveillance gear and my break-in kit in case we have to go with my plan."

"OK." She piles up another spoonful of white mush.

"I've never seen anyone eat grits as the main part of a meal, especially with nothing on them."

Campbell looks down at the mostly empty bowl. "Salt and pepper."

"I like butter and egg yolk on mine. Or gravy."

She shrugs. "I'm used to them this way. I really like them, but they're almost impossible to find in New England."

"Yeah, that doesn't surprise me. So, I don't think I need to tell you this, but if at any point you have suggestions or observations about the plan or what's going on, speak up."

"Yeah, you don't need to tell me—with my ass on the line, I'm going to be as helpful as I can."

Mac smiles, nods briefly. "For the drive down, we'll each take our own vehicle. I've already worked out the route to our hotel, so I'll lead, set the pace. It'll take us all day, but I'm going to keep us within five of the speed limit. My skin color attracts enough attention as it is without giving the local cops an excuse to pull me over."

Campbell looks surprised. "Really? But *you're* a cop."

Mac cocks an eyebrow. "Nothing on my car says that. Anyway, if either of us gets pulled over, the other keeps driving and we meet up at the next rest stop."

"OK. That sucks about the race thing—I didn't think that still went on."

Mac shrugs. "Sometimes—just the world we're living in. I fix what I can, deal with the rest." He shrugs again. "When I have a long drive ahead of me I pad my schedule to allow for delays, which is a good idea anyway—flat tires happen too. If either of us has some kind of car trouble, we both pull over. So you know what to do—any questions?"

She shakes her head.

"We'll take I-95 to I-85. There are a couple full-service rest areas near Greensboro, North Carolina—we'll pull into the second one for fuel, lunch, pit stops. That one is pretty close to half way, about 300 miles down the road from here. Sound all right?"

"Sure. I already topped off my tank when I got into town last night, so I'm ready to go."

Thirty-Two

The restaurant, on the outskirts of Atlanta, has a bright, clean, minimalist interior: polished blonde wood tables and chairs, a darker wood floor, and white walls. There's a wood and paper screening wall with the same color scheme in the back of the room, obscuring the doors to the kitchen.

After all day on the road and a skimpy meal of fries at a rest stop fast food outlet, I'm really hungry, and everything on the menu looks good to me. Mainly I want something starchy and filling—lots of noodles or rice.

"I realize you may be getting sick of seeing my face," MacIlwane says, "but I think there's some value in getting comfortable with one another before we're actually depending on each other, which could happen as early as tomorrow night."

I look up and nod. "Sure, that's fine; I feel the same way."

"So, do you see the sweet and sour section?" he asks, flipping back and forth through the menu's pages.

"That's Chinese, not Korean. Actually, I don't think it's even really Chinese, but they don't have that stuff here."

"I don't think I've ever been to a Korean place before. Any recommendations?" he asks, then adds hastily, "No wait—you said you're a vegan—that's some kind of vegetarian, right?"

"Yeah, I don't eat any animal products."

"OK, never mind—I'll pick something myself."

I know what to suggest, but would feel guilty doing it. Still, he's here because of me; he wanted to go to the Ground Round.

He senses me watching him and looks up.

"Animal rights advocates everywhere will be appalled," I say, "but I can tell you the *bulgogi* is a pretty accessible dish. It's Korean beef barbecue."

"But you've never tried it."

"No, I don't eat meat, but when I was stationed in Korea the carnivores I knew spoke highly of it."

"OK, I'll go with that, I guess. What are you having?"

"I think I'm going to have the tofu *chi gae*."

"What's that?"

"It's a spicy vegetable stew with tofu in it."

"Mmmm, *tofu*."

"Have you tried it?"

"Bean curd, right?"

I nod.

"Nope, I don't eat anything with the word 'curd' in it."

"Actually, it doesn't taste like much of anything on its own, but it tends to soak up whatever flavors are around it. That's the key to preparing tofu."

"Uh-huh."

Our waiter appears with a tray and places several small dishes of vegetables and greens on the table.

"Uh, I think there's been a mistake—we haven't ordered yet."

"This is *kimchee*," says the waiter.

"*Ney, kamsanidah*," I say to the waiter, my smattering of *Hangul* coming automatically.

"OK, obviously I missed something here."

"They always bring this stuff at the start of a meal—it's automatic," I say, taking a paper-wrapped pair of chopsticks from a jar in the middle of the table and jabbing one end into the table so the sticks rip through the other end. "This is kind of wasteful, but what can you do?" I say as I remove the wrapper and break the sticks apart.

MacIlwane looks around and realizes there are no western utensils on the table. "Oh, this isn't going to work."

"You've never used these?" I ask.

"My foreign area specialty in the Army was southwest Asia and Africa. I don't think there's a single pair of those in the entire region," he says, looking around for the waiter.

"Look, it's easy—I'll show you. Don't embarrass us by asking for a fork. Just take a set and open 'em up like I did."

He looks at me, then complies.

"OK, put one down and take the other and hold it like this." I demonstrate, laying the wide end of a stick against the webbing between my thumb and forefinger and routing it across one side of my middle finger near the tip. "This stick doesn't move—think of it as your anvil, and the other stick will be the hammer, OK?"

He copies me and nods.

"Now take the other stick and hold it between your thumb and forefinger. This stick actually runs the length of your forefinger, from this joint to the end, like an extension of the finger." I pause as he tries to copy me. "Well, line it up so the sticks end at the same point—yeah, like that. See? So the first stick just sits there, and the second moves with your finger. Use the full length of the sticks; that way they come together at an easy, natural angle and you have plenty of grip when you pick things up." I pick up a cube of turnip tinted red from one of the dishes and put it in my mouth.

MacIlwane opens and closes the sticks, tapping the tips together, and smiles, then looks at the dishes. "So what do we have here?"

"Do you like hot stuff? Because these are mostly hot, though these greens won't be hot at all. I'm not sure what they are, seaweed maybe, and they're served with sesame oil and seeds. This," I say, pointing at another dish, "is traditional pickled cabbage with chile peppers and garlic. It's probably what most people think of when they think kimchee."

"Yeah, people are thinking kimchee all the time."

"Well in Korea they are; kimchee can be part of all three meals there."

"Damn," he says. He uses his chopsticks to fish out one of the cubes I took. "What are these?"

"I think it's some kind of pickled turnip. It's a little hot—I mean, these are all cold, but spicy hot."

"I like hot," he says and puts it in his mouth. He chews thoughtfully and swallows. "Hmmm. Interesting."

"To be honest, kimchee was never my favorite; I think it's kind of an acquired taste."

Our waiter comes back, takes our orders, and is gone again.

"So how did you like Korea?" MacIlwane asks.

"It was fine. I mean, I didn't have any real interest in the place before I went there; I didn't even get a choice in my first assignment out of flight school. But the people were mostly friendly. I did tend to feel like a mercenary, though: more like a hired gun paid to defend someone else's government than an American soldier defending our country and the Constitution like the oath we took says."

He nods vigorously. "I hear that. I had that feeling a lot."

I shrug. "I guess that's the price of being a citizen of a superpower. But if I could have changed one thing about my time in Korea, I would have learned more Korean. I really wanted to talk to the people there. We always had a lot of kids come out to see the helicopter when we landed somewhere. Fortunately, one time we had a translator with us, so I gave a little class on the survival vest to a bunch of them. I used to save all the sweet stuff from my ration packs and hand the goodies out—that was always a crowd pleaser.

"And the flying was pretty cool. My unit did a lot of VIP transport up to the demilitarized zone, and those missions always took us over some amazingly beautiful mountain landscapes—a big contrast to the Seoul area, where we were based. Seoul was an ecological disaster area. Coming back out of the mountains, we'd see this enormous dome of brown air on the horizon long before we could see the city beneath it.

"But how 'bout you? What branch were you?"

"I went infantry out of West Point."

"Really?"

"Does that surprise you?"

"I guess—I mean, you're in law enforcement now, so I figured you would have been in military police."

"Yeah, no," he says, nodding then shaking his head. "I basically was looking for adventure, so I went infantry and snagged assignment to a Ranger battalion after doing a couple years with the 101st."

"The Rangers—I'll bet that was pretty hoo-ah."

He smiles a little. "Yeah, they put the hoo-ah in hoo-ah. Hoo-ah gets old after a while, though."

"It must have been a tiring pace of work."

"Well, mostly it was tiring because of all the macho bullshit. Don't get me wrong—they're excellent soldiers, but there was definitely this culture of bravado and posturing. I'm not saying they couldn't back it up, but it started to wear on me. The older I got, the less tolerant of bullshit I became. And anyway, I was always looking for the next thing, so I ended up branch-transferring to Special Forces, the thinking man's infantry," he says with a little smile.

"Wow—no kidding!"

He shrugs. "It's not as big a deal as it's sometimes made out to be. I mean, we got a lot of training and could do a lot of stuff, but in the end it's a job. I really liked it though; our focus was more on teaching and less on messing people up and breaking things, and the atmosphere was different. In Special Forces all that Ranger swagger is actually scorned: if you know what you're doing you don't need to advertise; you just know and do. I liked that, and I liked being able to use words with more than two syllables without being rejected for it.   In SF everyone was not only multi-syllabic, but multi-lingual."

"I think I know what you mean. An SF unit helped train us at West Point one summer, and those guys were laid back, but you could tell they knew their stuff."

"They didn't need to strut around to convey that; their competence showed through naturally, right?"

I nod.

"So what inspired you to go the Academy route?" he asks.

I look down automatically. The Bad isn't something I want to talk about, but since he already knows I guess I don't have to spell it out for him. "Invulnerability," I say, meeting his eyes.   "I figured if anyone knows how to protect themselves, it's the Army, and that's what I wanted for me. Plus, I had no interest in the college party scene—I actually wasn't planning on going to college at all until my school's guidance counselor told me about West Point. And I didn't have to rely on anyone's charity to pay my way—I could earn it myself. It made sense any way I looked at it."

He nods. "Sure, I'm with you; there was a lot of that in my decision to go there. And why Aviation?"

"Why not?   I got to *fly*.   Who wouldn't want to go Aviation?"

"Well, *I* didn't," he smiles. "But I'm surprised you didn't go Military Police, what with you stopping bad guys and protecting innocent people."

"Like I keep telling you, this thing I do now wasn't part of the original plan; this isn't the life I want to lead. Thing is, I'm really not a people person, so I didn't want a job that was all about dealing with people, especially people behaving badly. What I did like was whenever we got to ride around in helicopters as part of training, and I got more of that than most cadets because I was in the Tactics Club—did that exist when you were there?"

He smiles. "I was in Tactics Club too."

"Really? I loved training with them."

"I don't know if I would call it training so much. Mostly it was just a means of getting outside on the weekends to goof around and shoot off pyrotechnics. That was fun until we started a forest fire with a flare."

"Forest fire? Where was that?"

"Down by Lake Frederick. Luckily we got it put out before it went very far."

"Oh...well when I was there, Tactics Club was pretty serious—we emphasized planning and patrolling techniques. Sergeant Pike—he was our NCOIC—used to tell us to treat every exercise as if it were real, because things could turn real in a hurry. I knew how right he was, so I did Tactics Club and his Ranger School preparation to get as much—"

"They let you do that? I mean, Ranger School *is* still males only, isn't it? "

I smile. "Would it bother you if it weren't?"

He grins. "Hey, I'm an open-minded guy, but there are some things, like light infantry, that, generally speaking, men are just better suited to do."

"Sure, generally speaking, given the differences in physical strength, I'd say you're right. But you agree not *all* men are capable of succeeding as Rangers, or even as soldiers, right?"

"Of course, but—"

"And doesn't it stand to reason that not *all* women are incapable of succeeding at Ranger School? Shouldn't those of us who could succeed be allowed to attend since, after all, Ranger School is primarily a leadership, not an infantry, school?"

MacIlwane looks at me for a couple heartbeats, then sort of half nods and looks down. "You're right: I can't dispute that. But there's also the logistical considerations that come up when you have men and women together 24-7."

"Screw that. There are ways to deal with it, but there isn't the will. And that includes me: I didn't do Ranger prep as a political statement; I really just wanted the training, and I was fine with not going to Ranger School. I went to Jungle Warfare School down in Panama instead, and by the way there was less whining from all three of us women combined than from almost any one of the men in my squad.

"Anyway, it took some persuading, but Sergeant Pike was in charge of Ranger Orientation too, and we were friends by then, so he said I could stay in as long as I met the same standards as the guys."

"You've got a lot of hoo-ah yourself, Ms. Campbell."

I shrug and look down. "Like I said, I was just learning skills that might help me protect myself." Included in that skill set was learning to be around males without getting freaked out, but I don't mention that. "I liked patrolling because we learned to survive in the dark, in hostile territory, with no one to rely on but ourselves. Even if I don't ever use those exact skills, it was a good mindset to learn."

He nods. "I liked that too—I did the orientation program and Ranger School as a cadet. How much of the orientation program did you make it through?"

The question surprises me. "Well, all of it."

He pauses with his chopsticks mid-air. "Yeah?"

I nod. "They gave me—uh, yeah."

"They gave you what?"

I didn't mean to mention this but I guess it's OK, though it still makes me feel emotional. "The guys in the program, they chipped in and gave me a Fairbairn-Sykes dagger at the end because I couldn't go to Ranger School even though I'd completed the program with them." I look away, across the room, and I can feel myself smiling. "It was really cool. I liked that training stuff and those guys. It was fun." I feel goofy, and like maybe I said too much. I look down, then glance up to see if maybe he didn't notice, but he's looking at me and smiling.

"I propose a toast," he says, lifting his water glass. "To working together."

I feel one side of my mouth tug into a smile. I pick up my glass and clink it against his. "To working together."

Thirty-Three

Mac, wearing big padded headphones, turns on the receiver and listens to silence. He slaps the wall and hears, with the barest moment of delay, the sound repeated through the headphones. Then he hears her voice, in a clear, conversational tone: "Go tell the Spartans, passerby, That here, by Spartan law, we lie."

The epitaph for the 300 at Thermopylae?

She repeats the phrase again more softly, and then again in a whisper while he adjusts the settings on the machine. He slaps the wall again and she repeats the procedure. This time he hears even the whispered words clearly. He turns off the unit, removes the headphones, and goes back to her room, letting himself in with his copy of the key card. She's sitting on one of the beds, staring across the other bed and out the window.

"What's up with the Spartan poetry?"

"I just finished reading Frank Miller's rendering of the story—it kind of stuck in my head," she says flatly without looking at him.

"Who's Frank Miller?"

"He does graphic novels—comic books that have grown up. He just did one on the Spartan stand at Thermopylae."

"Really? The ultimate example of the warrior ethic, and one you always hope you won't have to live up to. OK, we should be all set," Mac says, sitting down on the other bed, in her line of sight. "Let's go over the plan. We'll wait for him to come back to his hotel—"

"What if he doesn't go back to his hotel?" Campbell asks. "And we don't know where he's staying yet."

"I'll call around this afternoon, starting with the chain he stayed at in Boston, ask to be put through to his room. When someone finally connects me, I'll know where he's staying and hang up. But you make a good point—there's a chance he might go directly from the trade show set up to his hunting ground. That seems unlikely, but to be safe we should pick up his trail as he's leaving the exhibition center. I'll still call around, though, to know in advance where he's staying and where he's likely to go. But that raises another question—we don't even know what vehicle he's driving. How will we know when he's leaving or which direction he's going in? There's probably a huge parking garage there with multiple exits."

"Yeah, it's not going to be easy, but I'll at least know when he's leaving, and if we know what hotel he's in then, if we have to, we can make an educated guess about what direction he'll be headed in and what roads he might take."

A question occurs to Mac; in fact, he's surprised he hadn't thought of it before. "The pain of your sense—you say it gets worse the closer you are to the source. Are you going to be able to hide what you're feeling when you're talking to this guy?"

She looks back at him. "Yes."

"No doubts?"

"I've hidden it before. No doubts."

"OK, so anyway, we hopefully track him to his hotel. If he doesn't go back to the hotel then we start driving a search grid downtown. What does this guy look like, anyway?"

"He's pretty big—tall, I mean, with a big frame. Athletic-looking. I've only seen him in a suit, but he seemed muscular—he has a thick neck. Blonde hair cut into a flattop, clean-shaven, tanned, pale blue eyes. Basically an Aryan poster boy."

Mac nods, trying to build a picture in his head. "How tall would you say?"

She pauses, thinking. "At least six feet, probably a little more."

Mac thinks of the police reports and crime scene photos from Baltimore and Boston, of how the victims were badly beaten before being killed: broken bones, extensive bruising, and teeth knocked out. "Listen, don't turn your back on this guy once you return here. As big as you say he is, he might actually knock you out with a punch, and then you won't be able to signal me when to intervene. We'd better talk about that now. The microphones in here are sound-activated, so as soon as you get in they'll start transmitting. I should get to my room just a minute or two after you arrive, and I'll be monitoring. Now for this to work, as you know, I need to catch him attacking you in some way, and that's what makes this hard, in part because the other two cases seem to have begun with consensual sex and only after that escalated to violence." Mac pauses, studying her face, which remains blankly impassive. "How do you want to handle that?"

She swallows. "We get back here, and I offer him a drink from the mini bar. We'll just talk, but when he starts coming on to me I'll tell him I don't do anything on a first date. I expect at that point he'll become more demanding, either gradually or abruptly—we'll just have to see how it goes. I'll continue to refuse, and eventually he'll get physical with me and either restrain me or hurt me. If he ties me up or pins me down, is that enough for you to arrest him?"

"Yes, any unwanted physical contact is assault. I'm out of my jurisdiction here, but I can still arrest him pending the arrival of the local police, which we'll contact as soon as we have the situation under control. But what if he does something quick to subdue you before you can verbally complain and bring me in? Especially since we're in a hotel here, he's not going to want you screaming for help."

"Well, if he gags me I can still make some kind of noise—would the microphones pick that up?"

"Yes. Let's make an alternate signal three quick repetitions of any one noise you can make—a sniffle, a cough, stamping your foot, anything."

"The listening system is sensitive enough to hear me sniffing?"

"Sure; you can try it out from my side—I'll set you up then make noise over here so you can hear what I'll be hearing. But let's also have one more signal—if I don't hear you make any noise for a full thirty seconds then I come in. But you need to be aware of that and be sure to keep making some noise—preferably say something—at least a couple times every minute so I don't intervene prematurely. If that happens, we have nothing."

She nods.

"OK, I'm going to remove the security latch on your door. If he asks about it, tell him you complained to the hotel staff, but they haven't done anything about it yet." Mac takes a phillips head screwdriver from his toolkit and begins removing the screws holding the hardware to the door jamb. "Look around—is there anything else in here he could use to barricade the door? I don't think he would, but just in case."

"No. I mean, I guess he could pull the armchair over, but I don't think he could wedge it so you couldn't get the door open."

Mac looks at the chair. "Yeah, you're right." He turns back to removing the screws. "It's unlikely he would do that anyway—he won't be expecting anyone to hear anything, and if they do, he won't be expecting them to barge in. Surprise is our best asset in this—we know what he is, and he's counting on us not knowing." Mac catches the last screw and the latch in his palm and pockets them as he walks back over to where she's sitting. "By the way, Campbell, you don't have a gun in here, do you?"

She looks up at him, and for a moment the stoic façade breaks. He can see the tension in her face and hear it even more in her voice. "No, I don't. I'm depending on you to save my ass. Don't let me down, Agent MacIlwane."

"I realize that, and I'll be with you," he says calmly. "I'll need you to feed me information—make conversation and verbalize what's going on. Make it seem natural, like 'why are you turning the lights off?' Any information about the situation will be helpful—where he is, what he's doing, and especially if he has any weapons. For example, being this close to his home base, he could certainly drive here and so bring his own gun, although from what I've seen that's not his style."

"OK." She nods, her composure restored. "What's your plan once you get my signal?"

"Obviously I'll be over here and in the room immediately, weapon out. I'll know what to expect based on what I've heard, and hopefully the speed and surprise of my entry will carry enough shock value to elicit compliance from him. If not, I'll fire on him, so stay low."

She nods again, staring down blankly at the carpet.

"Are you comfortable with the plan? Any feedback?"

She's quiet for several more seconds, then speaks without looking up. "I'm trying to think of what can go wrong. If he doesn't come back here, but we go someplace else—admittedly unlikely, but *if*—then I'll have that compact with the listening device you gave me in my purse. Not as good as what we have in here, but it'll give you some intel about what's happening with me when I'm not here. But what if you're right and he doesn't go for me at all? How do you know when to intervene if he's with someone else?"

"I have remote listening equipment in my car trunk of tricks—parabolic mike, shotgun mike, like that. We can use those to determine if and when to intervene. I also have my B and E kit with me in case I need to get in somewhere."

She looks up at him. "'B and E kit'? *That* doesn't sound kosher—isn't that kind of illegal?"

Mac shrugs, trying to look casual while debating whether to level with her—and himself. Instead he says simply "If someone's in imminent danger, I'm not going to worry about legality."

"That's *my* line."

"Then you know what I'm talking about. I'm beginning to appreciate what *you* told *me*: This sense of yours doesn't lend itself all that well to standard procedure."

"But it could, right?   I mean, if someone—*you* for example—vouched for its reality? That's what we're doing here, right? Proving it to you?"

Mac deliberately holds her gaze. "Let's just get through this mission first, all right?"

"What does *that* mean?"

"Just what I said," Mac replies, keeping his voice low and even, trying to calm her with it. "Right now, we need to focus on the task in front of us. It's dangerous and could turn violent, so let's give it our full attention."

She narrows her eyes, then looks away. "Fine, whatever. Let's get this thing done."

"Anything else?" he asks.

The green eyes find his again. "Yeah, what can I expect from him? You mentioned the other victims' encounters began consensually, then turned violent. What did he do?"

"First of all, keep in mind we don't know for sure *this* guy did anything—we don't have any evidence linking him to what happened in Boston and Baltimore."

"C'mon—you wouldn't be here if you didn't have some confidence in me. I admit I don't know for certain he hurt those two women, but I *do* know he's bad, and he was visiting both those places at the times of the killings. So just tell me what happened to those women."

"The UNSUB hit them," Mac says, then adds in a lower voice, "A lot. He used tie wraps—those plastic strips you can ratchet tight?"

She nods.

"The subject used those to restrain his victims." Mac hesitates, then decides to leave out the part about the degrading amputation. "If he puts the tie wraps on you, scream. I'll be in here before you close your mouth."

Her eyes hold his gaze for another second, then she closes them. "All right. Let's get some lunch," she says, a faint tremor barely detectable in her voice.

* * *

That afternoon, after about an hour of rest, Mac is just cinching up his tie when there's a knock on the door and the same "It's me," he heard that morning before they went for a run together, and again before breakfast. He looks through the peephole anyway, and it takes him a couple seconds to connect what he sees with the voice he just heard. He flips open the security latch and opens the door.

She almost glides in—even her movements are different now. The light green dress brings out the color in her eyes, which in turn contrasts with the pink she's added to her lips. He can tell she's wearing more makeup than the lipstick, but it's artfully applied and the result is a natural-seeming, enhanced appearance. As she passes him on her way into the room he notices she has breasts now; they're still small, but now there's a visible swelling at the top of her dress. The most striking difference, though, is the honey blonde, slightly wavy hair flowing down to the base of her neck.

She looks at him impatiently. "Well, what do you think? Everything look OK?" She turns slowly in place.

Mac smiles. "You clean up pretty good."

She glares at him over her shoulder. "I don't like looking this way. I know I can pull it off, but don't compliment me. Just tell me if everything looks all right for what we're doing, OK?"

Mac drops his smile and looks at her objectively, carefully. She's done a good job of transforming herself, right down to the strappy, matching green sandals and glossy toenails on her feet. He notices her arms, and realizes he's never seen them bare until now. While still slender enough to appear feminine, they're surprisingly muscular, with each group—delt, tricep, and bicep—set off from the other. He remembers seeing her leave for the gym a couple mornings while he was covertly watching after questioning her at the coffee shop, but he'd imagined she was just doing aerobics or something. Now he thinks she must do some weight training, and the muscle looks good on her. "OK, face me."

She turns. She's wearing a simple silver-colored necklace that stays close to her neck.

"I think you should lose the necklace—it could be used to hurt you. Are you wearing earrings?"

She reaches her hands up and moves the hair back, revealing dangly silver ornaments.

"Do you have any basic studs you can wear instead? If he pulls on those they'll tear your earlobes."

"They're just clip-ons—my ears aren't pierced anymore. If he pulls them it'll pinch a little, but there won't be any damage." She unfastens the necklace and puts it in the small purse she's carrying.

"Let me see your hands."

She holds them out, palms down. He leans forward a little and she raises her hands higher. The fingernails are short like before, of course, and still their natural color, but now they're glossy and the tips are smoothly curved. Still no jewelry on her hands, but the black G-Shock watch has been replaced by a slender, silver analog model. He straightens and meets her eyes. "What about the wig? Is it secure?"

She runs her fingers through it, and it looks like real hair. She tugs on it some and it stays in place. "It's glued to my scalp—it's actually pretty hard to remove it."

"Looks convincing," he agrees. He hesitates, but it could be important to know: "So are you a lesbian?"

Her eyebrows go up in surprise.

"I mean, your usual appearance—the men's clothing, the crew cut..."

"No—I wish. I tried, but it's just not in me. Closeness isn't an option for me."

"But you're all right with what you need to do, maybe as soon as tonight?"

She nods. "I can hold it together. I focus on what I need to do, and that keeps me too busy to think about anything else."

Mac stares at her face. A lot of guys, and maybe this Flashphaler guy, might find her attractive. Mac doesn't, but there *is* something he likes about her face. He has an urge to quit this, to tell her to go back to her room, take off the wig and makeup, change back to her regular clothes, and pack her bags. He'd pack it in too, and they could both be on their way home within the hour. "OK, you look ready," he says. "Let's get going—we can pick up sandwiches for dinner on the way to the convention center."

Thirty-Four

I finish my sandwich—basically a salad sandwich—without getting any of the Italian dressing from it on the dress. I rinse out with some mouth wash, open the passenger door of MacIlwane's car, and spit onto the parking lot's pavement. Then it's back to staring across the lot at the Jeep Cherokee we followed from the convention center to this hotel, listening to MacIlwane's jazz, and trying not to think too much about the constant scratching below my heart. "So, what's the deal with these guys?" I ask. "I mean, you study them—why do they hurt people? Why the cruelty?"

MacIlwane shifts in the driver's seat. "Different reasons with each of them. For some it's rage, others a sexual neurosis, others an inability to connect with people any other way." He pauses. "There are some commonalities, though. Usually they were abused, often sexually, as children, or simply not shown any affection, which is just another kind of abuse. And interestingly, a lot of them sustained a major head injury at some point in their past."

"Really? So for some it could just be a knock on the head?"

He glances over at her. "Well, it's always more than just a head injury, at least as far as I've seen and read, but that can be a factor. I've even read lately that lead poisoning can contribute to violent behavior. That's one theory for the spike in violent crime back in the seventies, before leaded gasoline was phased out. We're complicated machines, and sometimes when things go wrong with us, we do bad stuff."

That seems an odd word choice. "So do you think of yourself as a sort of blade runner?"

"You mean like in the movie?"

"Yeah—it sounds like you're saying these guys are machines gone bad, and you hunt them down."

He shrugs. "I said 'machine', but that's an over-simplification. Clearly, they're human, as human as we are. But a human is in many ways like a very complex, advanced machine, and like a machine, a human can break or malfunction. But some of the things that break us don't affect machines. Humans need love as children; that's not very machine-like, but without that love, a lot of us, maybe most of us, would break. Unfortunately, although parent is one of the hardest and most important jobs in our society, there's not much of a screening process for determining who gets to be one."

"Do you think any of us, given the wrong childhood, could be like them?"

He shakes his head, still staring ahead vacantly. "No. Different people react in different ways. Some become violent, some pathetic, some self-destruct. But it sounds like you're trying to get at something—do you think they're flat-out evil?"

"No, I'm not getting at anything; I'm just interested. I don't believe in good and evil anymore. Things are simply what they are, and the good versus evil angle is a human invention that doesn't really exist in the world. Good and evil are more subjective evaluations than measurable qualities. I guess I agree with you, though I've gotten used to thinking of habitual murderers as something different, something not like me."

MacIlwane nods and glances over at me before looking out the windshield again. "Sure—that's a normal response. We associate being human with the usual range of behavior and reactions, and these guys are well outside that range. Plus, since you fight them, and usually end up killing them, it's psychologically easier, maybe psychologically *necessary*, for you to not empathize with them and instead think of them as something completely different from yourself. You wouldn't normally harm a fellow human, and maybe it bothers you. It's easier to harm someone if you dehumanize him first, if you block that empathy you would normally have for him, because empathy is a basis for morality. When the Golden Rule tells you to treat others as you would be treated, it's telling you to recognize other people are like you and to consider their needs: 'How would *I* feel in his position?' But now you're breaking the Golden Rule, and that's easier if you don't empathize with your victim. I've done it. In combat you don't think of the enemy as people like yourself; they're the bad guys, monsters, demons. You asked where the cruelty comes from, and I think that's it: serial killers don't empathize with others, don't recognize others as having value. Their victims are objects to be used and disposed of. Or their empathy is psychotically distorted, and they think they're doing right by their victims despite all the evidence to the contrary."

"I guess that's why I'm a vegan," I say, thinking about what he said.

"I was wondering about that—if it were a health thing or what."

"Mostly it's about avoiding violence and respecting life."

He smiles, chuckles a little.

"What?" I ask, but that makes him laugh more. "What?"

He puts his hand up and stops laughing, but he's still grinning broadly. "First, I believe you—what you said fits with what I know about you, but you've gotta appreciate the irony of you saying that."

I do get the irony, but that doesn't make me want to smile. Instead I slump in the seat and cross my arms.

"Aw, c'mon Campbell—you're not the pouting type."

"I'm not pouting." I deliberately sit up and put my hands in my lap. "I hate my life."

"Please don't say that."

I look over and see his smile's gone and he's looking at me.

I sigh, feeling exasperated. "Anyway, after what you were saying, I'd have to say my being a vegan is really about empathy. Animals are innocent—they do what they do and don't seem to have much choice in it, or any idea of morality. And they're really at our mercy. I decided I didn't want to harm anything unnecessarily, especially if it has enough brain to be aware of itself and capable of suffering. Those qualities seem to be true for most of the animals people eat. Maybe these creatures aren't exactly like me, but they can feel pain and fear, and can suffer in captivity. I wouldn't want to be treated the way we treat animals, so I stopped eating them or anything produced by the factory farms that abuse them."

He nods, and is quiet for a minute or so. "Have you felt this way since…?"

"Since the Bad—I call it 'the Bad.'"

I'm not looking at him, but out of the corner of my eye I see him nod.

"I found out what it's like to be..." I pause, looking for the word. "...helpless." The word isn't nearly adequate, but so what.

We're both quiet for a while, then he says, "I'm sorry that happened to you."

"It's not your fault," I say irritably, then think about it. "But thanks," I add, working to change my tone. "After the Bad, all the philosophy, ethics, and religion there ever was didn't matter. I knew what was done to me and my parents was wrong. I wanted to go as far away from that, from violence and cruelty as I could, because I knew how it felt to be on the receiving end.

"I probably shouldn't be thinking about this now. Anyway, maybe it's naïve and ridiculous to empathize with animals that way; after all, pain, suffering, and violence are the norm here in Harold's world."

"Who's Harold?"

I look at him, surprised, then realize what I said. "Oh—nothing—just an expression."

"An expression?"

"Yeah...Harold is...what I call God."

"God's name is Harold?" he asks, smiling, but looking a little confused too.

"It's from when I was a kid. I thought the prayer was 'Our father, who art in heaven, Harold be thy name.'"

He smiles more broadly, laughs quietly. "I like that: 'Harold.'"

"I guess I use it because the word God carries a lot of baggage with me."

"Actually, I figured you for an atheist."

"That's what I mean; I was an atheist for a long time after the Bad. It's interesting: after that night I *wanted* God to exist so I could hate him, but it was too disturbing to think an omnipotent being existed and still permitted the world we inhabit. That's kind of scary, don't you think? I mean, *you* see a lot of really bad shit; don't you have a problem with the idea of an all-powerful deity who could make any world, making *this* world, with all the crap that happens in it? What kind of sick bastard would make monsters—or broken humans, whatever—like this guy?" I point with my chin at the hotel.

"We don't know for sure it's *this* guy."

"Well, whoever killed those women in Boston and Baltimore. Given the choice between a malevolent, wantonly cruel, but all-powerful being in the same universe as me, and nothing, I took nothing."

"But not anymore?   Or are you just kidding about Harold?" he asks, smiling again.

"Actually, it was this thing inside me, this ability...this sense I'm stuck with that made me re-think things. It's so consistently reliable...and I started noticing how well so many things work, how much order there is all around us, at every level from the sub-atomic to the universal. It just seemed too much of a stretch to say it all happened accidentally. I mean, theoretically it's possible, but what's the most likely explanation?"

"Harold?"

"You like that, don't you?" I say, smiling a little myself.

"I don't mean to be disrespectful—"

I wave my hand dismissively and let out a quick laugh. "Oh no, I didn't mean that—I don't have a personal stake or emotional investment in Harold—I don't even like it. It just seems to be the best explanation for the world I see around me."

"'It'? What's 'it'?

"Harold. Just because its name is Harold doesn't mean I think it's a guy. That would be crazy talk, that the vast infinity of the cosmos was created by a finite being with a gender; I mean, gender is only relevant for creatures that reproduce sexually, which wouldn't apply to something which pre-existed everything else."

"Sooo...do you feel like you're doing God's work when you go after these guys?"

I can hear, under his casual tone, the suspicion. "No," I answer truthfully, shaking my head for emphasis. "I'm doing this because I don't want anyone else to endure what that son of a bitch did to my parents and me. I don't think Harold has an agenda or any interest in what we do—it certainly didn't help me. So no, I'm not some wacko on a mission from God. Like you said, what I'm doing comes from empathy. I hadn't put it that way before, but you're right."

He's been watching me closely, but now he looks away, absently sweeping his eyes over the twilit parking lot and the hotel in front of us. "You say you're not an atheist anymore, but the world hasn't changed—it's still full of violence and cruelty."

"Yeah...it's scary to admit, but there's no getting around it now: it's Harold's world. I'm just doing the best I can in it."

"So how do you answer your question? What kind of sick bastard makes a world like this?"

"Obviously God isn't what we're told it is; it's not a kind and loving father. Maybe Harold *is* psychotic—maybe the guys we hunt are made in Harold's image, but I don't think so. It's probably vanity to think God is even interested enough to be cruel to us. My guess is Harold's pretty hands off. Sometimes I tell myself God built the machine, set it running, and walked away right after the Big Bang, not knowing how badly it'd turn out." I stop talking. MacIlwane says nothing, so after a while I ask him: "What do you think?"

He blows out the air in his lungs and looks away. "Maybe the world is a challenge, a test for us. Or maybe it's like lifting weights—you know, you traumatize your body so it will heal stronger. Only the world is training for the soul."

"Do you feel like you're getting stronger?"

He glances over, then looks away. After a couple seconds he says, "I hope so," and turns his head further away from me.

We're both quiet for a while, then he looks over and notices the goose bumps on my arms. "Why didn't you tell me you were cold? Here—drape my jacket over you."

"No, I'm fine."

"Look, I'm not using it. Just take it for now."

"OK." I arrange it over me; I *was* chilly and this helps. "So do *you* believe in God?"

"I was raised a Baptist. Both my parents were good church-going folks. Mom still is; Dad would be if he were still with us. I grew up just accepting it—didn't really think much about it one way or another until..." He pauses, trying to remember. "Well, there wasn't one event; more like an accumulation of experiences.

"In some of the units I was in we had a procedure called 'passage of lines' when we would pass through the main friendly forces and into potentially hostile territory where the patrol was pretty much on its own. Sometimes we had artillery or air support, but sometimes it was just us, depending on ourselves, our training, the equipment we had with us.

"I think a lot of people go through this passage of lines at some point in their lives and realize they're on their own— there really isn't anything like God looking out for them. You passed through when you were fifteen. I don't know exactly when I did, but once it happens, you realize all you have is your own judgment, your own thoughts, ideas, and whatever sources of strength you can find inside yourself. But unlike the military passage of lines, I'm not sure there's any going back. It's hard to un-think the thoughts that occur to you, to un-live the experiences you've had."

I nod. "But what do you think? About God, I mean."

He looks at me. "I think it's unknowable, and there's not much point in wondering about it. Like you said, if God exists, he—it—seems to have deserted us. And what I learned about God as a child doesn't seem applicable to the world I've lived in as an adult. Like turning the other cheek—that's noble, but not very practical. If you'd remained passive when you were attacked as a child, you'd be dead, and that son of a bitch would have tortured and killed more people. There's no way anyone could convince me it was wrong for you to fight back. I guess I'm an agnostic. Like you, it seems to me all this must have come from somewhere and, at least in mechanical terms, it works too well to be an accident. But beyond that, who's to say? It's unknowable and irrelevant. I rely on my own judgment."

I nod. "I think everyone is already beyond friendly lines—I don't think there *are* friendly lines. But not everyone realizes this. A lot, maybe most, kid themselves into believing without question in a God that cares, but really we're all on our own—we each have to make our own choices. Even if we choose to let someone else—like a church or the Bible or whatever—make our choices for us, that first choice is our own. It's inescapable."

We're quiet for a while. It becomes fully night, but the parking lot is well lit.

"So he's still here, right? You can feel him?" MacIlwane asks.

"Yeah, the itching is holding steady. Maybe he's having dinner in his room or the hotel restaurant."

MacIlwane nods. "How did you first find out you have this sense?"

"Initially I didn't know *what* was happening. The first time was less than a year after the Bad, when I was almost sixteen. I was waiting for a bus, and suddenly the pain started. I went to the doctor, thinking something was still damaged inside me, and they checked me out, but everything looked fine. They sent me to my shrink, telling me it was all in my head; said it was normal in cases of post-traumatic stress."

"It is."

"Yeah, I believed them. They said I might have smelled or heard something that reminded me of what happened, or of the guy that attacked me and my parents. The pain didn't happen often, but when it did, I figured it was just some kind of flashback."

"So what changed?"

"One Saturday night in Korea, while I was sitting up all night in the battalion headquarters as staff duty officer, the military police showed up with a soldier they'd arrested for beating a prostitute downtown. Before they even arrived, I started to hurt, and when they brought him in it was almost like I was being stabbed all over again. By that time I'd learned to not take the pain seriously, though. I knew there wasn't really anything wrong, so I just focused on logging the incident and signing CID's paperwork. As soon as the soldier was taken away, the pain diminished, then vanished."

"That still sounds like it could have been a flashback; I mean, you knew a violent man was being brought into the same place you were."

"Yeah, that's what I thought too—just another flashback. But an hour or so later, one of my required checks took me, without my realizing, past the detention facility where the prisoner was being held. I got the pain, though not as bad, twice then: once on the way out, and again on the way back. On the return trip I noticed the detention facility's sign and realized something weird was going on. The rest of the story—Florida and the rest—you already know."

A little after eight p.m. the itch converts to a scratch and continues to increase. "He's on his way."

We both sit up a little straighter and watch. He emerges from the front entrance, crosses the lot to his vehicle, and starts it up. When he leaves the parking lot we head out after him.

Thirty-Five

They follow Flashphaler's SUV down the highway running through the heart of Atlanta. Mac glances over at Campbell, sees her using his black Maglite held close to the map to illuminate it as she follows their progress. "How you doing?" he asks.

She glances over quickly, then looks back out the windshield at the signs and landmarks. "Fine."

"Scared?"

"Only as much as I need to be," she answers quietly, looking down at the map and inching her index finger along.

Good answer, Mac thinks. Flashphaler takes an exit near downtown. "He's taking exit 248—248*A*. I'm guessing he's headed for Underground Atlanta—that would make sense."

"I see it. If so, he'll be making a right down there. What's Underground Atlanta?"

"Yep, there he goes. Underground Atlanta is a complex built on and under the site of the old central train yard. It's sort of a multi-level mall with restaurants and clubs."

"According to the map there's parking near it."

They follow him through an intersection. "I see a parking sign up ahead," Mac says.

"That should be the lot—is he turning?"

"He's not there yet."

Out of the corner of his eye he sees her look up and watch. "There he goes."

Mac sees a fire hydrant and pulls over next to it. "OK, I'm letting you out here."

Campbell tosses the map on the floor by her feet and unfastens her seatbelt. "OK, see ya," she says as she opens the door.

"Hey Campbell, remember—if it starts going bad make a break for it, no matter where you are. He won't take precautions against you escaping until he starts doing his thing, and I'll be with you the whole way."

"OK," she says. "Get going or you won't see where he parks." She jumps out and closes the door.

Mac turns back into the street, drives the last several feet to the parking garage entrance. He takes the ticket and pulls through the automatic gate, glancing quickly around and glimpsing the dark green Jeep Cherokee turning down an aisle. Mac follows him up three levels and finds a space a few cars down from him.

Grabbing his suit jacket and the briefcase containing items for quick appearance changes, Mac jumps out and sees the target waiting for the elevator. Mac walks quickly down the aisle, but the elevator arrives before he does and Flashphaler steps in. "Hold the door please!" Mac calls, jogging the last few feet. The target complies. "Thanks," Mac says, stepping quickly to the back of the car to prevent Flashphaler from looking too closely at him.

"No problem," the tall man replies, releasing the door and pressing the button for street level.

They stand in silence on the way down, with Flashphaler remaining near the control panel and Mac staying near the back of the car where he can observe inconspicuously. Flashphaler is almost a head taller than him, about six-three Mac guesses, and like Campbell said, he's heavily muscled with a thick neck. The light blue dress shirt he's wearing is very broad across his shoulders and upper back, and tapers dramatically down to where it's tucked in to his khaki pants— the classic V shape bodybuilders aspire to. His close-cropped hair makes his head seem more narrow and his shoulders even wider. Mac shifts his eyes down. The target has big hands too. No rings on the left hand, but Mac can see the edge of a big gold watch peeking out below the cuff. *Long enough.*

Mac doesn't want the target to sense he's being observed, so Mac looks up at the numbers above the door: 1…L

The doors open.   The target strides forward without looking back. Mac steps out and puts on his suit jacket while allowing a gap to open between them.   When he reaches the sidewalk Mac sees Campbell up on the corner, partially obscured by shadows, observing them.

Flashphaler turns down a cobblestone street closed to vehicles, heading directly for Underground Atlanta, and Mac follows. The street is not crowded, but it's busy with people enjoying the cool spring evening, some of them gathered around a jazz trio playing near a fountain. Flashphaler walks without hesitation and at a quick pace, but his height makes him easy to follow, even at a distance. As they approach the entrances to a couple clubs, Mac can hear music filtering out to the street. Flashphaler enters a club called "Masquerade." Mac waits outside and several feet from the entrance until Campbell catches up.

"Hey," she says, slowing her pace as she nears him.

"You're in charge while we're in there—I'm following your lead," he says in a low voice. "When you leave, I'll be behind you. If he takes you to his car, he's parked on level three in the garage. I'll take the stairs instead of the elevator with you in case he might recognize me and get suspicious, but know I'm with you. I got a parking spot near him, so it won't be any trouble following you out. Hopefully he'll be headed to our hotel, but if he doesn't we've got the transmitter on his vehicle—I'll follow you and figure something out. And remember, if at any time you want to bail, do it."

She nods quickly and enters the club.

* * *

The big guys at the entrance wave me in; apparently Monday night is ladies night here. Inside I feel the strong pulsing of the music push against me. The room is bathed in a blue glow from hidden lights along the tops of the walls and several blue spots mounted in tracks on the ceiling. My eyes are drawn across the room to the bar, which is bright with white light coming from the translucent counter running around it. The place isn't crowded, with only about a dozen people on the vast dance floor—not surprising since it's a Monday night and probably still early for the kind of people who go to clubs. This is a good thing since it increases the chances of him coming on to me instead of someone else. My stomach clenches, but I force myself to focus on playing my part, doing the mission.

I move further into the club and away from the entrance, the sense humming along in me as a severe cramp at the top of my abdomen. I take the pain and look around, finally noticing the target at the bar. I skirt the dance floor to get to there, stopping at a bathroom on the way to empty my bladder and check my appearance. There's a woman at a sink fixing her makeup, but we ignore each other and I go into a stall to pee. While I'm finishing up I hear her leave; I have the bathroom to myself when I come out. I study the image in the mirror, neaten the wavy hair, touch up the lipstick, and confirm I haven't smudged the eye makeup. Looking over my shoulder I see some wrinkles in the back of the dress from sitting in MacIlwane's car, but they're not too bad and there's nothing I can do about them anyway. I drop the lipstick back in the little purse with the other makeup tools and my wallet. One last look at the mirror: I find my own eyes in this version of my face. The woman in the mirror tightens her lips slightly, and we give each other a tiny smile of encouragement.

At the bar, I take a stool at one end, several feet from Flashphaler's place near the center. *Don't want to be too obvious.* I'm not sure if I believe this rationalization or not, but it does seem sensible. The pain is almost at its maximum now, but I'm handling it. *It isn't real*, I tell myself and wipe

the sweat from my upper lip. I order a Coke and scan the
large room, looking for my competition, the potential victims.
There are several other unaccompanied women around, and I
wish I'd worn a more thickly-padded bra. I look down at my
chest and try to stick it out more. A tall blonde goes by on her
way to the bathroom; her body-hugging outfit has only a back
and front, with a few little ties crossing the sides of her body
and hips to hold the pieces together. I wish I could've worn
the little red dress with the tiny shoulder straps, but at least
this one still has the low neck line. Down the bar the target is
surveying the club too, and beyond him, at the opposite end
from me, MacIlwane, who's now wearing thick-framed
glasses, orders a drink from the bartender, then sits back away
from the lighted bar surface, his dark suit, shirt, and skin
becoming inconspicuous in the shadows.

   I look back at the target; he hasn't noticed me. He, like
most of the guys in here, is dressed more casually than
MacIlwane: khaki pants, no tie, and a light blue button-down
shirt he wears open at the neck. The shirt isn't tight, but the
way it drapes over his shoulders and chest makes his muscular
build obvious. I look away, the nausea in my stomach
competing with the stabbing below my heart.

   I see myself get up and walk right past Flashphaler to the
other end of the bar. MacIlwane gets up, and we walk out of
this hot, painful blueness and into the cool spring night.

   The bartender puts down a little napkin and my drink,
quoting a price as he does. I pay him and take a sip of soda,
which is watery and too cold from all the ice in it, but does
have one of those hyper-red little cherries.

   Let's do this. I swallow against the stabbing pain and
move to a stool two down from the big guy, who looks bigger
the closer I get to him. I look away before we can make eye
contact. Instead I continue gazing around, pretending to be
people watching, giving him time to notice me. After about a

minute I glance over at him, catch his eye, and manage a smile.

He smiles back, then looks away, back out at the main part of the room, maybe checking out a pair of barely dressed women dancing together nearby.

Is this right? I so don't know what I'm doing here. I was going to ask MacIlwane for advice, but he already seemed so doubtful of my ability to pull this off. I wait, but the target makes no further contact, though out of the corner of my eye I think I see him looking my way. I do something I saw in a movie: I take the cherry out of my glass and put it to my lips. Holding it by the stem and between my front teeth, I taste it with the tip of my tongue for a moment before putting it back in my drink. I put the straw in my mouth and sip, turning in my seat as I do to gauge the effect.

Drink in hand, he's walking away. He stops and stands in the shadows several feet away, looking out at the dance floor.

OK, how am I going to do this? I wonder.

Over the music I suddenly hear a male voice really close behind me say "How ya doing?" I almost jump off my stool, then turn quickly to see a man in his early forties with a comb-over leering at me from about six inches away. He jumps back a little too, with an exaggerated look of fear on his face before smiling broadly and laughing. "Didn't mean to scare ya, Cutie!"

"Uh, hi." I turn away and glance over at Mac, who looks quickly down, obviously trying to suppress a smile. *Yeah, real funny.*

I look at the large mirror behind the bar and notice the older guy next to me leaning in again.

"What I wouldn't give to be that dress you're wearing."

"All right, that's it," I mutter, taking my drink and walking fast toward Flashphaler, picking up his line of sight as I go.

* * *

Why the hell not? Flash had been planning to peruse the menu more, but it seems crazy to not take the easy route. She's attractive with a pretty face and great arms—nice muscularity, for a woman. Her breasts are really small, but breast size doesn't matter much to him anyway.

Guys who fixate on big breasts are really just trying to be children, to be close to mommy. The last thing Flash wants is to be around that bitch again. He just wishes he'd been the one to finish her, his way.

Anyway...Shy Girl has obviously locked in on him and, being so obviously uncomfortable and out of her element here, will probably be happy to leave. Besides, she may not pan out; as usual he needs the right combination of circumstances for his plan to succeed, so she's as good a starting point as any.

He looks over at the bar again and sees her actually headed his way, an uncomfortable look on her face. "Hi," Flash says, giving her the full blast of his smile.

Her face goes from unhappy to nervous surprise to gratitude in about a second and a half. "Hi," she says, "I feel like I'm swimming with sharks tonight." She moves her eyes and tips her head slightly.

Flash follows her gaze and sees a middle-aged guy watching them from his seat at the bar before quickly looking away. "Is it always like that here?" he asks.

"I don't know—I've never been here before. It's actually my first time in Atlanta." Her voice is lower and stronger than he imagined.

"Really? I'm from out of town too—I'm here for a software trade show," Flash says, hoping this is something she'll find interesting, or at least reassuring. Shy Girl looks like she might be the cerebral, geeky type.

"Wow—I wouldn't have pegged you for the computer type."

He notices her eyes—it's hard not to. He can't tell what color they are in the poor lighting of the club, but they're big and accented by downward-canted eyebrows and a little makeup. "What's the 'computer type'?"

"Well, smaller for one thing—skinnier."

Flash knows what she means, but pretends to be alarmed and sucks in his already concave stomach while making a show of checking his waist line. "Damn, I thought this shirt would hide that!"

She smiles. "No, I mean less, you know, *broad.* You know, in the chest and shoulders," she adds hastily.

"Oh, nice try—now the backpedaling and tap dancing begin."

She presses her lips together, suppressing her smile. "Obviously you know you have a nice bod, but I guess you've earned the right to be a little cocky and I'm certainly not complaining."

Flash is pleasantly surprised; he'd been expecting conversation with the wallflower to be stilted and awkward. And she's from out of town, maybe away from people she knows. "Would you like to sit down?" he asks, motioning to a small table with a couple chairs nearby.

"Sure."

As they sit down Flash introduces himself as Erik.

"Sharon Connor," she says, taking his offered hand.

He's careful not to squeeze her hand too hard. The return grip is surprisingly strong and sweaty, probably because she's so nervous. "So what brings you to Atlanta? Business or pleasure?" he asks.

"Both, actually—they don't have to be mutually exclusive, do they?"

Flash smiles back. "Of course not. I travel a lot for work, but always try to mix in some fun too. I mean, I get to visit all

these different cities and someone else picks up the tab—
might as well make the most of it."

"Totally," she says, nodding then taking a sip from the
straw in her drink.

"So what do you do?" he asks.

"I'm in market research—mostly I analyze data, look for
patterns, make predictions and recommendations, like that."

He nods. "Sounds…interesting…"

She smiles. "No, not really—it's probably more like
golf."

"You play golf?"

"No, I mean people who play golf must enjoy it, but
watching it or talking about it seems like it would be painfully
boring."

"So are you here for a conference or something?"

"No, I've been moderating focus groups for four days—I
just finished up today, and now I'm taking a couple days off
before I head home to Boston."

"No kidding? That's great. Unfortunately, I'm just
getting started—the show I'm exhibiting in doesn't even open
until tomorrow."

"What?"

Flash leans closer, across the little table. It seems as if the
music has gotten louder. "I said the trade show I'm here for
doesn't even start until tomorrow. So I'm here for a few
days."

"…–ay cool…here…out…"

He can see she's speaking to him, but the music has
definitely gotten louder and he's having trouble hearing her.
"You want to go outside?" he half shouts at her. "It's kind of
loud in here," he says, touching his ear.

She smiles and nods. "Sure," he thinks she says.

They abandon their drinks and head for the door.
Outside, even though they're in downtown Atlanta, it seems

almost rural quiet to Flash's slightly numbed ears. "So what were you saying?"

She shakes her head. "I was just saying maybe it's a good thing you're going to be around for a couple days. I mean, when I was planning these couple days off, I didn't take into account that I'd be in a town where I don't know anyone."

Flash suppresses his smile. "Yeah, I know that feeling. Like I was saying, I travel frequently, so I find myself wandering around alone in strange cities a lot. I don't want to just sit in my hotel room watching TV, but sometimes it feels weird—kind of standing on the edge, looking in."

"Totally!   That's it—you see all these people who obviously know each other, and you're on the outside, like peeking in through the windows."

"Well, I'm sorry I pulled you out of the club—now you really are on the outside."

She waves her hand dismissively. "To be honest, I didn't really like the music. I'm not into that techno house dance music, or whatever it's called." She looks at him. "I mean, not that there's anything wrong with it, it's just not my taste."

He smiles. "I don't really like it either. These guys sound pretty good, though," he says, motioning at the jazz trio performing nearby.

"I like jazz too," she says.

They stroll down the stone-paved street to the knot of people gathered around the musicians and listen for a little while. She throws a bill in the guitar case propped open in front of them, so Flash does too.

"So, you want to go someplace, maybe hang out for a while?" she asks him. He can hear the forced casualness.

"Sure," he says. "You have anyplace in mind?"

"There's a decent little bar in my hotel."

"Is it nearby?"

"No, we'll have to take a cab, but we can split it."

"Actually, I've got a car. I'm from North Carolina, so I just drove down for this trip. I get tired of sitting in a metal tube at thirty-thousand feet for hours on end."

"Yeah, I remember when I was a kid, flying seemed fun; that's definitely worn off now. So where did you park?"

"It's not far—there's a parking garage a couple blocks from here."

"Lead on, sir."

They chat about places they've visited as they walk, and end up comparing Philadelphia experiences. He realizes he's actually enjoying her company. She has a great smile, and there's a certain...he's not sure what—maybe vulnerability, that makes him feel almost protective of her.

But he knows better; he knows the truth women hide: the manipulative, domineering, parasitic bitch behind every carefully made up façade, every pretty smile, inside every stinking cunt. Regaining his focus, Flash finds himself looking forward to the moment of shock, when all the façades will drop away.

When they reach his vehicle, he opens the door for her. "Everything in?" he asks, playing the perfect gentleman before closing the door and walking around the back of the vehicle, scanning the vicinity as he goes. The door from the stairwell opens and a black guy emerges and walks down the aisle, keys in one hand and big shopping bag in the other. He notices the guy is wearing one of those knit skull caps, a white one that contrasts starkly with skin that is almost literally black. Flash thinks the cap is a Muslim thing. He quickly assesses the guy's walking pace, then opens the driver side door and slides in behind the steering wheel.

"So where's your radio?" she asks, nodding at the cavity in the center of the Cherokee's console.

"I take it out and put it under my seat when I park in the city. It's a pretty nice sound system—it would definitely be worth somebody's while to break in and take it. It's designed to pop out of the dash, so when I park I hide it." He leans forward and reaches under his seat, looking at her and scrunching up his face in mock effort as he does. He pulls the box-shaped component out and slides it carefully into its slot, latches it, and turns it on: Aerosmith.

"I love this song!" she says.

He looks at the lighted display on the stereo. "Sorry—I know I'm kind of weird about this thing," he says, reaching under his seat again and taking a handkerchief-sized cloth out of a zip-lock baggie. Holding the cloth in his left hand, he leans over and wipes off the front of the stereo. In one motion he launches across the low barrier between the two front seats, slamming his right upper arm across her chest, and clamping the cloth over her nostrils and mouth. The moment of stunned shock is followed by the expected frantic, useless thrashing. Again he's surprised by the strength in her small body, but she's no match for Flash, and the way he has her pinned prevents her arms above her elbows from doing anything. He holds the chemical-soaked cloth in place until she stops moving, then counts to sixty before removing it. He releases her but stays close, studying her face, her closed eyes, for any sign of consciousness, but there's none. Working quickly, he reclines his seat and reaches behind hers. He grabs the two pairs of handcuffs on the floor there and uses them to secure each wrist to the steel cable he attached to the seat's metal floor mounts. He takes large plastic ratchet ties out of the glove box and uses them to secure her ankles to a similar cable under the front of her seat. Finally he takes a light blanket from the back seat and drapes it over her body to block the garage attendant's view of the handcuffs and plastic ties.

He sits back and briefly admires his work, excitement and anticipation humming through his body, making his cock swell. He starts the engine and pulls out of the space, heading for the garage exit.

Thirty-Six

As he walks past Flashphaler on the way to his car, Mac is careful to look away, hoping the bastard is sufficiently distracted or oblivious to not recognize Mac as the man who rode down in the elevator with him about an hour earlier. To be safe, though, after leaving the club Mac put on a white knit cap from his briefcase. He also took out a large paper shopping bag, and put his tie and the briefcase in that.

Still walking, Mac hears the door on Flashphaler's Cherokee open and close. He opens his car's door, tosses the bag through to the passenger seat, and slides in behind the wheel. He opens his window slightly so he can hear Flashphaler start his car's engine. As he's waiting he turns on the switched pattern receiver for the small transmitter he attached to the underbody of Flashphaler's Jeep while they waited outside his hotel earlier in the evening. The set up is low-end, but sufficient to indicate direction and proximity up to about half a mile, and it's working now.

Mac doesn't hear anything from the target's SUV, and is about to pull out the receiver for the listening device in Campbell's purse to find out what's happening, when the other vehicle finally cranks. When Flashphaler backs out and begins to drive away, Mac starts his car and does the same. As expected, he ends up directly behind the Cherokee at the exit where they each have to stop to pay. While he's paying, Mac notes which way the suspect turns when he reaches the bottom of the garage's exit ramp, then the gate goes up and Mac drives off in pursuit.

As he turns on to the street, he can see the Cherokee stopped at a light a couple cars ahead. Mac checks the tracker again: still working. By the next light Mac has put himself right behind Flashphaler, but the suspect manages to make a left turn just after the light has turned red, leaving Mac stuck as cross traffic cuts off any possibility of pursuit until the light cycle comes around again. Still, so far they're headed in the right direction to get on the northbound highway back to the hotel, and the tracker will let Mac know if that's right or not.

Mac notices there's no dedicated left turn signal here, so he watches for the glow from the yellow light on the cross street. When he sees it, he gets ready and as soon as his light turns green Mac pulls into the intersection to make his turn before the oncoming traffic can stop him. A bright light to his left catches his attention. Instinctively he looks toward it and sees headlights very close. He slams on the brakes, but it's too late and he watches, without time to feel anything, the other car slam into his. He feels the impact, the irresistible motion, then nothing.

Thirty-Seven

Pain: the stabbing of the sense is at its peak. My eyes pop open; a line of red tail lights is in front of me, and I try to bring my hands up, but they jerk painfully against metal which bites into the skin of my wrists and grinds against the bones. It hurts but I can't help jerking on my hands again. I realize my wrists are handcuffed—shackled to something behind the seat, and my ankles are bound too. I feel dizzy, and like I might throw up. It's one of my nightmares; I pull against the handcuffs again, trying to wake myself, but it keeps hurting bad and nothing's changing.

"You awake?"

The sound of his voice makes me jerk spasmodically. *I'm in way too deep here; I want out I want out.* My throat's dry and sore, and making *uh, uh, uh* sounds. I can't get enough air and the harder I breathe the louder the noises get.

"Oh yeah, that panting's hot," he says.

"Fuck you!" I scream, "*fuck you!*" The rag he pressed against my face in the parking garage is gone now, but my lips and nose are burning, like there's a rash where the chemical touched them, and I can still smell the sweet scent it left behind. Whatever was on that cloth, it's in my head confusing me. *I want out I want out!* my brain shouts. I scream—no words, just crazy scared screaming—and strain against the cuffs and whatever's holding my ankles.

"Wooooooo! *Yeah!*" he yells, laughing. "That's what I'm talkin' about! Guess you're awake."

Wait, it's OK, I remind myself. *MacIlwane—* MacIlwane is following. This is our plan, our trap. This guy thinks he's captured me, but really MacIlwane and I are capturing *him*. MacIlwane's probably right behind us. My eyes shift around and I see the side mirror, see headlights behind. I mentally wave at him. He's right there, and when we stop he'll have a gun and arrest this fucker. I'm OK; this is all part of our plan—*my* plan.

"Don't stop now! I'm enjoying it."

He turned off the radio while I was screaming. I should keep acting scared so he isn't suspecting anything when MacIlwane makes his move. That shouldn't be difficult since I'm still freaking, but if I keep screaming now it might sound forced, so instead I drop my head and try to lean away from him, hoping he won't try to touch me before we get where MacIlwane can intervene.

"That's it? Well, there's plenty of time for more. That's the beauty of this—we have all kinds of time now."

I think of my purse with the listening device in it, but I don't know where the purse is now. I had it over my shoulder when I got in; maybe it's on my lap, under this blanket he threw over me. MacIlwane probably isn't listening now, but just in case I ask "Why—" then stop short before I can ask *that* stupid question again. Instead I say "What's happening? What are you doing?" I allow the fear, which isn't faked, to come through in my voice. Keeping my head bowed, I watch him out of the corner of my left eye.

He glances over, his gaze lingering on me for a couple seconds before returning to the highway. "I'm *living*. Everything else I do is just shit to get me here. This is my *real* life."

"I don't understand—where are we going? What's happening?"

He sighs loudly. "Shut up bitch," he says flatly.

"Please—please, can't we talk about this?" It seems like what he'd expect me to say at this point.

The back of his right hand snaps across the space between us and cracks against my cheek. Even on top of the incredible pain below my heart, this stings and surprises. I gasp and tears well up.

"You'll learn," he says, continuing in the same even, confident tone. "There's only one thing you need to know now: I am God. You are completely dependent on me: for the rest of your life, for your death. But for now, shut the fuck up." He turns the radio back on, and Eric Clapton sings *Leila*.

I keep quiet, my head bowed, staring at the blanket covering my lap, and sneaking looks at the side mirror to see if I can tell which set of headlights behind us is MacIlwane's. I'll be relieved when this is over, when I see MacIlwane again and he arrests this bastard. I wonder how much longer it'll be: probably not long after we stop. I look again at the lights in the mirror and imagine MacIlwane there, maybe less than a dozen yards away.

After three more songs and a commercial break we leave the highway for a major road, and not long after that we turn on to a secondary road. Through the tinted glass of the side window I see the lights of homes and the occasional closed business next to the road, illuminated by lights left on for security but obviously closed for the night. The radio broadcast gets static-y and he shuts it off. There are long stretches of time when there are no headlights behind us; MacIlwane is hanging back now, relying on the tracking device so as to not alert the target.

After another fifteen minutes or so the houses peter out, replaced by dark woods on either side. A few more miles and he slows the vehicle and turns right onto a dirt road. I check the side mirror and see only darkness. I hope the tracking device is still working. *MacIlwane won't let me down.* We're moving slowly now, the SUV bouncing gently over the occasional dip or bump in the road. The only light here is the headlights, illuminating packed red clay. Neither of us has said anything since he told me to shut up. Eventually he turns us left and the Jeep climbs a steep hill. At the top the headlights fall on the side of a log cabin. He pulls up close and parks, then cuts the engine and headlights.

Still he says nothing: only unfastens his seat belt and gets out. He opens the back door on his side of the vehicle, rustles around, then closes the door. I see him, lighting his way with a flashlight, walk up to the door of the cabin and use keys to remove a padlock. He goes inside, and after a minute or so some light spills out the open doorway. "OK, you can pull up any time, MacIlwane," I say quietly in case he's listening in via the device in my purse, which must be in here with me somewhere. "We went up a steep dirt driveway, and now we're parked outside a log cabin and he's gone inside. I'm handcuffed and my ankles are tied up too. So, if you're listening, now would be a great time to come in and arrest this fucker. I haven't seen any weapons." I'm watching out the window, and when Flashphaler appears in the cabin doorway I stop talking. He comes back to the truck, this time approaching my side.

My gut clenches.

The door behind mine opens. "I'm going to unlock the handcuffs now," he says from behind me. "I shouldn't even need to say this, but your legs are still bound. You can't get away. But if you try to, or if you lash out at me or do anything other than obey me completely and immediately, I will hurt you very badly *right now*. Clear?"

I nod my head.

"I asked you a question cunt: when I do that, you respond verbally and respectfully."

"Yes sir."

The vehicle tips slightly as he gets in. Keys jangle and he tugs on the handcuff around my left wrist, opening it and freeing that part of me, which I bring forward and lay in my lap. I feel him tugging on the right handcuffs, but with these he doesn't open the one on my wrist. Instead he pushes my still shackled wrist forward.

"Lean forward, put your left hand behind your back."

I consider my options, but with only one limb free, there's really nothing I can do. Better to minimize the damage to me and wait for MacIlwane.

"Lean *forward*, put your left hand *behind* your back!" he shouts, shoving me forward and pushing my right wrist painfully up my spine.

I gasp and quickly comply; the free handcuff closes on my left wrist. I remain leaning forward as he gets out, closes the back door and opens mine.

"You seem to be catching on, but one more time: do *not* resist me."

"Yes sir," I say quietly.

"Good." He pulls the blanket off me and takes my hand bag, then throws them aside on the ground. He shows me a small pair of wire cutters, then crouches down and reaches across my right leg. There's a small popping sound and whatever was binding my left ankle is gone. He backs up a little and does the same with my right ankle before quickly standing and yanking me out of the truck.

I don't get my legs under me fast enough; I tumble out of the vehicle and on to the ground, jerking my wrists against the cuffs when I instinctively try to break my fall. Since my hands are behind my back, I land on my right shoulder and my face. Fortunately the ground is covered with a relatively soft layer of pine needles.

"Get up." He stands a couple feet away as I struggle to my feet, then slips behind me and grabs the chain connecting the handcuffs. "Walk to the cabin."

The inside of the cabin is lit by a hissing propane lantern casting an intensely bright white light. I squint and duck my head, and have to keep my face pointed down—it's too bright to look anywhere near the lamp. The door closes behind me; I walk slowly and uncertainly since I don't know where he wants me to go. I raise my eyes a little and, squinting hard, look around. What I can see looks rough, dirty, and primitive except for a surreal brightly-colored child's swimming pool, mostly blue with lime green fish, a purple octopus, and an orange starfish imprinted on the rigid plastic sides.

"Go sit in the white chair."

I don't see a chair, but a moment later it comes into my squinty field of view—one of those molded chairs that are all one piece of plastic, sitting in the pool and near the log wall in front of me. I step into the otherwise empty wading pool and cross to the chair, then sit bent forward with my cuffed hands between me and the chair back.

"Not like that you imbecile." He doesn't shout, but his voice is exasperated angry. He steps quickly up to me, grabs my left wrist, and yanks it up causing pain to burst in my shoulders while my upper body is pushed down onto my thighs. "Put your arms behind the chair you stupid bitch!" He yanks back now, sitting me up straight, my arms hooked over the chair back. I feel a cold, heavy chain brush my arm, then the weight of it on the smaller chain connecting the handcuffs. More tugging, then a metallic click. He steps away and walks across the room.

My fingers reach out: the heavier chain is closed into a loop by a big padlock, and passes through a metal ring embedded in one of the massive logs that make up the wall. I'm left with only a few inches of movement in my hands and arms. My legs are free, but because of the height of the eyebolt and the short length of the chains, it would be impossible for me to stand up completely, even if the chair weren't in my way. Flashphaler didn't seem to do anything to lock the front door; I wonder how long it'll be before MacIlwane bursts in. *Any minute now.*

Flashphaler carries a straight-back wooden chair and sets it just outside the wading pool and to my right, then sits backward in it, straddling the narrow back rest with his legs and facing me. He says nothing, but stares at me silently. I don't look directly at him. Instead I try to stare straight ahead, but the light's glare still hurts my eyes, which aren't adjusting for some reason. Squinting hard, I shift my eyes and scan my surroundings. The cabin consists of a single sparsely-furnished room. I smell the gradual decay of wood over a long time in an enclosed space. Opposite me, against another wall, is a dusty, old-looking cast iron wood stove, its gray metal chimney going straight up then angling back and out the wall through a metal plate caulked with something. It's chilly in here, especially for me in this stupid dress, but I don't even see any firewood. Flashphaler is on my right, so I shift my eyes left. I'm not comfortable turning my head away from him, so I can't look directly at the door we entered by. I can see a window though, and in it a reflection of the opposite side of the room, where I think I see a sort of kitchen area with a wash basin, a long, low table against the wall, and a set of cupboards. I wonder if Mac is right outside, looking through the window, preparing to burst in and arrest this bastard.

Flashphaler continues to stare silently at me. *What the hell is MacIlwane waiting for? I'm tied up, aren't I? This is at least kidnapping. And what is this son of a bitch doing?* Not that I want him to do anything, but the staring is disturbing. I begin staring too, at the wood stove.

He stares for maybe another minute, then stands. "Would you like a mint?" he asks, producing a roll of candies from his pants pocket.

"No thanks."

He puts one in his mouth and starts making sucking and smacking noises. Staying close, he steps into the wading pool and circles around me. The wet sounds his mouth makes with the mint grate on me, but I keep my face neutral, empty.

When he's on my left side, he bends over and puts his mouth inches from my ear. "You're mine now."

More nasty sounds, close enough now I can smell the mint.

"I'm going to do whatever I want to you," he continues quietly, not whispering, but very low and close as if telling me some intimate secret. "The rest of your life is mine. *You're* mine—my property. It's hard for me to describe what a rush this is. I've had other women, killed them. That's a kind of power—power over their bodies and their lives at least, but it was always too short-lived. I had to sneak around to do what I wanted; it was demeaning. With you it's gonna be different. I'm gonna take my time, and my control of you will be total. By the time we're done here, I'll own you right to your core, through and through. You're as dependent on me now as the rabbits I keep at home. To them, I'm God. Now I'm *your* God. I bring life in the form of food, shelter, protection from other predators. And I bring death. Sometimes I'm merciful and death is quick. Sometimes it's slow and painful. I cut the hind legs off a rabbit once, then cauterized the wounds with a soldering iron so I could keep it alive. I roasted the legs, ate them in front of the double amputee as he sat in a pan on my table." Out of the corner of my eye I see him shrug. "Sometimes God is cruel—in that respect I'm no different from the God in the Bible.

"Rabbits, by the way, sound like children when they scream—I'll bet you didn't know that. It lived a day and a half after losing its legs. I wonder how long you would last in that situation? Maybe we'll get to find out."

Still bent close to me, his hands on his thighs, he drops his head momentarily and laughs a little, then looks back up at me. "Do you believe in God, Shailene?" His mouth, still close to my ear, makes noises with the mint while he waits.

I say nothing, considering my answer and deciding I'm not interested in a theological discussion with this bastard.

"Answer me." There's an edge in his voice, a threat.

"Yes." The answer surprises me, but I guess it's true.

"Really? So does he hate you or what?" Flashphaler laughs quietly again, then still smiling continues, "No, just kidding.   But seriously, where is he now?   Why doesn't he stop someone like me?"

"I didn't say he was good," I mutter.

"What?"

Oh shit, just shut the fuck up Shailene, I think, worried what I said will set him off, and wondering *again* where the fuck MacIlwane that son of a bitch is.

"Oh, hah!" He laughs again and straightens up. "I like that, so I'll let it slide, but you're wrong. I *told* you: *I'm God.*"

Or maybe not so wrong, I think, this time managing to keep my mouth shut.

"Look, I'm not delusional," he goes on, turning and stepping in front of me, then facing me again, gesturing as he speaks. "I'm not saying I'm the creator of the universe. He doesn't exist, or if he did, he's long gone now, abandoned us—abandoned you especially. I'm my own God. That's why I'm standing here and you're chained to the wall. But don't feel too bad; most people don't get it. Ever. I do: I'm God to me and, because of that, now I'm God to you. From now on you have to look to me for comfort and to keep you alive. You'll also get suffering and, eventually, death. By then you'll be praying to me for death, and when I'm ready, I'll answer your prayer. That's more than your God does. I really do hear your prayers, and sometimes I'll answer them." He stares at my face.

I keep squinting at the stove behind and to the right of him. For some reason my eyes still aren't adjusting to the light. Must be a side effect of whatever he used to knock me out.

"Do you want to pray to me now?"

"No."

I can see his broad, leering smile in my peripheral vision. "You will." He crunches the mint with his teeth, then turns and walks away. When he gets outside the kiddie pool again, he turns back toward me. "Do you need to use the bathroom?"

I hadn't thought of this, but as soon as he mentions it I become aware of pressure in my bladder. Then I think of my contingency plan, and admit the horrific possibility: maybe something has gone wrong with MacIlwane and he's not gonna show, and I'm all alone with this motherfucker and *fucking shackled to the fucking wall*. Maybe this is my chance and I have to take it. "Yes," I reply, my throat constricting behind the words.

"If you pray to me, I might take you to the outhouse."

For a second or two I actually consider it. *Fuck that*, I think. I'm not desperate enough yet to consent to mental rape.

"Or you can stay right where you are. That's why you're in the pool."

Bastard. "I can wait."

"How long?"

It won't be long, I think. *Mac's probably watching us now, just waiting for him to drop his guard or step outside or touch me.* Apparently soiling myself is part of the bastard's program, but he's going to be really disappointed.

He walks around the outside of the pool then steps in and approaches me from the left, putting his face very close to the side of my head. I hear him inhale deeply through his nose. "I can smell your fear," he whispers, so close I can feel his breath on my ear. "You smell good, but beneath the scent you chose to put on is the stench of fear. It's subtle now, but by tomorrow it'll fill the cabin. I love that smell." As he whispers these last, his lips actually graze the skin on my ear. I want to flinch away, but I hold steady.

"As much as I want to, I'm not even going to touch you tonight. I'm just going to think about you, about what I'm going to do to you. I really am in Atlanta for a trade show, but, like you, I've taken several days off after the trade show, and I'll be spending all that time with you. For now I'll savor the anticipation. I bet you will too." I feel his lips and the tip of his nose touch my cheek, the sensation light and lingering as he holds the kiss.

I close my eyes and imagine myself at home in my apartment, reading, safe, alone.

I hear his footsteps on the creaking wood floor; I open my eyes to slits. He's in the middle of the room now, fiddling with the lantern that's hanging there on a long chain. The light dims and goes out. There's a moment of complete darkness before his flashlight comes on and he walks out of the cabin, closing the door behind him and making my blindness total again.

I listen for the sound of MacIlwane's voice, or maybe just Flashphaler getting tackled. Even a gunshot. A couple seconds tick by. He secures the door with the padlock.

The silence stretches out and the sick feeling in me grows. *C'mon...c'mon...*

After maybe half a minute I hear the bastard's SUV start up.

"Oh fuck no," I whisper. "MacIlwane, where the fuck are you?"

The sound of its engine recedes, and with it the pain of the sense.

Then it's almost completely silent, except for the little whispered "no's" coming from my throat: "No, no, no, *NO!*" I scream *NO!* over and over, dragging it out, screaming and pulling at the cuffs, chains, and eyebolt holding my arms. "MacIlwane you bastard!"

A sharp pain in my wrist focuses my attention and brings me back to reality: I'll break my wrists before I break any of the metal holding me. My fingers are slick; they must be covered in blood. *I'm doing his work for him.*

Maybe that's what he wants.

I take deep breaths, try to relax my neck and shoulders, but instead tense up even more.

Breathe in, hold, breathe out. I keep at it, finally get to the point I can let my shoulders drop a little. I loosen my neck, my jaw, my arms. I'm doing pretty well until I think of him coming back for me, and then I lose it again, only now it's sobbing instead of screaming.

"I promised this would never happen again," I say out loud, my voice cracking. "I *promised*. Oh *fuck*."

I wonder what he's going to do to me—

Stop. I keep mentally silent for a few seconds before the fear and self-loathing start again.

Stop. I keep silent a little longer, and this time, before the panic comes back, I speak, keeping my voice as steady and calm as I can. "OK, think: is there any way to get out of this?"

The cuffs are tight; they're not cutting off blood or feeling, but there's no way I can deform my hands enough to slip them out, even with the added lubrication of the blood from my chafed wrists. If I were really some kind of hero, I'd know how to pick the locks on the handcuffs or the padlock, but I don't, and wouldn't I need a wire or something for that anyway? If I could break the connection to the wall I could at least move around and get my hands in front of me—I know to sit and bring my bound wrists under my butt and legs. But the loop of chain and the lock closing it are even stronger than the handcuffs, and the padlock is definitely—check to be sure—yep, definitely locked. Which leaves the eyebolt screwed into the wall. Stretching my arms back, I can touch it, and it feels even thicker than the chain, and there's no gap where the circle of iron meets the threaded bolt, which is all the way into the wall, right up to the eye. Even if I had something to pass through the eye and use as a lever, I'm not in a position to turn it: I'd have to turn with it. Anyway, I can't reach anything to use for a lever. Finally, it's all so tight I can't move around much, or even stand up. The looped chain is too tight to even get a hand through it, or to change my distance from the wall.

I pull stupidly on my arms again, but the pain puts a quick stop to that. I really hurt my left wrist pulling on it before; I can't afford to fuck around with this anymore.

I consider trying to so completely ruin my left hand it would fit through the closed cuff, but I don't know how I would do that or if I could go through with it. Maybe, if I get desperate enough, but not yet.

I close my eyes and focus on my breathing again, keeping my brain quiet. When I'm basically calm I speak quietly: "OK, how do I fight him?"

My mind goes to the contingency plan. I didn't tell MacIlwane about it—he would've nixed it, saying it wasn't necessary and could be used against me or him. But his ass wasn't on the line, and now guess what—I need it. It's not much of a plan, not really a plan at all, but it might be a chance. I've got other resources too—teeth, for one thing, and some skills I've picked up along the way. The key is to be on the lookout for opportunities, or thinking of ways to make opportunities, either to get free or to really damage Flashphaler.

Thinking like this helps. *Practical.* I've got my history too. The Bad was a worse situation; I survived that and I'm better prepared and stronger now. I just have to be ready—alert and looking for my chance. "I can do this," I whisper.

I remember what made me strong the first time, during the Bad. I was basically dead already; I knew that. I knew I had nothing to lose. I was still scared, but not as much as I would've been if I thought I had a chance.

Dammit. The tears start again, rolling down my face. *Fuck it.* Maybe I'm dead, but I'm gonna hurt him as much as I can on the way out. "He drops his guard for just a second and I'm takin' him out with me."

Thirty-Eight

Flash leans forward, the plastic tray, laden with the crumbs and debris from his lunch, pushed away to make room for his elbows. He sips his soda and marvels at how awake he is given how little sleep he had the night before. Usually the day after his night out he feels exhausted, but now he feels jazzed.

No surprises there, since this time instead of being done the morning after, he's *just getting started*. The days ahead are so full of promise it almost makes him feel like crying. After he got back to his hotel room last night, he laid awake until dawn planning all the things he would do to her, and make her do. He rehearsed it in his mind, wondering how long he'd be able to make her last.

He made a shopping list while eating his room service breakfast that morning; he'll pick up what he needs at a Wal-Mart on the way to the cabin this evening. At the top of the list is a fresh set of clothing for her and a package of those pre-moistened convenience wipes so he can make her clean herself up for him. He hopes she hasn't shit herself because the smell would probably linger even after taking the pool outside. He pulls out his list and adds air freshener and, as an after thought, scented candles with a question mark after the words. He debated about bringing food for her and decided to just bring for himself and eat dinner in front of her. She should be pretty hungry by then. He'll give her some water because he wants to keep her alive, but delay the food for another day, then make her earn it. He smiles; the ideas just keep coming. This is, hands down, the best thing he's ever done, the happiest he's ever been. A bitch all his own, trapped in his world, existing only to please him. *This* is what he's been looking for his whole life. This is it.

Flash sees a world of possibility opening up in front of him.   Even his rules can change—no more waiting for business trips when he can grab women from anywhere around here and take them the cabin. Eventually, maybe he'll keep two bitches there, make them do things together, to each other. He feels his sex stir in his pants and, not wanting to walk out of a McDonald's with a huge bulge pressing against the front of his pants, he puts the idea aside.

Anyway, he needs to get back to the trade show so Richard can get some lunch. Flash stands and walks toward the exit, abandoning the tray on the table. Putting on the sales persona is the last thing in the world he wants to do right now. The thought of three more hours of making conversation with all those drones, especially the geeky ones, is almost physically sickening, and he wishes life came with fast forward and slow settings so he could make the time he spends on the different parts of his life match his priorities. He pushes through the door and out into the stunningly beautiful day. At his Cherokee he pauses, savoring the feel of sunlight on his face before getting in and driving off.

Back at the convention center, Flash drives into the underground garage, parks, and kills the engine. He breathes in the trace of her scent still lingering in his vehicle. One last time he closes his eyes and pictures her sitting in his cabin, chained to the wall, waiting for his return.

Erik opens his eyes, takes the exhibitor badge off the passenger seat, and clips it to the lapel of his suit jacket. He gets out and locks the Jeep, then takes the elevator to the main exhibit floor.

Thirty-Nine

Looking out the one window that isn't boarded over, I can see it's sunny outside. It's frustrating and weird to be looking at such a normal—even beautiful—spring day outside, while being chained to a wall and sitting in a puddle of piss. Inside the cabin, with most of the windows covered, the air doesn't seem to be getting much warmer, and the puddle, almost hot at first, didn't take long to chill. I sit as still as I can because every time I move even a little some part of the wet not warmed by my body finds its way through my dress and underwear to my ass. I tipped the chair and drained off some of the liquid, but almost lost my balance and my seat. As bad as this position is, and as painful as it's becoming, it'd be *really* bad without something to sit on. There's almost no way I would be able to set the chair up again, and without it I'd be lucky if I could kneel or maybe squat. That'd get really old after about ten minutes. So I move as little as possible, except for the shivering, waiting for the bastard to return.

I've given up waiting for MacIlwane. Well, not completely, but I haven't been able to come up with an explanation for his absence which also includes him still showing up to get me out of this jam we put me in. Either something happened to him or, for some reason, he decided to fuck me over. That's hard to believe, but I'm cursing the fucking son of a bitch anyway.

OK, stay in control, I think.

I tried to sleep for a while, though between the fear and the growing pain in my immobile body and filling bladder, that was pretty hopeless too. Sometime after the light first appeared among the trees outside the window, I finally let my pee go. It smelled at first, but now I barely notice the odor.

Where the fuck is MacIlwane, anyway?   I stop myself from going down that dead end again.   I wonder if things would have turned out differently had I been doing this on my own.   The Glock was out anyway if I were going to use myself as bait.   But would I have done that?   Or would I have just taken him out like the one in Philadelphia?

I automatically cringe at the memory.   Like Trenton, that was a first.   Trenton was the first time I had a chance to think about it before taking a life.   I've been over all the justifications and rationales, including the skinny little boy in his underwear that I saved.   I know I did right, but what happened in that apartment won't leave me.   Philadelphia took another piece off me.   That was the first time I killed based only on the sense's say-so—no corroborating evidence.   That was a line I never wanted to cross.   I know I did right—waiting for another innocent person to get killed was not an option.   But still…all this is chipping away at the difference between me and them.

So would I have acted without looking for confirmation with this one?   Now that I know I'm capable of it?

I'm shaking my head before I realize I've answered my question.   I'm not going to be like these guys, killing just because a feeling tells me to, unless I have to.   MacIlwane or not, I'd have tried to get the target to choose me as his victim, and I'd still be sitting here.   I might've worn my knife rig under the dress, if I could have concealed it, but then Flashphaler might have found it when he knocked me out, and then he'd be more on his guard around me.   Better for things to be the way they are, with him thinking I'm just another unsuspecting victim.   That gives me a resource: surprise.

My teeth start chattering again.   I let them run for a while, then clamp them shut and spend several minutes trying to warm up by tensing and relaxing my muscles and kicking my legs.   I look over the room again, wondering what significance some of the objects will take on for me in the next several days: the folding cot with the air mattress on it, the wood stove, the long table, the shovel and ax leaning in the corner...

I'm freaking myself out again. And being stupid. *I still have options*, I remind myself. He'll get here tonight, and when he does, I can tell him I need to use the outhouse he mentioned. I'll even pray to him for it if that's the game he wants. Anything to get off this wall. I review what I learned about anatomy in the close quarter combat courses I took at the Military Academy: where the big arteries are close to the surface, the locations of the tendons that operate the hands, the places to insert a blade for a quick kill, the ways to inflict large amounts of pain in a hurry. I visualize the different moves we were taught and imagine using them on him. I wargame out stuff he might do and how I can counter, and imagine what openings I should look for because when they come, they might only last a second and I'll have to be ready. I systematically search the room with my eyes, thinking about each item and how it might be useful. I memorize the locations of the more promising objects—the edged tools; the long handles; chains, rope, and wires. Doing all this makes me feel a little more in control, takes my mind off being cold and scared and puts me, at least mentally, on the attack. Better predator than prey.

After a long time, I let my head drop and close my eyes. I wonder if I'll have to pee again before he comes back. As thirsty as I am, at least the lack of water is slowing the production of urine. I'm even more glad that, so far, I have no need to shit. *That* would be truly...well, whatever.

What else can I do? Is there anything else I can do to prepare, to gain some advantage? I think about what he said to me, especially after he dropped his normal guy act. Obviously this is all about power to him—all that wacky shit about him being God, answering prayers. *And what was that about rabbits?* I guess he raises them so he has a ready supply of torture victims. *Nice. If I get out of here...* What I need to do, would do if I were a real action hero, is figure out some psychological vulnerability I could exploit, something I could say that would get him to break down in tears or get so angry he'd screw up and I'd be ready to escape or, better yet, take him down. I close my eyes and replay as much of what he said as I can remember, trying to come up with some brilliant scheme as I do. But I have no more knowledge of how to break someone mentally than I do of picking locks. I get that he wants power, and frankly he's got it now, at least as far as I'm concerned, chained up in this cabin in the middle of nowhere like I am.

But that doesn't make him God, right? Is a predator God to its prey when it's making the kill? Even if it is, it's one thing to be God-*like* and another to actually *be God*. God is both the predator *and* the victim; it's everything put together.

Yeah, well, whatever Harold is, it's not helping me now. I'm *the only one who can help me.*

Who am I kidding? Really, it's pretty hopeless. I close my eyes tightly. I know I can't afford to think this way, but honestly: the guy is really big and strong. He completely pinned me in the car when he put the chemical-soaked rag over my face: I couldn't move, much less do anything to fight back.

But the Bad was a hopeless situation too, and I found a way out. *That* son of a bitch has been dead since then, and I'm still here. This one, Flashphaler, can chain me up, he can hurt me, he can even—I'm shaking my head, but it's true—he can even violate me, but he can't control me. I can still choose my response, even if all I have to fight back with are my thoughts. And since I'm as good as dead already, I have nothing to lose by fighting him every step of the way.

Just like the Bad.

OK, but be smart about it. Fight, but fight smart.

The thing that's different now is the handcuffs, and that's probably not gonna change.

Or…maybe it will.

Maybe I do know something about this fucker's mental state that can help. His God thing means he's too confident—he thinks I'm powerless against him, thinks he's too strong to be vulnerable. He won't expect me to fight back in any serious way. Maybe there *will* be a chance to use the contingency plan, or some other means for counter-attack, if I can get him to take the cuffs off, or at least get him to fasten my hands in front of me.

How do I talk him into that?

I think about it a while, then I get it. He's got me in this kiddie pool to keep things neat. It's OK if I wet myself, but he wants to contain the mess. And if he wants me around for a while to do stuff to me, he probably doesn't want me covered in shit. Maybe, if I tell him I need to take a dump, which isn't hard to believe, he'll let me have my hands in front of me so I can clean myself better. *It* could *work, maybe… It's a chance, anyway.*

If all else fails, if he puts his hands on me, and there isn't anything else to try, I'll make it as difficult as possible for him. Maybe I can take a piece of him with me, or at least get him to finish me off faster and ruin his fun.

My chin wrinkles unexpectedly and I bow my head. A couple tears fall in my lap. *Shit. OK, let it out now, before he gets here. He won't see this.* I let the sobs shake me.

Forty

Flash engages the parking break and gets out of his Cherokee. He pauses, looking at the cabin, savoring the anticipation. *We'll have a simple, clean fuck tonight, before I start breaking her down. Plenty of time to get nasty later.* He opens the padlock, then hesitates, wondering how messed up she might be already and if she shit herself. He came prepared with a new dress for her, and the handy wipes or whatever they're called. The door swings open; a swath of evening daylight shows the scared face looking back at him. He sniffs: urine, fear, but no shit. *Good.*

He feels like he should say something, but maybe it's better to be silent anyway. It's dim in here, so he crosses the room, gets the matches, and lights the propane lamp.

She's trembling and her teeth are clamped together to prevent them from chattering. Her cheeks are streaked black with eye makeup. He smiles: there'll be a lot more tears over the next several days.

He brings the bags of groceries and supplies in, setting them on the rough table in the kitchen area. It's chilly; he'll get a fire going in the wood stove, but first he wants to get her to the outhouse and back before she stinks things up more than they already are. He takes the plastic canister of handy wipes from one of the grocery bags, then turns and looks at his prize. Her face really is a mess. "You look like a sad clown," he says, laughing a little. "I'll bet you're hungry too," he says, deliberately raising her expectations, "but let's get you cleaned up first. I can smell you pissed yourself." He says this gently, but leaves the words hanging in the air for emphasis. "Do you need to go again?" he asks like he would to a child.

She nods. "Yes sir."

Pleased with her respectful response, he walks around behind her, avoiding stepping in the wading pool. As he unlocks the chain, he notices the seeping rawness of her wrists and wishes he'd brought some rubbing alcohol with him. *Tomorrow.* He lets the ends of the chain fall banging against the log wall, then hangs the open padlock from the eyebolt as well. "Stand up," he commands.

She tilts sideways and rotates to get her bound arms around the chair's back, then gets to her feet, but her legs are obviously stiff and wobbly from the hours of enforced sitting. She stumbles, and for a bright moment he thinks she will fall in the small puddle of urine, but she regains her footing and stands.

"Well, c'mon—let's go. The *out*house is *out*side."

"Um, sir," she says quietly, "I, uh, I have to do more than pee. Can I—if I'm going to clean myself, can I have my hands in front of me sir?"

That's a good point, he thinks. He wants to do a lot of things to her, but wiping her ass isn't one, and having her all shitty and smelly isn't his thing. *Bloody, but not shitty.* "All right, sit down." She obeys. "Here's how we're gonna do it: I'm gonna unlock your left wrist. You will then place your left hand in your lap, clear?"

He watches the back of her head nod. "Yes sir."

"If you do anything before I tell you to, I'll punish you. Is that clear?"

"Yes sir," she says, nodding some more.

He notices how careful she is to call him "sir." One night in captivity and she's already breaking down and becoming submissive. He takes the handcuff keys out of his pocket and frees the chafed and inflamed left wrist, which she dutifully places in her lap. *Good girl.* He carries the right arm with attached cuffs around from behind her, stepping into the kiddie pool but carefully avoiding the urine. He squats the length of his arm from her. Still holding her right wrist, he looks at her, but she keeps her eyes down, staring at the floor between them. He re-fastens the left handcuff, then looks back at her: eyes are still down. He studies the streaked but still very pretty face, which is partly hidden behind her honey-colored hair, so he reaches out and pushes one side of it back behind her ear. She flinches a little, but otherwise doesn't react. Flash can't decide if she really has given up hope or still has some fight in her. He doesn't want her too docile, but she's so quiet... *She'd better not shut down on me.*

He tugs on the chain linking the handcuffs and she lets out a gasp. *I'll make her less quiet tonight. Out here, I can make her scream as much as I want.* He straightens up, pulling her up with him by the handcuffs. She stands quickly and he let's go of the chain, grabs her shoulder, and shoves her toward the door. "After you."

By the time they reach the outhouse she's walking normally. He pulls the door open. It's clean inside and he installed a new toilet seat a couple weeks ago when he was up here preparing. It doesn't smell bad thanks to the lime and baking soda he sprinkled after the last time he used it. "There you go—do what you need to do." Flash watches her step in, turn, and face him. She says nothing, but it's clear she's waiting for him to close the door. "Oh no. I get to watch. Now go 'head, take your nasty panties off and place them next to you on the bench. After you're done, I've got these for you to clean up with," he says, gesturing with the plastic canister.

She looks at him for a few more seconds, then slowly bends at the waist and reaches up under the front of her dress. Flash takes a step closer. It's twilight now and dim in the outhouse; he wishes he'd brought a flashlight so he could shine a beam on this performance. She looks up at him, hesitating, obviously wishing he would turn away or close the door. He does neither and says nothing: only smiles, enjoying her shame. He's about to tell her to not be embarrassed now since he'll have her stripped and spread in an hour or two, but suddenly she's lunging across the three or four feet between them, leading with her manacled fists.

This surprises Flash, but he was hoping she still had some fight in her. Instinctively he catches and stops her shoulders, but her fists continue, hitting on either side of his crotch. He's about to laugh at her missing his balls when suddenly sharp pain flares in the places her fists hit. He throws her back and to the side, sending her crashing into the outhouse bench, then moves in to discipline her. As he does, he is aware of pain at the tops of his legs, on either side of his pubic hair, but his focus is on her. He grabs a handful of her hair and pulls her toward him, but she jerks her head away, and he's holding a full head of hair minus the head. Confused, he looks from the hair to the head it came from, but she's coming at him again. She grabs his hip—the pocket on his jeans—with her hand and starts hammering her other fist into the same place as before, to the right of his groin. More sharp, stabbing pain erupts in the top of his leg.

"YAAAHH!" he yells, backing away, but he's just dragging her with him and she's doing something vicious to him down there. He beats at her with his fists, but the nearly bald head is pressed against his abdomen, the face pointed down toward the ground, so he's just hitting the hard bone on the back and top of her skull, and at an awkward angle. He pounds the back of her neck and she starts to separate from his body, but she's still doing something he can't see to the top of his leg and it hurts like hell. Desperate, he grabs her neck and, squeezing hard, he lifts and pushes her. This gets her and she finally lets go, but even as he's throwing her back she gets one more blow in to his crotch and a new center of pain bursts at the root of his cock. "You fucking bitch!" he screams as she lands on the ground a few feet away. He looks down at his leg and sees his pant leg plastered against his thigh, warm and wet. *Blood?* he thinks, then looks up in time to see her scrambling to her feet.

He lunges at her, but she's already sprinting around him. There's no way she could outrun him, but she's small and agile, and instead of taking off down the dirt driveway she heads for the cabin. *Even better*, he thinks, reversing direction as quickly as he can. He feels dizzy for a second, then runs after her. His right sneaker makes a squelching sound as he runs, like it's full of water. The door to the cabin slams shut behind her, but a couple more steps and he grabs the handle and pushes through, just in time to see her pivot and run across the room at him, the shovel leveled like a spear.

Instinctively he steps aside and tries to deflect the weapon with his hands, but she adjusts and the metal blade is too fast and thin for him to get a grip on it. Instead, it pushes through his hands and the point of the metal blade hits just above his groin, driving him back out into the yard. The pain from his gut makes him feel sick, but he grabs the shovel's handle, gets the blade away from his body, and pulls hard. Instead of getting it away from her, though, she hangs on and he gets her with it, stumbling forward over her feet. His at last, he slams a fist into the side of her face, sending her sprawling.

She stays down, and Flash sees he finally got a good shot in: she's stunned. He spins the shovel around, and his head seems to spin with it for a second, but then he's OK again and steps toward her.

She looks sideways at him. Straightening her arms, she pushes herself up and pulls her knees under her, but she's moving slowly.

Gotta end this, he thinks, feeling a little sick. He adjusts his grip on the shovel, but his head feels light again, and the ground moves under his feet. He stops to get his balance. It's dark—*is it night already?* He refocuses on her, but she's moving, gathering herself to run away. He swings the shovel back. *Make her pay.*

Forty-One

The shovel goes up; I scream and launch myself at him, staying low and driving hard as I can with my legs, terror and rage making me faster and stronger. I get inside the arc in time to avoid the shovel blade, but his arms push me lower, so my head impacts about the same place I hit him with the shovel when I had it. I'm too small to knock him over with sheer force, but I grab one of his legs with my hands and he goes down backwards. I go with him, but I'm on top.

It's hard with my hands chained together, but I pump my legs and throw myself up his body. I don't know if I get a knee in his groin on my way, but I do get an elbow in his solar plexus and hear him gasp. He grabs my neck, but my fists are joined, making a wedge out of my forearms, and I hammer the wedge through, breaking his grip and connecting with his chin.

I scramble higher on his body and send both my hands out in another punch. The heel of one of them hits the point of his nose, but the punch is too weak and poorly-focused to break anything and send it back into his brain. Still, I keep the chain across his face and push, tilting his head back to expose his vibrating Adam's apple. Aiming just below it, mouth wide open, I turn my head and dive at his neck.

I bite, deep and hard as I can.

Forty-Two

Mac spots the next dirt track coming off the unpaved road and hits the brake while spinning the steering wheel on the rental car. He turns too far, but corrects before plowing into the woods. *OK, stay controlled*, he thinks, repressing the anxiety that's been building with each of the last three offshoots he's explored.

He presses the accelerator and drives fast up the hill, then eases off as the slope flattens out. The path turns, and suddenly the beams from the headlights show Flashphaler's dark green Jeep Cherokee with its South Carolina plate. Mac slams the brakes and shoves the transmission into park, then jumps out and crouches between the open door and the body of the car, drawing his weapon and scanning for the big man.

The lights from the rental car reveal a cleared area covered with pine straw. To one side is the SUV and a cabin, light spilling from its open door, to the other side a small shed, its door also op—

There's a body lying in the center of the clearing, and for a fraction of a second Mac suspects the worst until his brain registers the size of it and the same flannel shirt, jeans, and athletic shoes he saw Flashphaler wearing when he left his hotel in Atlanta earlier in the evening. Both arms up holding his Beretta, Mac moves forward, swinging his weapon left to the cabin, right to the shed, then to the woods beyond the clearing in front of him, then to the prone, motionless man at his feet.

There's something wrong with the head—Mac quickly scans—shed, cabin, woods—then looks back. "Holy shit," he breathes quietly. The head—Flashphaler's head—is separated from the rest, rolled to the side over the body's left shoulder.

Mac looks up at the open cabin door, into the lighted interior again, but still sees no one inside. "Sh—Shailene? Shailene?!" He scans the wood line, glances into the shed, which he now sees is an outhouse.

"MacIlwane?!" The voice—her voice, from somewhere in the woods in front of him—sounds panicked. "Is that you?!"

"Yeah! What are you doing?"

"Put your weapon away! He's dead."

"Yeah, I can see that."

"So put it away!"

"OK," he says, but keeps his weapon up, feeling uneasy because of the way she sounds. "But why? Are you all right? Why are you in the woods?"

"Just holster your gun damn it! I'm pretty fuckin' freaked right now, and I need you to do this."

"OK!" He puts the Beretta in its holster.

"And—and sit down."

"What?!"

"Just do it! You fucking owe me man! Just sit down!"

"OK, OK!" He slowly folds his legs, all the pains up and down his body from the car accident becoming noticeable again.

After he's sitting down, she steps out of the shadows of the woods, an ax in her hands.

Mac suppresses his instinct to go for his gun. "Shailene?"

She stops several feet away and stands looking at him. "I just—I just need to be in control here." He notices the wig is gone, and there's blood on her chin, her hands, arms, the dress—pretty much all over her.

"OK, I get it; *I* just want to make sure we're still on the same side."

"Where the hell were you?!" she screams, her voice breaking with the emotion.

"I'm sorry—I can't tell you *how* sorry, or how glad I am you're all right."

"I'm *not* all right!" she screams again. Her voice starts to break, on the verge of sobbing. "I'm *not* fucking all right! Where were you?!" Where it's not blood-stained or streaked with dirt, her face, contorted with rage, is almost red.

"I'm sorry—I got in a car accident—someone ran a red and plowed into me." Mac doesn't point out the neck brace and the gauze and tape on his head, but hopes they're obvious. Still looking at all the blood on her he asks, "Where are you hurt? If you let me get—"

"Augh!" she yells, the wail sounding strangled as she throws down the ax.

Mac starts to get to his feet.

"Stay down!" she shouts, then more quietly, "Just…just stay down for now, OK?"

"OK."

"Do you—" she raises her wrists, still joined by handcuffs. "Do you have a key to open these?"

"Yeah," he says, reaching in his pants pocket and taking out his keys.

"Toss 'em to me."

She doesn't try to catch them, instead letting them land on the pine needles at her feet, then squatting down to get them. The bunch of keys jingle softly and the little handcuff key makes a tapping sound as her shaking hands try to fit it into the lock. "Shit," she mutters.

"You want me to do it?"

"No!" she says sharply. "No, I got it." She rocks back and plants her butt on the pine needles. Bracing her elbows on her knees, she takes a deep breath and concentrates.

Mac looks over at the dead body and notices its right pant leg is soaking wet. His first thought is urine from the postmortem sphincter release, but the entire pant leg all the way down to the athletic shoe is wet and clinging.

After a few more metallic taps there's a click and the cuff releases. She passes the key to her left hand and starts working on the other cuff.

As she does, Mac notices the raw wound encircling her wrist. "Shailene, I am really sorry…"

There's a click and she rips the other cuff off and flings it against the wall of the cabin. She inspects the damage to her wrists.

Mac does too: they look bad. "Shailene, let me help you."

Her eyes snap up, fixing him with a glare. Without taking her eyes off his face, she stands and tosses his keys on the ground in front of him. "Tell me again what happened, from when I left the club with him."

"I followed you to the garage—took off my tie and put on a cap while you were listening to the jazz trio so he wouldn't recognize me as the guy who followed him out of the garage earlier. I saw him put you in the car, heard him get in. I got into my car, then waited for you guys to pull out."

"Yeah, that's when he was knocking me out."

"He hit you?"

"No, something on a rag, some kind of chemical."

Chloroform probably, Mac thinks. "I wondered why the delay, but figured you were just talking. When he pulled out I followed, but he went through a light just after it turned red, and I couldn't follow because the cross traffic was already in the intersection when I got to it. Even with the tracking device, I knew he was probably getting on the highway and I didn't want him to get too far ahead and lose him, so as soon as I got the green again I was going. That's when some idiot trying to beat the light slammed into me. I should've been more careful, but—well, I wasn't. Next thing I know I'm waking up in a hospital bed. I can't tell you how scared I was then."

"Probably almost as scared as I was when I woke up in his car on the highway, or when I was chained up in the cabin and realized you weren't going to show up," she says sarcastically.

"All right! How many times do you want me to apologize? I'm sorry I wasn't more careful!"

"Yeah, and how 'bout 'sorry I didn't trust you to begin with, Shailene, and get some more people from the FBI to help us out'? How 'bout that?"

"OK, yes, I'm sorry about that too," he says quietly.

She's quiet for several seconds, then "OK."

"I know it sounds ridiculous compared to what you've been through, but I really was freaked when I woke up in the hospital this morning. There was about two seconds of disorientation, and then it hit me all at once, like the ceiling falling in on me. The first thing I did after I left the hospital was go to your hotel room. I've never wanted and not wanted to do something so badly as open that door. After that, I was hoping he was keeping you alive somewhere, but I really didn't know. Following him was the only chance I had to find out. The tracking receiver was broken in the accident—my car was totaled. I rented that car," he gestures back over his shoulder, "and found him at the convention center, followed him from there. It was still daylight when he turned on to the dirt road coming in here, so I had to drop way back so he wouldn't notice me. I was worried if he thought he was being followed he might not come to you, and he was the only way I could find you. Then I didn't know where he turned off this road and I had to check each branch. That's why there was a delay between his arrival and mine."

She stands there looking down at him for a while, saying nothing. Finally, "OK, help me clean up here."

Forty-Three

"I'm open to suggestions," I say turning toward the body and seeing the shovel. "I'm exhausted, and I just want to get this cleaned up so no one can connect it to me." I step over the body and pick up the shovel. "You have any good ideas about how to do that, let me know. I figured I'd start by burying the body." I look back and see him painfully getting to his feet. "Can you help dig?"

He nods. "Yeah, but what about you? Where are you bleeding from?"

"Huh?" I look down at myself in the glare from the headlights. The dress, my hands, one of my knees—they're all red with blood. But except for my wrists, which kind of sting, and my head, which aches, I'm fairly pain free. Especially my scar—that's not hurting at all. I look back up at him. "I think it's mostly his blood. Except for my wrists, my skin is intact."

"Well here's a suggestion: Why don't we start by cleaning his blood off you and maybe seeing if there are some clean, warm clothes you can wear in there."

He's right; as soon as he says it, I want to clean the blood off me. And it is chilly. I remember the canister of wipes the target had been carrying when he took me to the outhouse. *How long ago was that?* It must have only been like twenty minutes—less maybe. Incredible. Still carrying the shovel, I walk to the shitter and find the white plastic canister laying on the ground. I cross the yard to the cabin, leaving the door open. MacIlwane follows me in.

"Maybe you can get a fire going in the woodstove," I say, thinking both of warmth and the impending need to burn things like the ax and shovel handles. "He brought those bags over there—maybe there's matches and stuff, and clothes, in them."

While MacIlwane goes through the bags, I go to the wooden chair the bastard sat in last night and set the canister and shovel down, then start wiping at my arms and legs with the little pre-moistened towelettes. It takes a while, but in that time MacIlwane drapes a clean dress and new underwear for me over the chair, and starts a fire with some wood he found outside.

He walks over again. "You've got blood on your face— you want me to clean it off for you?"

"No. Thanks for the dress. I don't suppose you have a jacket or sweater or something I could borrow in your car?"

"Here, take my jacket," he says, taking off the brown leather jacket he has on.

"No, that's OK," I say, feeling a little guilty for taking his coat.

"Shailene, seriously, take it. The rest of my clothes are a lot warmer than that dress; if either of us should have the jacket, it's you."

I look at the face I wanted to see so badly, then cursed so hatefully. Broad, rounded features on a lean face the color of dark chocolate. His dark eyes hold mine, and it's obvious he wants me to take the jacket. "Thanks. Give me a minute to change? I'll meet you outside."

"Sure. Don't forget to wash your face."

"OK."

"And bring the lantern with you when you come out— we'll need it to dig." He takes the shovel and leaves, closing the door behind him.

I wipe at my face and look at the nasty black and red combination of old makeup and fresh blood. I throw down the wipe and take another, and keep at it until the wipe comes away clean. I pull the old dress over my head and pull on the new one—a minimal piece of work in light blue, with spaghetti shoulder straps.   I'm really glad I borrowed MacIlwane's jacket, because this thing is giving me no insulation. The new underwear feels like a miracle. I wish I could change my shoes, but at least the ones I chose were flats instead of heels, so they're wearable. I zip up the jacket, then carry the bloody dress, pee-stained panties, and used wipes to the stove and throw them in, along with another couple sticks of wood. The warmth feels great, but I'm thirsty and I need to get going. I pull myself away, find a bottle of water in the grocery bags, and take several long drinks from it. I'm about to leave when I remember to look for the little push blade— half my contingency plan—that I dropped in here when I went for the shovel. I find it on the floor by the wall and pick it up. The one-inch serrated blade and rubber-covered T-handle are still sticky and red with his blood. I look at the little weapon that most likely was essential to me still being alive now, and think about keeping it. But it's a mess, and I don't want to carry his filth away from here. There's enough of that inscribed in my brain that I can't leave behind. Instead, I chuck the blade in the woodstove, throw in another stick for good measure, then carry the lantern outside.

The headlights are off, but I see a flashlight several yards off in the woods and go to it. MacIlwane is already digging. He looks up when I come near.

"Once we get through these roots, the digging should be easier he says."

We take turns—he digs, then I chop roots with the ax. After that the digging does go easier, but we're both pretty beat, so we quit when the hole's about three feet deep but not nearly long enough.

Before we use the ax to chop the body up into pieces that'll fit, I get the bastard's wallet.

"What are you doing?" MacIlwane asks.

I go through it until I find what I was looking for: "Driver's license. I'll burn the rest in the stove."

"What do you want with that?"

"Remind me—I'll explain later." I look and, luckily, also find the other push blade still lodged in the fabric of his jeans at the top of his leg. It takes some wiggling around, but I manage to get it back out through the slit it made in the denim.

"What's that?" MacIlwane asks.

"My backup plan." I display the small weapon in the palm of my hand. "I had this and its twin taped to the insides of my thighs up near my crotch. He thought I was reaching up to take my underwear off. He was wrong."

MacIlwane looks down at the body. "Looks like you went for his femoral arteries."

"Yeah. I think I missed with this one, but I was able to keep sawing with the other blade. Fortunately, I opened the artery on that side, judging from all the blood on that leg."

"Good thinking. Those blades weren't much to work with, but you figured out how to make them count."

I shrug. "I'm big on survival."

After the grave's filled in, we pack down the earth, scatter the leftover dirt as best we can, and distribute leaves and pine needles so it's not as obvious we've been digging there.

Back in the cabin we burn the tools, including the other push blade, and his wallet, and other stuff MacIlwane or I might have touched. I get my wig from the outhouse and my purse from the SUV, and they both go to the flames. The chair I was in is too big to burn, and too smooth and flexible to chop up with the ax, so we just wipe it down thoroughly, then drag it and the wading pool outside to let the weather at them.

"All right, almost there. All that's left is his truck," MacIlwane finally declares.

"What do we do with that?"

"Atlanta airport—long-term parking. We'll remove your trace once we get it there."

Forty-Four

About six a.m. I knock gently on MacIlwane's door. I wait maybe a minute and start to knock again when the door opens part way, revealing his haggard, unshaven face. "You look terrible," I say.

"Thanks. You wouldn't win any prizes either. How's your face? It looks painful."

I shrug. "It's not throbbing like it was last night, but the bruises are more colorful now, aren't they?" I shrug again. "I've had worse."

He looks at me for a beat, then says, "Give me a minute—I'm still trying to pull my pants on." He closes the door.

I look up and down the hall: still deserted. The door opens again, this time wider and MacIlwane, wearing jeans and a Newport Jazz Festival T-shirt, motions me in.

"How are you doing?" I ask.

"Really, really stiff. Everything hurts," he says, closing the door. "How 'bout you?"

"I'm all right," I say, not mentioning the nightmares. "Are you gonna be able to drive?"

He nods. "Yeah, I'll be all right. We really should get going. You all packed yet?"

I nod. "You?"

He shakes his head. "No, but it won't take me long."

After checking out, we decide to not stop for food until we make it across the state line into South Carolina. As far as we know we're not running from anyone, but we both want to put some distance between us and the dismembered body buried in the woods. It's a hungry hour and a half before we take an exit and stop in a little town just off the highway. Along the one main street there are a couple fast food franchises, but we choose a little restaurant in an old brick-front building. Inside it's small but bright and clean-looking, and about half the ten tables and booths are occupied. A waitress comes over and noticeably breaks stride as she draws near and gets a look at us.

"You here for breakfast?" she asks uncertainly.

I suddenly remember MacIlwane and I are different colors and genders in the rural southeast, and wonder if this is going to turn into some race thing. *I'm too tired to deal with this.*

"Yes," he says, a slight edge in his voice.

She doesn't look happy about it, but she says "OK...right this way." She leads us to the booth in the back corner by the kitchen door.

I'm embarrassed but say nothing, just reach for a menu.

"I don't think we're their preferred clientele," he says.

I meet his eyes. "Yeah, guess not; I'm sorry."

"Not your fault." He smiles a little at me. "Of course, it's almost like we're going out of our way to tweak them. Black man with a white woman, I look like I was in a bar fight, you look like a lesbian, and she probably figures *I* gave you that black eye."

I feel the smile spread across my mouth, and a short laugh escapes.

MacIlwane's smile broadens. "I didn't think you *could* laugh."

"It happens," I say. Suddenly, for no reason I can think of, I feel like crying. *Exhaustion,* I tell myself, swallowing hard and getting myself under control before MacIlwane notices. I examine the menu. "Damn, what I wouldn't give for a couple big veggie burgers now," I say, but even if it were lunch time, I doubt this place would have anything like that. My stomach growls loud enough for Mac to hear.

"Whoa—that's scary. Why don't you get the pancakes?"

"Nah—pancakes are made with eggs."

"And? You don't eat eggs?"

I glance up at him. "You really want to hear this?"

"About the eggs?"

"Yeah."

"Go ahead—surprise me."

"Most eggs in this country are laid by hens packed so tightly into cages they can't even open their wings. They have to cut the beaks off 'em because the constant extreme crowding makes them violent toward their fellow birds. So I don't eat eggs unless I know they're from hens which aren't kept in cages. Sorry—I don't mean to weird you out or anything, but you asked. Anyway, there's other stuff I can get—I'm hungry, but I'll be fine."

"You know, Shailene, I think you've earned a pass, at least for one meal."

I shrug and close the menu. "So," I begin a little uncertainly, "I notice I'm not 'Ms. Campbell,' to you anymore."

He meets my eyes and looks serious. "I'm sorry, I don't mean to be disrespectful—"

I wave dismissively, interrupting him. "No, no, that's not what I meant."

"It just seemed overly formal, given the circumstances."

"I agree, but that means I get to call you Silas, right?"

He smiles and looks down. "Only my mom calls me that. Everyone else calls me Mac."

"OK Mac," I say, reaching my hand out across the table to shake. "Thanks for coming looking for me last night." It feels right and awkward and hokey all at the same time, but he grasps my hand.

"I still feel bad—"

"It wasn't your fault. The main thing is you came back for me."

"There wasn't much for me to do when I got there."

"It's the thought that counts. But let's not talk about this anymore."

"OK. So, I'm curious: How did you survive in the Army as a vegan? What did you eat?"

"I made my own food whenever I could, but sometimes I just had to be flexible or go hungry. West Point was harder than the Army—I ate a lot of peanut butter sandwiches there—but it was never easy, obviously. That's one of the reasons I got out. How 'bout you?"

"I kind of liked the food, even the field rations."

"No, I mean, you weren't in long enough to retire—you're not old enough to have done that and be where you are in the FBI, are you?"

He sort of half smiles. "Is that a compliment?"

"No, it's a question."

The smile fades and he looks down. "Yeah, well, I felt like I wasn't where I should have been, like I was protecting the wrong people, doing what I did."

"You mean in Special Forces?"

He nods. "I ended up doing a lot of covert stuff, sometimes hurting people, sometimes protecting them, but I realized it was the wrong people either way."

The waitress comes to the table, looking like she has to clean up vomit. "Anything to drink?"

We both order black coffee and orange juice, then I add, "Actually, I'm ready to order now." I look over at Mac to see if he agrees.

"Can I ask you a question?" Mac asks.

She turns her head toward him, looking wary.

"The eggs here—were they laid by hens in cages?"

"What?"

"Never mind," I jump in. "I'd just like to get some side dishes—a couple orders of home fries, a couple orders of grits, and an order of toast."

She writes on her pad, then looks back at Mac.

"I'll have the tall stack of pancakes, but hold the meat," he says.

"No meat?"

"No, just the pancakes, and a side of home fries."

She raises her eyebrows and tips her head to the side as she jots this on her pad before heading to the kitchen.

"You don't have to be a vegetarian when you eat with me—I won't be offended," I say, putting my menu behind the napkin dispenser.

Mac shrugs. "I should probably cut back on that stuff anyway. Doctor says I need to watch my sodium intake and cholesterol."

We're both quiet. I stare past Mac at the window and the sunny morning outside, the occasional person or two walking by on the sidewalk, and start to feel weepy again. *Snap out of it.* Soon the waitress is back with the beverages. I drink about half the glass of OJ right away.

"So, listen, don't take this the wrong way," he says, "but if you want to crash at my place on your way home, there's room on my couch." Mac looks up from his cup of coffee, his face neutral. "Seriously. It's a long drive back to Boston from here," he says.

"Your wife won't mind?"

He compresses his lips for a second. "OK, again don't get the wrong idea, but my wife was killed thirteen years ago."

"I'm sorry," I say, automatically looking down at his left hand and confirming the gold band on the ring finger there.

He must notice because he gestures with that hand. "I'm still married. Maybe not legally, but," he taps his chest, "in here, where it counts. That's what I mean—when I say you can crash at my place, it's just that—a place to sleep, and breakfast before you start driving again."

I feel a little awkward, and look down.

"Even if I weren't married, you're not my type anyway—too short and pale."

I look up and see him smiling. I smile back, believing him, but the question is moot. "Actually, I'm not going home just yet."

Mac raises an eyebrow.

"The night he kidnapped me, after he chained me up, he talked at me for a while. Told me I would be like the rabbits he kept at home: completely at his mercy. Said he was like God to them, and they lived and died at his whim. Some he killed quickly, some he tortured, just like God. All the power over their world was with him, and he said it would be the same for me.

"But now *I* get to be God, and I'm gonna take those rabbits to an animal sanctuary out in Utah. It's a no-kill place, not like most local shelters, and they take great care of their animals."

"That why you wanted his driver's license? For his address?"

I nod. "You want to help me load them up tonight?"

He hesitates.

"I'm sorry," I say, suddenly realizing what I'm asking. "I'm not thinking—you must still be in pain, and can't take anything strong for it until you get home."

"I'm in."

I shake my head. "No, really—I'm so focused on this I honestly—"

"I'm in. I want to do it." The way he says it leaves no room for debate.

I look at him, then nod. "OK, thanks."

We're both quiet, staring into our coffees and OJ's. I think about what he said, debate with myself, and finally give in to my curiosity. "So, your wife—I don't mean to pry, but is that what you meant about protecting the wrong people?"

He looks up, a little startled. "I—let's not talk about that."

"Sorry."

"It's OK, just..." His voice trails off.

I wish I could take my question back.

"Why don't you tell me about what he said to you in the cabin," he suggests. "I usually interview these subjects when I can, to try to learn more about what makes them go."

"OK, well, like I said, he seemed to have this thing where he imagined himself as God. That was his main point."

"He actually told you he was God?"

"Well, yeah, but not in an insane way. What he said was he was God *to me*. And to the rabbits, and the women he killed. He knew he wasn't *God*, in an absolute sense, but more 'God' in relative terms. But he also said there was no God beyond him."

Mac nods. "It's funny, this being human," he says. "We all know—well most of us know—that we're pretty limited. Our bodies are only so strong, we only live so long, we're vulnerable, fearful, weak. And yet, we want to be so much more. I mean, obviously this guy was an extreme example—"

The waitress shows up with our food and Mac pauses while she places the dishes on the table.

"Thank you," he says.

"Um-hm," she replies quietly, then beats a hasty retreat.

We eat eagerly, silently for several minutes, before I remember Mac was interrupted. "So, what were you saying?"

"I don't know—what was I saying?"

"We were talking about...him, about what he said to me." Although no one is sitting near us, I avoid the name, as Mac has, not wanting to be overheard speaking it. "You started to say something about his God comments."

Mac chews thoughtfully, swallows, thinks some more. "Oh—just that as humans we're set up right from the start for struggle and frustration—we know we have limits, but we want to exceed them, either by being more powerful or more significant or longer-lived. Some try to resolve the situation by imposing their will. Others see the answer as being part of something bigger, like a cause or a family or a nation. Some combine the two. Whatever we do, it comes back to this conflict between our limits and our desire to exceed them, but it's more subtle in most of us. What's interesting about this guy, what you told me about him, is how naked this drive to transcend himself was. Most people have kids or go into politics or create art. This guy needed to experience power simply and directly, by torturing and killing, but I think at its core the dynamic is the same: limited humanity aspiring to the limitless."

"You make it sound so noble. Let me tell you, his intentions were anything but."

"Sorry—I didn't mean it that way. It can be noble, I guess, though that's a tricky, much-abused word. What I'm trying to say is the tension between what we are and what we long to be is typical of humans, but it gets expressed differently with each of us."

I'm still uncomfortable with the idea of any commonality between me and these monsters, but then something clicks into place.

"Look, I'll shut up—it's obviously coming out wrong," Mac says.

"No, actually, what you said about being human—the paradox of the limited aspiring to the limitless."

"Right," he says, nodding, "that's what drives us; that impulse comes out in different ways, but it's the same impulse."

"Well, maybe we *are* more than we seem."

"What do you mean?"

"I told you I've been trying to understand what Harold is. So far I know Harold exists, it's limitless, and it's paradoxical. The first two are really just the definition of Harold: the sourceless source. Everything comes from something, but ultimately there has to be something which has always been: Harold. God. The paradox part I noticed pretty recently: it's everywhere around us, from the universe itself, which is both chaotic and orderly, to atomic structures which are at once consistent and unpredictable.   But nothing embodies more paradox than us: love and hate, compassion and cruelty, mortality and desire for eternity—we could come up with tons of examples, and they're all in each of us.

"What I *hadn't* thought of, until just now listening to what you said, is if everything taken together is Harold, then we and Harold—God—whatever—are the same stuff.   This table, the diner, the air, you, me, the waitress—it's *all* God, because there's nothing else.   And the fact that we, like everything else, are loaded with paradox just confirms that. We *are* God."

Mac looks at me, his fork paused in mid-air.   "Oooh, my mama would slap you silly for that one."

"OK, that didn't come out right.   We're God, but God is us too—we're the same thing.   We're all parts of the biggest thing there is.   Maybe that's why we have this tension you're talking about.   We know we're just these limited human beings, but something in us, deep down, knows we're actually part of something much bigger, something infinite."   I look at him: he's still paused mid-motion, looking back at me. "Maybe I've said too much," I say, looking down at my bowl of grits and picking up a spoonful.

"I get it—I get what you're saying.   But, you're agreeing with him, saying he *was* God.   How can you say that?"

"No, he said *he* was God and *I* wasn't.   I'm saying we're *all* God, or at least taken together, all of us, plus everything else there is, is God.   He didn't have a monopoly on it. Obviously."

"Obviously.   Still, you're saying everything—good, bad; just, unjust—is equally part of God."

"Yeah, well, like I was saying before, maybe God isn't what we think it is, what we've been told it is.   Bad things happen; bad people happen. God can't really be all-powerful *and* loving and compassionate like we're told."

Mac shrugs and begins to cut off another bite of pancakes with the side of his fork. "Some say God is testing us, to separate out the worthy from the unworthy."

"But if God is the all-powerful creator religions—or rather, the people who made up religions—tell us he is, then why would God deliberately make unworthy people? If you were Harold, would you create inferior product? Plus, if God really is the ultimate source of everything, then there's no getting around the fact that everything is ultimately all the same stuff—all God. There's literally nothing else."

"So are you saying there's no difference, no meaningful difference, between good and evil?"

"What I'm saying is: good, bad, Harold is itself. We make up these distinctions—sin and virtue, justice and injustice—but they don't happen naturally or exist outside the world of humans."

"So again I ask, are you saying anything goes? It's all equally fine, whatever we feel like doing is OK? If I feel like abducting young women and torturing and raping them, that's OK?"

"No—no, you're right. I wouldn't say that. Maybe it's different with us—maybe good and evil, justice and injustice have meaning for people... But why should we be different from everything else?"

"Your food is getting cold," he points out.

We go back to eating for a while, but I keep thinking, feeling like I'm close to something and not quite getting it. "You know, we seem to be the only things on this planet that try to step back and understand ourselves and everything around us."

"Sounds like Aristotle—the human is that which reasons."

"Aristotle said that?"

"I think so. Something like that."

"Well even though Harold doesn't seem to care, most of us humans do. Most people expect justice and fairness, and treasure ideas of right and wrong. We bring that extra quality to the world. Some of us bring more, some less, and some, these monsters, bring none at all, or a twisted version of it. But if we're all part of Harold, then what we do, Harold does. Maybe, taken together, we're Harold's consciousness—Harold trying to sort itself out.

"Maybe that's where morality comes in: we each have to make choices, and we all have preferences and ideas we base those choices on. When my family and I were attacked, I was presented with a question: what do I do? We all get asked questions, and we ought to make the best answers we can because each answer, in a small way, defines the nature of the world, of God. We're all just pieces of the whole, tiny pieces of the big deal, but when we care, that's Harold caring. And if we don't care, there's shit for everyone. For God to be just, *I* have to be just. When someone is cruel, that's God being cruel. When we show compassion, Harold's compassionate. Each of us is responsible for helping determine the whole universe, for defining God with our choices."

He's staring at me; I've been raving like a maniac. "Or not," I say dismissively, and spear a potato with my fork.

"I'm not agreeing or disagreeing, but what you said…that's a dangerous idea. You know as well as I do people can't be trusted to make good choices. If we're all God's mind, then God is a crazed drunk stumbling around a dark room, looking for the light switch and destroying everything else in the process."

"Well," I say, smiling a little, "there you go: sounds like Harold's world to me. Only it's not just Harold's world—it's ours. We're responsible for it."

Forty-Five

Mac watches Shailene unscrew the license plate from the front bumper of her little car. "I see now why you repainted your car black. With the lights out it'll be practically invisible once it gets dark."

"Yeah, invisible comes in handy sometimes."

"You sure you want to do this?" he asks.

"Absolutely," she replies, nodding her head. "Besides, I got the cages and food and stuff now."

"Yeah, but Utah—isn't there any place closer? Or why not just let them go here?"

"I don't know much about it, but I don't think rabbits that have always lived in a hutch would know how to fend for themselves outside. As for shelters, I'm not taking them someplace just to have them put down if no one adopts them. There's a no-kill shelter up in Massachusetts, but they're just dogs and cats. I guess there are other places, but I don't have time to research it, and the place in Utah is a known good. Besides, I've heard Utah's canyons are pretty amazing, so I'll get to see something new and cool." She finishes detaching the license plate, straightens up, walks around to the side of the car, and throws the plate on the floor behind the driver's seat. "You sure you want to be in on this?" she asks, turning to face him. "It's not exactly legal."

"Legal is often over-rated. Besides, it'll be faster with two of us. Depending on how many there are, we can probably get the whole thing done and us gone in a couple minutes—maybe less."

They get in Shailene's car to wait for the sky to go black.

"So...Mac..." she says, sounding tentative.

"Yes?"

"I'm wondering what our next step is."

Mac is immediately on guard. He was hoping to put this conversation off until she had more time to recover, and had at least a few good nights of sleep under her belt. "Regarding what?" he asks needlessly, hoping this will somehow postpone the discussion.

"Regarding our working relationship. I mean, by now you must believe the sense is real, right?"

He considers saying something along the lines of "it could still be coincidental," but he'd either sound like a liar or an idiot—either way not a good approach, given what he wants to propose. "Yes I do. Like you, I don't understand how this can be true, but obviously it is. And I don't need to tell you what a powerful asset your ability is."

"So how are you going to do this? How are you going to convince people at the FBI I'm for real? What's the next step?"

He takes a deep breath. It's not like he hasn't thought about how to say this; he's rehearsed it in his head several times. He just wasn't planning to give the talk right now. "You need to understand: the Bureau is a bureaucracy—a giant, ponderous bureaucracy that, for the good of all of us, is heavily constrained by laws and regulation, not least the Constitution." He glances over at her to gauge how it's going.

The bruised face is glaring back at him.

Not good so far. "Shailene, what I'm trying to say is there really isn't any room—any provision—in the law for your ability, especially since there's no scientific basis for it, so there's really no way to integrate you—"

"What?!" she interrupts. "What do you mean? We could do a demonstration for them—bring a mix of convicts one at a time into a room with me, and let me pick out the psychopaths. There's the scientific basis—reproducible results."

"I'm saying don't get your hopes up," he replies quickly, adjusting on the fly.   "And look, even assuming the best case—the Bureau brings you on board, lets you consult on some cases, they're still going to have to follow legal procedure, which means gathering evidence, grand jury, trial—the works.   And even if—*if*—the *Bureau* buys the reality of your sense, I don't think there's a prosecutor alive who'd allow any mention of you and your sense in court, so how do they explain how they identified the defendant as the one who did the crimes?"

"All this is details—we can work those out later."

"Finally, once you and your ability are identified to law enforcement, you become as much a concern as an asset. Listen to what I'm telling you: You—*we*—would be much more effective outside the system, and you would be safer *from* the system.   And look, *I'm* with you all the way—you won't be alone in this."

"By 'not alone' do you mean 'not alone' like I was yesterday?   Chained in a cabin in the middle of the woods, waiting for a psycho motherfucker to come back and do unspeakable things to me before killing me? 'Not alone' like that? Because let—"

"C'mon, Shailene, that's not fair; it was—"

"Fair?! Mac, I—I—I don't even know how to respond to that.   You've got to *make* them believe you; you've got to make them believe the sense is real so I don't have to keep going up against these bastards myself! So I don't have to keep killing them!" She slams her fists on the steering wheel.

Mac studies her for a few seconds.   There are no tears, but he thinks they're not far off.   "Listen," he says softly, "why don't we talk about this later?   We'll do this thing tonight, you'll go on your trip—that's gonna take at least a week, right? Take a break—"

"Don't patronize me," she says quickly, gesturing to cut him off, her voice angry but under control again.   "What exactly do you have in mind? Pretend for a minute I don't matter—that shouldn't be hard."

"Shailene—"

She turns her head, stopping him with a look. "Tell me what your plan is."

Mac takes another deep breath, decides to lead with what he thinks will be the best part to her: "First of all, you won't be fighting or killing anyone anymore. I'll do that part. You just find the bad guys, and I'll take it from there."

"Sooo...what? You'll investigate them?"

"No, forget all that. I don't know how it works, but you've proven your sense over and over again. It's been verified enough. When you identify the source, I'll take him out. Anything else just increases the risk to innocent people, including, by the way, us."

"You trust the sense more than I do."

"I guess I do." He notices she always refers to it as "the" sense—not "her" sense like he's been calling it. To her the ability isn't hers, but something else residing in her.

She pushes the driver's seat back, hugs her knees to her chest and rests her heels on the front edge of the seat. She closes her eyes, then slowly shakes her head. "I don't know..." She pauses. "Mac, this isn't a comic book; we're not superheroes. You're talking about killing people."

"I'm talking about saving people from other, bad people who would hurt and kill them."

She stays closed up; Mac waits her out. Finally she says, "I don't see how this can work for you. For one thing, this time was unusual: I don't normally just stumble across the bad guy. Usually I see something in the news and I go to the place to start looking, and the search can take weeks. If you're gonna be there when I find the target, you're gonna have to be there with me while I'm looking. How are you going to take all that time off from the FBI? I had to quit the regular job *I* had, and I can't think it was anywhere near as demanding as what you do."

"I'd quit. I've been talking to a friend of mine from the Army—he has a security business now. He says he could use me; we'd work something out. I might even be able to get him and his people to help us, so see, you really wouldn't be alone, and you yourself wouldn't have to go against these guys anymore."

"Did you just think of that?"

"Well, that last part about his people helping us, yeah."

"I thought so."

He can't tell what her point is—that he's wrong to have been planning to keep her outside the legal system but didn't tell her until she confronted him, or that he's just making up any and every argument he can imagine to justify his scheme. Either way, he doesn't know what to say after that, so he stops talking.

She stays quiet too, for several minutes, her body still folded up, childlike.

Mac gazes out the windshield, watching the parking lot get darker, then the lights coming on. Trucks, minivans, and cars come and go, the drivers stopping for groceries before heading home to dinner.

"Maybe you're right." Her voice sounds strange after so much silence. "About this not being the best time to talk about this, I mean. I'm just damn tired. I don't like what you're saying, but I need a clearer head to think about it."

"Sure. Nothing's going to happen until you get back from this trip anyway."

"Yeah," then under her breath, almost too quiet for him to hear: "Hopefully." She straightens her legs, stretches them out in front of her, then adjusts the seat for driving. "Still not totally dark yet," she observes, and pushes a tape into the deck. That band she likes, the Radiators, comes out of the cheap speakers.

They sit and listen, watching the sky turn black.

When it does, she kills the music and they pull out of the strip mall parking lot and drive about a mile to 44 Red Oak Street. It's a quiet, suburban area, and the house is a brown single-level ranch. They drive by once and see no activity in or around the house, or on the street. They round the block and Shailene kills the car's lights just before turning on to the street for the second time. There's plenty of illumination from the street lights to find their way. She pauses just past the driveway for number 44, then shifts into reverse and backs smoothly and quickly into the driveway, the back up lights casting a dim glow, just enough to make out the end of the pavement and beginning of the back lawn. She stops, shifts to neutral, and engages the parking brake, but leaves the engine running. When they open the doors the dome light does not come on. They leave the doors open and Mac moves back into the yard behind the house, pausing just a couple seconds to listen and look while Shailene opens the car's back hatch. She comes up beside him and they walk silently across the grass, under a couple big trees with expansive branches.

The rabbit hutches, two of them side by side, are easy to find. Mac goes to the one on the left and shines his Maglite in. The red lens casts a dim glow, revealing three or four animals inside. He opens the latch and swings open the door. He hesitates, wondering if they bite, but he has gloves on. There's the sound of panicked rustling around, and then his hands close on a struggling body. He lifts it out, nudges the hutch door shut, and carries the rabbit back to the car. The tops of the cages in the car are already open. He lowers the warm ball of fur into a cage and turns. Shailene is coming up behind him with another. He side-steps her and jogs back to the hutches. He opens the door to his hutch again, feels around, and takes another animal. They continue this process until checks with their lights and hands show both hutches empty. They close the hutch doors and jog back to the car.

She closes the back hatch softly; they get in and close their doors quietly. She shifts into first, releases the parking break, and they're away. A couple houses down she turns the headlights on again, and they drive back to the strip mall.

Shailene pulls up next to Mac's car, shifts to neutral, and engages the parking brake again. "So…thanks…for helping with this."

"No prob." He's not sure what else to say. "Sorry the thing didn't go like we planned. I'm really sorry about what you went through."

She nods, but looks away.

"Call me when you get back, all right?"

She nods again, still not looking at him.

"Or call me sooner if you need to talk, or need help. You got your cell phone, right?"

"Yeah, OK; I should get going: I want to put some distance between me and here before I stop for the night. You should get some rest too—don't try to drive all the way home tonight, all right? I don't like your plans, but they're still better than what I've been doing, and they're not happening if you fall asleep on the highway and get killed."

"Yeah, I'm just going to Greensboro tonight. You be careful too." Mac realizes he doesn't want to say good-bye, and that confuses him. *Am I forgetting to tell her something?* he wonders.

She nods, then looks sideways at him. "OK, bye."

"See ya," he says, and gets out.

He closes the door and she pulls away, pauses at the parking lot exit, then turns on to the road and drives off.

Epilogue

It's evening when I pass the St. Louis Arch doing about fifty, heading west. Maybe this is a crazy idea, but I'm glad I'm doing it. Yes, it'll be over four-thousand miles out of my way by the time I get home, and sure, maybe Mac was right about it being unnecessary. After all, Flashphaler must've had someone stopping by to feed and water the rabbits; maybe that person would've adopted them. Or maybe they'd've been fine if I'd just let them run free. But either way, I can imagine more bad outcomes than good. I'm responsible for the animals now, and I'm gonna make damn sure they end up someplace safe and happy.

I looked into local shelters this morning before leaving Asheville. Well, not really. I got as far as looking up shelters in the yellow pages, but before I picked up the phone I started thinking about the place in Boston I volunteered at a few times. That shelter is probably one of the best, but even at that place there are so many animals that they have to be penned up in little cages crowded into noisy, stark, windowless rooms. The animals not adopted are killed—humanely killed, but killed—to make room for the inevitable new arrivals. I didn't want to rescue these guys just so they could be put down in a few weeks. The only no-kill shelter I know of that takes more than dogs and cats is the Best Friends sanctuary in Kanab, Utah. Somehow I got on their mailing list a while back and I get their newsletter. The rabbits there are housed in a big open building with protected access to the outside. No smelly, nasty, windowless rooms there. Yeah, it's a lot more driving, but to do otherwise would be a betrayal.

The rabbits don't seem to care about their change in fortune, but they don't know how it's going to turn out, and don't understand how it would have been if Flashphaler had come home to them, or if I'd just left them. They're always happy when the food appears though, and that makes me feel good.

Anyway, I'm glad it's a long trip: glad for the miles accumulating between me and all the bad stuff that's happened, for the places flashing past, the pavement speeding by a couple feet below me. The phrase "washing the blood off" keeps running through my head, and I think of the wind washing over Stacey, rushing by like a river.

Washing the blood off.

Hopefully nothing will happen to change this; hopefully I won't run into anyone bad. My mind flashes to the Glock under my seat, but...

I trace the scab encircling one wrist with the tip of a finger from the other hand. There are wounds inside my head too, giving me nightmares when I sleep, making me feel fragile when I'm awake.

I think about the rabbits, listen to one of them scratching around in the wood shavings and hay I put in the cages I bought yesterday, on my way to Charlotte. *Only yesterday.* It seems a long time ago now, and I take that as a good sign.

Washing the blood off.

* * *

I sit on the picnic table, my feet on the bench seat, and stir the soup in my blackened, slightly battered pot as I heat it on my little butane stove. The rest of the camping gear—the small nylon dome tent, two sleeping bags, a thin foam pad for under my sleeping bag—I bought at the same giant warehouse store where I bought the supplies for the rabbits.

It's getting dark now. I'd really wanted to make it out of Kansas before stopping for the night, but that was only for psychological reasons. After staring at the same two dots on the perfectly flat horizon all afternoon, never seeming to get any closer to them, I was pretty sick of Kansas. But it was more important to find a place to stay while there was still light for pitching the tent and getting the animals and me fed. I took exit 17 and followed the map to this empty, deserted campground.

I fed the rabbits first: carrots of course, lettuce, and an apple I cut up for them. They seemed pretty happy with that. I wonder what Flashphaler fed them. I didn't really look around inside their hutches except to make sure we didn't leave anyone behind.

The soup starts to boil; I stir in a cup of instant rice, put the lid on the pot, and kill the flame. It takes five minutes or so for the rice to soften, so I watch the rabbits having their dinner.

I see what Flashphaler meant about being like God to them, completely controlling their lives, their fates. The difference though, between him and me, is power makes me feel protective of them; I want to make their lives as happy as I can. Power provoked him, incited him to torture and kill. One species, two completely different reactions. Do we all— does each of us—contain the potential for both cruelty and compassion? I think of what Mac said about the importance of being loved when we're children, and also of how something as random as a head injury can make a difference.

I think of myself, driving these rabbits thousands of miles to guarantee their safety. I'm the same person who pushed the paring knife into a man's brainstem in Trenton, who beat someone to death with a tire iron in Florida, who tore a man's throat out with her teeth in Georgia. I wipe my hands over my face, making the bruises hurt. I concentrate on watching the rabbits eat.

The air is turning much cooler. A light breeze comes up; the air smells clean. I lift my face to it and feel it wash over my skin, think about how far away I am now. Gravel and sand filter subterranean water; the further the water flows, the cleaner it gets. I've already come a long way, and I'm still only about two-thirds of the way there. I look up at the sky, somewhere between azure and slate, with a purplish tint to it, and high, feathery clouds.

It's getting chilly. I move the whole show—rabbits, food, and gear—into the little tent. Inside I remove the lens end of the Maglite, allowing the tiny but powerful bare bulb to shine in all directions, lighting up the cramped domed room. Using the wrist cord, I suspend the small flashlight from a slit in the Tyvek tag sewn into the tent wall.

My food tastes good but a little bland; I wish I had hot sauce for it. I'll pick some up next time I stop for groceries. After dinner, I rinse out my pot with water from a gallon jug, then take off my jacket and sweatshirt and roll them up to make a pillow. I mostly cover the rabbit cages with one sleeping bag, and I slide into the other. The Glock goes under the pillow roll, then I reach up and replace the lens on the Maglite, screwing it down until the light is extinguished.

In the dark, I listen to the wind picking up and rustling the thin walls of the tent. I think about the rabbits, going someplace safe, someplace where danger, pain, and boredom might not even be remembered.

* * *

I wake up scared. *Just another nightmare.* I know this because the horrors were reruns: a mix from my past. The smell of the rabbits—the blend of urine, droppings, hay, and wood shavings—reminds me where and when I am, that I'm safe. I press the light button on my watch; it's a little past three in the morning. It'll be several more hours on the road between here and Kanab, but today the rabbits will arrive at their new home.

They'll be home, then I can go home. I picture my little apartment and the starter trays full of seedlings. I'll have to pick them up from Charlie's place when I get back.

Charlie's not really a friend—I'm paying him to care for the seedlings—but he's as close as I get anymore. For a while I'd been thinking Mac could be a friend, but I really don't know what to think about him.

I need to pee. I slide out of the sleeping bag. I slept in my jeans, socks, and an over-sized T-shirt, so I just pull on a sweatshirt and my Chucks, tuck the Glock into my waistband, and take the Maglite. Crouching, I pass through the tent's low opening into the chill night, zipping the door shut behind me to keep in the heat. There's enough faint illumination for me to see without using the flashlight. I look up to see the moon, and instinctively duck.

There's no moon out, but there are stars like I've almost never seen before: a vast array of countless tiny lights. Even the Milky Way is obvious as a denser, brighter cloud of stars forming a straight path across the sky. The sheer magnitude of the sight is almost enough to send me cowering back into the tent, and the reverence and awe of long-past cultures for the night sky suddenly seems logical and obvious. I stand bathed in ancient light, staring in silent astonishment for several minutes, until the fullness of my bladder and the cold of the desert night remind me why I came out here. This campground, like the others on this trip, is almost completely empty of people, but I'm still not comfortable with dropping my pants and squatting out here with the visible universe as an audience, so I make my way to the small building with the bathrooms.

After, as I walk back to the tent, I look up again. I know better, but I'm still thinking of the sky as an impressive, beautifully decorated dome above the Earth. I stop and remind myself the Milky Way is actually our galaxy, seen edge on. I picture myself in the greater context, standing on a speck of matter and looking out across the infinity of space, bathed in starlight that's traveled millions of years across an emptiness too large for my mind to appreciate, before impacting on my body, which is itself composed of ancient atoms forged in some long-vanished and distant supernova. For a few seconds I do it: I see my position, as much as I can, as it actually is: improbable and infinitesimal.

But being aware of this makes all the difference. My eyes tear up and my chin wrinkles spasmodically. Confused and embarrassed, I look down and walk quickly back to the tent.

* * *

The back of the car seems empty now that the rabbits and their stuff are gone, but I'm feeling good about bringing them here and undoing some of the bad in the world. It's not a big thing, but it's still weight on the other side of the scale, a change for the better. I rearrange my gear to fill the space more evenly, then close the back hatch and climb in behind the wheel. "Just you and me now, Stace," I say under my breath. I miss the animals a little.

On my way home I pass near Zion National Park again, and decide to take the rest of the day off and treat myself.

* * *

The side canyon is so narrow and deep it must be in shadow most of the time, yet somehow there are scattered trees and shrubs growing here, their roots sunk into the rock. The walls are smoothly rippled, like glazed ice which has melted and refrozen, rounding hard edges and curving angles. Touching the stone destroys the illusion: the surface is cool, not cold, and dry and rough like sandpaper.

The trail is wide and smooth, and no more challenging than a steep sidewalk—not exactly what I had in mind when I decided to visit this park, but it still feels good to use my body, to feel my muscles carrying me up the canyon, to breathe. *How cool it is to be here.* It's as if my whole body vibrates with the idea. As I walk and take it all in, I notice I'm smiling.

I prefer forests and oceans to desert, but this place is magical. It's similar to the Grand Canyon, but here the soaring, bare masses of stone are closer, more...intimate? That's not it exactly, but the narrow, shadowed spaces feel safe, and the whole place is more compact and less overwhelming. It's like the way I feel about New York and Boston: the Grand Canyon is the big spectacle that's fun to visit, but this place would be the more comfortable, manageable place I could make a home in. Here I can better appreciate the walls and mountains, the arches and pinnacles, the warm, radiant colors I don't normally associate with rock: mostly variants on orange, but rusty reds, bright yellows, and dark purples too.

Eventually I emerge from the small canyon, and the ground levels off and opens up. I pause, taking in the view and feeling the afternoon sun on my face while allowing my heart rate to slow to normal. I look down the main canyon to the southeast where an S-shaped stretch of river winds around a steep brownish-purple formation with rounded columns melted into it. To the right of that my view is blocked by a high, ridiculously vertical ridge: a massive red, brown, and black blade of terrain jutting out from the canyon floor and rising high above me.

I follow a steep, unpaved trail out and up along the blade's edge, the land falling away on either side, and there's only the path, in places marked by black chains held up to waist height by black metal poles sunk into the stone, and framed on either side by nearly straight drops of over a thousand feet. I think I can see the summit, but when I reach it, I'm not even halfway to the top. Although I know it has been here for at least thousands of years, the formation is so narrow and high it seems fragile. It makes me a little dizzy, afraid, and excited. I keep climbing, choosing my way carefully.

There are trees growing out of the rock here too, their trunks partially blocking my way, their roots disappearing into cracks. I don't think there can be any soil in those cracks, so how do they survive? Some of them are pretty big, despite the lack of soil and the winds, storms, and extremes of temperature they must endure. *Some bad ass trees.*

Except for the trees, I'm alone on the edge of the blade, maybe because it's early in the year and late in the day.

As I get higher, the blade gets sharper—now there's just five feet of walkable ground separating killer drops. The path is very uneven, and at times almost steep enough for me to use my hands. It's much cooler up here. I think nervously of wind gusts, and wonder if there are ever earthquakes here. I think I can actually feel the spin of the planet, and catch myself smiling broadly.

At last the ground widens and the slope shallows out. The summit is a relatively level area around 200 feet at its widest, and about four times as long, and I have it all to myself. I walk to the southern end; the view down the valley is awesome. The trees and brush I passed through a couple hours earlier look like brown and green moss clinging to the base of the canyon walls, which soar upward like ranks of massive, jagged stone teeth, weathered and gray on their pointed tops, their faces stained shades of orange, rust, and brown down to the mossy gums. Behind and below me, the start of the ridge trail is now in the shadow of a nearby mountain, but the summit is still catching the last golden sunlight of the day. I go over to the eastern edge and look down at the river, getting a thrill at the sight of a fourteen-hundred foot straight drop. There are no guard rails, and it would be easy to accidentally, or intentionally, exit the world from here.

I think about that: not for the first time, but only for a second and not seriously—not anymore. Even at the worst times, I always decided against killing myself because it would be handing a victory to the one who tried to kill me when I was a kid. Now it's more of a game, a way of asking "why not?" I'm not sure I have a rational answer yet, but I'm still not going to step off this cliff.

I roam around the summit some more, then sit near the southern end again and gaze down the length of the main canyon, thinking about heading home tomorrow.

What if I didn't? At first I think it as a kind of joke, but there's not a lot pulling me back to Massachusetts. Maybe I've done enough; maybe I can be done. If I don't scan the Internet or newspapers anymore, and move someplace remote where there aren't many people, maybe I'll never run into another human gone wrong. Hell, maybe I could get a job at the sanctuary—it could be *my* sanctuary too. *This* could be home. *Why not? Fuck it—why the hell not?* In the park's visitor center I read something about Zion being a Hebrew word meaning "place of refuge," and for a moment I'm ready to believe again in divine intervention and signs from Harold.

But I know better. There's no washing the blood off either. *Not really.*

Maybe I *have* done enough, though. When *can* I be done? After all, no matter how many monsters I stop, Harold's world will keep making more. Is it even possible to make a difference? Does anything I do matter?

If someone had stopped that bastard from killing my parents, from trying to kill me, it would have made a difference, for us at least.

The sun dips below the high ground to the west, and it becomes noticeably colder. I need to head back down before it gets too dark to follow that narrow trail safely. As I walk across the summit, I wonder if I can make it all the way through Colorado by this time tomorrow.   I think of the seedlings, and hope Charlie's remembering to mist them twice a day. *I wonder how tall they'll be when I get back.*

About The Author

Like Shailene, Max Salt is a graduate of the U.S. Military Academy and a former helicopter pilot. He now lives in Rhode Island in a re-purposed Grange hall on an acre of land he is transforming into a tiny nature preserve. This is his third novel about Shailene. You can learn more at maxsalt.com.